Published by Paradoxical, LLC

ISBN 979-8-9876263-0-6

Dedicated to my husband who made sense of the gibberish I wrote, and to my children who will be forced to read it ;)

Merrow Crescent
The Forgotten Secret
Book 1

by

Clara Horne

Chapter 1

Once upon a time. . . Well, that's how most stories like this one start, but not mine. While I'm sure you'll think what I'm saying is a fairy tale, a bedtime story, or even something I dreamed of one night, I'll tell you right now that everything that started that first day of summer is the truth. I pinkie swear it and cross my heart! I'm not going to say I hope to die, not because my story isn't true, I just think saying that sorta thing is what got me in this mess in the first place. And as my parents would say every time I sassed off to them and couldn't seem to respond to them in a more "respectable" manner, "Why make a bad thing worse?" OK, OK, I know I'm rambling on, and I should just get on with it already, and for that, I need to start at the beginning.

The sun was shining brightly down onto my face as the wind blew my long golden-brown hair back in an almost chaotic dance. It whipped around in every which way, and it seemed to sparkle as it did. I let my arms stretch out to both sides as if I was trying to let that very wind make me fly, but in a way, it already felt like I was. I was speeding along the blurry landscape of the rising morning sun, but I wasn't the one moving. I was a passenger. My gaze went down and saw a horse, but it wasn't a horse. It was a unicorn! Her coat was a pale caramel, and her long mane a deep brown. Her horn looked like it was made of silvery glass that glistened beautifully in the light. We were riding through a foreign yet familiar magical land.

I tried to see the world around me, but it went by so fast I couldn't entirely focus on any one thing long enough to know what I was looking at, but it didn't matter. I had never felt so free. Freer than I had ever felt in my entire life, but that feeling began to leave me as I saw something in the distance, something wrong, something evil? There was a giant blackened tower ahead of me, and it made me very scared, and then I heard it. *Jennifer . . . Jennifer . . .* and the whole world began to shake. What was going on? "Jennifer, Jennifer, wake up!" and with one more jolt, my eyes flew open.

When I awoke from the strangest dream I had ever had, I found my face pressed very uncomfortably against the car's window, my glasses slightly crooked and a thin line of drool seeping down my chin—gross! At first, everything was extraordinarily bright and out of focus, but after blinking hard a few times, rubbing my eyes, and of course, cleaning off my chin, I found myself very disappointed at what I was seeing. Outside the car was a very old and very run-down-looking farmhouse. I guessed it had to be two hundred years old and hadn't been painted in at least half that time. It was dirty, grimy, and just yuck.

"Jennifer Greenfell," the voice of my father from the front seat of the car called out to me.

With a sleepy yawn, I turned toward him. "Please tell me this isn't Uncle James's farm?"

With a roll of his eyes, my dad said in a less-than-pleasing voice, the voice he used a lot lately, "First off, how many times have I told you not to fall asleep with your glasses on." I responded to that comment by first fixing my glasses and then crossing my arms at him with a huff that was way more annoyed than the tone of his voice. "Secondly," he said sternly, "yes, this is Uncle James's farm, and you *will* remember to be polite while

2

you're a guest here."

"I don't want to be here," I mumbled under my breath.

"What was that?" he said sharply.

I tried to force myself to talk nicer. "Nothing. I didn't say anything."

I was sure I heard him mutter under his breath, "That's right, you didn't," but I chose to ignore it with another roll of my eyes.

My mom's softer voice broke through the tension. "Come on, honey. Be easy on her. You know she's feeling a bit down having to be away from her friends all summer." You could tell my dad wanted to disagree with her, but he bit his tongue.

For the last couple of weeks, he had been doing everything he could not to stress her out, and that's the reason I'm here in the first place. No, it's not that I'm bad, so stop thinking that right now, because I can already see the cogs spinning in your head. In fact, I would go so far as to say that I'm a pretty good kid compared to some of the kids I go to school with! Was it because my mom was pregnant? No, not just that. A few weeks ago, she started getting sick a lot and had to go to the emergency room. After that visit, the doctor put her on bed rest to keep her and the baby safe. It turned out my future brother or sister really wanted out, so my mom had to keep herself stress-free and happy. My dad thought it would be better if I went somewhere for the summer so that my mom could rest and not feel guilty about me being home all the time and bored. I argued that I could just hang out with my friends, but that wasn't good enough, as he figured that meant I would be at home all the time being loud. Whatever, Dad! I wasn't sure why my being home was stressful, but my dad seemed to think it was.

It probably wasn't the most intelligent move on my part, but when he didn't say anything back to my mom, I

3

sort of whispered the word "whipped" out loud. Granted, I had intended to think the word, but . . . I blamed not feeling 100 percent awake, and of course, I knew right away he had heard it because both his shoulders shot up, becoming rigid. He didn't say anything, but then I could see he was just about to say something to me when my Mom put her hand softly on his shoulder. It probably was going to be something along the lines of me being grounded all summer, which wouldn't have made sense since I was going to be hundreds of miles away from him, and there would have been no way for him to enforce said punishment, but he was pretty good at saying things without thinking them through sometimes. A trait I was told I inherited, obviously.

"Sweetie, try to remember that this is hard for her too. She's to be in a new, unfamiliar place away from her home, away from her friends, and away from us." It was the last part of what she said that seemed to make his shoulders slump back down, and so he held back the urge to protest, instead nodding in agreement, or maybe defeat. I wasn't sure which one it was.

Now, I coudn't say I knew a lot about my uncle James and aunt Tara. My uncle James was my dad's older brother. I only ever saw them maybe once a year at best, on Thanksgiving. Other than that, it was just the cards they sent me on my birthday. I didn't feel I knew much about them. If I were honest, when I did see them, I didn't talk to them much, as any time they were around all the grown-ups did was talk about grown-up things, boring things. I knew they owned a farm in the middle of nowhere near a town called Merrow Crescent, and that they had a lot of animals, crops, and stuff, but at this moment, I couldn't remember what kind. Also, to make things worse, they had no kids, so that meant there was no one to hang out with. I wasn't sure why they didn't have any, but my mom told me never to ask, something

4

along the lines of it being rude.

As I looked out the window, I saw Uncle James and Aunt Tara standing on the porch, smiling and waving at us in the car. They seemed excited as they waited for us to get out. Uncle James looked a lot like my dad, just a bit older and with slightly longer, messy brown hair. I guess when you work on a farm you don't have to care so much about stuff like that. Aunt Tara was stunning. She had long dark blond hair that she wore in a side braid, and she was always smiling. My mom said she was one of the sweetest people she knew. They didn't dress like I figured typical farmers would, with the classic overalls and flannel shirts, or was I thinking of lumberjacks? Uncle James just had jeans, and a blue T-shirt that looked weird over the blue jeans. I mean, who wears blue over blue? Aunt Tara was wearing some grey pants and a long, flowy green blouse. I honestly thought all farmers wore overalls, straw hats, and giant, mud-covered boots, but they looked like they could fit in easily in a coffee shop downtown.

As soon as my parents hopped out of the car, I heard a high-pitched squeal coming from Aunt Tara, and she ran quickly but carefully to hug them both. Seeing this over-the-top show of emotion didn't make me want to get out of the car any more than I already didn't, and I found myself staring at them through the window while they chatted, hugged, laughed, and hugged some more. Eventually, my mom looked over her shoulder and beckoned me with a wave of her hand to get out. I felt frozen for a bit as I really didn't like to be hugged, but when I saw my dad shoot dagger eyes at me a moment later, I let out a slight gulp before I forced myself to get out of the car and walk slowly and painfully to my doom. It turned out my slowness was in vain, as I soon found Aunt Tara rushing up to me and embracing me in a too-tight hug and another near-deafening squeal. She cooed about how big I was, how I was almost all grown up, and some other overly sugary thing adults say to kids. Yucksville!

Uncle James was soon standing by us as Aunt Tara finally decided to let me go. He looked down at me with a wide grin. "Jennifer, you've gotten so big. How old are you now?" and he paused before guessing "eight?"

I felt my nose wrinkle into a grimace as I responded with some bitterness, "Twelve, actually." Again I got another glare from my dad, so I faked a smile. Uncle James just laughed and then ruffled my hair. I quickly brushed it back against my neck since I'd worn it this way for a reason. You see, I had a birthmark on my neck that almost looked like a horn. My parents thought it was cute, especially since when I was much younger, I was obsessed with all things unicorn. I wasn't sure if I just loved them or if it was because for as long as I could remember, my dad would call me Uni because of the mark on my neck. I just felt embarrassed by it now. It wasn't that it was an ugly, gross mole or anything, but when it had been pointed out by everyone I ever saw since I could remember, it became a burden, and I wasn't the type who liked to stand out in a crowd. I wanted to blend in.

The adults soon started talking to each other again about all the usual boring things adults talk about, so I figured it was a good time to back a few steps away. You know, disappear before anyone could ask me any more personal questions, or worse, give me another hug. I let my eyes scan the area around me to get a better feel for my temporary new home. The house seemed OK from the outside; the typical white two-story farmhouse that you saw in many movies with a large porch that held several rocking chairs, none of which matched, and a big white porch swing. Of course, the road we drove in on was dirt, and along both sides were wooden fence posts. I wasn't sure how far away the actual road was since I had fallen asleep before we got here, but looking into the distance, I couldn't see anything that looked like a highway. All that lay before me was miles and miles of tall grass, or was it corn? I wasn't sure, but it was a plant, and that is all I really knew.

Looking behind me past the farmhouse, all I saw were more fields, more fences, and a few scattered buildings of different shapes and sizes. I was sure one of them was a barn, but it wasn't red like I thought all barns were. Instead, it was buttercup yellow, and there was a silo close next to it. Near the other side of the house was a small cottage-looking building; maybe it was for storage, but I wasn't sure. Honestly, I had no idea about any of this farm stuff. I wasn't sure how much more there was as it seemed like Uncle James's property went on forever.

Just as I was about to wander off to see what else I could spot—maybe some type of animal, I hadn't seen any of those yet—I heard my dad calling my name. With a groan, I turned around sharply to stare at him. He just stared as sharply back at me and motioned for me to go into the house. My mother and Aunt Tara were already walking up the steps to the porch, while Uncle James was heading over to help my dad get my cases from the back of the car. Uncle James was pulling out my large travel trunk. This was the first time I had been allowed to use it, as it was a lot bigger than any airplane would allow. That is, of course, unless you paid a small fortune for oversized luggage, or at least that was what my parents kept telling me. It was an old-timey trunk, the kind you would always see in movies about the past when people traveled by boats. I thought that it was really cool how they would have stickers on it from the places they had been, sort of like a passport other people could see. I, of course, never really traveled anywhere noteworthy, so instead, I put stickers on it of places I wanted to go! My plan was that when I am older, I can use my own money to take it with me and travel to all these places I dream of visiting.

As soon as he started to pull it free from the back, I could see that Uncle James wasn't ready for how heavy it was. Before I could utter a sound, his upper body was pulled down with my trunk as it slammed with a thud onto the ground below. I ran forward yelling something, more as a reaction than meaning to be angry. I think I said something like, "Watch what you're doing," or "Be careful with my stuff, stupid," or maybe I said both. Either way, my dad shot me a hard look, and you could tell he was just about to unleash a fury on me when Uncle James stood back upright and laughed. "Woah, girl, what do you got in here? I've picked up rocks lighter than this thing!" He then slapped my dad on the arm, getting his full attention "Help me take this thing inside, Greg." My father seemed to have forgotten what he wanted to yell and instead bent down to help Uncle James. I felt my face go hot and I was a little more than embarrassed about how I had talked to an uncle I didn't know that well. Then to see him being kind enough to keep me from getting into trouble for it made me feel all sorts of shame and guilt. Uncle James smiled at me and gave me a wink before he started to help my dad, who was already starting to sweat as he attempted to lift one side. I probably should have smiled back at him, but instead my stubbornness kicked in, and rolled my eyes instead, before I headed to the back seat to get my backpack.

I headed up the steps of the porch and noticed right away that one of them squeaked under my feet. "Haunted farmhouse, huh? Great," I moaned to myself.

Aunt Tara and my mom had stopped at the front door and were staring at all the commotion taking place at the car, looking confused. My poorly timed statement had clearly gotten my mom's attention, and now even she was starting to look a bit cross at me, just not as much as my dad was. "Jennifer. Be polite."

Aunt Tara laughed as she looked over at her. "Don't worry, Mary, she clearly just has a good imagination." She then looked at me with a bright smile that made me feel better for some reason. "This place is just old, so don't be scared if it creaks and groans," and with a wink, she added, "Probably just as much as your old man over there!" The three of us shared a small laugh.

I watched as my mom and Aunt Tara turned around to walk inside, still laughing with each other, and as soon as the screen door shut behind them, my laughing stopped. It wasn't that I thought what Aunt Tara had said wasn't funny, in fact, I thought it was hilarious. It was more that I had that sinking feeling about my parents leaving very soon and I wouldn't see them until the baby was born. My stomach churned just thinking of the creature that was growing inside my mom right now. I wanted to be happy to be having a brother or a sister, but I wasn't. It was just the three of us, and it felt perfect most of the time. I didn't see why we needed to mess with that, plus this baby was already causing me problems. I'd have to be stuck on a boring farm all summer, didn't have my friends to hang out with, and I was terrified about my mom's health. Sometimes I got scared thinking that she might die. And what about after this monster came into the world? Would they love me as much as they did before? Would we still do fun things together, like movies and bowling? Would they even have any time for me at all? Would I just be in the way as I clearly was now? The more I stood there thinking about it, the more I wanted to start crying or throw up, or maybe both.

With a lot of hesitation followed by a big, slow deep breath, I pushed open the wooden screen door and walked into the house. The first thing I noticed was the smell of meat cooking, though if I'm being honest, I wasn't sure what kind it was, but something told me I wouldn't like it. The ancient-looking wooden floor was covered by a pale green rug that just about matched the paint on the wall of the entryway. On the right, there was an L-shaped staircase that ran up the wall with an old wooden bench sitting in front of it, under which a whole bunch of dirty shoes were peeking out. There was also a bookshelf built into the stairs, which I thought was actually sorta cool, but just sorta. It was filled with old-looking books and random things. The staircase also had a doorway beneath its rise, which I was pretty sure led to the kitchen, as the smell of cooking meat grew stronger the nearer I approached. To the right was an ever so slightly open double door that led into a den. Through the thin gap between the doors I couldn't see if there was a TV, or anything fun to do. Across from the front door was a long hallway that had three doors: one on the left and one on the right and a window-paned one at the very end, of which I was sure led outside. There were tons of pictures hanging on the walls of people I didn't know and tons and tons of random knickknacks. That's what my mom called them, but Dad called them useless clutter. They seemed OK, though.

I was just about to look in the den, to investigate what fun my future may hold, when my mom and Aunt Tara came out of the kitchen door behind me. "Do you want to see your room?" Aunt Tara asked. I shrugged my shoulders at her, which I'm sure came across as impolite, but at this point, I was just trying to keep myself from crying. She smiled with a nod before beckoning my mom and me to follow her up the stairs. The green paint continued up the wall upstairs and led to an L-shaped hallway. Once we were there, Aunt Tara started pointing things out. "Here is James's and my room," she said as she pointed to the door to the right of the stairs. "If you need anything, don't be afraid to knock." She paused briefly, almost like she was waiting for me to say something before continuing, "Down there is a charming place to sit if you want to read a book. It gets great light in the morning." Looking down the hall, I could see the window with a built-in bench covered with a thick green cushion and a ton of pillows.

"Up here we have the attic, but I'd stay out of there, it's a bit of a mess," she said, and laughed. As we passed the attic door, I couldn't help but wonder what was up there. Treasure? Monsters? It could be anything, really. But my desire to explore and imagine was cut short as I noticed my mom and Aunt Tara had continued on walking without me. There was a door right next to the attic that held blankets and extra towels, Aunt Tara said, which seemed rather dull, but I guess it was something I should know if I got cold. Toward the end of the hall were two rooms. "This one on the left is my sewing room." My nose wrinkled at the thought. Sewing sounded like the most boring hobby anyone could ever have. "And here on the right is your room."

Aunt Tara opened the door slowly. I felt a tinge of excitement, hoping it would be a really awesome and cool place to hang out, so I allowed myself to smile, but once the door was open, my smile quickly deflated into a frown. There, in front of me, was one of the most boring rooms I had ever seen in my whole life! It had all the makings of dull. Plain wooden floors, check. Icky cream paint, check. Window with old creepy blue curtains, check. Oh, and let's not miss one old wooden bed covered with an even older yellow-and-black-plaid blanket, check. That was it, just a bed, no nightstand, no television. Not even a mirror, which I was glad for so I wouldn't have to see the disappointment on my face every day that I woke up in this deary existence. There was one door on the right, which I assumed had to be a closet.

I felt my mom nudge my shoulder, urging me to say something, and I noticed Aunt Tara was looking at me with a hopeful smile on her face. It dawned on me that I must have been staring at the room way too long and looking way too unhappy. "It looks comfy," I outright lied, all while eyeing the bed, thinking to myself that thing looked nothing near comfy.

Aunt Tara erupted with a laugh and said with a wink, "We gotta work on those lying skills," which made me blush with embarrassment. "I know it looks bad now, but . . ." She paused to smile up at my mom, who was also smiling. I felt entirely out of the loop as I looked between them both.

After a moment, I said slowly, "But?"

Aunt Tara bit her lower lip before saying in a questioning but very cheerful tone, "I thought that this room could use a makeover. So maybe, you and I can go into town tomorrow and you can help me pick out some new paint, bedding, maybe some cool furniture, and decor? You know, make it your own!"

I felt my eyes light up, and I couldn't help but let the excitement out. "You mean I can do anything I want?"

Aunt Tara laughed. "Well, within reason, yes. So long as you don't paint the wall black, I think it will be OK with Uncle James."

My nose wrinkled again. "Black wall . . . Ewww gross!"

My mom nudged me with a smile. "What? When I was your age, I thought black walls were sorta cool."

I eyed my mom suspiciously "Were you a . . . goth, Mom?"

Mom shared a laugh with Aunt Tara before she went on to say, "I'll tell you all about that another time." And she winked at me. I don't know why, but this just made them both laugh more, so I joined in. I didn't even know why, since I didn't understand the joke, but I guess I just felt like laughing. It felt good.

The laughter, however, abruptly stopped when I

heard my dad call us from downstairs. "Hey, hon, we need to get a move on if we want to get to the hotel before it gets too late." I felt my heart sink into my stomach. Up until this point, being away from my parents hadn't felt real, but now the realization of it all was crashing down on me. I followed Aunt Tara and Mom down the stairs and into the entryway. It felt like I was walking to my own funeral. Once we got downstairs, I saw that my trunk had been left near the front door, along with my other bags. I wondered how Uncle James would be able to get the trunk all the way up the stairs by himself. Right there next to it was my dad. He was just standing there, eyeing his watch carefully. He didn't like being late, and he also didn't like driving in the dark.

"Well, I think it is time we say goodbye." My mom's voice came out low and kind, but I couldn't seem to make myself look up at her. I felt like the second I looked at her face I would start crying, and I didn't want to do that.

My emotions were strong and I was torn between being sad and angry at the time time. Sad that they were leaving me here, but also angry that they were leaving me here. So I bit my lip and forced myself to speak. It came out more cold and uncaring than I meant it to. "Yeah, sure, whatever."

She lowered herself down to be more at my eye level, something that was a lot harder for her now that she was carrying a bowling ball around in her stomach. Then she placed one hand on the side of my face and spoke very softly. "I know this is hard, but you'll have a lot of fun if you let yourself, and the—" I didn't let her finish.

I just glared back at her, and I felt my whole face going red. A tear managed to escape my left eye before I snapped back with as much anger as I could show in my voice, "Fun? How could anyone have fun at this awful place? I bet it doesn't even have a TV or Wi-Fi!"

"Jennifer!" my dad yelled from the doorway, looking just as mad as I felt. My mom reached one hand out to his side to try to get him to stop before he said anything that might have made this situation worse, then she looked back at me. Her face was understanding, but I didn't see how she could be. After all, she wasn't the one who was being abandoned. Before she could say anything, she reached both hands down to her stomach and looked slightly pained. My dad rushed to her side to help her stand, along with Aunt Tara and Uncle James. "Sweetie, are you OK?" he said, his voice oozing with worry.

"It's . . . It's all right. I think maybe I have just been standing too long." She shot them a reassuring smile.

What happened next was something I regretted the moment it left my lips. "Well, just go, then. Maybe you should leave me here because it's clear you only love that thing now." I pointed at my mom's stomach. There was a flash of pain on my mom's and dad's faces as well as worry and concern on Uncle James's and Aunt Tara's. All I could think to do was to run upstairs as fast as I could.

I paused once I rounded the corner, out of sight from the adults downstairs. Softly I placed my back against the wall and carefully listened to what was going on. My mom said, her voice cracking as she did, "I need to go up there and talk to her," but as soon as she said it, I heard her make a strange, unpleasant noise.

"Sweetie, I don't think that's a good idea. You know the doctor told you not to overdo it." My dad's voice came out sounding so worried that I had to fight myself from going to her.

"I know." Then I heard her sigh loudly. "Can . . . can, you go talk to her, then?"

Before my dad could say a word, Uncle James cut him off. "Maybe you both should give her some time to calm down. I'm sure after we get some food in her and a good night's rest, she will come around." I peaked around the corner and could barely see my mom's head, but I could tell she was looking at the ground and appeared somewhat deflated, I thought.

"You're right." My dad spoke up, almost like he was cutting my mom off before she could protest. "We need to get you to the hotel so you can rest. We can call her when we get there . . . or in the morning." I felt the blood rushing from my face. Were they really going to leave without saying goodbye? No hug? No kiss? Not even I love you? I so badly wanted to run down the stairs and hug them both and tell them how sorry I was for what I said. I wanted to beg them to take me with them. But the hurt I was feeling was more potent than my wants—let's call it pride. So instead, I stood there, in the now darkening hall as the sun was slowly getting low enough that it didn't shine as brightly in the window as it had before. Tears were streaming down my face, and it took all I had not to let out a sob. There was so much hushed talking that I couldn't make out, and what sounded like agreement before I heard them say their farewell. All four of them walked out the door. When I heard the screen door shut, I ran off toward my room, dropping my backpack near the door before I hid under the ugly plaid blanket and started to sob.

I wasn't sure how long I had been lying there crying. All I knew was that when I heard a light knock on my door and peeked out from under the covers, it was almost completely dark outside. Then there was another knock, and I heard Aunt Tara talking from the other side. "Jennifer . . . hon . . . do you want to come down and join us for supper?"

"I'm not hungry!" I yelled back and covered my face once again with the blanket. There was a long pause, and I was sure I heard whispering from behind the door.

After a few moments, Uncle James said, "All right, well, if you change your mind, we are downstairs." I continued to lie there, not moving for what I figured was another hour, or maybe it was less. Time didn't seem to make sense in this empty room. I knew my phone was in the backpack I had dropped by the bedroom door, but part of me was too scared to get it, like they would hear me and come back. Part of me wanted them too, but the bigger, stubborn part of me didn't. There was then another knock at my door.

Aunt Tara's voice called out again, "Hon, if you change your mind, I'm going to leave a tray next to your—"

Before she could say another word, I shouted out again, "I said I'm not hungry. Why can't you just leave me alone?" Aunt Tara didn't say another word, but I heard her place something next to the door before she walked back down the hall. It started to dawn on me how hungry I was. I hadn't had anything to eat since we had stopped and gotten drive-through for lunch, and now it was way past the time I would usually have had my dinner. I wanted so badly to go out and grab the tray and eat whatever my be on it. Trying to fall asleep in jeans while also being hungry doesn't make for the best sleeping conditions.

So I lay there a long time, looking at the light that crept in from underneath the door, until finally, it switched off. I crept quickly into the darkness of my room, stubbing my toe on something along the way before slowly opening the world's creakiest door. There on the ground, barely visible in the pale white moonlight washing in from the window, was a tray with some form of stuff on it. I just couldn't tell what it was. I got down on my knees, and with a lot of care, I slowly pulled the tray into the room, holding my breath as I did. I don't didn't know why I thought holding my breath would make me quieter, or maybe even silent, I just did. Once I closed the door, I reached up to turn on the light and sat down next to the door.

On the tray, I saw what I thought was sweet tea, a ham sandwich with pickles and mayo, and, to my delight, my favorite brand chips. There was also a cup of grapes and, was that what I thought it was? Yes, a chocolate cupcake with sprinkles. A tinge of guilt flooded me looking down at all the food. I felt like such a brat, and Aunt Tara gave me a cupcake? But I couldn't help myself. I was so hungry, and the food all looked so good, and it did taste good. Well, the sweet ice was a bit watered down as I guessed Aunt Tara had put ice in it, which sadly had melted. She had cut all the grapes in half, something I thought that adults did for only toddlers or small kids. I didn't really care for them too much, but I was hungry, so I ate them all anyway. I saved the cupcake for last, and I don't think I have ever had a cupcake that tasted as good as that one. After my stomach felt full enough, I figured I could go to sleep, so I pushed the tray back into the hall and noticed that my trunk and bags had been left next to my door. I hadn't seen them before with how dark it was, and the light from my room made them stand out.

I grabbed one of my bags that had my toothbrush and pajamas, and when I turned around, I noticed there were two doors on the right side of my room, not one like I had thought before. I decided to check them out. One, of course, was a closet, and to my surprise, the other was my very own bathroom. I was overjoyed to see it. It meant I wouldn't have to sneak back out into the hall and risk bumping into anyone, seeing as, at this point, I really, *really* needed to use the bathroom. And there was the fact that I didn't recall my aunt ever pointing out a bathroom being upstairs. After I had put on my pajamas and brushed my teeth, I lay back in the bed, a bit colder than I had been before, but I decided I wasn't cold enough to try to sneak a blanket from the hallway. I lay there for a long time regretting how I had acted, wishing I had been able to get one last hug from my parents before they left.

Wishing I had acted differently. It felt like forever, but I finally felt myself slowly fall asleep.

Chapter 2

When I woke up the next morning and rolled over in bed, I had forgotten where I was and nearly scared myself to death when I almost rolled right off of it. The night before had felt more like a bad dream, and sadly I learned this bed was a lot smaller than what I was used to at home. My scare didn't last too long as I found myself blinded by the light coming in from the window. I couldn't help but roll back over the other way, pulling my pillow with me as I tried to guard myself against the harsh light pouring through the window. Sadly for me, in my haste, I had forgotten about the size of the bed and found myself falling to the floor, impacting with a big thud and dragging my blanket along with me for the ride. Thankfully I had a good enough grip on the pillow for it to soften the blow a bit. I lay there, thinking any moment Uncle James or Aunt Tara would come running into the room to see what happened, but after a while, it was clear no one was coming, which made me feel both relieved, as I wouldn't have to be embarrassed by my less than graceful exit from the bed, but also confused. If I was home, one or both of my parents would have been in my room in an instant, making sure I was all right.

There wasn't a clock in the room to help me figure out what time it was, and when I checked my phone, I found it was dead. I wanted to kick myself that I hadn't remembered to plug it in the night before. This left me with really only one option, I figured, to head downstairs.

I decided to forgo having a shower. I knew I hadn't taken one the night before, but I mean, after all, who was I going to be seeing that mattered in the middle of nowheresville? I did brush my hair, though; I wasn't a pig, even if I had to share a home near one. This made me wonder if they even owned any pigs. I hadn't exactly gotten the best look at the place, so who knew at this point. After I got my hair under control, I put on the first clothes I could find: a simple white shirt with rainbow poop emoji on it and a pair of blue shorts. Comfy and practical, I thought.

I wasn't sure why, but once I left my room, I found myself creeping slowly down the hallway, trying my best not to make any noise. I knew that was weird, as it was clearly later in the morning. How much later, I wasn't sure yet. But something about being in a new house with people who I felt I barely knew made me feel uneasy and also sort of like I was in the way, again. I was also feeling a tad bit embarrassed from the night before. I mean, I knew I couldn't avoid them all summer, but it didn't hurt trying, did it? I did learn that almost every step I took down the hallway made a creek or squeaking noise, and I didn't fair any better going down the stairs. I didn't remember any of those noises from the day before, so I couldn't understand why every step I took now that I was trying to be quiet seemed louder than my dad eating a bag of chips.

When I finally reached the kitchen door, I paused long enough to listen, making sure I wasn't about to walk into the middle of breakfast. Sure enough, I didn't hear anything on the other side, and slowly, I turned the handle and gently pushed the door open. The wooden floor carried on into the kitchen, which I now just assumed was the same way in the whole house. The first thing that caught my eye was that there was a door across from me. It had a window at the top half with a yellow-

and-green stained-glass border. I would have said it was pretty, but it had those frilly lace drapes near the top that I felt made it look old and way outdated. But I guess that fits in with the theme of the rest of the house. There was also a large wooden table that was way too high to eat at. I assumed it was meant to be a makeshift kitchen island, with a bowl of fruit on the top and lots of pots, pans, and mixing bowls randomly placed on a shelf under it.

There was a door to the left, and next to it was a large wooden cupboard with a corkboard on both doors haphazardly covered with postcards and small bits of paper. Spanning the gap from the cupboard to the door leading outside was a very worn-looking wooden counter with chipped yellow-painted doors that were just a bit lighter than the ancient-looking yellow floral wallpaper behind them. There was also a large sink, and I do mean large. I was sure you could wash a medium-sized dog in it. There was also a strange fridge with a curved top and a black stove. The stove had been most likely featured in one of my history textbooks, the kind they used before people had power. I think it was called a wood-burning stove. To the right of the room was a rectangular table covered with a yellow-and-white-checkered cloth and six mismatching chairs.

When I saw no one was there, I started to turn away to look elsewhere, but before I did, a white sheet of paper on the island caught my eye. It had a decorative horseshoe border and a handwritten note that read, "Sweetie, sorry, I had to go tend to the horses. There is breakfast for you keeping warm in the stove, Aunt Tara," and at the very bottom, "P.S. I hope you slept well." I felt my nose wrinkle at being called sweetie, so I showed my disdain for it to no one but myself by crumpling up the note and tossing it into the small white trash can that was next to the door I had just come through. I was a tad bit proud of myself when I managed to get it in in one shot.

Turning sharply on my heels, still feeling a bit cocky, I went over to peek inside the oven. When I opened the door, a rush of warm air engulfed my face, and sure enough, there was a plate of food waiting inside for me. It was a blue plate covered with scrambled eggs, bacon, and a slice of toast slathered with a red jam. It did look delicious, but the memories of the night before started to eat at me, along with how I had just acted about Aunt Tara's note, and then there was the big reason. I was missing my parents so much right now that I felt like I could break down crying at any moment. It made me lose my appetite big time. So with a little hesitation, I shut the oven door and turned around to face the fruit bowl. Inside there were some apples, pears, and oranges. After studying them for a while with no real intention of eating any of them, I picked up a large red apple and held it in my hand.

As I stood there studying the apple, I probably looked like someone who had never seen an apple before in their life, and I nearly dropped it when I heard a voice coming from the open doorway. "Good morning, sweetie." I looked over to see Aunt Tara smiling at me with a face slightly covered in what I hoped was mud. Her shirts and pants were also covered with it as well. I thought her note said she was tending horses, not fighting with them. I shrugged slightly as I quickly put the apple back into the bowl. Aunt Tara seemed to have taken note of it as she stepped forward with a frown, looking at the table where the note had been. "Oh, I'm so sorry, sweetie. I was sure I left you a note this morning," she said as she bent down to check all around the table. When she stood up, she looked at me, concerned. "You must be starving!"

I quickly shook my head before she could make her way to the stove, "No, no, I'm not really a breakfast person," I lied.

Aunt Tara looked at me unconvinced, but she didn't push the issue, like my parents would have. Instead, she smiled at me and said, "Well, we are closer to lunch now than we are to breakfast. How about you and I go into town and see if we can find some things for your room and maybe grab some lunch?" Despite my mood, the thought of going into town with a shopping trip to boot was enough to lift my spirits, so I nodded to her enthusiastically. Aunt Tara's smile got even bigger before she said she just needed to go upstairs to get changed. Before Aunt Tara could even turn around to head out of the kitchen, I bolted right past her toward the stairs as fast as I could. I was sure I heard Aunt Tara laugh before she shouted out to me, "Watch out for the fifth step, sweetie."

It's like my mind couldn't quite compute the words she was saying until it was too late. As my foot hit the fifth step at the speed I was going, it felt like it shifted ever so slightly. It was enough to disrupt my balance, and I found myself going headfirst toward the steps in front of me, and I felt a scream escape my lips. In an instant, everything felt like it was going in slow motion as the ground came closer and closer to my face. Time around me had slowed down, but my mind was still seeing everything at full speed. As soon as I lifted my hands in front of me in an attempt to break my fall, time suddenly and abruptly caught up without warning, like the stretching and sudden snap of an elastic band. Oddly, instead of hitting my face on the steps, I was lying on the steps, with my arms stretched out, unhurt. Aunt Tara ran into the room, looking at me, worried, "Are you OK, sweetie?"

I grabbed the railing and pulled myself up before nodding. "Yeah, I'm fine. Just got a bit scared, I guess." I smiled nervously back at her, still unsure what had happened. She nodded back with a thin smile. Before she could say anything else, I headed up the stairs again, but at a safer speed this time.

The thought of what had just happened kept playing in my mind as I approached my room. By the time I got to the door, I had decided that the lack of sleep was playing tricks on me. I picked up my now partly charged phone, discovering that it was almost ten a.m. How long had I slept, I wondered? That thought quickly left me when I noticed that I had no messages from my parents. My heart sank with the rush of thoughts and emotions and I had to fight the tears that wanted to form in my eyes. Were they really that mad at me that they wouldn't say they loved me, missed me, or even say a simple good night? Or worse, what if something bad had happened? I pushed the last thought out of my mind by reassuring myself that if something had happened, I would have known about it. It had to be the first one. I sucked in a deep breath and let the sadness that was forming turn into anger instead, and with an aggressive hand, I shoved the phone to the bottom of my small backpack before slinging it over my shoulders and storming out of the room. I shut the doorway behind me way too hard and then stomped back downstairs to wait for Aunt Tara.

I sat silently on the bench next to the steps as I tried to calm myself down, so I was thankful that it took her at least ten minutes to come back downstairs. It gave me a bit of time to allow for a cooler head, but probably not enough. I was sure I could still feel the frown lines on my forehead, or maybe I was just being self-conscious. I had to admit that I was a bit confused at how she had been so fast and there wasn't any dirt left on her. It would have taken my mom more than double that time just to brush her hair. I was rather impressed, but I guessed country living was not the same as being in the city. I could tell by the look in Aunt Tara's eyes that she knew something was off, but if she did, she wasn't saying anything about it. Instead, she motioned with her hand toward the door with a giant grin, "Well, come on, girly, what are you waiting for?" The relief that she wasn't going to pry made me happy, so I smiled back, and we both headed out to her red truck.

Chapter 3

Because I had been asleep when we arrived the day before, I wasn't prepared for how long and bumpy of a ride it was going to be as we left my aunt and uncle's farm. The fact that I hadn't woken up by smacking my head on the window was also surprising. Part of me was glad I hadn't eaten anything for breakfast, but another part of me wondered if I would have felt less sick right now if I had. I guess it didn't matter now because there was nothing I could do about it except try my best to pretend I wasn't about to dry heave all over the place. So when Aunt Tara looked over at me with a smile, as I held on so tightly to my seat in an attempt to ease the bumps while my knuckles started to turn white, I just smiled back at her. I kept trying to swallow the lump that was traveling up my throat and did my best to act like everything was A-OK. Aunt Tara must have seen right past my attempt because the truck slowly came to a stop, and she asked me very calmly, "Are you going to puke?" I feigned a look of offense when I shook my head in protest, but boy, was that a big mistake!

As soon as my head stopped, the feeling became so intense I didn't think I would be able to stop myself. As quickly as I could, I turned around and tried to open the door, which, to my terror, was stuck, and the more I tried to open it, the more panic bubbled up in my stomach. I heard Aunt Tara's calm voice behind me, trying to get my attention on how to get the door open, but my mind couldn't focus on her words. Instead, my full undivided attention was on the apricot horse with a dark brown mane staring at me from behind the fence that I was pretty sure wasn't there moments ago. At that moment, it felt like everything around me was moving so slowly again, and I started to wonder if this was all just some weird dream. So I did the only thing I could think of, which, to be honest, felt really stupid. I looked straight at the horse and tried to speak two simple words, though it felt like the sound never seemed to leave my lips: "Help me."

As soon as I said it, or, in this case, tried to say it, it suddenly felt like time had caught up with me. The truck door swung open so quickly that it pulled me along with it, and I found myself plummeting to the hard ground below. Half of me was expecting to feel a hard blow when I hit the dirt road, while the other half figured I was going to puke as soon as I hit it. Strangely enough, neither one of those things happened. It felt more like I had landed on a pile of pillows, and the extreme nausea that I'd had just seconds ago was gone entirely. For a short moment, I sat there stunned and really unsure about what had just happened. As soon as I heard Aunt Tara rushing around the truck yelling if everything was all right, I snapped out of it, and as soon as I did, my eyes darted quickly to the field in front of me and began searching for the horse that now appeared to have magically vanished. All I saw was a bunch of tall green plants, and now that I was looking at them more closely, I figured they might be corn. My plant knowledge was somewhat lacking, though, so they might have also been wheat, but then I was pretty sure wheat was probably brown. I shook my head slightly to break free of analyzing the crops because it didn't matter either way. The horse was nowhere to be seen, and I was getting concerned that I was having hallucinations, or maybe I just really needed a good night's sleep. Aunt Tara was soon on the ground kneeling next to me, checking me over for any signs of damage. When I was sure I couldn't see anything in the field, I asked her, "Where did the horse go?"

A worried look filled my aunt's face as she suddenly cupped my cheeks with both of her hands. She squinted her eyes as she peered into mine, and a flow of words began pouring out like, "Did you bump your head? Does anything hurt? Do you think you might have a concussion? Do you think I need to take you to the emergency room?"

"I'm fine." The words were barely understandable as they came out because she was squeezing my cheeks. Her hands slowly released me as a more relaxed, composed face replaced her worried one, and her whole body seemed to ease. "Well?" I asked again.

Aunt Tara looked at me very confused when she asked me, "Well, what?"

"The horse, where did it go?"

For a moment, Aunt Tara looked a bit befuddled by what I was asking her, then she laughed slightly and said with a bemused grin, "Sweetie, we do have horses, but they're kept back at the stables." The last word didn't even finish coming out of her mouth before a look of clarity came over her. She jumped to her feet and gazed out into the field, searching the area frantically. "What color horse did you see?" she asked, sounding rushed.

I shrugged slightly when I replied, "I dunno, it was apricot or golden, I guess."

Aunt Tara's body language swiftly changed from one of concern to one of irritation. "Oh, him" I heard her mutter but the rest of what she said was too low and angry for me to understand; though, I was pretty sure I heard something about a "stupid horse." She had a look on her face that made me think she was about to unleash a lot of words that she probably wouldn't want me to hear. The same face my dad got when he stubbed his toe, but when Aunt Tara's eyes came back to me, it was like she had forgotten I was there. She looked a bit embarrassed, and with a sheepish smile, she clearly tried to pretend like nothing was wrong, calmly saying, "Well, never mind that, your uncle can handle that later." She motioned for me to get back into the truck. "Well, if you're feeling better, let's get out of here and have some fun, shall we?"

I smiled at her, feeling a bit mischievous when I asked, "Stupid horse, huh?" My aunt gave me a grim smile with a quick shake of her head before she got into the truck without another word. I couldn't help but giggle to myself before I did the same.

Chapter 4

The rest of the ride down the never-ending road leading away from their house was in awkward silence. My aunt kept her eyes firmly on the road ahead. Her face seemed a bit off, almost a mix of concern and regret, and I wondered if she was feeling embarrassed because she had gotten angry in front of me. That's something most adults don't like to do in front of kids. It was OK for them to be mad at you, but being angry at other stuff seemed almost taboo. If she felt that way, I highly doubted she could feel more embarrassed than I did right now. I couldn't figure out what had just happened. First, it was the stairs before we left, and now this. Something in me couldn't help but wonder if there was a severe problem with my brain. Still, I quickly dismissed the idea and told myself that it had to be the lack of sleep, or all the crying I did, or how angry I had been, or maybe all three, or maybe, just maybe, it was all in my imagination. I mean, since I didn't want to be here, my brain had taken it upon itself to come up with reasons that might be good enough for my parents to take me home. Brains do that, right? Who was I kidding?! I doubted it was the last one. I'm sure if my brain were that clever, I would be in on it—I hoped. Either way, I was planning on going to bed real early tonight and trying not to get so upset about every little thing. The last part would be a big stretch, though.

As soon as we reached the paved road, I felt much better. I let out a long, low sigh as I felt my whole body relax, and I said under my breath, perhaps a little too loudly, "Ahhhh, civilization again at last." As soon as the words left my mouth and my brain realized I had said them out loud and not in my head as I should have, I felt my whole face turn red. I tried to sink my head into my shoulders, which made me feel silly because it became clear to me that I wasn't a turtle, so there was no shell there for me to hide in.

I made myself take a swift glance at my aunt's reaction, but to my relieved surprise, she was smiling at me, and she told me with a gleeful laugh, "I know what you mean. I keep telling your uncle we need to do something about that bumpy road." She paused for a moment before she added, "But if he is anything like your father . . ."

She let her sentence trail off, and then we both said in unison, with big grins, "They are stubborn." We laughed, and it was as if all the embarrassment I had felt melted away, along with the worries that had been floating in the back of my head.

When my eyes caught sight of the sign that read "Merrow Crescent, 3 Miles," my whole body began to feel giddy with excitement. I could imagine the tall buildings, the lively sounds of all the cars and people, the smells coming from bakeries and restaurants, all the fun things you could do, from parks to museums. Oh, and let's not forget the best part, all the shops to visit! It was my belief that you could never feel alone in a big city. Even at night, there was something going on somewhere. The idea that a city never slept seemed comforting to me for some reason. It took all the control I had not to start jumping in my seat. That was until something dawned on me. If we were only three miles away from the city, why wasn't I starting to see the tops of the skyscrapers and high-rises? No big deal, I reassured myself. Maybe it wasn't a super-big city like I was used to. It was probably just a smaller one, where the buildings were not as tall, like maybe only five or six stories tall. I held on to that hope as long as I could, but all the joy left me like a deflating balloon as the town came into view.

I mean, I guess you could still call it a town, but only barely. I wasn't sure what you called something that was smaller. Was it a village, or a hamlet, or something like that? As we got closer, I could see the buildings weren't in a style I was used to and looked really old. I wasn't sure if calling them old really did them justice to fully say how old they looked. Ancient, maybe? Nah, that seemed too old. They matched perfectly with the buildings I saw in the movies my mom liked to watch about English people in the past, when all the ladies spent all their time sitting near pianos, and no one had the internet or working toilets.

I looked at my aunt and smirked before asking, "Did we just drive into England or something?" What I said must have caught her by surprise because when she laughed, she also snorted, and she instantly looked embarrassed. To save herself, she started talking all about the buildings, about how old they were, and how most of the buildings were Tudor-style, built by the English colonists. She also said some weird things about the history of some of the buildings, and blah blah blah. I slowly let my eyes drift to the window while I hoped it looked like I was paying attention.

I inched closer to the window when I caught sight of what looked like water in the distance, nestled between two buildings. I couldn't help myself and cut my aunt's history lesson short: "Did I just see the ocean?!"

"Yes," she replied, her voice both amused and confused. "Didn't your parents tell you we lived near a harbor town?"

I turned away from the window and muttered as I sank back into my seat, "No, they failed to mention that."

"Maybe they wanted it to be a surprise," she said, seeming to understand my tone.

"Doubtful," I replied before crossing my arms over my chest and hoping it would give my aunt an indication that I didn't want to talk about it anymore. A part of me wanted to believe she was right, that they hadn't told me because they wanted it to be a surprise, but a more significant part believed they were just wrapped up in their new baby and they probably didn't even remember how much I loved the ocean.

I let my attention go to all the buildings we were passing, and I started to feel like I had entered a whole different world. None of the shops here were the brand names I knew. All the restaurants and shops were named with people's first or last names, or sometimes both. A lot of them had weird nautical-sounding names too. I guess everything in Merrow Crescent was family-owned businesses. I suppose in their own unique way, the buildings were all right. I mean, most of the buildings I saw in the city were modern, whereas the ones here had flower boxes and benches under their windows, and a few had weird-looking wooden statues of animals or other things decorating the outside of them. My dad would have called it street clutter; my mom would have called it enchanting. In fact, my mom would have loved it here. She would probably say "ooh" and "aah" and take a hundred pictures every few seconds. All the while, she would be babbling away, throwing in words like "charming," "quaint," and "picturesque," but to me, it just seemed somewhat pointless and boring. Why did they need to have so many flowers under their windows? Were they selling them? I doubted it. It was then that the car began to slow, and I realized we were about to park in front of a building that had a white sign with blue curvy writing that read "Susan's Antiques and Curios." I couldn't understand why, with so many free parking spaces, Aunt Tara had parked here, but then she turned off the engine and said with a big grin, "I'm sure we'll find all sorts of cool things in here for your room."

I had a sinking feeling in my chest as I looked again at the sign and then at the window that had all matter of weird junk sitting behind it. But what was I supposed to do? It was clear this town didn't have a department store, so I put on the best fake smile I could and looked back at her. At first I couldn't make myself say anything, but finally, I said, "Sure." I truly hoped she believed me.

Chapter 5

When Aunt Tara pushed open the door, a small hidden bell near the top softly rang and I heard a woman's voice from some unseen place call out, "I'll be right with you." My aunt quickly called back, "No rush, Susan, I'm just taking my niece shopping." There was a hint of pride in the way she said "my niece," and I couldn't help but smile because of it. It was nice to feel wanted for a change. Suddenly there was a loud sound of something being dropped, followed by many clanks and clatters from behind a shelf immediately behind a large wooden counter to our left. I figured it was the checkout counter; I mean, it did have a really old-looking copper-colored cash register on it, like the massive ones where the buttons stick out super high. A plump woman with very long, curly red hair wearing a green dress with a white collar appeared with a massive grin on her face, and her voice was high with excitement as she squealed, "Oh my word, is this her? This is baby Jennifer?!"

"Baby Jennifer?" I said with just a tinge of disgust as the woman rushed over to me. Before I even knew what was happening, she was squeezing both sides of my face, making me feel like a human fish, when she let out another high-pitched squeal. At that point, I would have thought she would have let go, but she just kept holding on to my face and staring at me, looking very pleased. I tried to speak, but the words only came out as muffles.

"Not so much a baby anymore, but yes, this is her,"

Aunt Tara said, laughing yet somewhat embarrassed. More so for me, I guessed. Susan's eyes left my face to look at my aunt, and only then did she finally release her iron grip. My hands instinctively went up to my face to rub at my cheeks, and I wondered if I was going to have bruises.

"Of course," she agreed, looking back at me with another big smile that made me take a defensive small step back. No way was I letting her get ahold of me again. Sadly I wasn't quick enough and she reached out to squeeze only one cheek, this time between her fingers. It felt like a crab had gotten ahold of my face between two very sharp claws. As she did, she spoke loud enough that I was sure anyone outside would have heard her. "Your aunt has been telling me all about you ever since you were in diapers!"

I could feel the blood starting to drain from my face as I roughly pushed her hand away and said bluntly, "Ewwww!"

Susan eyed me, confused, and she seemed poised to say something, maybe even tell me off, but my aunt asked her quickly, "So did your shipment come from Glenndenning yet?"

A brightness returned to Susan's eyes before she looked back at my aunt, thankfully forgetting about me, and squalled again. "Yes, this morning! You have to come in the back and see!"

Aunt Tara laughed and nodded in agreement before turning her attention back to me. She said cheerfully, "You'll be fine looking around by yourself, right?"

I nodded quickly in agreement. "Of course, don't worry about little me. You go looking at . . . stuff." Both of them smiled at me, and I was sure Aunt Tara gave me a quick wink before they disappeared behind the counter into a room while Susan continued squalling on about something I couldn't be bothered to care about. All I knew was I owed Aunt Tara big.

I waited until they were both out of sight before I let out a big sigh of relief, and I muttered under my breath, "What a nut job." As I let my eyes take in my surroundings, I couldn't help but notice that there was no sense of organization to anything in this place. In the stores I was used to, all the shelves were in perfect lines and aisles. These appeared to be placed at random angles and in odd places. How in the world do you find anything in here? I wondered. When I took a few steps forward, I noticed a table that was piled high with blankets on top of it. It seemed like here was no better place than any other to start looking. I mean, after all, a nice-looking blanket might help the room. But when I got closer to the table, I found myself very disappointed by what I saw. They all seemed so old and outdated, a lot of them like something you would see on an older person's bed, and quite a few of them were tinged slightly yellow from time and probably wear. It's not like I had anything against reused items. In fact, I thought it was a great idea, but I had to draw the line on used bedding. Bed bugs, anyone? No thanks! I moved the blankest around a bit, just in case there was a hidden gem underneath, but when I saw nothing, I let them fall back down. BIG mistake! It seemed Susan must not be a fan of cleaning because I soon found my whole face engulfed in a cloud of dust that had been waiting on the blankets for an unwitting victim. I couldn't help but gag and choke for a few moments as I tried in vain to waft the dust away from my face. That just made it swirl around me even more. I heard Aunt Tara call out to me, "Everything all right out there?"

I felt myself become more worried that Susan would come back to attack my cheeks again than I was about suffocating, so I yelled back between coughs, "Yeah . . . everything's OK . . . just swallowed wrong."

Swallowed wrong? Was that the best thing I could come up with?

Thankfully it didn't matter because Aunt Tara yelled back, "All right," and I knew I was safe, at least for now. I gave the blankets one hard nudge out of frustration before venturing deeper into the store.

As I walked around the shop, I saw lots of weird and strange things. Most of the items seemed like old, used junk, some of which I wasn't even sure what it was or what it could be used for. There were tall, alien-looking green statues tucked away in one corner that half hid under a dusty sheet; now that was creepy! I could also see a leg wearing a stocking lamp without a shade on a shelf, and I wasn't sure how many ornate picture frames I came across, but I'm sure no one would ever need that many. I gathered that this shop had more picture frames than people who lived in this entire town. But even with all these weird things, nothing caught my eye as something I'd ever want to have in my bedroom, even if it was just for the summer.

The more I wandered around, the more lost I started to feel. It was like I was in a maze, a very dusty, damp-smelling maze. Every twist and turn was getting me more and more lost, and there was the added bonus of some parts being dark and creepy. I felt a shiver run down my spine at the thought of what might be hiding in the dark spaces. I began to doubt that I even knew which way I had come from. Had I come across that teapot before, or was it a new one? Was this porcelain doll a twin of one I had seen before or, worse, had it moved? I had a flashback to a show I had seen my dad watch before, one about some guy who traveled around in a big blue box that was bigger on the inside. I let out a small laugh and said to myself— out loud, to calm the paranoid feelings— "I'm not in a TARDIS." I felt a bit stupid talking to myself like that, but something about doing it felt comforting, like "you're not alone" when you are very clearly alone, lost in a spooky, old-store maze.

I took a few calming breaths and gave myself a pep talk. I needed encouragement that I wasn't about to be murdered by a clown holding a bunch of balloons or one holding a puppy, just like in a painting that I had spotted leaning against a shelf. I decided to keep moving, hoping that I'd find my way out, or Aunt Tara would come looking for me. I was mostly hoping it was the latter. This place was getting creepier by the minute.

After rounding another shelf that I was sure I had seen at least two times before, I walked past an open doorway that had an old web- and dust-covered wooden sign that read "Books." I didn't particularly care about looking through stacks of books that probably were so old, they were handwritten. So I decided to walk right past it, but as I did, curiosity got the better of me, and I took a quick peek inside. The room was lit only by stained-glass windows inset in the roof, lighting all the bookshelves that lined both sides of the room. The light coming from them was almost magical, as the hued beams crossed paths with each other and practically made a rainbow in front of me. But that wasn't what had caught my eye. At the other end of the room, past all the full shelves and piles of books on the floor, was one bookshelf set apart from the others. On the very bottom, there was one beam of light that seemed brighter and different from all the rest. I found myself walking quietly and slowly toward it, and as I did, the dust that had settled in the room, which clearly no one had cleaned or been in for a long time, was kicked up and started to swirl around me. Something about how the dust seemed to dance around me seemed even more magical than it did before and somewhat calming. When I finally reached the bookshelf, I saw that there wasn't anything too special about it. It was much like all the rest, but I bent down onto my knees to examine the light more.

I smiled to myself as I let my fingers wave and sway around the small beam. I could almost feel the light, the tingle on my fingertips as they brushed around the edges of the beam. I followed it all the way down to where it was beckoning me to look. There was a large leather-bound book covered in a thick coat of dust lying there. After taking a very long, deep breath, I picked it up and tried my best to blow the dust off. Now, I would have thought, after the thing with the blankets, that I would have thought better of that, but no, I guess my dad was right; I did have the memory of a gold fish. After another choking and coughing fit and waving the remaining dust from my face, I looked down at what I had found. The book in my hands was still caked with lots of dust, like ancient dust that has been on something so long, it's almost moist or turned into one solid layer, but I could tell there was something underneath it. I remembered seeing a stack of dishcloths a few shelves down before coming in here, so I took the book with me to find them.

I was thrilled that I was able to find the cloths again. It made me feel like there was hope, that I would find myself out of this labyrinth yet. I picked up a dark gray one from the pile, figuring it would do best at hiding anything gross that I might wipe off from the book, and after a few strong wipes with it, I was able to see most of what was underneath all the grime. The book in my hands was a light tan color and was, in fact, made of leather or the hide of some animal. On the cover was an intricately engraved image of a beautiful unicorn head, surrounded on all sides by an ornate border. I turned the book in my hand every which way, examining it from many angles. It was then that I noticed a small scratch on the neck of the unicorn. "That's a shame," I said out loud to myself. "Someone nicked it."

"Nicked what?" a voice said from behind me. I

instantly let out a high-pitched scream, and I jerked forward and into the air reflexively. The cloth fell from my hand, and I almost dropped the book but was quickly able to hug it to my chest as I spun around to see Aunt Tara smiling at me.

"Oh, it's just you," I blurted out, sounding relieved.

She raised her eyebrow at me curiously before she asked, "Who else would I be?"

I shrugged as I hugged the journal a bit tighter to my chest. "I don't know, maybe a murderous clown with a dog," I muttered.

"A what?!" she asked, looking a bit alarmed.

I shook my head, smiled, and said, "Nothing, just a creepy painting I saw in here." She laughed.

Her eyes went down to the journal and then back to mine. "So, what's nicked?"

"Nicked?" I replied, then remembered what I was holding. "Oh, just this book I found," and I turned it to show her.

Her eyes studied it for a moment before simply saying, "That's pretty. Did you find anything else you liked?"

I gave her a pained smile, speaking through my teeth while feeling a bit embarrassed. "Not . . . really."

My aunt's eyes gazed at the area before she nodded in agreement. "Yeah, this probably wasn't the best place to look," and she smiled in a way that reached her eyes. "Maybe we can look online tonight and order something?" I felt a surge of warmth spread through my body at the word "online," and all I could do was smile back at her and nod with as much enthusiasm as I could. "All right," she said as she started to turn, "just the book, then?"

I hesitated for a moment, feeling a little lost for words. The only thing that came out was "Well, I was just looking . . . I mean." Aunt Tara chuckled as she reached out and took it from me.

She quickly flipped through the pages, much like someone would a magazine at a checkout counter before buying it, then nodded, satisfied, and said, "It's OK, Jennifer, you can use it to write in about all your summer adventures," and she gave me a wink, then gestured with her head for me to follow her.

I wasn't sure if Aunt Tara came to this store a lot, or if she just had the best sense of direction ever, because after only a few turns we were standing back at the front of the store. I looked back to where we had come from, feeling very confused, as I had been so close to the front all this time. I couldn't tell if this had anything to do with the other two things that happened this morning or if I was being overdramatic. Either way, I was glad to finally be closer to freedom and fresh air. Aunt Tara placed the book on the counter in front of Susan, who was looking through a stack of papers. She was now wearing a thick pair of glasses that had a bright purple beaded chain on them. Susan lowered the glasses slightly before looking at the book, a little bit perplexed. "I don't recall ever seeing this book before." With the mountains of things in this store, I wasn't sure how she could.

When her eyes met mine, her whole facial expression changed. It looked vacant, maybe even replaced somehow, and I couldn't help but feel like I had done something really, really bad. She just stared at me for what felt like forever, and I could feel my mouth go dry. Even a bit of me fought the urge to gulp. Then, without a blink, the look vanished from her face as she said cheerfully, "The book's on the house. Think of it as a welcome gift," and she picked it up to hand it to me.

I took it from her slowly with a sheepish smile and told her, "Thanks," and she giggled at me with delight before she went back to finish my aunt's order. I was pretty sure this lady was a bit wacky. I slowly moved as close to the door as I could so that when Aunt Tara picked up her box once Susan had finished packing, I could quickly open the door and we could leave. I didn't know what I'd do while I was here this summer, but I now knew what I didn't want to do, and that was return to this creepy place.

Chapter 6

I got into the truck while Aunt Tara took her box to the back. After looking back at her through the rear window, it seemed like it might take her a few minutes to try to figure out how to fit her box in what appeared to be an already full truck bed. I smiled to myself as I settled back in my seat and looked down at my reward for making it out of the creepy maze of doom and dust alive! I was a bit confused when I opened it to the first page, as someone had already written in it. That was very disappointing; I mean, who would want a partly used journal? Having a quick glance in the book, the writing was mostly in cursive, and it looked a bit hard to make out. I turned to the next page and what was on there caught my eye instantly.

There was a beautiful drawing of a unicorn standing on top of some tall grass. The picture looked so real that the grass under it seemed to be blowing in the wind. I could easily have mistaken it for a photograph rather than a hand-drawn sketch, if it had been colored that is. The picture took up a good chunk of the top left corner of the page, probably a good third of it, in fact. The rest of the page seemed to be a list of what looked like species names, colors . . . Before I could fully process what I was looking at, Aunt Tara opened her door and got in, and I nearly dropped the book. Fumbling for a second, I regained my hold on the book and swiftly shut it. I placed it on the seat between us, hoping she didn't notice that she scared me AGAIN. Fortunately, she didn't seem to take note of it or at least was doing well at not showing that she did. Instead, she put on her seat belt and started to reverse into the street behind us.

Once we got going, she quickly glanced over to me and asked, "So how do a greasy burger and fries sound?"

I felt my eyes widen when I told her, excitedly, "Sounds awesome!"

My aunt couldn't hold back a laugh when she said, "And that's why you're my favorite niece."

This one statement made me feel happy but then confused. I looked over at her curiously when I asked her, "You have another niece?" Aunt Tara's whole face changed when it seemed to dawn on her what she had just said, kind of like the face my friend Alice at school had when she accidentally admitted she had a crush on a boy.

She paused for a moment before she spoke again, "Well, yes, a few of them, in fact."

I waited for a moment to see if she'd add any more, but when she didn't, I continued by asking, "Where do they live?"

The car slowed down at a stop sign, and Aunt Tara's focus appeared to be on seeing if any cars were coming from the side streets when she said, sounding very much distracted, "Most of them live in other states."

"Most of them?" I quickly asked. There was a strange look that overcame my aunt, almost like she had regretted how she answered the last question.

It felt like an eternity before she finally said, "Yes, I have one that lives in town." There was a hint of sadness in the way she said it, along with a melancholy look in her eyes, and I couldn't help but wonder why that would be. But before I could ask anything else, the car came to a stop, and my aunt loudly announced, "We're here!"

Lunch was fine, except it started to feel more like an interrogation, as my aunt kept the conversation going with endless questions about my life: "How is school? Do you have lots of friends? What are your hobbies?" I wasn't sure if she was genuinely this interested in my life or if she was trying to keep me from asking her any more questions about the niece she had in town. The one she clearly didn't want to talk about.

Anytime I would even try to ask her, she cut me off and asked what I felt was another set of random questions. It made me second-guess if I really wanted to keep asking her my own. Adults are so weird sometimes. Once we were finished with what was truly a good plate of burger and fries, she glanced over at the menu hanging on the wall behind the counter and said cheerfully, "Oh, good, they have pecan pie today! Yum!"

"A what pie?" I asked quizzically.

She tilted her head slightly before she said in a strange tone, "Don't tell me you've never had pecan pie."

I couldn't help but feel a little attacked, so I said in my most unimpressed voice, "What's a pecan?"

"It's a nut."

"A nut pie," I said back, wrinkling my nose to show how gross I thought it was. She chuckled as she scooted out from the booth.

Once she was out and standing, she looked back at me with a smile and said, "I'm going to head to the ladies' room. When I come back, I'll get us those pies. Trust me, you'll love it!" and with that, she headed toward the restroom.

As I sat waiting, I played with the napkin on the empty plates in front of me before looking around the room. The restaurant my aunt had brought me to, "Krakens Feast," was a mix of those old greasy spoon restaurants—the ones with booths lining the walls and a big, long counter with stools in the middle—and the inside of a pirate ship. It was weird for sure but also a bit fun. When I caught a glimpse of a man playing a game on his phone at the counter, it reminded me that I had mine in my bag. This seemed like the perfect time, if any, to see if my friends had messaged me and also to check their social media to see what I might be missing. I never made it that far, though, because when I switched it on, the first thing that greeted me was a cacophony of dings, indicating a whole bunch of missed text messages and phone calls.

Most of them were from my dad. Apparently, he had been trying to call and text me incessantly since not long after they had left. But the theme seemed to be him saying things like, "Why aren't you picking up your phone, Jennifer?" "You're hurting your mother's feelings by not answering." "Why are you being such a brat?" "I'm so disappointed with your attitude right now." After several more of these types of texts, his mood changed completely, like Dr. Jekyll and Mr. Hyde, "Sorry I was so hard on you. Your aunt said you went to bed right after we left. I'm sorry for what I said. Please call your mother. We love you!" I wasn't sure if I was mad at him or missed him, but it was probably both.

There was only one message from my mom. It simply said, "I'm sorry how we left things. I wasn't feeling well, but I'm doing fine now, so please don't worry. I know you're upset and I'm sure you don't believe me when I tell you I understand. If you need a few days to call me that is OK. Take the time you need. Know that no matter what, we love you. Mom." I felt my eyes begin to tear up. Part of me wanted to cry because I felt terrible about how I'd acted toward them. Part of me wanted to laugh because she signed her text messages with "Mom," like, did she not know how text messages work or what? I tried to keep myself from crying as I let my gaze turn to the window. One really nice thing about this restaurant, beyond the juicy burger I had just devoured, was the ocean view. There was something calming about it, but I wasn't sure if it was going to be enough to keep me from crying.

Outside the window, across the street, I could see the beach and a long boardwalk that had quite a lot of people on it. They appeared mostly to be kids my age, who, unlike me, I'm sure, were enjoying their summer with their friends, not stuck on a farm with their uncle and aunt. Lucky. Pondering this and enjoying the dream of what could have been, I hadn't even noticed that Aunt Tara had returned. She was standing beside me, but when I looked up at her, I could see she was also looking at the groups of kids. Her face softened as if she had just figured something out, and when she looked down at me, she said, "Sorry, kiddo, it seems they have only one slice of pie left."

"Bummer," I said, trying to sound disappointed.

My aunt attempted to hide a laugh before she suggested, "Well, since it is my favorite after all, and you don't seem too eager to try it, maybe you would like me to give you some cash, and you can go and get yourself an ice-cream cone at the pier?" She moved back a bit while producing a few dollars from her hand, offering them to me.

I couldn't help but feel overwhelmed with excitement when I replied, "Really?" I wasn't entirely sure what I was more excited about, not having to eat a pie made from a nut or being allowed to go across the street without an adult. This is something my parents would have never let me do in my city.

She gave me a quick nod and smiled. I quickly found myself jumping out of the booth, snatching the money from her hands, and rushing toward the door. When I got to the door, however, I suddenly froze when the realization came to me that I was acting a bit, you know, rude, maybe? I quickly turned around to see that Aunt Tara, who didn't seem to think much of it, was getting ready to sit down to wait for her pie. When she saw me, I quickly went back and hugged her, and before she could say anything, I said, "Thanks."

She laughed a little before whispering back, "OK, get already, so I can eat my pie—and have fun!" And with those words, acting like a gust of wind, I was gone.

Chapter 7

When I walked out of Krakens Feast, I found my face bathed by the warm, salty breeze that came from the waters ahead of me. It felt wonderful, energizing in fact, especially with the way the sun warmed my skin, just like being covered in a toasty blanket. The water ahead of me is what I guess you could call part of the ocean. I mean it was connected to one, somewhere. The ocean I was used to had what seemed like endless beaches, and when you looked out to the distance, all you could see were water and sky, but here the beach is a lot different. I wouldn't say it was the most petite beach in the world, but I'm sure it made it on the list, and when you looked across the water, you saw land.

I couldn't see from above, but I assumed that was why the town had "Crescent" in its name, that maybe it was shaped like a crescent. I guess it didn't matter. If there was water, sand, and sun, I could live.

Despite how small the town was, it did seem packed. I wasn't sure if everyone in town was from here or maybe this place got a lot of tourists. If it were the latter, I was starting to doubt I'd have much fun this summer. I liked the beach, but not every day. Even in my negative mood, it appeared that everyone else was having a blast, from riding their bikes down the road to building sandcastles, and even a few at the end of the pier who were fishing. I muttered to myself, "The only one keeping you from having fun is you!" and with those words, I stood up a little straighter, took a deep, calming breath, and headed across the street.

I had been excited at first about the idea of meeting kids my age and maybe hanging out, but the closer I got to the pier, the more doubt started to set in. What was I going to do? Walk up to a group of kids I didn't know and say, "Hey, my name is Jennifer. I'm here for the summer. Wanna hang out?" I tried to put myself and my friends in their place. If some random kid came up to us at the park and asked the same thing, we would probably have been weirded out and left the area at the first opportunity, or worse, laughed. I wouldn't have laughed, obviously, but a few of my friends might have. Then something worse dawned on me, what was I wearing? I quickly looked down at my shirt as I stepped onto the sidewalk and saw it. I was wearing my stupid rainbow poop emoji shirt, the lamest thing in my whole suitcase! Something I only wore on lazy Saturdays at home when I knew no one would see me. I quickly hugged my chest, trying to cover it up as much as I could, when I walked past a group of girls in what appeared to be fancy riding uniforms. Not a single one of them seemed to notice me. Part of me was happy about that so I wouldn't have to feel embarrassed. The other part of me felt invisible. In fact, not even a single one of the kids I walked past gave me a second look! Maybe they were just used to lots of new faces in town, but it still didn't help me feel any better about my situation. Oh well, at this point, my best bet would be to go and get an ice-cream cone and then return to the restaurant to wait for Aunt Tara to finish.

The line for the ice cream stand wasn't too long, thankfully, but when it got to be my turn, they were all out of my favorite flavors: mint chocolate chip, cookies and cream—there wasn't even vanilla or strawberry. After quickly evaluating the situation, and with a sense of panic setting in, I decided on chocolate, which wasn't the worst ice cream but certainly not my favorite either. Chocolate ice cream by itself was just so boring. I turned around, with ice cream in hand, ready to head back, when I saw a girl a few yards ahead of me, smiling and waving. I felt excitement bubble up inside me, and I quickly waved back at her. It was then that a girl from behind ran past me up to her. They both started laughing and hugging each other. I felt my whole face go red—like, my shirt was embarrassing enough, but waving at someone who wasn't waving at you was so much worse.

I turned sharply on my heels and attempted to rush away in the opposite direction. Sadly for me, I didn't make it very far, as I found myself smashing right into someone and promptly felt the cold ice cream through the front of my shirt. All I could do was stand there in shock, with my arms spread out to my side, still holding on to the now empty cone. I stared down at the horrible mess of ice cream that was slowly creeping down my front.

"I'm soooo sorry," I heard a boy say. When I looked up, I saw a kid about my age staring back at me, looking as horrible as I felt.

He was a little bit shorter than me, and most of his face was hidden beneath his messy brown hair. Which, I might add, was in real bad need of a haircut! I could also just make out that he was wearing a pair of dark-framed glasses. He had on what I would call a fishing vest, as it was covered in weird hooks of all types and sizes. I assumed he really liked fishing.

Before I could utter a word, though, he asked, "Can you hold this for a moment?" while he handed me a string of fish, not giving me a chance to say yes or no. I stared at it, feeling utterly grossed out. Eating fish was one thing, but holding dead ones was too much. He quickly pulled a cloth from his back pocket and then proceeded to clean the ice cream off my shirt! Apparently, this boy didn't know what boundaries were. Now, I say clean, but no, that was not what was happening. If anything, all the action did was just move the mess from one spot to another, leaving a trail of brown stains in its wake. I then noticed something strange about the cloth. It had large, slimy silvery-gray chunks attached to it and the unmistakable smell of fish.

"Ewww," I squawked, "what is on there?" The boy stopped for a moment to look at the cloth closer, then his face went red.

He sheepishly replied, "Sorry, they're fish scales." He then quickly put the cloth back into his pocket.

"What kind of person carries a rag covered in fish scales?" I demanded to know.

"Sorry," he said again, "I like to dry them off before I take them home." All the embarrassment vanished as he stuck out his hand and said, "I'm Chuck Dunbar, by the way."

I couldn't help but stare at his hand while I wondered if this guy was for real. Did he *really* think that I wanted to shake his smelly fish hands? Maybe it was rude, but at this point, I didn't care; I shoved the line back into his hand and muttered "Jennifer" under my breath. Chuck nodded at me, looking somewhat pleased that I had given him my name. This guy was getting weirder by the minute. He surprised me, though, when he proceeded to make it even more bizarre.

Chuck pointed to my shirt and chuckled slightly. "You know, it is funny if you think about it."

"How so?" I replied in confusion.

"Well, your shirt has a poop emoji on it, and the ice cream looks like poop!" He paused to laugh a bit more, but this time he sounded a tad nervous, probably due to the look I was giving him. "Well, now it looks like the poop went poop." He stared at me as if he was willing me to see the comedy in it, but all I could do was glare back at him with a clenched jaw. He gulped before adding, "Which is

absurd! Scientifically it's impossible for poop to defecate."
I was still mad, but I'm pretty sure my face read as more
confused than anything else. So not only was this guy
short and weird, but he was also a giant nerd.

I couldn't help but feel a shiver down my spine
when I heard a chorus of giggles coming from my side,
and when I looked over, to my complete horror, I saw that
same group of girls who were wearing the fancy riding
clothes. They were all looking at me, whispering, giggling,
and pointing with malicious glee. They all looked the
same, pretty with perfect hair, and right then, I knew
they were probably the popular girls in town. You know
the ones. They either liked you, so everyone else did too,
didn't notice you, or sadly, in my case, noticed you and
didn't like what they saw. They were the type of girls who
could make my summer here a living hell if they wanted.

Chuck broke my thoughts when he asked me, "You
want me to get you some napkins from the stand?"

When I looked back at him, I said in almost a snarl,
"I think you've done enough!" I was about to say
something else quite mean when I was interrupted by the
sound of Aunt Tara calling my name from behind me. She
glanced at my shirt but didn't say anything.

Instead, she looked at Chuck and smiled. "Hey,
Chuck, I see you got lucky with fishing today."

He smiled down at the fish before replying, "That's
right, Mrs. Greenfell. I got five of them today!" His smile
was big and full of pride. She then looked between us.

"I see you also met my niece, then." Chuck looked
a bit sheepish but nodded. I just shrugged.

I could see my aunt was about to ask if everything
was all right when she was cut off by the sound of a
bubbly and musical voice calling out, "Hi, Aunt Tara."

When I looked over to where the voice had come
from, I noticed one of the girls from the group who had
just been giggling was coming over to us with a wide grin.

She was taller than me, but not by much I thought, with long honey-blond hair in a perfect braid, not one strand out of place. Everything about her screamed perfect.

"Hi, Brittany," my aunt replied, sounding strained as if she was trying to be happy but clearly faking it. Brittany either didn't notice or didn't care, and I suddenly understood why my aunt had hidden her existence or at least failed to tell me about her.

Brittany glanced over at me and then back to my aunt and said in that same cheerful tone, "And who's your messy little friend?"

I could see from my aunt's face that she was conflicted, though I wasn't sure why, when she answered, "This is my niece Jennifer. She's staying with us this summer." Brittany looked me up and down with a smug smile that screamed, "I'm better than you." Never had I ever so badly wanted to punch someone. Well, Chuck was a close second.

Chuck chimed in to the conversation with "Oh, does that mean you both are cousins?"

Brittany and I just stared at him, and I'm pretty sure we both looked disgusted by the idea that we were somehow related to each other, but Brittany beat me to it when she said, her voice mirroring her face, "By marriage, which doesn't count. It means that she's nothing to me." She gave me a sideways glance. I was glad about this, but at the same time, I felt offended that she had just called me "nothing."

"Brittany," my aunt started to say, not sounding very pleased. I guessed Brittany's attitude had finally passed a line that Aunt Tara wasn't going to let go. That being said, I didn't want to make things worse for myself, so I interrupted her.

"Can we go home now?" Aunt Tara seemed to understand, so she nodded, and we both began walking back to the car. Sneaking a glance behind me, I could see that Chuck was already walking away, but Brittany was still standing there, staring at me with what I felt was an insidious grin, then she raised one hand and gave me a slow, posh wave. I felt a lump in my throat and decided that it would be best never to leave the farm again.

Chapter 8

The ride back to the farm was eerily quiet, and I wasn't sure which one of us avoided talking more. The girl covered in fishy-smelling ice cream or the woman who failed to hide the fact that she had one of the world's worst nieces on the planet. My money was on my aunt; after all, I could fix my problem with a shower. I doubted there was enough soap in the world to fix Brittany. After a while, the silence was starting to get to me, so I decided to ask her a question. "Can I ask you a question, Aunt Tara?" I noticed right away that her whole body became rigid. Yeah, she was definitely more on edge.

"Sure, what's on your mind?" she finally asked, seeming reluctant.

"Why did you paint your barn yellow?" I asked her.

"Well, she's just—" but before my aunt could say another word, she stopped and looked at me a bit perplexed before continuing, "Wait, what was your question?"

"Never mind my question," I told her, hardly able to keep the excitement and curiosity from my voice. "I want to hear more about what you were saying!" Aunt Tara honestly looked lost for words, and I couldn't help feeling just a tad bit sorry for her, but only a tad. When it became clear she wasn't going to go on with her last statement about the "she," who I could only assume was Britany, I said again, a bit more bitterly this time, "I asked why your barn was yellow. I mean, aren't they normally red or something?"

Aunt Tara clearly became more relaxed and smiled after letting out a long, low breath she must have been holding in. "Oh, that, well, that's an easy one," she told me. "You see, we have a bull; his name is Maurice," then she paused for a moment before adding, "and, well, he really, and I mean he really *really* hates red."

"Don't most bulls hate red?" I asked, thinking about all the times on TV I had seen a bull careening after a red flag some guy, who must have had a death wish, was holding on to.

She chuckled softly. "True, I guess, but he has a stronger hate for it, I think. After the third"—she paused to think about that last part before continuing—"or maybe the fifth time, he had almost completely demolished most of the barn walls. We just decided it would be best if we chose another color."

"And that worked? It calmed the savage beast, I mean."

That got me another chuckle and a nod before my aunt said, "Yeah, you could say that. He's still an ornery old boy but just a little less destructive.

We were getting closer to the road that led to the farm when my aunt's phone rang. She answered it. This action surprised me a bit, as my parents had a strict rule about not talking on the phone in the car. They made sure I knew that it was unsafe at every opportunity. I had no idea who she was talking to, but her tone and face went through a range of emotions, from concerned to relieved to annoyed. Her side of the conversation was just too cryptic that I couldn't understand what it was about. She said, "Any good news yet?" followed by "Oh, thank goodness, you found him!" After a short pause, she replied, "Really? Eating their apples again? How much is this going to cost us?" and then finally, "All right, I'll be there soon.

When she finally put her phone down on the seat next to her, I stared at her until she looked at me with a "What's wrong?" look. I folded my arms across my chest and, copying the tone my parents used on me when I'd done something I knew I shouldn't have, I said, "And what was so important that you put our lives at risk?" She got a peculiar look on her face as she processed my words, and then all of a sudden, she burst into laughter. A booming and big laugh, the kind that makes your whole face go red and your eyes start to water. Add this to the list of not the best things I thought an adult should do while driving. When she saw I was serious about my question, the laughing trickled away.

She cleared her throat and then said with a sincere voice, "You're actually right, Jennifer. I should have known better than to use my phone while driving. Believe me, I normally don't; it's just that I was waiting for some important news."

I unfolded my arms, curious as to what was going on. "What news?" For a moment, I was worried it had to do with my parents, but the whole apple thing wouldn't have made any sense.

"Well, you remember that horse you saw this morning?"

"Yeah," I said doubtfully, still not sure if it had been real.

"Well, that was our resident mischief-maker, Cliffton."

I couldn't help but wrinkle my nose at the name Cliffton. What kind of horse name was that? Then she continued, thankfully not noticing my expression as her focus was on turning onto the dirt road. "He somehow, and don't ask me how, escapes continually, and most of the time we find him in a nearby pasture eating our neighbor's apples."

I settled back in my seat, wondering if he was

really breaking out for apples or because they named him Cliffton. This thought made me chuckle slightly, and my aunt asked me, "Why is that funny?"

The first thing that came to mind besides the harsh truth of their bad naming choices was "Oh, I was just thinking that maybe, if you grew your own apple tree, he wouldn't have any reason to escape." Then I faked a grin, hoping she believed me.

Her face looked genuinely thoughtful about what I said, and she nodded in agreement, sounding very pleased when she told me, "You know, that's a pretty good idea. I'm going to have to talk to your uncle about this when we get to the stables."

I couldn't help but smile that my brain, for once, had come up with a good enough lie that somehow also was a good idea, but then my brain caught up with me. "We're going to the stables?" I asked.

She nodded and smiled as we turned onto a different dirt road. "We sure are."

My aunt and uncle's stables were pretty nice from the outside. Of course, I wasn't exactly sure what a stable was meant to look like. It was made from different sizes of gray brick that were framed within a dark wooden trim and topped off with a matching wood roof. As we walked into the stable, I asked my aunt, "So how many horses do you have?"

She paused briefly at the large wooden door that had been left slightly open. "Four," she said, but then she quickly corrected it to three. I wasn't sure how she could get that wrong. It's not like horses were small things after all, but when she corrected herself, I could briefly see a look of pain cross her face, so I decided it was best not to inquire as to why. As soon as the look passed, she pushed open the door and went inside.

When I walked in behind her, the first thing that hit me was the smell. It wasn't bad, but I wouldn't say it was good either. It was just weird, like someone had mixed grass, dirt, something sweet, and something a bit foul all together. Was this what horses smelled like, or was it the smell of their food, or worse, what came out of them? Now, seeing as it was a closed building, I decided to guess that it was probably all three.

The room itself was dim, with the light coming only from the windows on both sides of the rectangular room. The floor was dirt-covered with patches of what I thought was straw, or maybe it was hay. I wasn't entirely sure what the difference was, though. There were four stalls on both sides of the room, but most of them were empty. The ones on the left were filled with bales, and I assumed those were hay. In a couple of the stalls were tools like brooms and shovels. Two of the stalls on the right side each contained a horse. My aunt and uncle were standing and talking in front of one. The horse in that stall was the apricot one I had seen that morning. In the stall next to it was another horse with tan fur with a white patch going down the front of its head and a white, almost cream-colored mane. I saw a wooden sign on the stall door that read "Eloise." I stood there for a moment, admiring her. She was a beautiful horse. Something about the way she stood seemed regal, like she *knew* she looked good. I turned to look at the other two stalls, but I didn't see anything. One of the doors had a faded spot where a wooden sign had once been before. The other one had a sign that read "Thor." I started to go toward the door to look in when my attention was taken by a loud neigh that came from behind me.

I turned around just in time to see my aunt and uncle trying to calm down the horse that she said was called Cliffton. My head abruptly jerked backward. It took a second to realize that something had grabbed ahold of my hair and was trying to pull me back and downward. I let out a loud scream as I was unable to halt being pulled back. My uncle and aunt both yelled in unison, "Thor, no!" as they rushed over. Whatever Thor was listened to them, and I found myself free.

After taking a few steps for safety away from whatever Thor was, I turned around. I expected to find myself face-to-face with the biggest horse I'd ever seen, but instead, I was greeted by a short, stocky one. His fur looked more like that of a cow in pattern, colored dark red and white. He had so much wild and unkempt hair coming from the top of his head that you could barely see his eyes. I felt myself starting to laugh, but the look Thor was giving me made me feel like I had somehow offended him, which made me wonder, could a horse be offended?

"Are you all right?" my uncle asked.

I then heard my aunt whisper to him, "I don't know if we are bad at taking care of kids or if she's just unlucky." I could have responded with a million things like, "Maybe it's both" or "Now I know why you don't have kids!" but I decided to pretend I hadn't heard her.

"I'm fine," I mumbled as I rubbed at the sore spot on the back of my head.

"Do you want to pet him?" my aunt asked me. I glanced angrily at Thor.

"Him? Heck no! He just tried to murder me!" They both chuckled, but I didn't see how it was so amusing.

I wasn't sure if a horse could laugh, but the way Thor neighed and moved his head seemed a lot like a laugh to me. My aunt laughed some more before adding, "No, no, not Thor. He's a bit of a biter, as you now know. I was talking about Cliffton."

I looked over at Cliffton, who was standing there looking, well, not threatening, and I shrugged. "I don't know. Is he going to eat my brains as well?" Again, Thor made that weird horse laughing sound.

"You'll probably be fine if you give him a gift," my uncle told me, and then he handed me a large red apple.

Cliffton must have eyed the apple because he started moving about, looking all excited. I found myself hesitating for a moment before I finally decided it was safe. I took the apple and headed over to Cliffton. The horse leaned his head toward the apple in my hand. I wanted to pet him, but I was a little afraid to try. Cliffton's mouth opened, and he went to grab the apple with his teeth, but he stopped just short of it. He looked at the apple, and then he reached his head just a bit closer and started to stiff me. I don't think I've ever seen an animal's eyes, or anyone's eyes for that matter, get as big as his did. The next thing I knew, Cliffton was backing away as quickly as he could while making a very displeased sound on his way into the corner of the stall.

"That's odd," my uncle said as he came over to stand next to me.

"Guess he doesn't like me," I said begrudgingly.

"Nah, that's not it," my uncle reassured me. "He likes everyone. He probably has a cut somewhere because he had to go through some rosebushes in his great escape today. I better give him a good grooming." He then headed into the stall, but before he closed the door, he looked at me and smiled, saying, "Your aunt told me your idea about an apple tree. That's a pretty clever idea you had. You must get your smarts from your mother." We both laughed a bit before he shut the door and headed over to Cliffton, who didn't seem as annoyed as he had been a moment ago. After a small sniff of the air around me, my aunt decided it was an excellent time to head back to the house so I could get cleaned up. I gave my hand a sniff and found myself wincing at the aroma of sickly sweet–smelling fish. Yeah, maybe I did need a shower.

Chapter 9

It felt like it took me forever to scrub the smell of fish from my skin. It took so long that I started to worry about having any skin left at all. I used to like to eat fish sticks or fish and chips when I wanted to feel worldly, but now, knowing how foul and gross they smelled, I wasn't sure I wanted to ever see another fish again, even in a tank. Clean at last and in fresh clothes, I headed out of the bathroom. The smell of some food cooking wafted into my nostrils, though I couldn't tell what it was. Looking at the clock on my phone, I saw I had been in the shower for nearly an hour. I hoped this hadn't upset my aunt and uncle as this would have been the type of thing that would have sent my dad through the roof! OK, maybe not the roof, but I would have had to listen to him lecture me about wasting water and everyone doing their part not to leave a big carbon footprint. I mean, it's not like I disagree with him, but sometimes you must pay the price for fish funk.

I decided that since no one had called me for dinner, it might be a good time for me to text my parents. I sat on the bed with the pillow propped behind my head, and after taking a long deep breath to calm my nerves, I typed a short message to them both in a group chat.

"Hi." Short and simple, I thought.

I waited for a moment while I watched the bubbles where my text should have appeared, but then it finally said, "Unable to send." "What?" I said out loud but then felt sort of silly doing so since no one else was in the room with me. Next, I tried to call my dad, but I got an "Unable to connect" message, and then I got the same with my mom. The last thing I tried was to connect to my social media account, but unsurprisingly, I found myself unable to log in. With an angry huff, I tossed my phone to the end of the bed and folded my arms, feeling defeated.

I'm not sure how long I sat there, glaring at my phone at the end of the bed before there was a knock at my door, and my uncle said from the other side, "Jennifer, dinner is ready."

I quickly responded with, "OK, I'll be down in a minute," and then I heard footsteps moving away. There was no reason for me to have not just gotten up and gone with him, but I was still in a brooding mood and didn't want to have to deal with any chitchat on the way to the kitchen. So after I was sure he was way ahead of me, I left the room and made my way there.

There were so many smells that got stronger and stronger as I walked down the stairs. It smelled good, but that really didn't mean much. I've smelled food before that smelled and looked like it would have tasted delicious, only to be very disappointed. I remember thinking ratatouille looked delicious after seeing it in an animated movie. I know that is probably not the best place to look for foods, but meh. After begging my mom for several weeks, she finally made some. It took all day, and it smelled like it was going be the most delicious thing I'd ever taste, but it ended up being one of the worst foods. It's like I had completely forgotten that I hated most of the vegetables that were in the dish. Lesson learned!

I pushed open the door to the kitchen just in time to see Uncle James and Aunt Tara placing some bowls and plates of food on the table. My aunt smiled at me as I came into the room, and she motioned for me to come and sit down. "Come on, kiddo, before it gets cold."

I sat down and scrutinized all the food. Some of it looked normal, but as for the rest, I wasn't sure what it was. There were rolls, mashed potatoes, green beans, corn, and some form of meat. It was covered in a gooey-looking grayish-white slime. I couldn't help but eye it suspiciously. Aunt Tara noticed my intense quizzical look so she asked, "Haven't you ever had country-fried steak before?"

"I've never seen a steak look like that," I said, doubtful she really knew what a steak was.

She giggled at me just before she plopped one onto my plate and told me reassuringly, "Trust me, it tastes a lot better than it looks."

I poked at it with my fork before mumbling, "I seriously doubt that."

My uncle chuckled and added, "Don't worry, at least we've got some pecan pie to look forward to. Your aunt here got us some for dessert from Krakens Feast today, and let me tell you, they have the best pecan pie I've ever tasted!"

I looked at Aunt Tara, who was staring at my uncle, looking a bit pale, and asked her curiously, "I thought you said they had only one slice left?"

Aunt Tara's face reddened just a bit before she said confidently, "Oh, well, they came out with another whole pie right after you left." I couldn't help but smirk as I poked at my food again.

After a few hurried bites of everything on the plate, except for the weird meat, I said, "I tried to call my parents, but for some reason, my phone is not working."

They both exchanged a confused look with each other. "What do you mean?" my aunt asked.

"It won't let me text them, call them, or even search online, but it did when we were in town."

My uncle nodded slightly, now understanding what I meant. "Ah, yeah, sometimes we have trouble with our cells near the house. I think we are just a little bit too far away from the tower." He then took another big bite of his food. I felt a sense of dread come over me. Was I *really* going to have to go all summer without access to the outside world?

Aunt Tara smiled and reached over to touch the top of my hand. "I'm sure you're uncle James wouldn't mind taking your phone into town tomorrow to see if there is anything they can do to make it work," and she paused before continuing, "or at least partly functional."

Uncle James looked up from his plate at the mentioning of his name, still chewing away when he said, "Oh yeah, sure." He quickly wiped at his mouth as a bit of mash potato tried to escape.

My aunt eyed him for a moment and shook her head at his manners before she added, "But until then, you're more than welcome to use the computer in the office for the internet and the landline for any phone calls."

My eyebrows shot up. "What's a landline?" They shared another look between each other while trying to keep themselves from laughing.

"It's a phone," my uncle said while motioning to the wall behind me. There, next to the kitchen door, was an old, dingy phone hanging on the wall. The only time I think I have ever seen one like it was in a movie, and quite honestly, that is where they were meant to stay. Did they really want me to use that thing?

I turned back and told them both, "Oh, right, I just never heard anyone call it a landline before." I paused before adding sarcastically, "I know what a phone is." This got a smirk from my uncle.

He matched my tone, responding with, "Sure you do." I smiled at him despite myself. He may have won this time, but not next time!

I continued to play with my food, daring enough to try only a few bites of the weird steak and discovering that it tasted nothing like steak. It wasn't bad, but it wasn't good either. Uncle James and Aunt Tara had started talking about some farm-related thing after they drilled me about my first day. I was zoning out a bit, pushing some of the remaining potatoes around my plate, when my aunt asked me "Would you like to call them now?"

"Huh?" I responded when I looked up at her.

She motioned over to the phone on the wall with a tilt of her chin. "Your parents, would you like to call them?" For a moment I debated it.

I did want to talk to them, but with a whole day having have passed since the drama that happened, I really didn't want to talk to them for the first time with an audience, so I lied and told her, "Nah, I'm good, but can I go upstairs?"

"Don't you want some pie?" my uncle asked, looking at me like I'd be silly not to.

At this point, I just wanted to be alone, so I wrinkled my nose and shook my head, implying I was grossed out about it. This caused an even stranger look from my uncle in response. Aunt Tara, though, seemed to get the hint, so she just smiled and nodded. "Go ahead."

As soon as I got the OK, I darted out of the kitchen before my eyes could tear up. I didn't know why I was being such a baby. I really did want to call them and with my phone not working, I had no idea how long it would be before I could get a private moment. Add to that, that even though the pie sounded gross, I found myself wanting to have some. Why did I make things so hard for myself? Oh, that right, like my dad had told me countless times before, I was stubborn.

When I was finally done taking another shower (this one just to relax my mind), brushing my teeth, and putting on some pajamas, I found that someone had put a small wooden round table next to my bed. On top of it there was a plain white lamp along with a plate holding a good-sized slice of pie and a glass of milk. I was really surprised that someone had managed to set it up without me hearing, but I was also glad that clearly my aunt had seen through my fibs about not wanting any pie. I was starting to think she and I were going to get along.

With a heavy sigh, I got under the covers and sat in the bed. When I picked up the plate, I saw something else. It was the journal that I had forgotten to bring in from the truck, along with some sharped pencils. I took a small bite of the pie, which by the way, was soooo good, and then placed the plate on my lap. I picked up the journal and flipped to the first page. I wanted to see if I could read it this time. The page was stained, which I could only assume was from age, and the writing was faded in various spots but not enough that you couldn't see the words. On the readability scale, though, I would give it a 2 out of 10! It said, "I write these pages so that the knowledge of the creature that once walked among us will not be lost."

There was a break in the line, and below it, a different style of writing, still vibrant in its blue ink, "I have hidden the key right under our enemy's noses. The burning tree will never find it."

I held the book farther away from me, and I was sure I was looking at it a lot longer than I should have. Still, I quickly decided that was wrong. Whoever had the journal before me, they were either not in their right mind or perhaps trying to write a story. I wasn't sure which, so with a shrug, I turned to the next page, the one with the pretty drawing of the unicorn.

After turning the page, I noticed that there were remnants of pages that should have been there. The jagged edges close to the spine made it look like they had been ripped out in a hurry. Thumbing my finger along the rough edges, I could make out that maybe there were six or seven pages no longer present in the book. What could have been on them? Maybe attempts to draw a unicorn that didn't come out quite right? The more I thought about it, the more I realized I had wasted Aunt Tara's money on such a damaged journal. Taking a deep breath to calm the frustration, I decided not to dwell on thoughts of the missing pages for long, and I went on to focus on the page before me.

I studied the drawing longer this time. The page seemed aged, and at the bottom, there were strange small brown dots of different sizes, which seemed like a really odd design, though who was I to judge the artist. I found myself wondering who they were. I assumed it was whoever wrote the top part of the first page, as the handwriting seemed to match. I snuggled into the pillow behind me just a bit more, continuing to eat my pie as I read.

Species: Land Unicorn
Life Range: Unknown
Color: They share the same colors as their cousin, the horse, but I've seen a few with stripes.
Size: 12 hands to 17 hands
Favorite Food: Fruits of all kinds, but most really enjoy apples.

I paused for a moment and giggled, thinking of Cliffton before I went on.

Power: More studies must be done.
Biological Relatives: Unknown, though literature is filled with flying unicorns, so that cannot be ruled out.
Dislike: Unicorns seem to be very sensitive to the smell of death and will do anything they can to get away from it.

I'm not sure why, but this caught me as odd as I thought more about Cliffton and the way he acted around me. Did he smell the fish on me? Was he afraid of that? I shook my head before I went back to the book. I was disappointed that there was nothing else written. The letters "Li" were written but nothing else. It would seem rational to assume they were writing "Likes," but abruptly stopping part way through a word was strange. I found myself studying the strange brown dots longer, and a wild idea came to my mind: Was that blood? I didn't know if it was blood, but the very idea of it freaked me out so much that I dropped the book and quickly pushed it off the bed with a loud thud.

With just some crumbs remaining on the plate, I quickly placed it on the table and guzzled down my milk before turning off the light and swiftly hiding under my covers. I knew I should have brushed my teeth again, but something about the thought that I was in the room with something that may have blood on it creeped me out. What if it was haunted? I tried to tell myself I was just silly, but being away from home and with the darkness of a foreign room, it was just too much for me to push aside. I closed my eyes tightly and begged that sleep would soon come.

Chapter 10

The room was still dark when I felt myself being pulled out of a comfortable sleep. I usually sleep through the night without waking up, but tonight I was being woken up by my body shivering from the cold. I reached down to grab my blankets but found myself grasping at air. "This can't be right?" I thought. Forcing my eyes open, I peered down the bed to see where my blankets had gone. I felt my forehead tighten with the confusion that I suddenly felt. Not only from not seeing my blankets, but also that the curtains in my room were blowing with the breeze. "What?" I muttered into the dark room, rubbing my eyes before looking again. There was no doubting what I was seeing. The window in my bedroom was completely open, but I don't remember opening it, and I don't think it opened by itself when I went to bed. However it had happened, I had to do something about it. I hopped out of bed, nearly tripping on the blanket that was in a heap on the floor. This made me mutter even more. With a growl, I picked it up and tossed it onto the bed behind me before I made my way to the window.

I reached up with both arms, and just as I was about to pull it down, I found myself frozen. I wasn't sure if it was the breeze or what I was looking at that suddenly made my veins grow cold, but a dark figure was out on the grass outside my window. Whoever, or whatever it was, was standing perfectly still in the darkness below, and if it hadn't been for how wildly what I assumed was a cloak was blowing in the wind, I wasn't even sure if I would have seen it. I wasn't sure what it was or where it was facing, but the bitter, churning feeling in my stomach made me feel like it was looking up right at me. We both just stood there, neither moving, as if we were locked in a staring contest. A contest I was getting more and more scared about losing. I was too afraid even to blink.

A cloud above crept just enough to let some moonlight shine down. Something strange caught my eyes in that short moment of time, and I felt them widen. The figure on the ground below me was clutching something tight to the middle of its form, something that looked really familiar to me. "It can't be," I whispered before quickly turning to look at the floor, but it was true. The space on the floor where I had pushed my book was empty. Only the faint outline of where it had landed in the dust remained.

I felt a surge of anger coarse through my whole body before I turned back to confront the thief, yelling, "Hey, that's my book!" but when I did so, the figure was already heading away. This made me even madder! Someone had come into my room, stolen from me, and then had the nerve to turn away while I was yelling at them. I wasn't really sure what overcame me, but without even thinking it through, I turned around, and before I knew it, I was standing outside in my pajamas.

Standing in front of the porch, I scanned the darkness in the direction where I had last seen the figure. At first, I didn't see anything, and I was just about to give up and go back inside when suddenly, another beam of light illuminated the area where the figure had gone. It seemed to be standing in front of the cornfield as if it had been waiting for me to see it, because when I did, it turned away from me, disappearing into the darkness of the tall stalks. For a moment, I could have sworn I heard it laugh. Deep down, I was petrified. The laugh sent shivers down my spine, and this should have been the alarm bell that told me this was dangerous. The voices at the back of my head said, "Don't go after it, you idiot! Go back inside!" and "Nothing good ever happens in a cornfield! Especially at night! And was that cornfield even there yesterday?" But I didn't listen. Instead, I let the primal emotion of anger overwhelm my common sense. I stood there for just a moment, readying myself, before I felt a smirk spread across my lips.

I whispered to myself, "I got you now!" with a sense of triumph

I don't think I have ever run so fast in my entire life. It felt like the wind pushed me forward, faster and faster as I flew through the tall plants. Bits of corn and leaves were exploding around me in every which way I broke through them. I hoped I wasn't destroying my uncle's crops, but even with that thought, I kept going anyway.

When the field ended, I found myself standing in a small gap between it and the very dark trees ahead. The figure again appeared to be waiting, just steps within the woods, but it melted into the darkness and vanished when it saw me. I could feel myself hesitate for a moment as I stared into the spot where it had just been. Behind the first few rows of trees, there seemed to be nothing but endless darkness.

After a few calming breaths, I took one brave step forward. Anticipating something to happen, I was surprised when nothing weird or strange occurred. Nothing jumped out from behind a tree to attack me. In fact, everything seemed perfectly normal. Well, as normal as the woods at night could be, which was dark and scary, but that was normal, right? After I took a few more steps forward, all that changed. At first, it started with just a breeze, but the farther along I walked, the more the wind around me picked up. I stopped for a moment to look around. That was a big mistake. When I looked behind me, all I saw was darkness, and even though I was sure I hadn't walked that far into the woods, I could no longer see where I had come from. A panicked feeling grew inside me, and the more scared I became, the more it felt like the darkness around me was creeping in closer and closer. The shades of black looked like strange faces, each with eyes peering back at me, and the sounds of rustling branches were like growls. So, I did the only thing I could think to do, I ran! And the more I ran, the faster and stronger the wind around me grew, so strong I had to grab at anything I could in front of me to keep myself from being pushed back.

After what felt like an eternity, I finally saw the figure again ahead of me. It was just the incentive that I needed to muster all the energy I could and vault myself toward it, but when I landed, it wasn't there anymore, and I found myself kneeling on the edge of a circular clearing. Of course, the figure was nowhere to be seen. Even stranger, the moment I entered the clearing, the wind that had been blowing stronger than any storm I'd ever felt just stopped. It wasn't like it slowly went away either. It was just gone, like it had never been there in the first place. It felt so creepy when I noticed that not only was there no wind, but there was also no sound of any kind. It was dead silence. The only sounds I did hear were the ones of my own making. The fast thumps of my heart beating, the air swooshing into my lungs as I desperately tried to catch my breath.

Once I felt like I could finally breathe again, I stood up slowly. I felt nervous as I scanned the trees around me before finally searching the clearing. The area was well lit from the beams of moonlight that broke through the clouds above. The trees beyond, though, were pitch-black as if all the light around this one spot had been sucked away.

Something caught my eye. In the middle of the clearing, on the ground, I could just make out my book lying there, a small beam of light giving it the appearance that it was glowing. I made myself take a cautious step forward. I waited for a moment after that step, testing nature and whatever else was going on. Nothing happened, and after a quick scan around me, I felt a bit better, so I moved forward again. After my third step, I heard the lowest of whispers. I couldn't make them out at first, but when I took another step, they grew in volume, then another step, and another until they became loud enough to make out.

"Help them," one voice said urgently.

"Beware the burning tree," said another.

"He needs you!" begged one.

"Please save us!" yelled another from the darkness.

All the whispers I heard grew louder and more desperate the closer I got to my book. Each one was vying for my attention, talking over each other till they were one. They became so loud that I had to cover my ears with my hands just to try to block them out. I could feel my jaw tighten, and my body ached the closer I got. As the whispers crescendoed to a scream, I found myself screaming back at them, "Shut up! Leave me alone! Please stop; you're hurting me!"

I finally reached the book and quickly snatched it up with the plan of darting back through the woods as fast as my feet could carry me. The moment I turned around while holding the book tightly to my chest with both arms, the screams stopped. The void of silence was also gone, replaced with the sound of a light breeze ruffling through the trees. I could hear the sounds of crickets chirping and a few hoots of an owl in the distance.

I had to let the scene around me settle in my brain before I started to take a few small steps forward. For the first time, I noticed the feel of the damp leaves under my feet, and I couldn't help but look down at them as I squashed them between my toes with a dull crunching sound. I felt somewhat calm, staring down at them. It was so serene how the moonlight made the drops of dew shimmer. The peaceful feeling, however, was soon replaced by fear as I found myself frozen when the light from above me dramatically shifted. I was too scared to turn around, and I was sure I felt a warm gust of wind hit my neck, or was it a breath? Was that someone's breath? I instinctively hugged the book tighter to my body, and I squeezed my eyelids shut before I heard the faintest whisper in my ear say, "Jennifer, you have to help him."

The next thing I knew, I was shooting up from my pillow with a loud, ear-piercing scream. My room was still dark, but there was enough light coming from the window that I could see. Within just a few moments, I heard my uncle and aunt quickly leaving their room, followed by loud, rushed steps. A light came on in the hallway, which I could see shining through the crack under my door. My uncle practically burst into the room, holding a baseball bat and yelling something like, "Who's in here!"

He stood in front of my bed like he was wielding a sword, his eyes scanning the room, searching for a threat. My aunt entered behind him, appearing calmer, holding a small lantern with one hand and clutching her robe tight at her neck with her other. Her voice was soft and calm when she spoke. "Jennifer, are you all right?"

I couldn't find my words, so instead, I nodded at her, and she came over to sit on the bed next to me. Uncle James and I just stared at each other for a moment, but once he was happy that everything was all right, he lowered his um, weapon, and stood there looking confused and unsure about what he was meant to do next. When my aunt suddenly grabbed my hand, it made me jump.

"Bad dream?" she asked.

"Yeah," I said slowly, "you could say that."

I could make out her smile as she added, "Must have been a bad one; you're all sweaty," but then she paused before asking, "Are you feeling sick?"

"No," I told her firmly, "it was just a bad dream, but I'm OK now." I could tell she wanted to say more, but she nodded instead before getting up from the bed and walking to the door with my uncle.

Before she shut the door, she looked back at me and told me, "If you need anything, don't be afraid to wake us up, all right?"

I could tell she wasn't going to leave without a reply, so I nodded and said, "Really, I'm all right." Aunt Tara sighed just slightly before she nodded again and softly shut the door behind her.

As soon as they were gone, I lay back down, feeling completely awake. I checked my phone to see what time it was, and joy of joys, it was only just past midnight. Great, now how was I meant to get any sleep? I tried to shut my eyes, but as soon as I did, I opened them right back up and hopped out of bed. I snatched up the journal that was on my floor and took it back into bed with me, holding it tightly to my chest, much like I used to with Mr. Wiggles, my stuffed sloth, when I was small. Something about having the book with me now made me feel safer, so safe I felt like I could fall back to sleep. That was until I moved and felt something hard under my hip. I reached down, searching the bed under me until I found the item, and grabbed it, whatever it was. Holding it in front of my face, I gasped and muttered, "You've got to be kidding me!" as I stared at a small kernel of corn between my fingers. It was going to be a long night.

Chapter 11

I never did quite feel like I fell back to sleep, more like I was stuck someplace between awake and unconscious. Thoughts just kept filling my head while I lay there, mainly about the nightmare, my new journal, and the weird behavior I had seen in Cliffton. I indeed had to admit to myself that I knew absolutely nothing about horses, but I was sure even my uncle seemed to be confused by Cliffton's sudden jolt away from me. Did all these things have a common thread? Was I secretly looking for something to give me a reason to go home? Was my brain even clever enough to manipulate myself that way? I doubted that. The more I thought about it, the more Cliffton's behavior and what I read in that journal made me consider something that I would have thought was ridiculous just days ago. Were unicorns real?

I woke up ages before I had the day before, and in fact, I was pretty sure I had gotten ready and dressed for the day before my aunt and uncle even left their bedroom. I decided to stay in my room as long as I could, even though I had no access to the internet. I preferred to be bored out of my mind. Why, you ask? Well, part of me really wanted to avoid any talks about last night, but the main reason was that I had a plan.

As soon as I was sure breakfast was ready, or at least almost ready from the smell of cooked meat I had smelled waffling down the hall, I headed out of my room. I made my way down the stairs into the kitchen, just in time to see Aunt Tara finishing up cooking a pan full of what looked like bacon and sausage.

I quickly sat down as Aunt Tara scooped a giant mound of scrambled eggs onto my plate, along with a few pieces of bacon and sausage. I was hungry, and it did look really good, but for a second, I felt a bit put off by it when it suddenly occurred to me that this food could have been from animals here on the farm. I didn't consider myself a vegetarian, but my family never consumed two different types of meat at the same meal, unless you counted a buffet or party. And it wasn't like I was friends with any of these animals either, well, at least not yet. Still, after seeing them going about living their lives, it did make me feel a tinge of guilt. I pushed the thought aside when my hungry stomach got a better whiff of the food on my plate. It smelled so good that my mouth began to water, and after all, I didn't want their lives to have been in vain, right? With that last thought, I began to shovel a large forkful of eggs into my mouth.

Right when I had a mouth full of eggs, that was the exact time my aunt decided to sit down and ask me a question. "So bad dreams, huh?" she said, peering at me from above the rim of her cup of coffee. I knew this question was coming! I mean, how could it not? What adult is going to run into the room of a screaming kid, in the middle of the night, and not ask about it the next day? I was really hoping she wouldn't, but I knew I was kidding myself about feeling that lucky. Since my mouth was clearly full, I used it to my advantage and just shrugged at her before shoving another mouthful of eggs into my mouth. Aunt Tara nodded at me, seeming to understand I didn't want to talk about it before she started eating some of her own food. I had to give her points for trying, at least. Uncle James seemed more interested in his breakfast and the paper he kept glancing at. It was a strange sight to see as I didn't realize people still read those things.

It wasn't long before I noticed that Aunt Tara was giving Uncle James an odd look, almost as if she was willing him to speak with her mind. When he finally took notice of her, he lowered his paper just enough to look at me before saying, "You know, Jennifer, you can talk to your aunt and me about anything that's bothering you." The look of concern on his face and the tone of his voice made me feel it was more forced than natural.

I quickly took a gulp of my orange juice to help finish off my mouthful of eggs before I told him, "OK, thanks, but I'm fine." Uncle James smiled and nodded, looking proud of himself like he had solved some great mystery, and happily went back to his paper. Aunt Tara, on the other hand, didn't look convinced.

It seemed like now was the best time to begin my plan. I got another forkful of eggs, this time a much smaller one, before I said, "So, I was thinking, maybe I could take the horses some apples this morning? You know, so they get to know me better." I quickly took another bite, pretending to be nonchalant about it, while I read their expressions.

Uncle James looked complexed for a moment before he flatly said, "It's way too early for them to be eating apples, maybe later." When I saw Aunt Tara nod in agreement, I knew I had to act fast, so I gave her one of my world-famous pouts before I looked pitifully down at my plate, using my fork to play with my food.

I had to keep myself from smiling when I heard my aunt say in a very sweet and slightly worried tone, "Well, it wouldn't hurt just this once." Before my uncle could even finish the bacon he had just put into his mouth to protest, she was already getting up from the table and heading over to a bowl where there were some apples and other fruits. She came over to me in less than a minute, holding a small paper bag into which she had placed a few handfuls of apples she had sliced up.

Not giving my uncle a chance to say anything or for my aunt to change her mind, I snatched the bag from her hands and grabbed a few still-warm slices of bacon from the plate as I rushed to leave the kitchen, telling them, "I'll just grab a few for the road."

I had almost made it to the door when my uncle called out my name, causing me to freeze midstep. So close! I thought. When he asked me, "Do you want me to take your phone to be looked at today?" I was a bit surprised as I had been fearing he was going to keep me from going to see the horses.

"Oh," I murmured before telling him, "sure, it's on my bed," then I hurried out the door before anyone could stop me again. I was sure I heard them both chuckle slightly before the kitchen door swung closed behind me.

The bacon wasn't really for the road, as it was part of my grand plan, and I was happy that my aunt had made it for breakfast. Otherwise, I wasn't sure what I was going to do. I wasn't too far from the house when I heard the sound of a car coming down the road, but I didn't bother looking behind me. I didn't want anything or anyone getting in the way of my plans. I almost felt like a scientist or an adventurer about to make a great discovery.

When I got to the stables, the door was shut. I wasn't too surprised by that. I was, however, surprised by how hard it was for me to pull it open. Clearly, the slices of bacon I was holding in one hand and a bag of sliced apples in the other weren't doing me any favors, but after a few hard pulls, I was able to open it just enough to squeeze myself through, barely. Before I did, though, I put the slices of bacon in my back pocket and hoped that they didn't stain.

As I entered, all three of the horses turned their

heads toward me as I slowly approached them. They all seemed a bit startled by my appearance, and I wondered if I had woken them up. I ignored both Eloise's and Thor's stables and went right for Cliffton. He took a few steps away from me, and I smiled slightly before showing him the bag of apples and asking, "You want some apples, boy?" I am sure that at that moment, he looked less scared and a bit excited. Now, I know horses don't smile or anything, but there was just something that changed about him that made me feel he was happier.

Cliffton walked toward me after I took out the first slice, and he hungrily ate it from my hand. The other two horses slightly whinnied as if they were trying to tell me they wanted some too. "Don't worry," I said, "there is more than enough for all of you." I took another slice of apple out, and this time I let the bag drop carefully to the floor. As Cliffton started to eat the apple, my other hand went for the bacon, and I whispered to myself, "But I got to see something first." Before Cliffton could finish the apple, I put a slice of bacon next to his nose, and I swear his eyes grew larger than I thought they could and he bucked into the air. I fell backward onto my butt in shock, taking in how tall a horse could be when standing on two feet like that. Cliffton quickly steadied himself before cowering into the corner of his stall again like he did yesterday. "Interesting," I murmured, but before I could say another word, I heard some voices, and then the door behind me opened more. I jumped to my feet as fast as I could and grabbed the bag of apples from the ground.

Chapter 12

I couldn't help but let out a sigh of relief when I saw Aunt Tara poke her head around the door. I wasn't sure who I thought it could have been, but part of me felt I would have gotten a talking to if they knew I was shoving slices of bacon under a horse's nose. Aunt Tara smiled at me just as it dawned on me that I was still holding the bacon, so in a move of panic, I quickly shoved it into my front pocket with a sinking squish. I was really going to regret that later, I thought with a grimace. "You have a guest," my aunt said, sounding so excited. So excited that I could imagine only two people she thought I'd be that happy to see, Mom and Dad. I felt a smile spread over my face as I quickly raced to the door, but when I got to it and looked out, I didn't see my parents. Instead, it was that boy from yesterday, Chuck, and some girl who was taller than him by a good few inches.

"Oh," I said disappointingly, which caused Aunt Tara to give me one of those "don't be rude" looks as Chuck looked down at his feet. I had a moment of panic, as it wasn't my intention to have sounded so rude. I was just upset it wasn't who I wanted to see. So, with a deep breath, I said as happily as I could, "It's Chuck, right?"

Chuck looked up from his shoes at me, a big grin on his face, nodding as he replied, "Yeah, and this is my friend Jade." I looked over at the Jade standing a bit behind Chuck. She had a tan complexion, and her dark brown hair was pulled back in a ponytail. Her eyes were a deep shade of green, which I thought suited her name really well.

I gave a slight wave of my hand at her and smiled, which she returned with a bubbly grin of her own. She seemed nice, I thought. Before I could say anything, Chuck stepped between us more and said excitedly, "I got you a present!" Before my brain could wrap around what he was doing, he had slung his backpack in front of him and proceeded to dip inside for a moment before pulling out what appeared to be a large tub of chocolate ice cream. My eyebrow arched up in confusion as he thrust the tub that had quite clearly started to melt toward me. "For the ice cream I ruined yesterday," he told me, answering my unasked question. "I figured it was your favorite," he added with a proud grin.

I wasn't entirely sure why I had picked it yesterday since it wasn't really one I would typically have picked. Probably more panic on my part. I'd never been good at choosing food from a menu when someone was staring at me. I always got the feeling that they were annoyed that I hadn't instantly known what I wanted. This feeling had, in turn, gotten me several bad meals.

I tried my best to smile, and I said, "Thanks," but I didn't reach out to grab it. It looked way too sticky. Rude or not, I wasn't going to take it from him.

Thankfully Aunt Tara did, with what looked like a forced smile when she realized how sticky the tub was. "I'll take that, Chuck, and get it in the freezer before it melts. You kids have fun," and with that, she turned away and rushed back toward the house, leaving a small trail of chocolate along the way.

The three of us stood there looking at each other in an awkward silence that felt so long, and the longer it got, the harder it was to break. I decided that I had no choice but to be the one to break it. At precisely the same time, Chuck and Jade also tried to, and the three of us spoke at once. Then, for another but shorter period of silence, we each stared, debating who would speak first. This time it was Jade. "So, Chuck tells me you're visiting for the summer?"

"Yep," I said, nodding at her.

"That's cool." She smiled before asking, "So where are you from?"

"New York City," I replied before I scuffled my feet slightly. I felt uncomfortable as I recalled being made fun of when I was much younger for being from the city by a group of kids. They had called me "city slicker" and "city girl" and laughed at me like I was strange. But that feeling faded somewhat when Jade's face lit up.

She about squalled in excitement. "Oh my gosh, oh my gosh, that is so cool! You have to tell me all about it! I've always wanted to go there!" I felt my face redden.

"I told you she was cool!" Chuck blurted out, and then he had a strange look on his face like he wanted that to have remained a secret. His cheeks reddened, and he tried not to make eye contact. I swear, boys are weird.

I was more than willing to tell Jade all about where I was from. In fact, I was feeling really excited about the idea, but there was a much bigger question to ask, and so I did. "So why are you both here?" looking from one to the other.

"Oh," Jade said, looking suddenly a bit sheepish, and she quickly looked to Chuck, who just smiled. "I thought we could show you around town," then he added with a much bigger, somewhat prouder smile, "Well, the cool spots at least." I highly doubted that Chuck knew anything cool. I wasn't trying to be mean, but . . . well, I guess he did know Jade, so maybe he did.

I shrugged at them both. "I'll need to ask my aunt and uncle first," I told them.

"They already said it was all right," Chuck said, beaming.

"Oh," I said, feeling a little annoyed. If I wanted to get out of this, I had just lost my chance and couldn't fall back on the "Oh, sorry, they said I can't today" lie. I faked a smile when an idea came to me. Hoping my sarcastic tone wasn't heard, I replied, "Well, how are we getting to these cool and amazing places?" Chuck smiled, and he looked over his shoulder. I followed his gaze, and I saw two bikes lying on the ground a little distance behind them. "Ummm," I said while I kept my eyes on the bikes, "there are only two of them."

I caught Jade giving Chuck a look that almost said, "Told you so," which instantly made Chuck look embarrassed. "Well," he said, trying not to sound as embarrassed as he looked, "you could always ride on the back of mine," and he gave a weak smile. I felt my nose instinctively wrinkle up, but before I could say a word, I spotted Uncle James coming toward us from the house, pushing along what appeared to be a bike.

"Great," I muttered to myself, hoping no one heard me after I said it, or if they had, they thought I meant GREAT! Like, yay, I'm happy and not "great" like it was another nail in my coffin. I undeniably wasn't feeling the first one, and the closer Uncle James got to me, the more dread I felt.

When the bike was close enough to inspect, the first thing I observed was that it was obviously too small for me. Next, it was the nastiest shade of green I'd ever seen, almost like a pukey-green pea soup color. It also looked so old I wondered if it had been Uncle James's when he had been a boy.

My uncle looked at me with a wide grin as he motioned to the bike at his side. "You're aunt said you guys were going on a bike ride, so I thought you could use this."

"Can I?" I said, doubting I'd be able to.

My uncle took my question more like I was asking

if he was sure it would be OK, replying, "Of course you can, kiddo!" He let the bike drop down onto the grass with a light thud before he said, "You kids have fun." He paused briefly, then turn around with a silly grin and said, "But not too much fun."

"We'll try not to," I said with a fake grin. "We won't," I mumbled under my breath as I walked over to the bike. Yep, it was old, and it might have also been a bit rusty in a few spots, which made me wonder if I was up to date on my tetanus shots.

It wasn't long until the three of us were slowly, and I do mean slowly, making our way down the road leading out of the farm. I suddenly understood how Sisyphus felt in that ancient Roman or Greek story. The one where Zeus punished him by making him push a giant boulder up a hill eternally. That's what this felt like. No matter how fast I peddled, which wasn't very fast since the bike was clearly made for a much smaller child, I moved at such a slow speed that Chuck and Jade were able to make loops and loops around me. I felt like my body's battery was already at 50 percent as beads of sweat started to form all over my body.

We had probably made it halfway to the road when Jade stopped, got off her bike, and looked me over before saying, "This is not going to work. That bike is crap."

Chuck's eyes nearly bulged out from their sockets when he looked at her with his mouth agape, "You shouldn't talk like that."

Jade rolled her eyes and gave him a strange look. "You got a better word for that bike, Chucky?"

Chuck seemed to cringe at the nickname. Clearly, he didn't like it, but he shook his head, adding, "Yeah, you're right, it is crap." The three of us shared a look before we broke into a laugh. All right, maybe this day wasn't going to be entirely bad. At least they both had a sense of humor.

103

Once the laughter died down, I asked, "So what are we going to do about this?" motioning to the bike under me.

Chuck and Jade both thought it over before Jade spoke. "Maybe we can just walk it?" and she glanced over to Chuck to see if he agreed.

Chuck didn't, as he emphatically shook his head, saying, "No way, it would take ages to get down if she has to pull that thing along." Then there seemed to be a hint of hope in his voice when he added, "Well, I mean, she could just ride on the back of mine. I don't mind at all."

Jade and I exchanged a glance before I said doubtfully, "Let's call that one plan B." Jade practically snorted as she added, "Or, C, D. Heck, let's just call it plan Z." Chuck gave Jade a mean glare with a scrunched-up nose before he muttered something that sounded like "whatever." Jade returned the exchange with a mischievous giggle.

I was all ready to suggest that maybe it would be best if we tried this another time, but before I could get the words out, I heard the sound of a vehicle approaching from behind us, and when I looked behind me, I saw a tan truck. When the truck came to a stop beside us, I saw my uncle looking at us, somewhat perplexed. I hadn't realized that he had his own truck. Seemed a bit overkill, but maybe they needed two, so they could do double the work or something. He rolled down the window, and with an arched eyebrow, said, "Um, I would have thought you three would have reached the town by now."

"Well," I said, stopping while I tried to think of the best way to approach this without offending my uncle.

Still, before I could think up anything, Jade chimed in, saying, both truthfully and respectfully, "This bike is no good, Mr. Greenfell." Embarrassment flashed across my uncle's face before it was replaced with that look adults got when they got something wrong but pretended they knew it all along.

He smiled and nodded. "Yeah, I was a bit worried about that, but I thought it was worth a shot. How about you kids put your bikes in the back, and I'll give you a lift."

Jade and Chuck didn't hesitate and swiftly lifted their bikes up into the truck and hopped in the front, so I followed suit and joined them. It was not as easy as they had made it look. Thankfully, Jade got back out and helped me with the slightest of grins.

"Where to?" my uncle asked, looking at Chuck, who was seated right next to him.

"Merrow Crescent Stables," he said cheerfully.

Chapter 13

Uncle James didn't say much after he started driving. In fact, anytime I looked over at him, he grew more and more uneasy. I found myself wondering what could possibly be the problem. Chuck and Jade seemed oblivious to it as they kept talking and pointing out random things to me as we drove past them. So oblivious that when Chuck decided to ask my uncle, "Mr. Greenfell, did you use to go Merrow Crescent Stables when you were our age too?" his whole body stiffened slightly from the question.

He grumbled back, "Um, not really." It was becoming clearer that my uncle was not as approachable as my aunt was, or maybe he just didn't like kids too much, which would explain why they never had any of their own. The more I looked at him and saw how uncomfortable and out of place he seemed, the more sure of it I was. Chuck didn't appear to notice because he continued to ask my uncle questions.

"Oh, why not?" Chuck asked, sounding very curious.

"Because I didn't," he replied flatly.

"Why not? My mom told me all the kids used to go there when she was younger."

"Yeah, well, I didn't," he grumbled back, the flat tone starting to become just a hint annoyed.

"But my mom," Chuck said, staring at my uncle almost suspiciously.

"Your mom doesn't know everything, Chuck," he

said, the tone of his voice sounding a bit more annoyed.

"Oh, well, she knows a lot of—" Chuck proudly started to say, but he suddenly stopped when Uncle James turned just enough to look down at him. His voice seethed with a warning when he said only Chuck's name.

I was sure I heard Chuck swallow before he quickly turned away to Jade and me. There was a long moment of silence before Jade announced, both sounding happy and relieved, "We're here." When I turned to look out the window, we had just passed a very large, very expensive rectangular wooden green sign with a white border that read "Merrow Crescent Stables" in large, pretty letters, and a year written underneath, which I didn't quite see.

My uncle pulled over to park next to the sign. I was rather confused as he didn't turn down the paved road that led toward the stables. Still, before I could ask what he was doing, he told us, "You kids can make it the rest of the way on your bikes from here," and before anyone could protest or complain, he quickly got out of the truck and started unloading the bikes, seemingly rushed to do so.

All three of us stared at each other. Jade and Chuck looked just as confused as I felt, but we all shrugged and hopped out of the truck. Uncle James had just gotten the last bike out of the truck bed as we all reached him. "If you need another ride, just give me a call," he said before he turned toward Chuck and asked, "You got my number, correct?"

Chuck proudly nodded as he said, "Yes, sir, I know it by heart."

My uncle's eyebrows shot up for just a moment before he said, "Riiiiight," sounding a bit weirded out. And with that, he shut the tailgate and gave us a wave over his shoulder without looking back, telling us, "All right, kids, you have fun."

"Thanks," I said, but I was sure he hadn't heard me

because he'd already shut the door and was back on the road driving away within just a few seconds, leaving a trail of dust flying at us. I couldn't help but cough a bit as I tried not to choke on the cloud that was slowly dissipating around me. Chuck and Jade didn't seem bothered, but they had already started walking toward the stables, leaving me there staring at my uncle's truck as he drove away, or fled might have been more accurate. He wasn't speeding or anything or even being reckless, but you could tell he was in a hurry, making me wonder why. But adults were weird, so I decided it probably didn't really matter.

The Merrow Crescent Stables was a short distance from the road, well, short if we had driven down the rest of the way to it. Pushing the bike alongside me was longer than I would have wanted it to be between the heaviness of the bike that was hindering every step I took and the heat that seemed to become increasingly hotter by the minute. The flattened dirt road that led toward the stables curved and gently bent left as we went, which I thought was rather picturesque and looked a lot better than if it had been straight. I guess, in a way, it looked more natural than made by someone. There were clusters of birch and oak trees on both sides of the road with bushes and flowers between them. I was sure someone must have planted them there, but they did it in such a way that the whole area felt like you had traveled into a forbidden forest, especially with the way the light streaked through the canopy of branches that hung over the road above us. There was also a strong, sweet smell that wafted in the air around me. I couldn't place it, but when I asked Jade about it, she smiled and told me it was honeysuckles. It wasn't until we got a lot closer that the stables came into view, and by then, I felt like I needed a shower. Also maybe a gallon of water by the time we were able to abandon our bikes next to the mossy stone wall that bordered the clearing ahead. The stables were amazing, if I were being honest. It felt as though I had walked right into a fairy tale. I didn't know a lot about stables. In fact, the only ones I had ever seen before these were my aunt and uncle's, and this one made theirs look, well, dull.

It was obviously old, but how old I had no idea. The buildings were made from misshapen gray stones, and the roof was a dark wood. From the outside, it seemed like just a large square building that had random patches of ivy growing up the walls and lots of pretty trees, bushes, and flowers landscaped around the outside. There was a large arched opening on the side that we walked into. I was amazed to find that after at least thirty feet of walking through it, the passageway opened into a large courtyard area.

The courtyard center had a small rectangular walled-off grassy area with a wooden fence and some old sturdy-looking wooden tables and chairs. Outside that, the ground was well-worn dirt with lots of hoof prints. The walls around the courtyard were lined with many dutch doors. Each one had an oval nameplate on the bottom half that bore the horse's name inside. All four walls of the courtyard had an archway just like the one we had entered that led to other areas. I found myself taking a deep breath. The air oddly didn't smell bad at all, and I found myself feeling a strange sense of peace and excitement. I never really thought I was the type of person who would want to ride a horse, but now I found myself strangely wishing to.

I quickly found the happy feeling I was so fondly enjoying vanish as I felt Chuck pat me on the shoulder, exclaiming, "It's great here!"

"Sure is," I said, flashing him a fake smile before looking away and mumbling to myself, "Or at least it was."

"What'd you say?" he asked. I felt my face flush red

when I realized what I had just said was out loud and not in my head like it should have been.

"Oh," I said, stumbling to find the right words to say so as not to hurt his feelings. He stared back at me, and the look in his eyes reminded me a lot of a lost puppy dog, which just made me feel guilty and bad, so I did the only thing I could think of and asked him a question instead, "So why did you bring me to this clearly awesome place?" I follow it with the best smile I could muster. Chuck bought it, thankfully, because his whole face lighted up.

"To see my horse," he told me.

"Our horse," Jade corrected him, looking a bit slighted.

"Yeah, our horse," Chuck said, looking a bit defeated.

"You share a horse?" I asked, then asked another question, not giving either of them a chance to answer the first one, "How can you share a horse?"

"It's complicated," Jade said as she shoved her hands into her pockets, looking a bit embarrassed as she did.

"How so?" I asked, looking between them.

"Well," Chuck said, letting the words draw out.

When Jade saw I wasn't going to accept "well" as a suitable response, she told me, "Since we both live in town, neither one of us has enough land to house a horse, and well"—she looked at the ground trying to avoid my eyes—

"this place is pretty expensive. Between our allowances, we could only afford one stall." Chuck finished for her by adding, "So we decided to share one, but it works out anyway because it means we share the jobs of brushing and cleaning the stall out. If anything, it is actually better!" Chuck smiled like he was trying to believe his own lies.

"Well, half the work is better than all the work,

right?" I said, smiling at them both but still wondering if they got into fights about whose turn it was to ride. Chuck smiled at me before gesturing for me to follow him. Jade only looked at me briefly before quickly turning away and following Chuck.

I took a quick peek inside some of the other stables as we passed them, and I saw so many beautiful horses in them. Some were with their owners being groomed, and others were alone munching on hay. Some even had their manes braided or decorated with ribbons and bows. One I passed had to be the most beautiful horse I'd ever seen. It was a white horse with flecks of gray down its neck leading to its chest and this almost shimmery light golden-brown mane. The sign under the door read "Moonlight." I noticed that Chuck and Jade had stopped walking, and for a moment, I thought that maybe this was their horse. That was until a moment later when I realized they were standing in front of the stall next to it.

I gave Moonlight one more longing look before I moved away to the other stall. The nameplate on the door read "Cumberbunch." That's a weird name, I thought, thankfully not accidentally voicing it out loud this time. When I looked into the stall, though, it suddenly didn't feel weird enough. Now, I never thought I'd be a person who would say an animal was ugly, but well, I could never in my entire life look at the animal I was looking at now and say it was pretty either. That whole "the face only a mother could love" phrase suddenly made a lot of sense to me. Cumberbunch looked more like a cross between a mule and a zebra than a horse. His mane seemed to be super dry and short, sticking up much like you would expect a zebra's would. His coat was dirty, I thought, or maybe the coloring just gave him that look. I wasn't sure if he was white, gray, or brown, or perhaps all three. Either way, he was a sight to behold, and that was before I noticed that his teeth seemed way too big for his mouth.

The more I looked at them, the more I wondered if a few of them were slightly crooked.

I wasn't exactly sure how long I had been standing there, staring at the horselike creature, before I heard Jade ask me, "So what do you think?"

Her words broke me out of my trance, and I found myself quickly trying to process the right words to say. Thankfully none of the thoughts that swam inside my head, like "Is that really a horse?" or "What happened to his face?" came out. Instead, I managed to simply say, "He's adorable." Jade and Chuck both smiled at each other in unison, as if somehow my approval of their horse had been really important.

I gave Cumberbunch one last look, hoping that maybe if I gazed at him again, I'd see what they clearly saw in him, but nope, he was still just an extraordinarily strange-looking horse. "Adorable?" a shrill voice said from behind me.

"More like abnormal." There was a chorus of laughter, and when I turned around, I saw that girl from the pier, Brittany, standing along with what I assume were her three lackeys. I had to admit to myself that I hadn't paid much attention to her the day we met, seeing as my brain only registered her as a mean-looking rich girl. I had my doubts we would ever cross paths again, or at least I was hoping we wouldn't.

After looking at her a bit more closely this time, had I not known better, I would have thought she looked like an almost lovely person. Brittany was definitely pretty, the sort of pretty that often leads to being the popular girl in school, which totally explained her lousy attitude. Popular and mean usually went together like hamburgers and fries. She wore her wavy honey-blond hair in a tight ponytail under her riding helmet. The three girls who stood behind her were almost her clones in the way they dressed. All of them were in black riding uniforms, which matched their attitudes, but that is where the similarities ended.

I was trying to think of some witty comeback, but I lost my train of thought when Chuck said in a babyish voice, "Don't listen to the mean girl. You're a handsome man." He then proceeded to grab Cumberbunch by the muzzle and started giving him a fury of kisses, and all the while kept saying, "Aren't you, aren't you?"

There was a loud collective "Ewww" from the four girls who stood behind us. Even Jade looked a bit disgusted by Chuck, but she was loyal enough of a friend not to admit it.

Instead, Jade crossed her arms and looked Brittany over from head to toe, almost like she was trying to decide if she could take her, before she asked sharply, "Did you need something, Myrick?" Brittany scoffed at her, looking amused.

"From you, Callaghan, or are you going by your mother's surname? What was it again, Lopez, Guzman, or something?" She paused just long enough to look at her friends and roll her eyes, which got another chorus of giggles, before she added, "There's nothing you could ever help me with."

Jade's body deflated before she broke eye contact with Brittany. She quickly turned her attention to Cumberbunch, grabbing a nearby brush and stroking his coat with it. I don't know why I suddenly felt the urge to protect Chuck and Jade; it wasn't like they were my friends or I knew anything about them, really, but right now, it felt right. I looked at Brittany and gave her my best "I don't like you" look and asked, "Did you want something?" my voice dripping with boredom.

Brittany seemed shocked for just a moment, but she hid it well. I was sure I saw just a bit of panic in her eyes before she told me, sounding proud, "Well, I thought I'd give you a chance to hang out with the cool girls, instead of"—she gestured over toward Chuck and Jade who were still doting over their horse.

I took one glance over my shoulders, pretending I had no idea what she was talking about, and noticed they both looked a bit crushed, so I quickly turned my head back around to face Brittany and told her flatly, "Yeah, I'm good where I'm at."

Brittany scowled before she lifted her chin, as if in defiance at me, nearly growling as she replied, "Your loss, loser!" She turned sharply on her heels and stomped off, two of the girls following suit. The remaining girl looked over at Jade for just a moment. The look on her face seemed regretful. But whatever it was she wanted to say or do quickly passed and she changed her mind, scurrying away to join her friends.

"So, what was that all about?" I asked as I turned back to face Chuck and Jade. Their moods appeared lifted compared to moments before. They both looked at each other silently for a moment before I had to ask again, "Well?"

Chuck started to say something, but Jade cut him off, telling me, "It's complicated," and the look on her face was pleading for me to let it go.

"Fine," I groaned with a roll of my eyes, "but can you at least tell me what their names are?" I'm pretty sure Jade wanted to say no but refrained from saying so because she couldn't come up with a good reason as to why. When Chuck saw this quandary on Jade's face, he jumped in front of her and pointed at the girls who had wandered far enough away that they couldn't hear us.

He first pointed to the one who looked the most similar to Brittany. They both had nearly the same color hair and style, and fair complexion. Still, the other one seemed just a little less pretty than Brittany, and I wondered if that was by design. If I knew anything about the queen bee of the popular girls, they didn't like to get outshined by their lackeys. Chuck told me her name was Jessica Baker. The girl next to her was named April Collins. She had her black hair pulled back into a bun, light green eyes that stood out as they looked between us, and dark skin. She kept giving me mean looks once she noticed us looking their way. The last one he pointed at was the girl who had hesitated to leave. Her name was Hazel Foster. Her thick red hair almost looked like it wanted to escape her tight braid, her eyes were bright green, and a blanket of freckles covered her nose and cheeks. From the interaction, she appeared to be the most friendly of the four, almost a bit unsure of herself, like she was trying to fit in but wasn't sure if she was.

Once Chuck had finished telling me their names, I finally asked, "So what now? Are we going to ride him or what?" Chuck looked a bit sheepish, while Jade looked unsure. When neither of them said anything, I was forced to say, "Well?"

Finally, Jade spoke. Her voice wobbled slightly, and I wasn't sure if she was embarrassed or just caught off guard. "Probably not today."

"Why not today?" I responded, not understanding why they had dragged me all the way here to see a horse and then not ride him. I mean, I could have done that on the farm.

"He's not really ride-ready," Chuck finally admitted.

"Ride-ready?" I asked. "But he's a horse," the last word came out a bit slower, partly in a questioning tone, as I still wasn't 100 percent sure he was a horse, and if he wasn't, I didn't want to upset them by not knowing that.

"Yeah, I know," Jade told me grimly. "He's just, well." She paused, looking Cumberbunch over. "He's not ready for that yet." I flew both my hands up in surrender. Whatever the issue was with their horse, they clearly weren't ready to tell me about, and honestly, I was getting a bit fed up with the both of them being so secretive. Yeah,

I knew we didn't know each other yet, but the pair of them had more secrets than Area 51. Seeing my obvious irritation, Chuck quickly apologized and changed the subject by suggesting we head to our next destination for the day.

After we left the stables, Uncle James picked us up and took us to Krakens Feast since it was close to lunchtime. Thankfully, this time, he seemed a little less stiff, but still, something felt off to me. I was gladder than anything that he simply handed me some money to treat my "new friends," as he called them, to lunch and left, saying he would pick me back up at this spot in three hours. Chuck and Jade talked about all sorts of stuff, but honestly, my brain didn't want to pay too much attention. I might have been distracted by our journey to the stables, but now sitting here eating another burger, my mind just kept thinking about Cliffton. The logical side of my brain would tell me I was being stupid, unicorns are not real, and I was acting like a little kid. The adventurous side of my brain, though, was certain that he had to be a unicorn because he checked off so many boxes from the book. How could he be anything else? Thankfully, neither noticed my lack of attention as they kept going on and on, and I assumed they thought I was just intently listening.

We didn't do too much in the time before my uncle was meant to pick me up, mostly walking within a mile or so of the diner. But I did find out there was an arcade called Poseidon's Quest, and it was mostly full of older, retro games. Many of them looked like they were from long before my time, but surely they could still be fun, right? I also saw an ice cream parlor, the Salty Seas Witch, which I was very keen on having my aunt take me to. Chuck told me they were famous for their sea salt caramel sundae. Then there was the bakery, the Sea Biscuit Bakery, which was full of yummy bread, cakes, and cookies. The smell that wafted out the door was divine. Other than that, most everything else was knickknack shops or small businesses, nothing that really caught my eye. By the time we returned to the diner, my feet were killing me along with any desire I had a few hours ago to try to uncover the mystery that was Cliffton. That would have to wait until tomorrow, I reassured myself. So with a big thanks to Jade and Chuck for the day of fun and the promise of getting together soon to do it again, I headed back to the house with Uncle James. The only plans were to have dinner, shower, and bed. Then I was going to get some answers.

Chapter 14

It is hilarious how life works sometimes. You make plans to do a thing, and they fall through, so you make plans again with pretty much the same result. Then, you stupidly say to yourself, hey, let's make some more plans, and then you're somehow surprised that you have to change them once again. Well, apparently, that was what my life was now.

When I walked into the house, I was fully expecting to smell food cooking, which I did, and it smelled incredible. Then I expected to go into the kitchen and tell my aunt and uncle about my day while we ate before heading upstairs. That, however, is where reality and expectation parted ways. Before I headed into the kitchen, I could hear my aunt on the other side talking, but I only heard her voice, so I wasn't too surprised to see that she was on the phone when I entered. What surprised me was when she turned to me and said, "Oh, here she is now," and she held the phone out to me with a smile. I stood there unmoving, knowing very well who was on the other end. It had to be my parents. I didn't feel like talking to them. Well, I guess I did but just not in front of my aunt or uncle, who had now just walked in behind me. When I didn't take the phone from her, my aunt peered at me, confused, before she whispered, "It's your dad." I guess she didn't understand that I knew who it was. It felt like my body, brain, and mouth were all working against me because I just kept staring between my aunt and the phone like it was a foreign object that I had no clue how to use.

My uncle got the hint before my aunt for the first time, and he whispered, "Maybe she wants some privacy." My aunt put the phone back to her mouth, and she told my dad to give her a moment. Then Uncle James gestured for me to follow him out of the room. I wasn't sure where we were going at first, but he brought me through the double doors that led into the room across from the kitchen. The den was as I expected. Everything was a bit old and outdated, much like everything else in the house. The wooden flooring continued from the entryway, but the walls in this room were a lot different. They were painted eggshell white, with wooden slats going down every few feet. It reminded me a lot of the Tudor buildings in town, except I didn't think I'd ever seen someone do that design on the inside of a house before. I sort of liked it. The paint looked old and chipped like it hadn't been painted in a decade, but most of the walls were covered in a wide range of photos and paintings placed in no particular order. None of them seemed to go with each other, nor did they seem to follow any kind of theme. In the center of the room, there was an oversized pale blue couch with two matching chairs, one on each side, that made a U shape in front of the large stone fireplace. Each stone differed in size, ranging from the size of a marble to that of a baseball. Behind the couch was a tall, thick wooden table covered in small plant pots, knickknacks, and a large pile of mail. The table matched the coffee tables in front of the couch pretty closely, I thought, except the coffee tables were literally covered with coffee mug rings, and I wondered if they knew what coasters were for.

Uncle James pointed to the small round table that was squeezed in between the couch and one of the chairs. There, an ancient phone sat next to an even older blue-shaded lamp with a tarnished-looking silver base. I nodded to him and waited until he left the room before I went over and sat down. I paused just a moment before I picked up the phone. While I did, I couldn't help but notice the absence of something above the fireplace. Right in the center, where you'd usually expect a painting to be, or in my uncle's case, a mounted deer head, there was nothing. There was nothing physical, at least, but there was a strange discoloration in the shape of a rectangle, suggesting there may have been a photo there at one time. The area was severely stained, and I knew it didn't matter, but something about the vacancy of that spot made me feel wrong for some reason. Then again, maybe I was just looking for reasons not to pick up the phone. I took one long, last deep breath before picking up the receiver, placing it to my ear, and saying "Hello," with as little emotion as I could.

There was a strange clicking noise, which I assumed might have been my aunt hanging up the other phone, before I heard "Hey, Uni," my father's voice chirping on the other end, and I felt my nose wrinkle slightly. He had called me that since I was a baby, his own little unique nickname, he said. I never minded him calling me that, but something about it now bothered me a lot. There was a short silence, and when I didn't say anything back, he asked, "Are you there?"

"Yeah, I'm here," I said bitterly. There was a long, irritated sigh on the other end before my dad's voice changed from the cheerful tone he had just greeted me with to his boss-dad-mode one.

"You're not still sulking, are you?"

"I'm not sulking!" I protested.

I could almost feel the smirk on his face when he told me, "Sure you're not."

"I'm not!" I demanded.

"OK, that's enough of your little pity party, Jennifer," he said. It wasn't a yell, but it was much louder than I thought I had ever heard him talk on a phone before. I stood there frozen for a moment, part of me wanting to cry, and the other part of me wanting to scream at him. My eyes searched around the room for a moment while I tried to decide which way to go: say I was sorry, or slam the phone down. It was then that I noticed that something was missing from the room. There wasn't a television anywhere. Now, really, this wasn't the most significant thing in the world. It's not like I could see myself sitting down in the den with my aunt and uncle, watching some of my favorite shows or anything like that. Honestly, them not having a television made a lot of sense for some reason, but that didn't matter, at least not in my head right now. It was just one more bad thing in an otherwise large ball of bad, and I was going to cling to it like a life preserver.

"Pity party," I spat, like my words were full of venom. "Just because I'm miserable because you sent me to the worst place in the world doesn't mean I'm having a pity party." I put as much emphasis on the last word as I could. This, of course, made my dad more upset with me, and he matched my tone without a beat

"Now listen here, little missy, maybe you could try to be grateful for once in your life." Those words stung hard. I never thought of myself as an ungrateful person. Was that really what he thought of me?

"Yeah, well," I argued, "it's not like they even want me here. Uncle James has made that clear." I'm not sure why I blamed this all on Uncle James, I mean, he did act weird in the car, but it seemed more toward Chuck than anyone else. Anger made me say stupid things sometimes.

"Why would he want you there with the way you've been acting?" My dad's words caught me off guard. Did he *really* just agree with me that I wasn't wanted here? Did I hear him right? He went silent for a moment, and even though I couldn't see him, I was sure he realized what a big mistake he had made. His voice softened a lot as he started to tell me, "Jennifer, I—" but I wasn't going to let him apologize, not after that, not for a long time. So I cut him off with my own declaration,

"Well, clearly, I wasn't welcome at my own home. Why would I be welcome here either?" The only thing he said back was my nickname, like he didn't know what he could say to fix it. I added one last thing. "Maybe the next time you think I'm a burden to your happy, perfect life, you can at least send me someplace where I might be wanted." With those last words, I slammed the phone down.

I felt my eyes begin to water like I was about to let a whole flood escape from them. I felt my lips begin to tremble from the overwhelming and rather conflicting emotions that filled me. I wasn't sure if I was more sad or angry. Angrad? Sangry, maybe? But the sound of creaking boards and footsteps attempting, and failing, to quietly move away from the shut door behind me snapped me out of my introspection. Had someone been eavesdropping on my conversation? Instantly I was flooded by embarrassment. I swiftly wiped away any tears from my eyes and took a few long deep breaths, trying to get control over the emotions I wasn't so sure I could control.

With one last breath, I forced myself out of the chair and opened the doors. No one was on the other side, so I decided maybe I should give them the benefit of the doubt and assumed whatever I thought I heard was just the sounds of a really dusty old house. Still, that doubt faded when I walked into the kitchen and saw the expressions on their faces. It was somewhere between guilt and pity.

Aunt Tara smiled at me as she finished placing some food on the table and asked, "Enjoy your chat?" A worried look flashed over her briefly, like she wondered if she had said the right thing or not. Uncle James gave her a side glance before smiling, like he was trying to reassure me that he did like me and did not indeed hate my guts.

"Um, sure, I guess," I whispered before sitting down, staring at my plate.

A rush of guilt came over me, urging me to call my dad right back and tell him how sorry I was. I looked up at Uncle James and asked him softly, the words barely coming out as I continued to battle the tears that so badly wanted to be free, "Can I have my phone back, please?"

His whole face went pale as he reached for a bread roll from underneath a cloth covering a small wicker basket. "Well." He paused. "I took it in today to be looked at."

There was at least some good news, I thought, but why did he look so scared? I thought about it for a moment and then asked something that I knew deep down I should have waited until tomorrow to ask, "When will I get it back?"

"Um," he said with a very, very tiny gulp. "The man who can fix it wasn't there when I dropped it off, and . . ." I felt my face stiffen. Whatever he was going to say next wasn't going to make me happy, and he knew it. Uncle James looked over at my aunt like he was pleading for some backup, and she did just that.

Aunt Tara smiled softly and said, "Well, Mr. Jimmy is home sick, so it might be a few days before he can look at it."

I wanted to be mad. I wanted to yell and scream and have a fit, I wanted to ask why he left it at all, but a few days shouldn't be the end of the world, so instead, I nodded and stood up from the table, asking, "I'm not really hungry. Can I please be excused?" They exchanged a look before my uncle nodded, and I walked out of the room without another word.

That night was pretty hard on me. I took yet

another long shower to try to wash all the bad of the day away . . . spoiler, it didn't work. I had peaked into the hallway and saw that someone had left a plate of food covered with foil, no doubt to keep it warm, a glass of what might have been lemonade, and a chocolate cookie, all on a tray. I quietly shut the door and, after a few moments, opened it again, dragged the food into my room, and shut the door. Then, after a moment of thought, I pushed it back out.

I was indeed super hungry, but I was feeling way too guilty to eat any of it. Guilt over how I had acted toward my dad. Embarrassment and shame for not knowing how much my aunt and uncle might have heard me say. At that moment, I felt like the worst person in the world who didn't deserve any of my aunt's yummy food. I ended up just lying in bed after that, telling my stomach to get over itself. It wasn't listening, though. It wasn't until sometime later that I heard my door creak open, and a beam of light shined on the wall in front of me, and I could feel two pairs of eyes peering in at me in the dark.

The muffled whispers of my aunt saying, "Maybe she wasn't hungry after all?" and my uncle agreeing by telling her, "Well, I'm sure they had a big lunch. Girls have weird food habits anyway, don't they, what with all those fad diets?"

There was a strange noise followed by a low groan before my uncle, sounding a bit out of breath, said, "What the heck was that for?"

I smiled to myself, knowing full well neither of them could see me, and figured that my aunt must have smacked him or something before she said, "You better never let her hear you say anything stupid like that. You hear me?" My uncle didn't say anything, but I assumed he must have agreed in some nonverbal way because shortly after, the light that had softly lit the wall in front of me disappeared once again, leaving me alone with my growing hunger.

After many hours had passed, I decided I could let myself cry, and I cried a lot. So much so that I was pretty sure it was the only reason I had been able to fall asleep as my stomach growled and screamed at me for even just one bite of that cookie. This appeared to have become a new pattern for me, going to my room at night without food. The last thing I remember thinking was that perhaps I needed to hide some snacks in my room, just in case it happened again.

Chapter 15

Even though the light coming from the window wasn't exactly what you would call bright, it still stung my eyes anyway. It was an adverse side effect of a night of crying, and now I regretted having forgotten to shut my curtains. This was yet another item on an ever-growing list of remorse. I felt tired, too tired for it to be morning. So tired that I decided a morning shower wasn't worth it and opted to wash my face with some cold water instead, which I sadly learned didn't wake you up as portrayed in movies. Instead, it just made the edges of my hair wet and dialed up my crankiness level.

I picked out some comfortable clothes, a pair of blue shorts and a plain-looking white-and-yellow striped shirt. I wasn't going to get caught today wearing anything babyish or silly again. I went and grabbed the handle of my door to leave the room but found myself backing up and sitting back on the bed, deciding I wasn't ready to face anyone, at least not yet. I went and reached for my phone only to find it missing. This, sadly, was the third time I had reached for my phone this morning, each time forgetting it wasn't there. The first time was to see what time it was, and the second time, which made me feel really stupid, was just moments before I had decided to leave the room only to chicken out.

My stomach, of course, was hungry, which made the cranky beast inside me stir more and more, but those thoughts shifted to anxiousness when there was a soft rapping sound at my door. I sat there for a moment, not wanting to move. Finally, I made myself speak. "Hello?" I called out, my voice sounding tired and slightly hoarse.

Uncle James poked his head in and smiled at me warmly before asking, "Can I come in, kiddo?" I nodded in reply, not having any faith in my vocal cords anymore. He came in and sat next to me on the bed, looking almost unsure before sounding very regretful. "First, let me say I'm sorry that I overheard some of your call yesterday." His sudden confession wasn't expected, and it made me wince, but I didn't interrupt him. "I'm probably not the best child expert," he admitted, "so if I said or did something that made you feel unwelcome, I'm truly sorry."

I didn't know Uncle James very well, but I felt like he was being honest with me. He seemed to be waiting for me to speak, and thankfully my voice worked when I responded, "No, it's not you," and I paused as I decided whether to be honest with myself. "Well, only partly. The things I said were mostly because I was just mad at—"

"Your dad," he finished for me when I appeared stumped if I should say who, and I nodded in agreement. Uncle James smiled with a knowing grin, and he nodded. "Yeah, I know how he can be." And in unison, we said, "Stubborn!" This got a tiny chuckle from us both, but my uncle's laugh died quicker than mine, and sounding curious, he asked, "So what did I do?"

"Do?" I replied, totally forgetting I had just admitted it was partly him. "Oh," I said, hesitating for just a moment. "The way you acted in the truck yesterday. I guess I felt like you just wanted to get away from me."

Uncle James thought for a moment before it dawned on him, and his laugh came out load and uncomfortable. It took him a few moments to gain control. He wiped away a tear that had formed in the corner of his eye and admitted, "No. No! I wanted to get away from Chuck!"

"Ohhhh!" I said, and it suddenly made a lot more sense. "Because he kept asking about the stables," I responded. The very statement made my uncle's face stiffen slightly, but I decided not to say anything else about it. After a moment of me not asking any follow-up questions on the topic, he relaxed a bit and his shoulders slumped down slightly.

"I was thinking," he said, breaking the slowly growing uncomfortable silence, "that maybe you might want to come out with me this morning and help with a few chores?" I debated that for a moment. I wasn't really the get-out-and-get-dirty chore kind of a person, and I was pretty sure anything my uncle called a chore had to be a dirty job, or worse, cleaning up after all the animals. Then again, this seemed like a good chance for me to maybe bond with him or, at the very least, gain some favor after the way I had been acting since I'd gotten here. So with some reluctance, I smiled and gave him a nod. A moment later, my stomach made the loudest, angriest sound I think I had ever heard, causing both myself and my uncle to look down at it in disbelief. He chuckled slightly and told me as he was pushing himself from the bed with his hands, "After a quick breakfast first, that is," and I agreed with him with a grin. "Yeah, after breakfast."

I didn't think I had ever seen a person eat as fast as my uncle. He practically stuffed an entire stack of pancakes into his mouth in only a few bites. I found myself feeling slightly impressed and grossed out at the same time. To be honest, I was probably no better. I mean, I didn't eat as fast as he did, if you could call what he was doing eating, as it was more like consuming at an incredible speed, but I was going at my breakfast like I hadn't eaten in weeks. A night without food had made me ravenous. Aunt Tara just looked between us as she slowly and calmly sipped her coffee. Possibly afraid that if she spoke, we might try to eat her as well! But there was, however, a smile behind her mug. When she finally decided to ask us, "So where's the fire at?" Uncle James replied, "Fire?" as he chewed a large mouthful of pancake, causing a tiny bit to almost fall out of the corner of his mouth. He quickly reached up and wiped at it before he swallowed it down, asking again, "What fire?"

"The one that you're both clearly racing to!" she replied with a smirk. She eyed our nearly empty plates and then motioned to her own, which was more than half full.

He got a sheepish grin on his face, clearly trying to show he was going to try to slow down his meal, before admitting, "You're right. I'm sorry, it's just that I've got—" He paused to correct himself as he grinned over at me. "—we've got a lot of things to get done this morning."

"Oh," my aunt replied, looking between us and taking another sip of her coffee. Uncle James waited until she was no longer looking at him before shoving the last large chunk of pancake into his mouth and jumped up from the table. He paused just long enough to kiss my aunt on the top of her head and motioned for me to follow him with a tilt of his head. I attempted to take a long final big last bite, though it wasn't as impressive as the one he had taken. I then quickly got up and joined him, not copying his kissing my aunt! I didn't think our relationship was quite to that point yet. I grabbed the small backpack that I had placed next to the kitchen door. Earlier I had decided to put my journal inside, just in case these chores brought us near the horses and I had time to investigate. It felt like a long shot, but it was better to be prepared, I thought.

I had no clue what Uncle James had meant by chores, but our first stop, thankfully, was the stables. Unfortunately, none of the horses stayed around long enough for me to test anything because my uncle quickly let them all out into the pasture to roam free, so no testing anything on them, at least not yet. I remained optimistic. Things started off all right. I had what I thought was a simple job of sweeping out old hay from the floors of the main area of the stables along with the stalls. The stalls I cleared all seemed to be mostly full of bales of hay and random tool bits, so nothing too gross. My uncle took on the bigger job of cleaning out the horse stalls. I was very happy I didn't have that job. It was easy at first, but the longer I swept, the more my arms began to ache and the more exhausted I felt. I never knew sweeping was such a workout. Foolishly I expected that once I was done, that would be it, but no, that was just the beginning. I was starting to wonder if I had made a big mistake.

Our next task was to bring in new hay bales from the back of a trailer. The rectangular bale was way too big and awkward for me even to attempt to try to carry like my uncle was doing, so I did the next best thing, I dragged it. I felt proud of myself once I finally pulled the first one inside the stall, my fingers aching and burning from how the thin red rope had dug into my fingers and left behind indents in my skin. Then I looked over to see that my uncle had single-handedly brought in all the rest, a good thirty of them, if not more. I felt deflated and honestly embarrassed. My uncle just smiled at me, and at first, I wanted to believe it was an "I know you did your best, good job" type of smile, but it was a smile that didn't quite reach beyond his mouth. More like a "did I just make a big mistake bringing you out here" type of smile.

Things just got worse from there. I ended up knocking over a whole box of nails, which took forever to clean up, and I wasn't entirely sure I got them all. I then dropped a bucket of chicken feed before getting it to their bowls, or was it a trough? This caused all the chickens to go into some weird feeding frenzy, and I barely managed to get away with my life. Then right after, I dropped at least three of five eggs that I had been trying to put into a pail. I wasn't sure how I'd clean up that mess, but one of the chickens cleaned up for me by eating it all up. So today was a day of me dropping things, apparently. After all this, my uncle told me I could have a break. I wasn't really sure if he was asking or telling me to take one, but I did so without question. I was feeling so defeated by the day thus far that I didn't want to risk anything worse happening. I wasn't sure what could be worse beyond the wake of chaos I had already left behind, except for maybe setting all the chickens free. I shuddered at the thought. I sulked away, letting my feelings of worthlessness fester inside me like a growing storm while my uncle continued to collect eggs.

I never knew that chickens ate their eggs, and honestly, after seeing them do it, I wish I didn't know. The knowledge that chickens had secretly been cannibals all this time wasn't something I really wanted to know.

I walked off with no real purpose or destination, though I soon found myself standing in front of the fence surrounding the large pasture. The smell of smoke wafted in the air behind me from an old barrel burning some weeds. Thor and Eloise were a fair distance away, with Cliffton being the closest. I leaned on the fence, and it felt strong, so I wasn't scared it would break. The thought that it might and the fallout that would occur if I let the horses out was enough to make sure I didn't put my whole weight on it, just in case.

I watched Cliffton for a while, admiring how much nicer he looked in the sun than standing in the dark, mucky stable. His coat shimmered in the light. He really was a beautiful horse, despite having such an awful name, the thought of which still made me snicker slightly to myself. I decided to give this another shot. With a click of my tongue, I tried to get his attention, and even though I was sure I saw his ear twitch to the sound, he wouldn't look at me. I then tried calling out his name and, once again, not even a glance. I tried one more name, this time I called out, "Here, unicorn, come here, boy," but was left with nothing but silence. I knew it was stupid to think he was a unicorn, even more foolish to think I could get a horse that didn't know me to come to my call, but it made me feel so angry.

"Fine!" I half yelled, making sure I wasn't too loud that my uncle would hear me. I took the journal from my backpack, raised it above my head, and violently shook it. "I knew you weren't real," and with that acknowledgment, I turned sharply on my heels and stomped to the barrel that was several feet behind me. In the back of my mind, I thought I heard some horse noises behind me, but I quickly decided either I imagined it or it had no connection to me. When I got to the barrel, I stared at the journal in my hands, feeling a fury of emotions from sadness to hope to rage, and even though tears were beginning to form in my eyes, I let that rage overpower anything else I was feeling, and I released the book, letting it fall toward the barrel below. I was full of regret when it started to fall, but a strange feeling overcame me in the next moment. Just like the day before, everything slowed down. So slow, I could see the wings flapping on a bee that hovered not too far from my face. Then, in the very next moment, time caught up like the snap of an elastic band. I saw my journal suddenly jerk backward in the direction of the horses as if it was on an invisible string. When I turned to look behind me, Cliffton was right next to the fence staring at me, looking angry, with the journal hanging out of his mouth.

Chapter 16

Cliffton and I both just stood there for what felt like an eternity, just staring each other down. I was staring at him in disbelief while he looked back at me with what looked like disdain. I wasn't sure why I labeled him with that, as truthfully, his face didn't change at all. He reminded me of those shirts with different emotions listed, but all the pictures were the same. It was more a feeling I was getting in the pit of my stomach as I stared into the darkness of his large brown eyes.

Once the shock of it had passed, like a receding wave, and my brain felt like it had been lifted out of all-consuming wet sand, I stomped right back over to the horse and quickly reached for the book in his mouth. This must have been an unexpected move to him because once it clicked in him what I was doing, he attempted to move away, but I managed to reach for him and get both hands on the book before he could flee. From there, we stood fighting over it. Cliffton desperately tried to jerk the book out of my grip, shaking it every which way he could. Left, right, up, down, but my hold was tighter. There was no way I would be beaten by a horse, even if my arms did feel like they were about to be pulled from their sockets.

"Let go of my book!" I growled through gritted teeth, attempting to place both my feet on the bottom rail of the fence, using my entire body weight to push at it. Then there was a voice.

It was somewhere between annoyance and

exhaustion. "It's . . . not . . . yours!" The sudden unexpectedness of the voice startled me so much that I lost my grip on the book and plummeted hard onto the ground, landing flat on my back. My entire body throbbed from the impact, and all I could do was roll onto my side and curl into a ball, groaning from the pain. Thankfully I was pretty sure I hadn't hit my head.

After the pain eased from bolts of lightning searing through my nervous system down to more of a dull throb, I pushed my body upward using my arms and looked around. I expected to see my uncle, seeing as how the voice I heard sounded male, but to my surprise, there was no one there. Had they run off when I fell, I wondered? Then again . . . I turned my head sharply to look straight at Cliffton, who happened to be just as confused as I was. "Did you say that?" I asked, staring at him. I thought about how stupid I was being. Did I hit my head and just not realize it yet? But, after asking the question, his head jerked back, and he looked from side to side as if he was trying to imply, "What? Are you talking to me?"

I carefully got to my feet, dusted the dirt off my body as I did, and took a small step forward. "Well, did you?" I asked him again. My question was only met with silence, but instead of giving up, I asked a different question. "Whose book is it?" I didn't break eye contact with Cliffton, studying his every muscle twitch as he processed my question. I could see a flood of emotions flicker behind his eyes. There was once again a very long and rather uncomfortable silence before, finally, I got a reply.

"I don't remember," the voice admitted. I looked all around me again to make sure someone wasn't playing a trick on me before I let myself believe, or at least try to, that the fantastical possibility that the voice I had just heard hadn't come from the bushes or my imagination but, in fact, had come from the horse that was still holding my gaze in front of me.

"Did you—" I began to ask, but he cut me off when he said, "Just talk?"

I didn't see his mouth move, which seemed a bit weird, but at the same time, I was a bit grateful for it. One time, my dad tried to get me to watch some black-and-white show about a talking horse. Trust me, it's unsettling at best to see a horse's mouth move to words. "Why didn't your mouth move?" I asked Cliffton, still feeling the need to stare at his mouth in case I was missing something.

Cliffton's eyes darted around for a moment like he was searching to make sure no one was watching. When he appeared satisfied that we were alone, he lowered his head slightly before a swirl of thick white smoke appeared on the top of his head. When it dissipated, a long white horn was revealed. "With this," he replied, sounding almost smug.

I was sure my mouth must have been gaping open. After a few seconds of shock, I was able to find my words again, well, a few words. "You're a—a—a," I said, not seeming to be able to say that last word.

"Unicorn," Cliffton finished for me before nodding. This time when he spoke, I noticed that his horn vibrated ever so slightly. Just from the single word, I saw that it moved like a tuning fork, though in a much more complex manner to be able to imitate human speech.

"Yeah," I said as I exhaled deeply. It took a moment before the thought "This can't be real" started to form in my head, and I felt the strong urge to voice it. "But unicorns . . ."

"Aren't real," Cliffton finished. There was a short silence between us, but just like an itch that needed to be scratched, I didn't think I'd feel satisfied until I said it myself. "Unicorns aren't real!" I blurted out fast enough that he wouldn't have time to interrupt me this time.

Cliffton snorted at my sudden outburst before it trailed into a dumbfounded laugh.

"What's so funny?" I asked, not entirely sure if he thought what I said was funny or just dumb.

He looked thoughtfully at me for a moment before he looked away. His voice seemed tired and almost spiteful when he told me, "All you humans are just the same."

I couldn't help but feel a bit offended, even though I wasn't sure why I would need to be, but I asked him nevertheless, "What is that supposed to mean?"

Cliffton turned his head back to look at me. "None of you can believe anything unless you see it with your own eyes. It's really quite pathetic if you think about it."

I could feel my cheeks flush with anger, "Oh, so because I don't believe in unicorns, which by the way no one does, that means I'm pathetic?!"

"Ding, ding, we have a winner!" he replied, his voice seething with gleeful sarcasm.

"That's not true!" I argued, fighting the urge to hit the fence with my hand. Instead, I turned away from the fence so that I wouldn't give in to the impulse. I heard him laugh a bit more behind my back, and so I whipped around to face him with an even stronger glare. "What now?" I almost yelled.

Cliffton didn't seem fazed one bit, replying, "You know, if you think about it, here you are looking at me, talking with me, but yet you stand there arguing with me about how I'm not real!" He paused in thought before adding, "If humans never sailed the seas to other lands, would you argue that a zebra or giraffe wasn't real because you had never seen one before? Even if it was standing right in front of you?"

I didn't even bother to think about what he just asked. I replied by instinct when I told him, "No, of course not. Zebras and giraffes are real!" I put a lot of emphasis on that last word.

Cliffton snickered again. "What about all those little cells and DNA you have floating inside your body? You can't see them, yet you trust some scientist who says they are real."

"That's different," I argued.

"How so?" he quipped back, this time his voice calm and maybe a little curious.

The anger in me vanished, like someone dumping a bucket of water onto a fire. I hugged my arms to my chest, something I did a lot when I felt upset. There was just something about the feeling that was calming to me before I finally admitted to him and myself, "I'm not sure."

I wasn't sure why my brain decided that this was the right moment, but before I could even try to stop myself, tears were pouring out of my eyes, and the sudden weight of everything that had happened over the last few days, maybe even the last few weeks, felt like it was crushing me so hard, almost like gravity pulling me down. I let it, and within a blink of an eye, I was sitting on the ground, burying my face into my knees and sobbing. I must have sat there for a few minutes crying and sobbing before I heard him clear his throat, and when I peeked up, Cliffton was bending his head over the fence as close as he could to me. His eyes glistened, pupils wide, almost radiating warmth. I would even say that there was a bit of pity in his look. With a thud, he dropped the journal on the ground a few inches in front of my feet.

"I'm sorry," he whispered, lifting his head back up before adding, "I didn't mean to hurt your feelings."

I slowly reached for the journal and picked it up, hugging it to my chest before admitting, "No, you're right, I'm horrible." Something about saying it out loud made me feel a hundred times worse, and I buried my head again, letting out another burst of ugly sobs.

Cliffton's voice seemed worried or maybe even a bit

uneasy. "No, shh, shh," he begged. "Don't cry. I'm sure I can fix this if you let me. Um, um." He hesitated before asking me, "Do you want to go for a ride? That could be fun," he added, doing his best to sound happy.

I think we were both caught off guard when a distraught British lady's voice said sternly, "What are you doing?"

When I looked back up again, I found myself to be the only human around still, but behind Cliffton, I spotted Eloise standing there, pawing her hoof into the ground, looking very frustrated as the grass and dirt flew around her in large chunks. Quicker than it appeared, the horn atop of Cliffton's head vanished in another puff of swirly white smoke, and he turned slowly to face her. They stared at each other for a moment, but when it was clear Cliffton had nothing to say, Eloise told him with a growl, "What has gotten into you? You're going to get us caught! You know better than this, Cliffton!"

I jumped to my feet and, without thinking, blurted out, "You're a unicorn too?!" Eloise turned her neck when she heard my voice. I saw a hint of panic in her eyes before she let out a loud, ear-piercing scream that was so shrill that I had to cover my ears. Even doing that, my body instinctively curled into itself, as if shielding me was going to help somehow, but I quickly found out it didn't. My ears felt like they were ringing when I finally decided to uncover them to see if she had stopped. Cliffton was in front of Eloise, nuzzling her muzzle with his own. I think they were talking to each other, but they were speaking low enough that I couldn't make anything out, especially with the throbbing pain that was starting to fade from my ears.

That's when Thor decided to trot over, seemingly oblivious to what had happened but coming over to see why Eloise had just screamed. When he spotted me behind the fence, he stopped just short of reaching the others, and he quickly pretended to eat some grass. I cleared my throat before asking, "Can all three of you talk?"

Thor's head shot up, and when he saw me looking at him, he quickly turned away, trying his best not to see me, until Cliffton said, "Yes, he can talk as well."

Thor bucked his feet into the air before falling dramatically to the ground. Laying his head to the side, he stuck his tongue out as far as he could and shut his eyes. I couldn't help but giggle at the scene. He looked ridiculous! Cliffton walked over to him and nudged him with the tip of his hoof. "Pretending you're dead isn't going to fix this, Thor," he groaned. Thor didn't move, he just kept lying there, and I was sure he tried to stick his tongue out just a bit farther. It hung out so much in fact that just a part of it seemed to lay on the dirt below. When Eloise came over and bent down to bite him on one of his legs, which were sticking high into the air, his eyes popped open, and he let out a long whinny before quickly rolling over to get to his feet.

"It would have worked if you two joined in," he shouted. He sounded arrogant, which surprised me for some reason. I'm not sure why, especially since only a few moments ago, I would have never believed unicorns could talk.

"I can't believe what's happening," I breathed before I pinched myself on the arm to make sure I was awake. I let out a sharp yelp. Apparently, my pinch hurt a lot more than I thought it would, and all I got from that test was a sharp pain and a lot of confused looks from the horse, er, unicorns. Oh, I really wasn't sure what to call them yet.

"Did the human child just inflict pain on herself?" Thor asked, sounding bewildered.

Eloise snorted a giggle before she looked down at

him. "Humans are bizarre creatures. I've told you this many a time now." Cliffton and Thor exchanged some strange looks before they both let out a small laugh.

"What?!" I shouted, feeling quite embarrassed and upset that I was being made fun of by unicorns. "I was making sure I was awake!" I protested.

Eloise said between her fit of giggles, "You have yet to learn if you're . . . awake!" The laughs between the three of them got even stronger, leaving me staring at them as the anger bubbled to the surface. I felt my arms grow tight as they fell to my side, and my hands both balled into fists. Fortunately, before I could even think of what to say, or yell I wasn't sure which direction I was about to take, the laughter abruptly stopped.

My arms relaxed when I heard quick footsteps approaching from behind, followed by the familiar voice of my uncle. "Jennifer, are you OK? I thought I heard a scream."

A wave of panic filled me, and I was pretty sure I saw the same response in the three unicorns in front of me, but when I turned to face my uncle, who was just about to reach me, I already had a calming smile on my face. I tried to look as embarrassed as I could when I told him, "Sorry, I just thought I saw a snake."

Uncle James's face paled a bit when he realized all three horses were staring and looking unsettled, and he must have believed it because he said, "Well, that explains why the three of them are just standing there like that. Let's get you inside, and I'll come back to see if I can track it down before it causes any harm."

I felt a bit guilty, as this seemed rather mean to make Uncle James go and hunt down a snake that wasn't there. I mean, how long would he look before giving up? Sadly I just didn't have any other excuse I could give him. It wasn't like I was going to say that "Eloise screamed because she's a unicorn who can talk!" Not only was I sure he wouldn't believe me, but it was entirely possible he would lock me up in my room for the rest of the summer. Maybe even send me away. Whatever the outcome of saying that, I knew that it wouldn't end well. Instead, I nodded and started walking back toward the house, with Uncle James leading the way. I paused only long enough to look back at the unicorns over my shoulder to see all three of them still watching over me. It might have been over right now, but I'd be back and with a whole list of questions.

Chapter 17

I can't say things went to plan after I returned to the house. In my mind, I figured after searching for the nonexistent snake for maybe a couple of hours tops that Uncle James would give up, thinking either I saw a stick or that it had gone far, far away, but no, that's not what ended up happening. It was near dinnertime before he came back, looking both worn-out and worried, letting me and Aunt Tara know how the horses had kept acting scared the entire day, despite seeing no evidence of a snake. However, since the horses continued acting panicked, it made him believe there must still be a snake around out there somewhere. Adding to my horror, he said that until the horses calmed down or he came across the snake, it would be much safer if I stayed inside. I had thought Aunt Tara would have backed me up when I assured them I'd be careful, but she agreed with my uncle. It was apparent that both my uncle and aunt were more on the deep end of the paranoia and safety spectrum than I had thought. They said many things, like how it was their job to keep me safe, there were lots I could do inside, and they were sure it'd only be for a day or two. Well, they were right about one thing, I was safe inside, safe, and incredibly bored. Sadly for me, the other two things they claimed had proved to be false.

I spent most of my time wandering from room to room, staring out the window, and since I still didn't have my phone, there was pretty much nothing for me to do. I searched most of the house for any sign of a TV or even a book that didn't seem less boring than staring blankly at the wall. I even attempted to use the computer to search for things for my room like my aunt had suggested but found the internet so painfully slow it didn't feel worth the time. I deeply regretted that I hadn't asked Chuck or Jade for their numbers. I had no way to contact them, not that I knew them enough to just call them out of the blue. Oh, and the whole day or two was way off. Way, way, way off! Try five days, yes, five days of mind-numbing boredom. I sat there usually alone, as Aunt Tara had decided to help my uncle with the great snake hunt. It was going on as long as it had because of the stupid horses, er, unicorns. Every day my aunt and uncle would come back saying no sign of the snake but that the horses had kept acting scared. This meant that it just had to be around somewhere because horses could sense things like that or something.

I knew the truth, though; they just didn't want me to get anywhere near them again. I had even caught them doing it! It was day three of lockup when I had been watching Thor standing peacefully eating some grass, acting like he didn't have a care in the whole world. Then, as soon as he got sight of my uncle, he started bucking and acting up. This grabbed the attention of my uncle, causing him to drop what he was doing and rush over, big little faker! They were causing all this just to keep me away, but I had to give it to them, they were clever. Mean but clever.

I replayed the whole event, often thinking of all the lies I could have said that might have changed the outcome for me. I had to kick myself for not thinking of them sooner. Why didn't I just say I hit my leg or stubbed my toe? Would that have made my uncle make me wear iron boots? I doubted it. Instead, all I could do was sit there and wallow in my many, many regrets. And here I was, once again, on day five, being a prisoner of my own making.

I lay on the couch in the den, staring at a spot on the wall where only the dim light of the rising sun spotlighted, wishing a TV would magically appear. So when my aunt called my name from the doorway, looking for me, I nearly jumped in fright.

"There you are!" she said cheerfully before asking me, "I didn't scare you, did I?"

I, of course, lied when I told her no. Her eyes twinkled ever so slightly, matching her grin. "Well, I got good news."

I sat up straight and beamed at her. "You found the snake?" I questioned hopefully, then felt rather foolish since I knew there wasn't one.

She laughed at my excitement before shaking her head and replying, "No."

I felt my body go limp with disappointment, certain my face mirrored the action. Aunt Tara raised both her hands, almost the same way as when I saw her from the window when she was trying to calm the horses. I honestly felt a bit offended by the gesture. She then spoke to me in a soft, reassuring voice. "But honestly, Jennifer, I think it's time for your uncle to abandon that quest once and for all." This brought a smile to my face, but before I could ask if that meant I could have my freedom again, she added, "We are, however, going out today."

I felt my lip curl into a smile as I asked her, "Really, where?!"

"We're taking the horses to the town's horse show at Merrow Crescent Stables.

"Oh," I said, trying not to sound disappointed, "awesome." Aunt Tara laughed at me, clearly seeing right through my facade.

"Don't worry, there's more to do there than just watch horses, and I'm sure Chuck and Jade will be there too," she told me, looking hopeful.

I wasn't sure how I felt about the pair of them yet. I guessed there was potential for a friendship, but they hadn't sought me out during my imprisonment, so I wasn't sure how they felt about me either. But to spare my Aunt Tara any bad feelings about me, I gave her the best smile I could muster and told her, "Sounds great." Her smile was much more at ease this time, and when she walked out of the room, I sighed a huff of relief, having for once managed to pull it off. If I got anything from this summer, it might be becoming a better liar. I wasn't sure if that was a good or bad thing. Only time would tell!

There wasn't a lot of time between my aunt telling me about us going and us leaving. This meant I didn't get a chance to ask her what a horse show was. From what I could understand, it sounded a lot like a dog show, but with horses, with some of them being ridden. OK, I guess maybe not like a dog show. Aunt Tara had said people entered their horses into different competitions, like riding, looks, tricks, and some other thing I couldn't remember anymore. Still, it sounded like something most of the town showed up for, and it was a big event everyone loved. She also said there was other stuff going on, sort of like a fair but with no rides, though they had games and food.

I had partly feared I'd be given work to do, but when we arrived, Uncle James handed me a wad of money, told me where I could find them if they needed anything, and told me to have fun. Part of me wanted to be offended, as I assumed my lack of skills in the days prior probably made him not want me anywhere where I might mess things up, especially since I had been waiting forever to get a chance to see the unicorns again. On the other hand, I was also relieved I didn't have to get all dirty and gross and, after thinking about it, realized this probably was not the best place to try to talk to the unicorns again anyway. You know, what with them wanting nothing to do with me and the fear that someone would see me and think I was nuts. So with a big smile, I thanked my uncle and aunt, and we parted ways.

Even though I had just been to Merrow Crescent Stables a few days before, I found myself feeling surprised at how much bigger it was than I had originally thought. The lawn had seemed pretty large when I first saw it, even if I had only been there briefly. The front lawn now was full of booths and tables. There were simple games, people selling homemade wares, and yummy-looking treats. My aunt was right as well; I was sure every single person from town was here, and maybe the one nearby, so moving around from booth to booth wasn't going to be the easiest thing. I wandered off a short distance, since I hadn't particularly felt like battling a crowd yet, and decided to see where the people who went behind the stables were going. I followed a flat dirt path that ran along the side of the building, towering trees on the other, until I reached the end. I was amazed to see the large field behind it, filled with every type of obstacle, which I figured had been made for horses. Even more impressive was the towering two- or three-story building off in the distance. It made the stables look tiny in comparison, and I felt a bit silly for not having seen it the first time I'd visited, not that I had been behind the stables. Thinking more of it, I wasn't sure if it could be seen from the front with all the trees.

I sheepishly asked an older lady wearing a large yellow hat adorned in a forest of flowers and a matching yellow pants suit, "Excuse me, miss, can you tell me what that building is?"

She took one look at me, taking in my simple pair of green shorts, tennis shoes, and white shirt with a rainbow line across the chest, and sneered at me when she said, sounding both bored and off-put, "It's where they have the showmanship." Her tone silently added, "You silly, unkempt girl."

I thanked her and walked away, feeling none the wiser about what that building was. Part of me wondered if the big building was where the unicorns were right now. It wasn't exactly as if my aunt and uncle had told me where I could find them, and I found myself pretty tempted to look, but as it seemed that my gut lately was intent on leading me down the wrong paths, I decided against it and went back to the front, where all the booths and tables were. After all, I had a pocket full of money, and it needed to be spent!

I walked around for a good twenty minutes, not seeing anything I wanted to buy. I mean, don't get me wrong, there were lots of cute things, mostly horse-themed, but nothing that caught my eye. Most of the games either felt like baby ones or didn't have a prize that I wanted to try to win. Looking after a goldfish in a bag for the whole day or carrying around a giant bear didn't sound as fun now if there wasn't a parent to carry it for me. The food did smell good, but I wasn't hungry after the big plate of waffles I'd had earlier that morning.

My boredom level was about to hit the red line, so when I heard a feminine voice call my name and turned around to see Chuck and Jade hurrying my way, I felt a jolt of happiness, more than I expected I would have.

"Hey, Jennifer!" Chuck said between labored breaths after coming to a sudden stop from his run to me. Jade was right on his heels but not looking as tired as he did.

"You are one hard girl to track down," Jade told me with a smirk before asking, "Where have you been hiding, anyway?"

My shoulders slumped slightly. "Been under house arrest," I told them.

They both looked at me confused, then Jade,

looking at me suspiciously and with just a hint of approval, asked, "What did you do?"

"Oh," I said before putting my hands out defensively in front of me, "no, no, no. There was a snake, so I wasn't allowed outside." I paused to take in the confused looks before adding, "I didn't do anything wrong. It's just they're really protective of me or something." Chuck and Jade both laughed.

"Sounds like it," Jade said sympathetically, patting me on the shoulder as Chuck nodded in agreement.

"So," I said, drawing out the "o" since I was feeling just a bit unsure or maybe embarrassed and wasn't sure what to say.

"So," Jade said, sounding very bubbly, "now we have some fun."

We spent the next hour and a half having just that. My mood that morning hindered me from really seeing the potential of fun around me, or maybe I just wasn't feeling like doing any of it alone. Something I would have thought I'd be used to by now after so many days in exile, but either way, I was having a blast now. I think we played almost every game they had, even the ones clearly aimed at a much younger crowd. We didn't win any of them, but I don't think any of us cared. Chuck did, however, win at a game called Duck Hunt, which was as exciting as it sounds. It was an old wooden washing tub, filled with not quite clear water and a few rubber ducks floating in it. If you found the duck with a red spot on its bottom, you won. After winning, Chuck proclaimed that his mother was deathly allergic to fish and so he didn't want the prize. That didn't make much sense to me, seeing as how the first time I had met him, he was covered in them, or bits of them really, but I think it had more to do with the small girl who he saw burying her face in her mother's dress, sobbing because she lost and had no more tickets. I was impressed by him when he

handed her the fish, saying he couldn't keep it himself
and asking her to take good care of it for him, causing her
whole face to light up. Her mother's face, on the other
hand, was a mix of gratitude and exasperation. Jade and
I had to keep ourselves from giggling. Chuck was a bit
weird, I had to admit, but he was a nice weird.

One of my favorite games of the day had to be the
archery booth. You got to shoot an arrow with a tip
covered in some strange-looking bean bag at some
randomly placed targets that included soup cans painted
to look like small wild animals and some small painted
pumpkins that I guess were meant to be the bad guys.
The whole setup looked like a tacky medieval scene with
a knight on a horse, an evil wizard, a princess in a tower,
and, behind it all, a large board with some trees painted
on it. The only detracting factor about it was that it was
all made of random junk. The knight's horse was made of
several bales of hay with, what I assumed was, the head
of a rocking horse attached to it. The knight clearly
looked like a scarecrow from someone's farm but with a
large rusty bucket over its head and a cardboard sword
and shield tied to its hands. The princess was pretty
much the same, just in a dress and a ratty blond wig. The
wizard, however, was the most impressive part. They had
dressed an old store mannequin in a very long, dark
hooded black cloak that shimmered in the light. It looked
a little bit silly with an excessive amount of silver glitter
stars pinned all around the hem. It seemed rather
expensive, or at least I thought so minus the stars
hanging off it. I could definitely imagine that someone
had used it for a Halloween costume contest in the past,
but so long ago that it had been downgraded for use at
silly fair games.

Besides the games, we did spend some of the time
browsing the many wears that were being sold. Nothing
stuck out at me as something I could see myself buying,

as most of it was aimed at either adults or very small children. Items ranged from knitted blankets and carved wooden toys to jams and jelly. I wasn't really sure what the difference was between jam and jelly, but there seemed to be a bickering match between two older women whose booth tables were right next to each other as to which was better. Honestly, I didn't get it. Most of the items being sold fell into one category, horses. Just about everything I saw had one or more horses on it. It made sense seeing as what was going on today, but it also felt like a bit overkill. The more I looked at the things around me, the more I thought of my aunt, and I couldn't help but smile to myself, wondering if any new items would appear in the house today. I then realized that I wasn't sure how busy she was with whatever it was they were doing, so who knows if she would have time to look at any of it. A pang of guilt swept over me. I couldn't say why, but it did, and I felt a strange urge to buy her something. As I stood in front of one booth, deciding between a square pot holder with a horse on it and a mug also with a horse on it, Chuck and Jade ran over, grabbed my arm, and quickly dragged me away. They were talking so fast and excitedly that I couldn't understand any of the words coming out of their mouths.

When they finally released me, we were in front of a large rainbow-colored boot with a sign that read "Ocean Breeze Taffy." Probably a stand from the local candy store, I thought. On the table and the shelves behind it were jars and jars filled with what appeared to be saltwater taffy. I was a little confused as to why this was such a big deal. It's not that I thought saltwater taffy was terrible. In fact, I rather liked it on the rare occasions I got to have any, as it was often a treat my parents got when we went on vacation. Usually, they would buy some for us when we were in a scenic area like a national park or beach town. When Jade noticed that I wasn't getting it, she grabbed me by the tip of my chin and turned my head next to a stack of brown paper bags with the shop's name stamped on the front and a bright color sticker that read, "Free Taffy, Try All 100!"

"Ohhh!" I exclaimed, finally understanding, and a smile crossed my face. Chuck added, with just as much delight as I was feeling, "Free candy!"

Fifteen minutes after discovering the free candy, the three of us were sprawled out on the ground, surrounded by a sea of wrappers, staring blankly at the sky in what could only be described as a sugar coma. Before we started devouring our treats, Chuck had found what he thought was the perfect spot to eat them. A grassy area bathed in sunlight which was away from the crowds but still close enough to get more candy if needed. Something I was sure he no longer felt like doing, as low painful moans emanated from him while he rubbed his belly. I thought the spot Chuck had picked had looked fine enough, but now lying on the ground with no desire to make my body move, I partly regretted it after learning the unexpected grass spot that had looked soft and inviting before was actually quite bumpy, and there was a sharp rock poking me in the back. No matter how hard I tried to fish it out from under me without, you know, moving or getting up, I couldn't seem to find it. When Jade pointed up at the clouds and said one looked a lot like their horse, Cumberbunch, and Chuck agreed with her statement, I gave up my rock hunt and gazed up at it too. I wasn't seeing anything that came anything close to looking like a horse, it looked more like a blob, but I agreed anyway, which seemed to make them happy. Then again, I still wasn't wholly convinced that Cumberbunch was a horse, but I wasn't about to say that.

Jade and Chuck continued pointing out clouds to each other that looked nothing like what they said they looked like. It was at the point when I was starting to think either I was really bad at cloud spotting or they were hallucinating from a sugar rush that I started to get a bit bored.

"So, what are we doing next?" I asked, sounding hopeful as I pushed myself into a sitting position. Chuck and Jade soon followed suit.

"Well, we didn't try all the flavors of taffy," Chuck suggested, causing both Jade and me to groan. "Or not," he said, rubbing his stomach as if he suddenly remembered it was still hurting.

"Well," Jade said thoughtfully, "we could always go look at the horses that aren't being shown right now."

"Aren't being shown?" I asked, confused.

Chuck jumped up to his feet and gave his whole body a shake, trying to get the dirt and grass off. His movements reminded me of a dog shaking water from its coat, and I had to hide my smirk. "Yeah, they keep all the horses in a staging area in the main building between the events, because they can't all come out at once, and not all the horses are part of the same events."

"Oh, I get it," I told him. I sort of did, but I guess I sort of didn't. Animal showings of any kind weren't something I really had any experience with, but I assumed it was like the Olympics; you couldn't have swimmers on the same field as a runner. At least, I thought it was like that.

"All right!" I told him, and he held out both hands to help Jade and me to our feet. Then both of us brushed the bits of dirt and grass off in a much less strange manner than Chuck had, but I wasn't sure he noticed the difference.

I have to admit I was feeling a little sluggish as we made our way to the large building behind the stables. It suddenly felt like it was miles away, and I promised myself I would never eat candy again, well, at least not anymore today. The building itself wasn't as impressive as the main stable area I had visited before. It looked more like a giant warehouse that was made from wood rather than metal. Most of the people who were headed to it walked through a nearly two-story door that led into a large staging area. For some reason, it reminded me of the circus, minus all the creepy clowns and colors. We didn't go in, but I saw it had stands on both sides where people were sitting. In the large area between them were lots of poles and obstacles spread apart, which I assumed was an extreme jumping test for the horse, seeing as the horse that was currently running seemed a bit tired. Once we walked past the door, I heard many people clapping, so I guess they did well. I had no clue about any of this, but clapping often meant good, right?

We walked all the way around the building, which felt like it took us forever. I wasn't sure if the building itself was so big or because the path we had to walk was covered in white rocks, making every step I took felt like a cautious one. I'm sure there was no danger of tripping on them, and it probably was a silly thing to be afraid of, but something deep, *deep* inside of me was terrified I was going to trip, skin my knee, and then lay there crying, looking like a big crybaby. I wondered if something like it had happened when I was much younger, and it had left a deep-seated primal fear in my subconscious. I guess it ultimately didn't matter. So long as I took it slow, I was sure I'd be all right.

The longer we walked to where the horses were being kept, the more something felt wrong, so when I asked out loud, "Are there normally so few people back here with the horses?" both Jade and Chuck stopped midstep, looked at me, then looked at each other strangely before they both looked around them. Chuck was the first to speak after a few aguishly long moments of silence that made me wonder if my question had been really stupid.

"No, not normally," he admitted.

"There are usually lots of people back here. Some checking on their horse, some just coming to see them," Jade added. A strange look quickly filled her eyes, one of suspicion.

"So, is that strange, then?" I asked, looking between the two of them, nervous and anxious feelings growing in the pit of my stomach. Chuck and Jade glanced at each other once again before looking at me. Their faces were blank and somewhat unreadable. I must have looked petrified because before I could form any words, or give in to my brain's message about fleeing, Chuck, with Jade following only moments later, started laughing at me like I was hilarious.

"What?!" I barked, sounding offended, which I was. I forced myself to try to sound a bit more lighthearted when I continued, "What's so funny?

"You!" Chuck said between snorted laughs. He then proceeded to double over, clutching at his stomach as his laughter got louder. Jade pointed at me between the steady streams of tears that were running from her eyes.

"You should see your face!" she howled before trying to wipe her tears away with the shoulder of her shirt. I could feel my cheeks redden with a mix of embarrassment and overwhelming anger, but to save myself any more humiliation, I attempted to join in the laughter, though I was sure it didn't sound real. Jade seemed to catch on to that as her laughter suddenly died, and she seemed to give me a look that said, "Sorry."

On the other hand, Chuck just kept laughing until Jade asked him smugly, "Did you have an accident, Chuck?" and she glanced behind him.

Chuck's whole face reddened, and then he attempted to look behind him, which reminded me a lot of a dog chasing his tail. I felt a pang of guilt that I kept comparing him to a dog in my mind. Jade and I both

161

shared a laugh over how Chuck was going around and around in circles, trying to see his backside. Chuck snapped back, "Hey, it's not funny!" and he wiped at a patch of dirt that he had missed before muttering, "It's just dirt, geez."

"Come on," Jade said without missing a beat, acting like the whole thing that had just happened hadn't happened at all, or at least didn't matter. The two of us followed behind her. The mood was a bit better by the time we reached the doorway. Beyond the doorframe were two long, wide hallways. The first one led straight ahead and had stalls on both sides of it. The other one led to the left and only had stalls that faced the interior walls.

When I looked down both hallways long enough, I was sure that the one that led straight ahead had a path that also led to the left, and the one to the left had a hallway that led to the right. I was puzzled by the layout, but I asked anyway, "So, it's like, what, a giant square hallway?"

Jade looked at me strangely, but Chuck nodded. "Yeah, pretty much."

Jade smiled slyly before admitting, "I never really thought about it, to be honest, but yeah."

"Probably just wanted to fit in as many stables for the event as they could," Chuck said, shrugging and looking a little confused that this even mattered. I decided to let the whole thing go even though something in the pit of my stomach felt really weirded out. It was as though there was something right under my nose that I was missing, but I just couldn't see it.

Chuck motioned for us to follow him down the left hallway. "I think this is the fastest way to your uncle and aunt's horse," he told us when we didn't follow him right away.

When Chuck got to the very end of the hallway and turned, he stopped. I mean, just stopped. He was like a statue, not moving. It didn't even look like he was breathing. I could see from the side of his face that there was a mix of confusion, shock, and maybe even fear.

"What's wrong?" Jade asked as she walked up to him. She turned to see what he was staring at and mirrored him perfectly. A part of me was screaming not to follow suit. I wondered if this is how Medusa had managed to turn so many people into stone, one person after another going to see what was around the corner even though the person in front of them had just been turned into a statue. My feet didn't want to listen to that warning, or maybe the curiosity was just too strong to resist. So with one calming breath, I stepped out and looked down the hallway. What I saw in front of me was so much more unbelievable than if it had been Medusa herself.

Chapter 18

I definitely wasn't expecting what I saw when I rounded the corner, and by the expressions on Jade's and Chuck's faces, I was really expecting to see something more along the lines of two teens getting caught making out or maybe the mayor having a secret exchange with a mob boss. I wasn't expecting to see a dark hooded figure wearing a long flowing cloak holding a very long gnarled-looking wooden staff with a large glowing red orb at the top, which he, or she, was pointing right at Cliffton. I couldn't make out who this person was, not that I had anything to go on as it wasn't like I knew many people in town, but their long pale arm protruding from under the cloak looked sickly and withered. The arm seemed too old and weak even to be able to hold up the staff that was taller than them.

After watching for what could have been only seconds to maybe as long as a minute, I noticed that the arms shifted just slightly. I don't mean that they moved, but the look of them changed. The arms began to look healthy?! The wrinkled flesh stretched out, becoming smoother, and the once pale tone gained a healthy glow, looking more tan than white. Why was that? I wondered, and I found myself studying the wooden staff more. A strange bright light was going into the very visible horn on the top of Cliffton's head from the now pulsating red orb at the end. I looked at Cliffton and realized I was wrong. He looked tired and weak like life was literally being sucked right out of him. I was sure he would soon collapse, his body swaying back and forth. It was then that I knew it wasn't a light going into him, but instead, it was the light that was being sucked out.

I didn't think my next moves through too much. I just went with instinct. I yelled out as loudly as possible at the creepy cloaked figure, the words feeling shaky in my throat as they came out, "Hey, stay away from him!" The light suddenly ceased, and the figure turned quickly to face me, their face obscured by the shadows of the large drooping hood.

The unexpected loudness of my voice and the presence of the three of us appeared to catch the cloaked figure off guard. It also snapped Chuck and Jade out of their shocked gaze. For a very long, tense moment, all we did was stare at each other. That was until my friends decided to start asking questions.

"Was that a horn on top of that horse's head?" Chuck asked, sounding more excited than confused.

"And what was that light?" Jade added, her voice tangled with suspicion.

"Better question," Chuck added, taking a courageous step forward and stretching one arm out in front of him, pointing accusingly at the figure ahead of him, "who the heck are you?"

Jade and I followed suit and moved forward so that we were both flanking Chuck, giving him much-needed backup. The figure didn't respond and instead hesitated, taking in their predicament, then quickly looked back and forth between Cliffton and us as if they were deciding what to do. I felt my heart sink and a wave of fear consumed every inch of my body when the figure suddenly sprinted toward us. It appeared to change its mind right before reaching us, grabbing something from within its cloak and tossing it on the ground. A swirling green smoke spiraled up from the ground, engulfing the figure, and caused the three of us to choke and gag. A smell that reminded me faintly of soot wafted in the air.

"What the heck was that?" Jade said, nearly choking on her own words.

"My eyes burn!" Chuck groaned as he attempted to rub at them underneath his glasses.

Once the smoke finally cleared and we all could see and, more importantly, breathe again, I saw that the figure was gone. We just stood there in silence, each one waiting for the other to speak first. The longer we stood that way, the more bizarre the events that had just unfolded seemed. Then, sure enough, Chuck and Jade both started asking questions again at the same time and at such a high speed that my brain couldn't make them out. Chuck's questions leaned more toward the whole "Is your uncle's horse a unicorn?" while Jade's were more about the hooded figure.

Neither one of them wanted to stop the continuous stream of questions, and the longer it went on, the louder they got. I stole a quick glance over at Cliffton, whose horn had vanished again and who was now flanked by Eloise and Thor, both of whom appeared to be seeing if he was OK or maybe even comforting him. He looked pretty tired, but not as bad as he had been while the light was being ripped out of him, so I assumed whatever effect it had on him was wearing off.

Once my initial fear for his health was eased, the realization that Chuck and Jade would expose hid secret was at the forefront of my mind. I first tried asking them in a hushed tone to calm down, but neither of them noticed me as they continued getting louder and more hysterical. I finally stomped my foot as hard as I could. This didn't get the desired effect I wanted—the ground was hard cement covered with a light scattering of hay, and my tennis shoes didn't make much of a noise. What it did accomplish, however, was sending a shock of pain up my leg that made me yelp slightly, but that I would have to deal with later.

I had to turn to my voice again. I tried, slightly louder but hopefully not too loud to attract any unwanted attention. "Guys, you need to stop before someone hears us." Once again, I was ignored or unheard. "Please! Stop!" I begged this time, using my normal speaking voice, and once again got nothing in response. Finally, I yelled louder than the both of them, "Can you both shut up for one minute, for crying out loud!"

They both stopped midsentence and turned to stare at me with wide eyes. Jade looked confused by my outburst, and Chuck a tad scared.

"Thank you," I said softly, and for Chuck's sake, as sweetly as I could make myself sound. "Look, I know you have a lot of questions," looking around once more just in case my yelling had caught anyone's attention. I leaned in and continued in a quieter voice, "I don't know everything. Heck, I don't know much at all, and I definitely don't know who that was, but if you meet me at my house after this event is over—" I paused when I called it my house. It felt strange, but I guess I was starting to assume that I would be stuck there forever at this point. I had to shake that line of thought out of my head for later pondering, and I finished by adding, "I'll explain the whole horn thing there, or at least as much as I know."

Neither one of them said a word, so I quizzically asked, "All right?" Chuck and Jade looked at each other for a long moment. So long, in fact, I was starting to wonder if they knew some form of secret language through eye blinking or, with all the other extraordinary things I had seen, could they be reading each other's minds? Finally, Chuck and Jade both turned to me and nodded in agreement.

Once the events and shows were over, we met up with my aunt and uncle. Aunt Tara had bought as many new random knickknacks as Uncle James could carry, and Uncle James bought as many sweets as he could without Aunt Tara seeing him, which of course, she did but pretended not to. Finally, they loaded all the horses into the back of a trailer, and we were on our way back to the house.

My mood must have clearly been off because it wasn't Aunt Tara who asked about it, but rather, my uncle. "Everything okay, kiddo?"

I had to admit there was a tiny spot in the back of my mind that screamed to just blurt out all the things I'd seen over the last few days. I mean, after all, they were adults and would surely be able to figure out what to do better than I ever could. The other part, the larger, more stubborn part, told me to keep my mouth shut because all of it sounded completely made up. So I faked a smile and said as confidently as I could make myself, "Yeah, just ate too much taffy."

Uncle James looked down at me, and there was the slightest hint of what I thought was suspicion and I had to keep myself from gulping. Then it dawned on me that he wasn't looking at me as much as he was at the very large sack of saltwater taffy on my lap he had asked me to hold. His expression turned to a more humorous one as he told me, "Maybe you should let your aunt hold on to those. I don't want you eating all of them before I've had a chance to get a few!" and he followed it up with a joking grin. We all shared a chuckle, but when I stole a quick look at my aunt, I was sure even though she was laughing and smiling, something in me told me that she wasn't buying my story.

I waited until we got closer to the farm before I finally dared to ask, "So, I was wondering if it would be okay if Chuck and Jade came over today?"

Uncle James didn't reply, but he looked over to my aunt, clearly waiting for her to make this decision. She looked thoughtfully for a long moment before she said softly, like she was afraid to upset me, "Well, it's almost dinnertime, so I'm sure their parents wouldn't let them come this late," and smiled apologetically.

I felt my heart sink into my chest. Was I *really* going to have to wait until tomorrow? What if they told someone? What if that creepy hooded guy came after us to keep us quiet or went after the unicorns again? What if . . . The last thought was cut short when Uncle James said, "Why don't you see if they can spend the night?"

Aunt Tara looked at him, surprised he had said it, and when he noticed her staring, he shrugged like it wasn't a big deal. "Well, we do have a couple of air mattresses in the shed we could use."

Aunt Tara looked thoughtful, like the idea of this happening was still being debated in her head. After what felt like the longest, most painful silence in history, she agreed, "Sure, you can invite them over if you want. I mean, we might have to take a broom to the mattresses with how much dust must be on them since the last time we used them, but otherwise, I guess it's all right." She said the last part with a sly grin. I would have hugged my uncle at that moment if he hadn't still been driving, and if it wouldn't have been enormously awkward, so instead, I just said thank you.

Chapter 19

Both Chuck and Jade had seemed very eager to come over, except that Chuck apparently had to do some begging on his end. His parents, or should I say his mother, seemed to be very protective of him. Chuck was like a Jedi Knight swinging his lightsaber around, countering every reason his mother could throw at him as to why it was not a good night. Once he had worn her down, she did insist that she talk to my uncle and aunt when she dropped him off, and no matter how he begged, she clearly was not going to concede on that point.

They arrived in a dull yellow Ford Focus half an hour later. When Chuck's mother got out, I saw a very nervous, tense lady with the same brown hair as her son. I could tell under all the lines of worry on her face that, more than likely, she normally had a sweet, happy demeanor. The moment her eyes caught a glimpse of Jade and me sitting on the porch swing, it was almost like a weight had been lifted off her shoulders, and the lines that had once crinkled her worried brow faded away and were replaced with a soft smile that could light up a room. She didn't stay as long as I had thought she would, only a minute or two, and she didn't come over to talk to us like I had expected either. Instead, she gave Jade and me a warm smile before she turned to kiss Chuck on the top of his head. This caused his cheeks to instantly redden. With a half wave to us all, she headed to her car.

I glanced questionably over at Jade while Chuck

attempted to hide his embarrassment by turning away from us to wave to his mother. Jade quickly leaned over to whisper, "He gets bullied a lot by the boys at school." I guess that made sense in a way, but it also didn't, as some girls could be five times worse than any boys I'd ever seen. Chuck could also have saved himself a lot of headaches with his mother if he had just told her who he was seeing instead, but then again, boys never seemed to follow the same rules of logic that girls did.

When Chuck finally reached us with a duffle bag that was way too big for a sleepover, I jumped to my feet, causing the swing to creek slightly from the pressure. I was more than ready to usher them up to my room so we could chat. Still, before the words "Follow me" could leave my lips beyond a sound that was more like "Fa," Aunt Tara interrupted me by saying, "OK, kids, go to the kitchen and wash up. James will be back with some pizza any minute." I hadn't even realized he was gone, but dealing with the whole mess of Chuck's mom had kept me pretty distracted. Jade and I both looked at each other, sharing an "Oh, great" look, while Chuck, on the other hand, became super excited and started questioning my aunt all about the pizza as he followed her closely inside.

"Oh, oh, what kind of pizza did you get?" Chuck asked.

"Ham," she replied.

"Just ham?" Chuck asked, sounding a little disappointed.

My aunt thought about that for a moment before adding, "And pineapple."

"That's called Hawaiian pizza," Chuck replied, sounding proud of knowing its name. "It's one of my favorites!"

"Yes, I know, your mother told me all about that on the phone." She seemed amused by that fact but also slightly annoyed, which had me wondering what exactly

Chuck's mom had said before she agreed to let him come over. I mostly ignored the rest of the conversation, but from the snippets I heard, it continued about what type the other ordered pizza was. Chuck also had a deep concern if my uncle remembered to get breadsticks or garlic knots.

Jade grabbed me by the arm before we could walk in and, in a low, desperate voice, said, "Do you think your aunt and uncle will let us eat in your room? I *need* to know what's going on."

All I could do was shrug at her question and promise, "I'll see what I can do." Jade nodded at me before she let my arm go, and we both headed inside.

Jade, Chuck, and I pleaded and begged with my aunt and then did the same thing with my uncle as soon as he walked in through the front door. He was holding a stack of three pizza boxes with another box of garlic knots, on top of which were two precariously balanced large bottles of soda. We still kept getting no after no for letting us eat in my room. I thought I did pretty well arguing, but they were having none of it.

My aunt first claimed she didn't want any ants upstairs, which seemed pretty weird since I had already eaten several meals in my room now. Even when I promised we would be careful and pointed out that I'd eaten there already, she quickly switched to another point, like pizza time was family time. When I rebutted that with the fact that two of the three of us kids were not family, she just shrugged it off and said they were just as good as family.

We were able to whisper to Chuck just long enough to tell him that we needed to eat in a rush so we could get upstairs to talk. Chuck didn't get the memo, though, and I couldn't decide if he was purposefully trying to slow us down or if he was just the world's slowest eater.

My aunt's and uncle's endless questions about our

day sure didn't help us out either. Jade and I gave simple, short replies, but Chuck went on and on about every little detail he could remember. It was like he was a talking novel, painting the scene with his words in great agonizing detail. When he got to the part about how we went into the back stables area to visit the horses, he said, "And when we rounded the corner, you won't believe what we saw—OW!" Jade and I had both given him a sharp kick under the table to keep him from saying too much.

It seemed our kicks hadn't gone unnoticed because Jade and I got the strangest looks from my aunt and uncle both before my aunt turned to Chuck, smiled sweetly, and said, "You were saying, Chuck?"

Chuck shot a quick, nervous glance at the both of us before he rubbed at the back of his neck and simply said, "Um, well." He paused for a moment, buying himself some time to think. He made it look like he was about to sneeze, then it slowly turned into a yawn before he finished with, "Just two teenagers smooching in the shadows."

Jade and I gave Chuck the slightest of nods. My uncle looked quizzically at Chuck before shoving another bite of pizza into his mouth. My aunt didn't seem 100 percent sold on the story, saying, "Hmm, strange thing to be so secretive about," as she gave Jade and me a strange look before adding, "But then again, it's been ages since I was young," and she shrugged almost like she was trying to convince herself that was true.

Whether she believed him or not, Aunt Tara didn't bring it up again, and the questions slowly shifted to other topics like what we planned on doing that night and if we had any big plans for the week. Jade had taken over most of the conversation, being as short and simple in replies as she could with, "Talk, and just hanging out." She had to take over because it was clear Chuck was a bit of a blabbermouth!

Once we had all finished our food, and my aunt and uncle seemed *mostly* satisfied that we weren't up to no good, we were finally allowed to leave the table and head up to my room. Jade and I practically ran up the stairs as she carried a very small bag that I was sure was only big enough to hold some pj's and maybe a toothbrush. Chuck lagged behind us, trying his best to catch up while he panted, carrying a huge duffle bag over his shoulder. I wasn't sure if he had overpacked or if it had been his overprotective mother. I figured it had to be the latter.

Chuck barely had enough time to set his bag down on the floor before Jade shut the door behind him, quickly turning to me with a face full of anticipation and excitement, matching the urgency in her voice when she told me, "OK, now spill the beans!"

I sat down on the bed with a long huff, and a sudden feeling of anxiety overcame me that I couldn't quite place. It wasn't like I had done anything wrong, but I couldn't shake the feeling that somehow I was responsible for all of this. Yes, part of me wanted to tell them everything I knew, even if that wasn't much. Knowing something like this and being the only one was torture. I knew I couldn't go screaming through town that unicorns were real, not unless I wanted everyone to think I was living in a fantasy world, but another part of me felt almost guilty. Like somehow, I was betraying the unicorns by telling their secret. As my mother would have said, I had to acknowledge that the proverbial cat was out of the bag. Honestly, that saying was super creepy. Did they really keep cats in bags in the past, and if so, why? I shuddered at the thought and decided I didn't want to know. Anyway, Jade and Chuck had seen for themselves, and they just hadn't realize yet what they'd seen.

I took a few calming breaths while Chuck sat on the floor in front of me and Jade leaned against the wall. The way she had her head tilted told me she was going to

177

keep an ear out for any eavesdroppers. Once she nodded to me that the coast was clear, I opened the floodgates and told them everything, and I mean everything. From the strange slowness of time I had experienced to the journal I found, the dream, and of course, the fact that my aunt and uncles' horses were unicorns pretending to be horses.

There was a very, very long uncomfortable silence after I finished talking. So long that I was starting to really doubt myself for telling them everything that I just did. Did they believe me? I mean, honestly, I don't see how they couldn't after what we had all just witnessed that afternoon. Then again, humans didn't always have the best track record about that sort of thing; well, at least adults didn't. Always finding ways to argue the facts that were right in front of them. Maybe kids were different?

After a bit more silence, I found out that, yes, kids were different. Jade let out a very long sigh, then she rubbed one hand down the back of her head while she slid down against the wall, locking her knees in place so that it almost looked like she was sitting in an invisible chair.

"Well, that's a lot to absorb," she simply said with no hint of any emotion, so I couldn't quite read her yet.

Jade's speaking broke Chuck out of whatever daydream or thought he was having because his once-confused face suddenly brightened, and he nearly shouted, "Magic is real! Woo-hoo, that's amazing!" Jade and I both had to hush him, and he quickly lowered his head and muttered, "Sorry, sorry. I forgot."

I was just about to speak again when Chuck jumped to his feet and turned quickly to face Jade, the excitement back in every movement he made, but this time he made sure not to yell when he asked Jade, "Are you thinking what I'm thinking?" Jade looked at him, confused at first, then thoughtful, and then the same excitement came over her as well and she jumped to her feet too. They took two steps so that they were standing right in front of each other.

In unison, they said, "Do you think Cumberbunch is a unicorn?" Glee and hope filled every word.

The idea that that weird-looking horse was a unicorn seemed pretty ridiculous to me, but Thor was also a unicorn, and he didn't exactly meet the build I would have expected either. The very thought made me feel even more silly as the whole unicorn thing was something my brain still had a hard time accepting. I half expected that at any minute, I was going to wake up back home in my own bed to find that this whole summer-on-a-farm thing had been a very strange dream that I would have most likely forgotten before breakfast. I thought about that longer than I should have because when I snapped out of my fantasy, I found Jade and Chuck standing in front of me, looking very happy and partly anxious.

I blinked a few times, feeling like I must have missed something, when Jade finally asked me, "Well?" The smile on her face was even bigger than it had been before she asked her question.

"Um, well, what?" I asked, hoping I hadn't hurt their feelings when I went into my daze.

Chuck snorted before replying, "Do you think he might be?"

"He who?" I responded, mentally kicking myself that I had forgotten what they had just been talking about.

"Do you think Cumberbunch is a unicorn too?" Jade asked, partly trying to keep her smiling face, but her eyes told me she had gotten a bit cross.

"Oh, that," I said while quickly trying to think how to reply. Clearly, I wanted to say no because, honestly, I didn't see that happening, but I didn't want to hurt their feelings either. So I decided to lie, and with a shrug and my voice trying to sound as encouraging as I could make it, I said, "I don't see why not."

Jade and Chuck beamed at me before turning toward each other and holding hands. They then jumped around excitedly in almost a dance, all the while chanting, "Unicorns, unicorns, unicorns!" A light, rapid knock at the door suddenly cut off their gleeful chant. Jade and Chuck just stood there, still holding hands, looking very much like deer caught in headlights. I probably didn't look much different. There was a short pause before another knock came. This time I said, "Come in." Uncle James walked into the room, holding a tray somehow with just one hand. On it were three large glasses of milk and a plate piled so high with chocolate chip cookies that if we ate them all, I was sure one of us would end up in a sugar coma.

"Your aunt thought your guests might want a snack," he said. His normal expression was quickly replaced by confusion as he took in what he saw, his eyes darting to Jade and Chuck, who were still holding hands. When they noticed his look, they quickly moved away from each other. Uncle James looked between them before finally setting his gaze on me. "Did I hear something about unicorns?" he asked.

I'm not sure why I said this or even how my mind had come up with it so fast, but I soon found myself giving him a warm smile before saying, "Yeah, they were just showing me their secret handshake for the unicorn club."

Jade and Chuck quickly turned to me, looking both confused and alarmed, before a look of realization came over Jade, and she mirrored my smile, adding, "Yeah, we love unicorns." She pumped her fist into the air with mock enthusiasm.

On the other hand, Chuck took longer to get the hint when he asked, "What club?" That got him a sudden jab to the ribs from Jade. He winced, and when he looked at the even more confused look on my uncle's face, he came up with his own lie. "Sorry, I thought it was a secret club."

"It is," Jade admitted, and then gave my uncle a look that could only say, "Hey, maybe you could go away now." He got the hint because he quickly handed the tray of food over to Jade since Chuck's hands were busy rubbing at the spot where Jade had just jabbed him.

He walked to the door, and we thought we were in the clear, but he paused, turned, and looked at Jade, partly amused, partly all "I'm a grownup, so you'll listen to me" sort of way before telling her, "Try not to hurt Chuck anymore. I don't think his mother wants him all covered in bruises."

"Aye, aye, Captain," she said, and gave him a strange little salute. He shook his head like he wanted to say something else but quickly thought better of it before turning and walking away. He shut the door behind him. I was sure I heard him mutter something to himself as soon as the door was shut.

Jade waited all about twenty seconds, just long enough for the footstep sounds of my uncle to fade before she turned and gave Chuck another sharp jab to his ribs. "Owww!" he cried while taking a significant step away from her and placing his hands in front of him as protection from other attacks. "What was that for?" he whined.

Jade shot him an icy glare, "You couldn't figure out what we were doing, Chuck?!" and she placed two fingers into the air, holding them only about an inch apart, as she added, "Is that *really* the best thing your tiny, tiny brain could come up with?"

Chuck's whole face reddened, and he quickly looked at his feet. "Sorry, I panicked," he told her softly.

The anger that once filled Jade's whole face softened a bit by Chuck's response, but instead of going on or even saying she was sorry, she simply waved both hands in the air in front of her before turning to face me.

"What do we do now?" she asked.

I wasn't sure why she thought I would know. It's not like I am a walking library about *real unicorns.* When I saw the look in her eyes, though, a look that pleaded for me to give some great answer or idea, the same look Chuck himself was now giving me, I did the first thing that came to mind. I shrugged and said, "Maybe we should see what the unicorns know?"

They both stared at me thoughtfully before Jade smiled brightly and nodded in approval, and Chuck exclaimed, "That's a brilliant idea!" They both turned away and started for the door. I didn't say anything, clearing my throat instead to get their attention. They both turned to give me a puzzled look, and so I gestured to my bedroom window where the sun had set, the very last rays of light leaving a deep red glow on the horizon.

"Oh, right," Jade said disappointingly.

"So it's a bit dark," Chuck said as he looked between us like we had lost our minds. "Are you guys scared of the dark or something?" he added with a tiny smirk. Jade growled before she gave him a light but still painful-looking punch to the arm, for which he quickly let out a loud yelp before rubbing it.

"No, but you are, Mister Night-Light!" A flash of embarrassment filled Chuck's face, and he stole a quick peek at me before he looked down at his arm and muttered something about "there's going to be a bruise."

I decided to ease the tension that was growing by simply telling him, "No, but if I asked them if we can go see the horses now, I think they might get a bit suspicious."

"And that's the last thing we need right now, adults getting in our way," Jade was quick to add. Chuck nodded, finally understanding, "Yeah, that's a good point." After that, we decided to keep the unicorn talk to a minimum. Jade wasn't confident that my aunt and uncle wouldn't spy on us after the whole unicorn club thing. I wasn't sure why but I agreed, and we spent the rest of the night talking about anything else while enjoying our cookies and milk. Where Jade and I kept our number of cookies to just one or two, I was disturbingly surprised by how many cookies Chuck had eaten, especially considering the amount of taffy he had before.

Soon my aunt poked her head in, telling us it was lights out, and we complied. Typically I think we might have stayed up longer talking, but I think the three of us were too anxious about getting up early to question the unicorns about that creepy person in the robe. Before I shut off the light, I caught a glimpse of what appeared to be a superhero night-light at the top of Chuck's bag when he put his toothbrush back. Part of me wanted to tell him he could plug it in if he wanted, but the other part didn't want to embarrass him. So instead, I flipped off the light and lay down on my bed, the silhouettes of Jade and Chuck lying on the air mattress on my floor, barely visible under the moonlight coming from my window. I hoped that was enough light for him, but I hoped even more that I didn't have any more dreams, especially any with haunting cloaked figures, and with that last dread-filled thought, I let myself drift off to sleep.

Chapter 20

We had every intention of waking up super early the following day. Jade even set an alarm clock on her phone to wake us up. But Jade either sleepily pushed the snooze button before it could wake up anyone else, or she forgot to turn up the volume. She had claimed it was the latter, but I was sure I saw a hint of guilt in her eyes that made me believe it was probably the former. So, the plans of talking to the unicorns before the adults could wake up and make breakfast were clearly foiled as I awoke to the blinding light flooding through my window and the smells of food I couldn't identify. It sure did smell great, though. We got dressed and hurried downstairs to find a table full of pancakes, eggs, bacon, some random cut-up fruits, and a massive pitcher of what I assumed was orange juice.

I did try to eat fast, at first at least, but all the food was so good, and for some reason, my stomach felt like I hadn't eaten in days. So I allowed myself to enjoy every single delightful bite. After all, after we left the house to question the unicorns, I had no idea what was going to happen. So it made sense that I might as well fill up while I still could.

Jade and Chuck, however, appeared to be thinking the same thing because they also were shoving the food into their mouths like this was the first time they had seen food. Uncle James didn't seem to notice as he was consuming his food pretty much the same way, but Aunt Tara did.

She watched us curiously while slowly sipping at her coffee. I could partially see the gears turning in her head with a look that screamed she wanted to ask us a million questions, something we definitely didn't have time for this morning. When I saw her go to put her cup down, an alarm inside my head alerted me that those questions would come as soon as that cup hit the table. So with a gentle nudge with my foot, I quickly and softly kicked at Jade's and Chuck's feet under the table, though I was sure not to do it hard enough so Chuck wouldn't give me away with another loud whine, and said quickly, "Is it OK that we go out to see the horses?" I turned my eyes to Uncle James, avoiding looking at Aunt Tara so that hopefully she wouldn't be the one to reply.

He gave me a confused look as a forkful of dripping pancakes hung on his fork, his eyes darting quickly between it and me. Thankfully his hunger overtook his chance to think about it, and he said, "Sure, I don't see why not," before shoving the large bite into his mouth. The three of us swiftly got out of our seats without missing a beat. Aunt Tara looked at me, dazed and confused as her brain tried to catch up with what had just happened, and a babble of words came out of her mouth. It almost sounded like a protest, but it didn't quite get there. The three of us didn't give her the chance to get her words figured out before we thanked her for breakfast and hurried out the door, leaving Uncle James happily eating his food and Aunt Tara stunned, still unable to fully wrap her head around what had just happened.

A sense of anxiety pulsed through every inch of my body as we approached the barn doors. Part of it was that I couldn't get to them quick enough, worried any minute that my aunt would run outside and call for us to come back. The other part of me was still somehow concerned that this was all in my head, or at least the talking unicorns talking part. I really couldn't deny what happened yesterday anymore as I wasn't the only one who saw it, but only I had heard them speak. The closer I got, the more my brain pleaded with my body to just go quicker, and once we finally pushed the doors open, quickly went inside, and then shut them behind us, it was like a giant weight had been removed from me.

"You all right?" Jade asked, snapping me out of the fears still wanting to bubble to the surface.

"Yeah, why?" I replied, and, for the first time, noticed how out of breath I was. Jade gestured to my chest, which, at this point, was rising and falling like I had run a marathon.

"Oh," I breathed, and faked a smile. "Guess I was worried she would stop us." Jade looked at me thoughtfully for a moment before nodding in agreement.

"Your aunt totally did look a bit sus, didn't she?"

"Yeah!" I agreed. Chuck cleared his throat, and when we both turned to look at him, he had both hands on his waist and was tapping one foot impatiently.

"Well, maybe we should go see the horses in case she decided to follow us out here!" he told us both, his voice a mix of anticipation and worry.

"He's got a point," Jade agreed, and I nodded to the both of them. The three of us all turned in the direction of the horse stalls simultaneously and slowly made our way forward. None of the horses, er, unicorns, seemed to take much notice of us being there, though when Cliffton spotted how we were looking at them, more importantly at him, he looked a little nervous. His eyes darted from Jade to Chuck to me and back to Jade for quite a while before finally settling on me, and it wasn't until one of my friends cleared their throat that I suddenly realized I must have been standing there looking at him for a lot longer than I thought I was.

"What?" I said, and it came out a bit snippier than I had intended it to be.

"Are you going to make him talk or what?" Jade asked, returning my attitude with an even meaner-sounding one.

"Yeah!" Chuck added. I shot him a stern look, causing him to look away quickly.

I had to think about this for a moment before I said, "I'll try." I mean, after all, was there really anything else I could do if they didn't want to talk? It's not like I was the boss of all unicorns or something.

They both gave me doubtful looks before I turned away from them. I suddenly felt really nervous, the kind of nervous you get when you stand onstage, and everyone looks at you just as a spotlight blinds you. I wasn't sure why I felt this way. Was it Jade and Chuck watching me, or was it the unicorns I was suddenly being so shy around? I told myself it didn't matter. With a deep breath, I straightened myself as tall as I could and let both arms go rigid down by my sides before I cleared my throat and said, a lot quieter than I had meant to, "I was hoping we could ask you some—" but Jade cut me off.

"What did you say?" she asked. This time I tried a bit louder, but not loud enough to spook them.

"Sorry. Again, I was hoping we could ask you a few questions about yesterday." Cliffton just stared at me for a very long agonizing moment before he lowered his head and began munching on some loose hay near his feet.

"Cliffton," I said softly, but he didn't budge. When this got me nowhere, I switched to a more upbeat voice. "Come on, boy, you can talk to us." This time I thought I saw just the slightest twitch of his eyes before he tilted his head in a slightly different direction to gobble up another mouthful of hay.

"Come on!" I urged him, this time talking in a lower whisper between gritted teeth. "You're embarrassing me," and again, he ignored me.

Gosh, I was starting to really hate unicorns.

Cliffton briefly lifted his head and stared at me, giving my heart a sudden surge of hope. He let out a weird-sounding snort, and then he was back to eating. Jade grumbled something behind me that I couldn't quite understand, but despite the feeling that I should ignore it, I turned and asked, "What was that?"

Jade practically glared at me before placing both hands on her hips, giving me a look that screamed, "I'm over this," and her voice was full of some more snark and sass that hit me like a brick. "I'm starting to think we got pulled into a girl's delusions," she spat.

"Excuse me?!" I shouted back, but it came out more like a half yell, half whisper, as if the words had started out strong and suddenly lost life when they poured out of my mouth. I cleared my throat again before I said, this time calmer, "You saw that creepy hooded thing yesterday too, Jade."

She rolled her eyes before giving Chuck a side glance, his face pale like he had seen a ghost and somehow forgotten how to move or speak. "Do we *really* know what we saw? I mean, we ate lots of sugar. Maybe we were just on a major sugar high?" Chuck looked at her with an expression like he wanted to agree, but something seemed to click in his head that quickly made him shake it at her. Jade went on, as if she needed to convince Chuck I was losing my mind, evil, or both. "Maybe she drugged us?"

"What?!" I shouted in protest. This time, Chuck looked like he could believe that weird lie. "With what?" I asked while gesturing wildly around the whole stable with my hands.

"Maybe something you found around here," she admitted while looking me over, "or maybe something you brought from your home. Where did you say you came from again?"

"What does that have to do with anything?" I

growled back. "And I didn't drug anyone."

"So you claim," she snarled back before reaching over and grabbing Chuck's hand, who had still not said a single word. "We're leaving, Chuck," she insisted as she started stomping off, dragging the still frightened Chuck behind her.

"Good!" I yelled back. "I don't need your help anyway!" I turned my back to them both. At this moment, a new voice filled the air, a soft female British-sounding one.

"We need their help, Cliffton" the voice begged. I felt frozen for a moment then I sprang around to see Jade and Chuck had both stopped midstep and then turned to face me. Jade waited for a moment before the confused-teetering-on-the-verge-of-being-scared look on her face swiftly morphed into an even angrier one than she had before.

"Oh, very funny, Jennifer. Nice accent." She was about to walk off again when Eloise approached her stall door and looked at Jade.

"I said it," Eloise told her with a small flourish of her head. A soft white puff of swirling smoke left behind a twirled white horn near the top of her head. Compared to Eloise's horn, Cliffton's almost seemed plain.

Jade's eyes grew wide, so did Chuck's, but only Jade spoke, if you could call it that. The only words she managed to get out were "Holy . . . " before her eyes rolled to the back of her head, and she fell backward, almost taking Chuck down with her.

A few minutes later, when Jade came to, she found Chuck and me standing over her, Chuck looking very much concerned. Me, on the other hand, not so much, and I did all I could not to smile down at her, which I knew I was failing at because I could just feel the slightest of tugs in the corner of my lips. Was I being mean? I wasn't sure, but the way she had just talked to me and accused me of poisoning them of all things, something about her passing out made it feel a bit more even, that and proving her wrong. But now wasn't the time to celebrate my rightness. There were unicorns to be questioned.

Putting aside my majorly hurt feelings, I offered my hand to her. Jade appeared confused before she reluctantly took it, and I helped her up to her feet. For the first time, I realized either I was relatively weak or Jade was a lot heavier than she looked.

"What just happened?" Jade asked as she yanked her hand away from me and began checking her head and body for any injuries.

"You passed out," I said flatly in response, and she shot me a sharp glare.

"And she talked," Chuck added, looking both delighted and a bit scared as his eyes darted nervously between us and the watching eyes of unicorns.

Jade thought that over for a moment before she shook her head. "Nah, Jennifer clearly said it," she said firmly before adding with a smirk, "and with such an awful British accent too."

"I beg your pardon?" a voice said from Jade's side. Quickly turning toward it, she found Eloise's face inches away from her own. "There is nothing fake about my voice in the slightest I'll have you know."

Jade's jaw flung open, and nothing but a bunch of unformed words seemed to want to come out again.

"Also, you have some dirt on your rear, darling. You might want to do something about that before the others see," Eloise told her in a whisper before flinging her head back so that her mane swooshed and bounced. It reminded me a lot of what women did in movies when they were trying to seem alluring and confident at the same time. "And besides," Eloise continued, giving Jade side-eye, "didn't you see the most stunning horn appear on top of my head just moments before you?" Eloise

191

paused just long enough to let out a sarcastic-sounding snort. "Or did you miss that with your, well, quite frankly, overdramatic fainting spell, my dear? You must be as blind as you are poorly dressed."

Jade's fists curled into tight balls at her side, so I quickly stepped between them both, asking, "You said you needed our help?" I was hopeful the subject change would diffuse the situation before it could get any worse. I wasn't sure if Jade would go as far as to hit a horse, but after the many times I'd seen her smack Chuck, I wasn't about to test it.

Eloise turned her attention to me. "Why yes, I did, didn't I?" Her tone seemed a little off.

There was a sudden low growl preceding a voice from Cliffton's stall. "You should have kept your mouth shut. They're kids. They can't help us."

Then there was a bang from Thor's stall, and when I looked over, I saw he had somehow managed to get his two front legs over the stall door and was just barely managing to keep himself there when he added, "You tell her, Cliffton."

Eloise responded to him with a very mean glare, and when Thor saw her, he sheepishly sank back behind the door. I decided to ignore both the boys and turned my attention to Eloise. "What do you need help with?"

Eloise tilted her head slightly as if she was contemplating the question, and after a long, drawn-out moment, she admitted, "I'm not entirely sure, actually."

"You're not sure?" Chuck echoed, finally stepping closer to where Jade and I were standing.

"How can you need help but not know with what?" Jade asked as she crossed her arms over her chest, her hands still held in fists.

"I'm, er, it's, well, it's just . . ." Eloise stuttered before trailing off. Forcing herself to regain some sense of composure, she continued, "It's just, it's a tad bit embarrassing, the situation that the three of us have found ourselves in, that is."

"And that situation would be?" I asked, trying my best to sound reassuring. Eloise avoided eye contact with any of us, and the look on her face made me wonder if unicorns could blush, not that you would see it under all the hair. There was a loud sigh from Cliffton's stall before he poked his head back out and turned to face us. "We lost our memories," he confessed.

"Lost your memories?" echoed the three of us simultaneously, and Chuck couldn't help but say "Jinx" at the end, which no one paid any attention to. He mumbled something under his breath about none of us being any fun, which we ignored too.

"Go on," I urged Cliffton. There was an unease that fell over Cliffton like a blanket, and he stood there, locking eyes with me. I wondered if he was debating whether he should say anything else. Finally, his whole body slumped just a tiny bit, as if he had decided to accept his fate.

"It's hard to explain," he told us, stealing a quick look at Eloise and Thor before he went on. "For a few years now, or at least we think it's only been a few years, we seemed to have forgotten almost everything."

"Almost?" I asked, starting to feel like a questioning parrot. He nodded solemnly.

"Sometimes it feels like we are just on the verge of remembering something, and then it's gone just as quickly as it surfaced."

"What do you remember?" Jade asked as she moved to stand right next to me. Chuck followed suit and stood on my other side. This time Thor decided to chime in after he positioned himself over the stall door again with a little more ease this time.

"Well, we know we are unicorns," and he paused before adding in a laughing tone, "which we learned is not normal." I couldn't help but nod to him in agreement, though saying that it was not normal seemed like an understatement.

"Anything else?" Chuck asked when neither of them offered any more information. Cliffton nodded sadly.

"We're pretty sure this isn't where we are from, and there's this strange feeling we keep getting that we're . . . well, I don't know how to . . . " and he trailed off, deep in thought.

"That we're protecting something," Elosie continued without missing a beat, causing Cliffton to snap out of whatever thought he had been having.

"Protecting what?" the three of us asked. Just as Chuck's mouth was opening and the hint of a sound of a word came out, "Ji—" Jade shot him a stern and he clamped his mouth shut without finishing.

Cliffton shook his head, looking miserable. "We don't know. It's just a feeling we all get sometimes."

"Especially when certain people come by," Thor added.

"What people?" I inquired, taking a small step closer to Thor, which caused him to recoil from me silently before he answered, "I can't remember."

This news caused me to frown. I wasn't sure if he was being honest, as part of me worried that he was talking about me. That thought triggered an itchy thought at the back of my head, causing me to quickly spin around and face Cliffton, my voice accusatory when I pointed my finger at him and announced, "That's why you tried to steal my journal, isn't it?"

Cliffton looked caught off guard, but after a moment, he let out of long, loud laugh. It took him a while to calm down, but when he did, he told me, still slightly laughing, "No, not at all." He continued on, reassuring me, "We don't get any bad vibes from you like we get from others."

194

"Did you get bad vibes from that hooded figure yesterday?" Jade inquired, which caused all three of them to become restless, much like a horse might when it sensed danger.

"Precisely, my dear, we most definitely got bad vibes from that person," Eloise agreed.

"Do you know who they were?" Jade continued.

Eloise mulled that question over before telling her, "I think I did, but I forget now," her voice was heavy with regret and melancholy. I felt like I had waited patiently enough. I mean, the questions that were being asked were important, I had no doubt about that, but I still hadn't been given a full answer to the one I had just asked.

"But why did you try to take my journal then?" I asked, only looking at Cliffton.

There was a sudden seriousness to his voice with just a hint of grief when he admitted to me, "It's not yours."

I felt disappointed since he had already made that fact clear before, and it forced me to ask, "Then whose is it?"

Cliffton looked away from me, embarrassed, before he replied, barely in a whisper, "I don't remember." I had to admit that I wasn't satisfied with that answer, and I was ready to demand a better one when I was cut off by the sound of the stable doors opening behind us. This caused Thor to drop back down into his stall with a thud and Eloise to wander away to the back corner of her stall. Cliffton took one long look at me, and I could see a world of sorrow behind his big brown eyes before he looked away and went to munching at the hay by his feet. I wanted to spend all day talking to them, but when I glanced over my shoulder, I could already see Uncle James coming in, starting his day, so I knew that would have to wait.

He gave us a strange look, but Jade smiled at him reassuringly and said, "You really do have some of the best-looking horses in town, Mr. Greenfell." This caused him to beam; apparently, Jade knew how to play to someone's ego. Maybe I could learn a thing or two from her, well, maybe after I forgave her for calling me a poisoning liar!

The three of us walked single file past my uncle, who went on with his business, not asking any questions as to why we were there or even seeming to care. I stole one last glance at Cliffton before we walked out the door. He was looking at me, still as sad and miserable as he had been moments before. I don't know why. It's not like we were friends. I wasn't even sure he liked me, but looking at him this way just made my heart ache for him.

Chapter 21

At first, the three of us had all been in agreement that we would wait until Uncle James finished doing his chores in the stables, and when he was out of eyesight, we would sneak back in to ask more questions. At least, that was the plan. After sitting in an area where we wouldn't look suspicious but still had a good view for over an hour and a half, it was clear that wasn't going to happen. Every time Uncle James left the stables and we thought we were in the clear, he would suddenly pop back, each time from some new direction. One time we even got to the door just as he reappeared and barely managed to duck behind a few crates that he had left there the last time he had gone past. So then we sat there, looking at each other, not knowing what to do next, until Chuck suddenly announced, "I got it!" It caught me off guard, and I almost fell off the bench I was sitting on.

"Goodness, Chuck!" I exclaimed as I hopped up from my seat. He gave me a puzzled look.

Jade snickered as she patted him on the shoulder. "You've got to learn to tone it down a bit," and when she saw he wasn't getting it, she added, "You know, don't be so dramatic all the time." All he could do was frown and look embarrassed until she asked him, "So did you have an idea or what?"

Chuck smiled, but it didn't quite reach his eyes, and I wondered if we had been too hard on him too many times. I mean, he did keep completely missing the point of, well, I don't even know, and it wasn't like I was keeping count of his mistakes, but something told me that Jade and I needed to stop being so hard on him when he did.

"Well, since it's clear Mr. Greenfell isn't going to be leaving the stables for very long today, maybe we could check the library?"

Jade about snorted and rolled her eyes. "That sounds boring," she declared.

I ignored her, giving Chuck my best smile when I told him, "That's actually a wonderful idea, Chuck. Great thinking!"

The look on Chuck's face was priceless, like all the self-doubt he had been feeling just wafted away, and he returned my smile with an even bigger one. Jade, on the other hand, wasn't so convinced. "Um, yeah. Count me out. It's summer, and there's no way you're going to get me into that book graveyard."

I chuckled at her slightly. I had never heard of a library being called a book graveyard before, but then again, I liked to read. Obviously Jade didn't, so I shrugged and said nonchalantly, "Well, it's not like we are having much fun here either, but if you want to watch Uncle James by yourself while Chuck and I go on an adventure, suit yourself."

With those last words, I motioned for Chuck to follow me. He hesitated for a moment but quickly caught up once he decided he was going. Jade waited for a moment longer, looking anxiously back and forth between the stables and us, before she called out, "Wait for me," and ran to catch up. Once she did, she said, slightly out of breath, "But I'm not reading any books!" and crossed her arms defiantly across her chest.

Before we could make our way to the library, we had to ask my aunt's permission. Since neither Jade nor Chuck had brought their bikes with them, and the one I had used before would have taken me until my next birthday to get into town, my aunt agreed to take us. She did seem to think it was a bit odd that we would want to go to the library—she even said as much—but Chuck told her they both had a summer assignment to do and that they wanted to get it done so that it wasn't looming over them, ruining their whole summer. Aunt Tara appeared to believe this, and she had gone into a whole rant about how homework was "just work for the parents" and "what kind of teacher gives schoolwork to kids during the summer?" I had to admit, I agreed. But something about how passionate she was about it felt strange, especially since she didn't have any kids. I had to assume maybe she had helped some of these nieces and nephews I knew nothing about, but even that didn't fit. I decided to shrug it off, though. Add that to the weird things about this area list!

She pulled up in front of the library, but before letting us go, she asked me to call her when we needed a ride home. I had to remind her that I still didn't have my phone, and she looked a bit hesitant about leaving us there alone. Thankfully Jade pulled out her phone and promised her that she would call her as soon as we were finished. Aunt Tara hesitated slightly before finally agreeing, and she even left me with some money in case we wanted to get some lunch or ice cream.

Merrow Crescent Library was both smaller and bigger than I had imagined. I wasn't sure what I had expected—it's not like I spent my time thinking about libraries—but after the weirdness of the last few days, there was just a tiny, tiny thought in the back of my head that it would be this huge creepy old building with gargoyles flanking large imposing wooden doors. Inside, it would be big and dimly lit with towering dark mahogany shelves, spiderwebs adorning them all. The books would be so old that each one was covered in a thick layer of dust, which you could use to accurately date them, probably hundreds of years. Oh, and the librarian would be just as old and look all dark and menacing, the kind of menacing that would throw you into a dark basement if you talked above a whisper. The very thought was enough to send shivers down my spine.

Upon reflection, it was clear I had thought about it way too much. I had been completely wrong about most of it. Outside it was a simple brick building with two large windows next to two large glass doors, so clearly, it wasn't going to be dark inside. It wasn't what I would call modern upon entering, but it wasn't hundreds of years old either.

The room was painted in a light shade of blue that seemed closer to white than blue after looking at it more. It made the whole area feel bright and calm. There was, of course, a very large selection of bookshelves that were filled to the brim with books, but the shelves didn't look too old, and the books that lined them didn't appear old at all. Usually, the old books were various shades of brown, but all the books I saw were bright in color. Something about them felt so inviting, like they were urging me to come and read them. What can I say? I love to read. On one side of the doorway, there was also an area with computers, and on the other, lots of comfy-looking couches and chairs in bright shades of teal for people to read.

I felt a tiny tinge of pride when I got one thing right: the librarian did, in fact, look a hundred years old, and when we came in, she barely even looked at us. I just knew she had to be secretly evil! She wore a high-necked plain burgundy blouse with a silver-looking flower pin placed in the middle of her neck. She wore her light gray hair tightly in a bun on top of her head. It was so tight, in fact, that it appeared to pull the skin on her whole face back. And, of course, she wore the classic thick, black-framed glasses you only saw in movies, but they swung under her face, held by a beaded crystal chain attached to both ends. The bottom half of her body was hidden behind the reception counter. For some reason, I imagine her having octopus legs.

Chuck walked right up to her and said brightly, "Morning, Mrs. Higgins," in a voice that was most definitely too loud for any library that I've ever been to.

Instead of glaring at him, hushing him, or giving him really any sort of reprimand, she beamed back at him and looked genuinely happy to see him when she said, almost as loud, "Oh, Chuck, back for another book so soon? Didn't you just get three books last week?"

Chuck shook his head before telling her, "Not this time, just doing some research with my friends," and he motioned back toward Jade and me with his arm. I had to admit I felt a bit confused. I hadn't realized Chuck liked books, possibly more than I did, but I didn't know him that much, so I wasn't too concerned, but Jade looked a bit confused. Had Chuck hidden this from her? I wondered to myself. That seemed like a weird thing to hide, but again it wasn't like I knew either one of them that well.

By the time I vacated my mind thinking about the whole book thing, Chuck had finished his small talk with the librarian that he seemed to know pretty well. She told us to let her know if we needed any help before she went back to doing whatever she was doing before we arrived. Jade and I followed close behind Chuck since he clearly knew his way around more than either of us did.

It could have been thirty minutes. It could have been thirty hours at this point. After looking from shelf to shelf, none of us could find any books on unicorns, or at least none that weren't silly kids' stories. There wasn't even anything about the history of the town or one that would have clicked as possibly being relevant. After way too long of looking, it became clear that all the books we were seeing were new, or at least new enough not to be of much help with giving us any clues as to how to help Cliffton and the others.

We even spent a big chunk of time searching on the computer, typing in "Merrow Crescent unicorns," "Merrow Crescent magic," and "Merrow Crescent history." Every result was either very dull and not at all helpful or about some magic show the town had done a few years back, and I wondered if that's where that clock at the game had come from. The silly kids' magic definitely was not the sucking-out-a-unicorn's-life-force magic. We all slumped back in our chairs, tired and drained, before Chuck offered, "Maybe it's time to bring in the big guns." I must have given him a really weird look because he put up his hands almost defensively. "No, no, not real guns," he corrected. "That's just a saying."

His whole facial expression screamed nervousness. I couldn't help but laugh at him when I said, "I know the saying, Chuck."

Jade gave me a big roll of her eyes. "She probably just wanted to know what your idea was, dork!"

Chuck visibly exhaled, looking relieved but also a bit annoyed by Jade's comment. "I was just meaning; maybe it is time to ask Mrs. Higgins?"

It was probably a good idea, but at the same time, I didn't want to be going around asking about town magic and unicorns either, and I asked him, "Yeah, maybe, but do we really want people looking at us like we are nuts?"

Chuck nodded slightly. "You got a good point. I'll just be discreet."

The three of us pushed ourselves from the computers and wandered over to where Mrs. Higgins was still standing. I wondered if she had ever moved. If she had, I never saw her, and that definitely would make my octopus-like theory more plausible. Chuck approached the counter and said, this time in a quieter, library-worthy tone, "Mrs. Higgins, can I ask you a question?"

She shut the book that had been out of sight behind the counter and placed it on the pile of books in front of her. "What can I help you with, dear?" she responded in an almost singsong tone.

"Well," he said, then cleared his throat, which I assumed was to give himself a bit more time to choose his words wisely. "We wanted to learn more about Merrow Crescent's history, but we can't find any good books on the subject."

Mrs. Higgins seemed to mull this over before asking, "And how far back are you wanting to look?"

"To the beginning," Jade cut in.

Mrs. Higgins's eyebrow shot up, and she eyed Jade suspiciously.

Chuck chimed in with a nervous smile, "Well, as far back as we can."

"This town is very old, dear," Mrs. Higgins replied, more to Chuck than Jade, but she eyed her up and down the whole time. It was clear Mrs. Higgins either didn't trust Jade or didn't like her very much.

"We know," Chuck told her, trying to keep his smile in place. That seemed to be enough to draw her attention away from Jade, who stepped back slightly once Mrs. Higgins was no longer looking at her.

"Why do you need this, Chuck?" Mrs. Higgins quizzed him, her voice oozing with mistrust and unease.

With a clear hint of confusion on his face, because he hadn't anticipated her asking why, he started to mouth words, but nothing came out. Quickly I said, "My teacher back home gave everyone in my class this ridiculous assignment to learn about the history and customs of the places they visited while on vacation." I paused and shrugged. "And, well, since I'm going to be here all summer this was my only option."

Mrs. Higgins gave me a small smile that didn't reach her eyes—there was definitely some mistrust in those eyes—but she seemed to buy my explanation. She nodded before telling us apologetically, "Well, I'm very sorry to be the bearer of bad news, but a few years back, most books and archives were taken away to make the library more, well"—she dramatically gestured with one hand at the room before saying with an almost sigh— "modern." She thought for a moment and added, "They were going to digitize everything, since a lot of the books and documents had gotten so old there was a risk of them being lost or damaged, but I'm not exactly sure what happened with that." She looked perplexed by the whole thing, as if all that information had suddenly flooded her mind after having been long forgotten.

"Where did they take it all?" Jade pushed, which got her another suspicious look from Mrs. Higgins.

"If you don't mind us asking?" Chuck quickly chimed in, in the sweetest way possible. This caused her attention to snap back to Chuck, which Jade looked very happy about, and we both exchanged confused looks as to why Mrs. Higgins obviously didn't like her much.

Mrs. Higgins drummed her fingers on the counter in front of her, the loud tapping of her nails echoing all over as she thought about it before answering. "I do believe they took them all to Susan's Antiques and Curios." My heart sank slightly in my chest. After my first visit, that was the last place I ever wanted to go again.

Chuck thanked her for her time, and we all made our way to the front door. I paused just long enough at the doorway to look over my shoulder, only to see that Mrs. Higgins was no longer behind the counter. In fact, she was nowhere to be seen.

"Creepy," I said softly under my breath before striding out the door and letting it shut behind me with an eerie creek I hadn't noticed before.

Chapter 22

As soon as we reached the bottom of the steps, I asked, "Did anyone else get some majorly weirded-out vibes from the librarian?" Jade nodded enthusiastically in agreement while Chuck shook his head.

"Why would you say such a rude thing?" Chuck questioned me, looking offended. "Mrs. Higgins is a gem and a town treasure!"

This caused Jade to snort out a laugh before she replied, "Well, she probably is old enough to be considered a treasure." She shot me a smirk, which caused Chuck to scowl at both of us before she went on, "Also, she was way rude to me, Chuck, or didn't you catch all her mean looks?" She crossed her arms over her chest, adding a bit of dramatic effect to her question.

Chuck's scowl quickly faded, and he rubbed at the back of his head shyly before shrugging. "Maybe a bit, I guess." Jade huffed, rolling her eyes once more before turning away from him.

"So," I said, letting the word linger in the air a little, hoping to make them both realize that I didn't want to be any part of whatever this was turning into. "Should we head to Susan's?"

Jade gave me a bored expression, her voice even more so when she told me, "Why can't we go do something more fun, like the arcade?" I had to admit that sounded fun, but a strange feeling of urgency bubbling down in my gut made me feel we needed to get this done. Something about the librarian's sudden disappearance felt wrong when she had been there the whole time.

"No," I said firmly, "I think this is more important." Jade looked like she was about to let me have it when Chuck interrupted with a suggestion of his own,

"Well, maybe we could grab some food first? I know I'm starving." He rubbed at his stomach with one hand, during which I was sure I heard a gurgle. I was about to protest, but then my stomach decided to harmonize with Chuck's. Looking to Jade for her approval, she nodded begrudgingly before stalking off in front of us, leading us in the direction of food.

There had been some bickering between Jade and Chuck about where to eat. Chuck wanted tacos, while Jade was dead set on pizza. They decided I should pick in the end, and since I didn't know much about my options, I opted for the only place I knew, Krakens Feast. This seemed to be an acceptable choice for them both as the arguing finally came to a close. I figured the selection was big enough to give anyone a choice, and I also thought maybe if I brought Aunt Tara a slice of pecan pie, perhaps she wouldn't ask me too many questions about my day. It was probably far-fetched but worth a try, I thought.

Even though Jade and Chuck clearly wanted different types of food, they both ended up eating hamburgers, and not wanting to be the odd man out, er, odd girl out, I decided to do the same. We avoided any conversations about unicorns, magic, or even the town. Instead, we mostly ate in silence. There was a weird tension growing between my two friends. I felt a bit more at ease thinking of them this way. After all, it is friends who you go on weird adventures with and have even weirder secrets with, right?

As soon as we finished, I left a small tip and grabbed my plastic bag containing five small boxes that held the pecan pies. The bag was definitely overfilled, but

I felt Uncle James might get a bit jealous if I didn't get him one. That then led me to wonder if I wanted one too, and from there, it just felt rude if I didn't also get a slice for Chuck and Jade. The waitress asked me if I just wanted one whole pie, but I declined, which I now regretted. The bag would have probably been a whole lot easier to carry, but it was too late to change my mind now.

We didn't run to Susan's Antiques and Curios, but I felt our pace was definitely more hurried than our normal walking one and probably much faster than it should have been with the way the bag with the pies swung around, threatening to burst at any moment. I felt pretty pleased with myself once when we made it to the shop without losing a single one. Any joy I had managed to make myself feel all but evaporated though when I looked at the door leading into the antiques store.

A feeling of dread flooded me, much like waiting to be seen by the doctor when you knew you had a shot coming, or even worse, waiting for your grade on a test. Something told me most people would have thought the first one was worse. But no matter how much I tried to tell myself I was being utterly ridiculous, that feeling surged through every inch of my body like hot burning lava and screamed for me to flee and run away, but my legs wouldn't obey it. Instead, with one final nod to my companions, I pushed the door open. The sound of the bell softly chiming above alerted the owner to our presence before we walked inside.

At first, I didn't see her, for which I was incredibly thankful, but after waiting for a few moments and there still being no sign of her, that relief I had been feeling turned into a sour feeling in my stomach. Either that or I ate too many fries. Chuck must have been feeling it too, but instead of being perfectly happy being quiet like Jade and I had been, he asked in a cracked, shaky voice, "Hello . . . is anyone here?"

Again we were met with nothing but silence, though not for long. There was a low rustling sound from the room behind the counter, and moments later, Susan appeared looking both happy to see us but also somehow not. She was smiling, but her eyes appeared cold, almost void of feeling. "Oh, sorry," she announced, with a voice that seemed so overly happy that it felt fake. "I didn't hear the door." Something told me that wasn't true.

"No problem," Chuck replied, still looking a bit worried.

"What can I help you kids with?" she said, placing both hands on the counter in front of her before her eyes landed on me, her smile weirdly deepening into her face. "Jennifer, you came back to see me! What a wonderfully unexpected surprise." I gave her a small, half-hearted smile in return when she kept staring at me.

"Mrs. Higgins said all the old books and stuff from the library were sent here, and we were wondering if we could look through it?" Jade said as flatly and disinterestedly as she could.

"Oh," Susan said, sounding once again overly happy, almost chipper, and I couldn't help but notice she kept her gaze firmly on me. Was every adult in this town so creepy, or was I just really unlucky today?

Susan placed one finger on the left side of her chin and crooked her head ever so slightly, looking thoughtful before telling us, bewildered, "What a curious and marvelous request."

"So, does that mean we can look at them or what?" Jade asked, confused by how Susan had answered.

Susan lowered her hand as she chuckled softly, responding, "Of course you can. They do belong to the city, after all. And since you are citizens of Merrow Crescent, they belong to you just as much as they do to me." Something about the way she said all that was very unsettling to me. She finally looked at all three of us for the first time and motioned for us to follow her.

The store looked much the same as it had the first time I had visited, but at the same time, everything felt different and wrong somehow, but I couldn't put my finger on exactly why. Not that it felt right before or anything, but something was definitely off. I had to tell myself that it was my imagination with all these strange and sometimes terrifying things I had experienced over the last few days, but was it really so hard to believe this store was any different from all the other unbelievable things? Probably not.

I was sure that I saw Susan looking over her shoulder at me every now and then, and I couldn't help but wonder why she seemed so interested in me compared to the others, but the attention was truly starting to freak me out. Finally, she stopped in front of a large simple-looking wood door at what I thought might be at the very back of the shop. There was nothing special or strange about it. There was a thin layer of dust, giving the impression that it hadn't been disturbed in quite a long time.

Susan pulled out a key and went to the long task of trying to unlock it, making me wonder what was so important that it needed to be locked away. The faint click of the lock snapped me out of my train of thought, and as she opened the door, my whole insides twisted with dread.

I didn't know what I was expecting to be behind it. All I knew was that I didn't expect to see a long dark stairwell leading below.

"Down there?" Chuck asked with a trembling voice. I couldn't help but shiver when a gust of cold air pushed up from the darkness from some unseen place. That was undeniably odd.

"What are you waiting for?" Susan asked, her voice sounding just as cheerful as it had before. The three of us exchanged a few awkward glances before Jade finally decided she was the bravest of us all and stepped confidently toward the stairs as if it didn't bother her at all. Susan flipped a switch that I hadn't noticed before next to the door, causing a small light bulb to flicker on, illuminating a very dim path toward the bottom. With some hesitation, Chuck and I followed behind her. I have to admit, I was a bit scared that Susan would shut us in, or worse, turn off the lights, but when I heard her following behind us, I relaxed just a tad.

With each step, the stairs creaked and groaned, as if at any moment with my next step, I might suddenly break through the old-looking wooden stairs. Reaching the bottom of the stairs, I exhaled, releasing some pent-up fear and feeling a wash of relief flow over me. That feeling didn't last long, though, as I took in our surroundings and saw that we had been led into a dead end. However, before the fear grew into outright panic, I noticed in the very dim light that there were two doors, one on both sides of the small nook we had ended at.

Susan pushed past the three of us, which was a lot harder with so many people in such a tight space, making me wonder why she hadn't just led the way herself. With a lot of effort on her part and narrowly missing Chuck's head with her elbow, she reached for a key that was hidden above one of the doorframes. With just as much work as the first door, she was able to unlock the door.

The room inside was lit dimly from a small rectangular window near the very top of the ceiling. From what I could see through visibly dirty glass looked to be another building, so I guessed it was a view into an alley. The room itself was lined with lots of shelves, each one unique, all stacked with boxes and boxes, so many boxes. The floor wasn't much different as it, too, was covered in a collection of boxes. Some were by themselves, while others were stacked on top of each other. Most were taped shut but a few here and there had been left open. There were also various books and stacks of paper with no rhyme or reason as to their placement. Chuck pointed eagerly to one corner, looking excited. I wasn't sure why but when I glanced to where he was pointing, I saw one of those large chunky microfilm readers, the ones that used to be in most libraries before computers and the internet. Next to it were several stacks of microfilm reels that probably held all the old newspapers.

Since Susan was still in front of us, she had no choice but to enter the room first. With some effort, she pushed a box next to the door aside so she could stand there and let the rest of us enter. As we entered, I had this sudden feeling deep inside me that this was a terrible mistake. When I turned back to look at Susan, she was placing the key under the collar of her red-and-white polka-dot dress. She noticed me looking and smiled before asking in a pleased but curious tone, "So what are you three looking for? I might be able to lead you in the right direction."

Chuck opened his mouth to speak, but before he could, Jade answered, "Just helping Jennifer with a school project."

Susan's eyebrows arched slightly, "And what kind of school project are we working on?"

Jade hesitated, clearly assuming her first answer would have been enough. "I just need to learn some cool facts and history about where I'm spending my summer," I offered.

Susan's face relaxed just a little, a few years dropping from her face as her furrowed brow faded, making me realize that it wasn't usually there. Her smile was now more natural also. She let out a tiny, trapped breath. "That's all?" she mused. "Well, that shouldn't be a problem at all. What sort of history are we looking for? Maybe important town events or the city's traditions," she continued before turning her back and looking through a stack of books like she knew exactly where to find the things she was talking about.

As she managed to get a lid off one of the boxes near her, Chuck chimed in, saying, "We're looking for things a bit more magical, actually." There was a sudden chill down my spine, and it felt like everything in the room was filled with a deafening silence. The lid that was in Susan's hand dropped to the floor with a loud thud, and she appeared frozen in place.

Jade and I exchanged awkward glances about what had just happened. Chuck didn't think anything of it because he started messing with a box next to him. Susan abruptly came to life again, glancing over her shoulder at me, a strange, awkward smile having replaced the natural one she had before. "Can you excuse me for a moment? I think I heard the front bell ring," she said before she turned and walked out the door at a hurried pace.

I thought about this for a moment. I hadn't heard any bell, and even if there had been one like she claimed, I had to question how she managed to hear it all the way down here when she hadn't heard it when we first came in. She had been *a lot* closer at the time, after all. Without giving it another thought, I decided to follow her, but when Susan saw me coming, she quickly slammed the door shut behind her, and I heard the loud click of the lock just as my hand reached the doorknob. It was stuck, and no matter how much I tried to turn it, it wouldn't budge.

I found Jade right next to me, slamming her fist wildly at the door, screaming to be let out right now. A strange noise emanated from the other side of the door, and I urged Jade to be quiet. As we listened, we could barely make out Susan talking, clearly on the phone, as there were no other voices besides hers: "Yes, they came here like you said. . . . Worse than you thought. . . . I have them locked away. . . . Yes, yes, I'll call Mr. Woodwick right now."

I looked at Jade, asking her in a whisper, feeling both confused and terrified, "Who is Mr. Woodwick?"

Jade thought for a moment before she told me, "Some rich old guy whose family has been here since, like"—she paused—"like before the town was even a town or something. The Woodwicks are a big deal in town because they're one of the founding families." She rolled her eyes at me, showing how little she thought about that.

I tried to open the door again, one more time. I felt a bit ridiculous for trying, since I knew it was locked, but I felt it was worth a shot. As I tried, I heard Susan's footsteps, no doubt heading up the stairs, swiftly followed by another loud slam of a door.

"Are we trapped?" Chuck asked us both in a trembling voice, still standing where he had been moments ago.

"Yeah," Jade spat. "No thanks to you and your big mouth"

"Whaaa?" Chuck asked, looking offended. "What did I do?"

"Magical?" Jade patronized him with a stern look.

Chuck shrugged, clearly not understanding yet what he did that was so wrong, and blurted out defensively, "Yeah, so what's the big deal? She's an adult!"

This made Jade roll her eyes so far back in her head, I half expected either for her to pass out or for them to get stuck up there. With a snort, she told him, "Chuck, adults are the enemy."

Chuck shook his head, not wanting to believe this statement, and when Jade motioned to the door as proof, Chuck looked down at his feet, finally seeming to realize the mistake he had made. "Sorry," he muttered under his breath.

Jade looked like she was about to release a world of fury on him. I knew we didn't have time for this, so I stepped between them, stretching out both arms wide so there was a good distance between them. "We don't have time for this," I told them both. When it was clear that neither of them was going to argue about it, I went on, "We need to find a way out of here before she comes back with others."

"What are they going to do, Jennifer? They're adults. It's not like they're going to harm us," Chuck said, his voice even now conveying that he was still in denial about our situation.

"What kind of adults lock kids in a basement, Chuck?" Jade asked him sarcastically.

"Good point," Chuck agreed with a sigh.

"How are we going to get out, though?" Jade asked, turning to the door and trying once again in vain to pull or even push it open. I was sure I heard it creek slightly from the pressure but didn't feel entirely confident that we could break it down. "We can't get out without a key," she added with a tired huff.

"Pick the lock?" Chuck asked hopefully.

Jade shot him another annoyed look. "Did you learn how to pick locks without telling me, Chuck?" she quizzed him in an accusatory tone. He shook his head before looking at me hopefully.

All I could do was shake my head, causing all three of us to slump slightly. When I looked back up, my attention went to the window above us. It wasn't a big window or anything, but after studying it for a moment, I was sure it was just big enough that we could squeeze through it. I tilted my head toward the window. "That's our way out."

Thankfully most of the boxes were just about light enough for us to move but still heavy and robust enough that I thought they could hold our weight, or at least most of it. With a lot of effort from all three of us, we were able to build a sturdy-looking tower to climb, well, sort of at least. Clearly, the first level had been the easiest, but each one after had become dramatically harder to do. Pushing a box was one thing. Lifting it over your head was an entirely different story. By the time we had raised the last box as high as we could manage, all three of us were panting with exhaustion and soaked with sweat.

"Think it will hold?" Jade asked, looking our creation over doubtfully.

"I'm not so sure about this, guys," Chuck said, gazing at the box at the top. Now that I was looking at it more closely, it looked like it was already close to falling off. I had my doubts that it was going to offer us any support, assuming we even got up that far before everything came crashing down around us. Then there was the fact that even that box would only get us chest-high to the window.

"Um" was the only thing that was able to leave my lips before I heard a familiar noise. Someone was at the door at the top of the stairs, trying to get it unlocked again. "No time to test it," I said hastily before urging Chuck and Jade to start climbing.

During the long construction, we had already decided that Jade would be the first to go up. She was the most confident in her abilities to get the window open. Chuck would follow after her because she figured he might need some help climbing, and I would take up the tail end so I could help push Chuck up if, for any reason, she wasn't strong enough to pull him by herself. Once Jade got to the top, making it look effortless, and without many of the boxes wobbling under her, she started trying to get the window open. Time slowed. Thirty seconds passed but it felt more like ten minutes. My heart was pounding, trying to beat its way right out of my chest, and I found my gaze continuously switching between what Jade was doing and the door. What if I had missed any sounds of the door above being opened? Or the sound of footsteps or voices? I feared that the door could swing open at any moment. So very, very scary.

I quickly looked up to Jade, asking her in a hushed and urgent voice, "What's taking so long?!"

"It's jammed," she said between gritted teeth as she struggled to open it. "I think it's painted shut or something!"

Chuck was halfway up the box tower at this point. He reached inside his pocket, and a few moments later, he pulled out a small Swiss Army knife. He tugged on the back of Jade's pant leg to get her attention. When Jade peered down at him, she looked confused then annoyed, asking him, "Did you really have that this whole blasted time?" All Chuck did was shrug before it got yanked from his hand, and Jade immediately went to the task of trying to pry open the window while muttering something about talking about this later. Jade made quick work of the window after that, and I wasn't sure if her annoyance with Chuck had given her the adrenaline she finally needed to get it open.

"Give me a push," she demanded after she attempted to get the top half of her body through the window and found she wasn't quite able to get herself through. Chuck moved in closer, and after a long, struggling push from him, she managed to get through, nearly kicking Chuck in the head in the process. By the time Chuck had reached the top box, I was already behind him. Just before he reached for the windowsill, we both stopped and turned toward the sound of loud, almost thundering footsteps coming down the stairs.

"What did she do, bring the whole town?" I asked in a low whisper. Chuck gulped so loud that I was sure whoever was coming down the stairs right now heard it. "Hurry up," I urged him in a whispered scream. It took everything in me not to start screaming at the top of my lungs.

Once Chuck got the top part of his body through the window, Jade began yanking on him, and we soon discovered that it was a lot harder for him to fit through than for Jade. "Push him!" Jade demanded from the street. I lifted his legs with all my strength while pushing with my legs against the boxes below to force him through. The moment Chuck's body went soaring through the window, like a cork from a bottle, so did the box right under my feet. I felt gravity trying to suck me down, but right before I started hurtling to the floor, something caught hold of me. I looked up to see Jade holding on to one of my wrists.

There was a loud sound of boxes crashing under me. Apparently, our tower was not as strong as we'd wanted to believe, as the one box that had been on the top had managed to take out the rest of them. "What was that noise?" an unrecognizable female voice from behind the door yelled. The question was quickly followed by a rustling of keys and a panicked scuffling noise as whoever it was quickly tried their best to get the door unlocked.

"Hurry!" I yelled this time, not bothering to try to be quiet. Jade attempted to pull me up while my other hand reached for the windowsill, trying as much as I could to get a grip on it, my feet kicking wildly beneath me. Jade looked beyond tired, and I was sure I saw a hint of fear in her eyes that quickly turned into sorrow, like she knew she couldn't do it and she was really sorry about that fact.

"Please don't drop me!" I begged. If I hadn't been so scared, I was sure that I would have started crying right then. Chuck reached through, next to Jade, and grabbed me by my other wrist. The two of them tried to pull me as hard as they could. I felt my body start to inch up the wall, and I had to force myself to stop kicking my feet in case that made it harder for them.

My heart sank when I heard the door fly open with

a loud bang as it smacked into the wall. It was more like someone had kicked it in instead of unlocking it. "Don't let her escape!" I heard Susan's voice yell followed by another shrill female voice urging, "Hurry! Hurry! She's getting away!"

Their voices were followed by a rough male's voice that ordered, "Grab her feet!"

Hearing this made me quickly attempt to lift my legs as fast and as high as I could, but before I could make it very far with this plan, I felt something, or should I say someone, grabbing at them. Whoever it was managed to get ahold of just one of my feet, and they were desperately trying to pull me back down. I was too scared to look down to see who it was, almost like doing so would be enough to make me fall down. After a quick moment of internal panic, it dawned on me that I did have another foot, and so I did my best to kick at what I hoped was going to be the person's hand while I screamed up at my friends, "Pull harder!"

Jade and Chuck responded to my call, giving one big, long pull just as I managed to make contact with the person's hand with my free foot as hard as I could. There was a loud painful yelp from below, and then my other foot was free, allowing my body to be pulled to the safety of the street above.

As soon as I was out, none of us dared to look back inside. Instead, we darted down the alley, and I could swear I heard the voice of the person I assumed was in charge ordering the others, "What are you waiting for, go after them!"

We didn't stop running until we were sure we hadn't been followed, ducking behind a dumpster several blocks away. All three of us were breathless and panting for air. We didn't have to say it, the realization of whatever was going on was written all over our faces. What did we do now? Who could we trust? Where would we be safe? These were the only questions that kept racing through my head, and I didn't have an answer for any of them.

Chapter 23

We had waited in the alley for close to half an hour before either one of us dared to move, let alone speak. I had so many questions in my head now that I wanted to ask, but in the end, Jade was the first to speak, and her question was definitely the least important.

"Why didn't you remember you had that pocket knife a lot sooner, Chuck?" she asked accusingly.

Chuck shot her a peculiar look before he replied, "What difference would that have made?"

"I don't know. Maybe we could have gotten the door open instead of having to make our way out a cramped window like we were a bunch of common criminals?" Her tone was both angry and mocking.

Chuck had done a pretty good job up to this point at not returning her attitude, but it seemed that ship had finally sailed. "I don't know, Jade," he said, spreading out both arms upward in front of himself. "Maybe because neither of us can pick a lock with a pocketknife!" His voice was a lot louder than I wanted him to be at this point. I quietly shushed both of them before I allowed myself to glance around the dumpster to make sure no one was coming.

Jade crossed her arms tight to her chest, staring daggers at him before replying, "Well, I don't know, maybe you could have used—" She stopped to place one finger on the side of her chin like she was thinking about it, but it was clear she was just mocking him some more before she snapped back, adding, "*The screwdriver* to unhinge the door."

This didn't faze him, though, as he barked back, "And what about the second door, Jade? And then making our way through the whole store unnoticed?" Sarcasm and anger was seeping into his tone.

He did make a good point. I seriously doubted the three of us could have managed to unscrew two doors and lower them both to the ground without making a lot of noise, let alone not get crushed by one, as I had no idea how heavy a door might be, and then somehow after all that get out. With our luck, we would have only gotten one door down, maybe two at best, before the adults showed up. Then it would have been game over.

Jade just crossed her arms and fumed, not wanting to believe what Chuck was saying, so I did the best I could not to sound like I was taking anyone's side when I said, "Those doors were so old they probably would have taken ages to get down anyway." When Jade shot me a look, I added with a shrug, "We barely had time to build our death trap tower before they got there."

Jade's face softened slightly as if she was finally allowing herself to see the flaw of her thinking, but instead of apologizing or even just admitting she was wrong, she shrugged at both of us and looked away.

I wasn't sure what the problem was, but I was growing increasingly tired of it. "I don't know why you both are getting so mad at each other, but it needs to stop now," I said, pointing at them both accusingly in turn. "You're both friends, best friends from what I can tell, for I don't know how long, but right now, you're acting nothing like it." I noticed my voice was starting to rise a few decibels, but I didn't think it was loud enough to draw anyone's attention from the street. Still, I tried to lower it while still giving it the edge I had gained.

"Maybe it's time you both just say you're sorry for

whatever"—I made a wild gesture at the air between them—"this is all about, and just move on already. I think we all have more important things to worry about right now than hurt feelings, you know, like maybe the whole town being after us for all we know!"

Jade and Chuck looked taken aback by my sudden outburst, both looking a bit embarrassed and remorseful. Jade opened her mouth and pointed her finger at Chuck, only managing to get the words "But he—" out before I shut her up with the same glare my mom would have given me if I tried to talk back.

I was hoping Chuck would leave it alone since he was the more logical of the two, but instead, he had to respond. "But me what?" His tone was not angry but somewhat worried.

Jade couldn't make eye contact with him, instead turning her attention to her shoes and replying softly, "It's like you've been living a secret life without me."

"Huh?" was the only thing Chuck was able to think to say to that.

With a shrug, Jade told him, "Like, I didn't know you spent all your free time at the library." She paused to correct herself. "I mean, I know you like your boring books and everything, I'm not stupid, but—"

Sounding very confused, he cut her off to say, "You're mad I read too much?"

Jade shook her head, and it was clear she wasn't being frank with him, but with an eye roll, she admitted, "You didn't defend me or even appear to care when your librarian friend was treating me like I was nothing."

I noticed the slightest hint of moisture starting to form in the corner of one of her eyes, which she quickly cleared before it could become anything or Chuck noticed. "Oh," Chuck said, flabbergasted. Contemplating it for some time, he finally replied, the worry in his voice replaced with warmth. "You're so much tougher than I am," he admitted. "I guess I just figured you wouldn't want me to fight your battles for you." He shrugged before adding in a low whisper, "I'm sorry I let you down, Jade."

Jade's shoulders slumped as if all the fight had left her, and she turned to face him with a shy smile, her voice almost betraying the confident look she tried to have on her face. "Yeah, well, I'm sorry, I was being a jerk too."

Chuck returned her smile before teasing her with "That's not the word I would have used, but OK."

Jade's mouth opened in a wide gasp before her whole face brightened, and she playfully punched him in the shoulder, not hard enough to hurt him but enough to make him cower slightly back. "You big jerk!" she said.

I leaned back against the dumpster with a sigh, glad that the drama was finally over. I could deal with only one major drama at a time. I immediately moved away from the dumpster with a jolt when I realized what I had done. There was no way in the world I wanted any part of my body touching garbage. It wasn't like it was the grossest dumpster I'd ever seen, but that wasn't the point. This day was bad enough without being covered in dumpster stink, gross!

I waited a few more minutes, watching the alleyway closely to make sure no one was coming. I turned to my friends and asked, "So what do we do now?" Neither Jade nor Chuck seemed to be willing to give me an answer. That definitely wasn't going to be helpful. It's not like I could make all the decisions here after all.

I was moments away from throwing my hands up in desperation when Chuck finally offered, "Maybe we should call your aunt and have her pick us up? It might be safer to figure out what to do next from . . . " Pausing, he took a quick, nervous look around before continuing, "You know, where we aren't so exposed."

He did make a pretty good point. There was a certain foreboding feeling that at any moment, a hand might reach out from the shadows and grab us. Being at home, even if it wasn't really my home, felt a lot safer than being in a dirty, damp alleyway in a town I barely knew. Jade appeared to be in agreement with me. She was looking tired and borderline paranoid the way she was now searching the street ahead with her eyes.

It didn't take too long for Aunt Tara to pick us up. The alley we had hidden in hadn't been too far from the arcade, so that was where Jade had asked her to pick us up. I would have much rather had her pick us up from the alley, but no matter how many ways I tried, I couldn't think of a logical reason we would be there. So the arcade was our best bet.

The whole five or so minutes it had taken us to walk there was nerve-racking, to say the least. I couldn't shake the feeling that every adult we walked past gave us weird looks of suspicion, and every window we walked by had someone inside watching us, but I didn't dare look in to find out if I was right. Even the few minutes we had to wait outside the arcade felt like an endless eternity. My imagination got the better of me, and I expected the black van that was coming down the road to stop in front of us and drag us inside to be never seen again. When it turned down another street, I felt a bit more relaxed, well, only a bit. Thankfully for us, my aunt had been in town running some errands when Jade had called her.

The three of us raced to be the first in the truck, basically crawling over each other. Chuck ended up getting in first with Jade behind him, leaving me next to the door, which I quickly shut with some force, making a loud bang. "Careful with the door," my aunt said. When she noticed the wide-eyed expression on my face, she added with a laugh, "This old girl is on her last leg as it." I tried to smile in response but wasn't exactly feeling joyful right now.

Aunt Tara pulled away from the curb, beginning

the journey home, when I almost jumped in my seat as Jade tapped my shoulder. My full attention was on the sidewalk, looking for anyone who seemed out of place. I gave her an annoyed expression but felt a bit confused by the worried look she was giving me. Actually, it was the worried look they were both giving me. Chuck's eyes darted down to where his feet were, and that's when I saw it. Was that the bag of pies I had taken down into Susan's creepy basement? It wasn't until now that I remembered even buying them. It wasn't like saving pies was on the top of my list when we made a daring and nearly failed escape.

"Um, Aunt Tara?" I asked as I kept my eyes on the bag.

"Yes?" she said without even looking my way, keeping her eyes fixed firmly on the road and giving a half wave to someone outside the car. Looking out the window, I didn't see anyone I knew, let alone anyone who looked like they had just waved at her.

I sucked in a deep calming breath. "Where did you get that bag?" I questioned, trying to keep any hint of emotion from my voice.

At first, she didn't say anything, then ultimately responded, "What bag?" Before I could answer, she remembered, "Oh," she said, her voice perking up, "I ran into Susan before I came to pick you all up. She had told me you forgot it while you were at her shop and had been looking all over town for you."

None of us said a word. Instead, we exchanged nervous glances. "Why were you at the antiques shop, anyhow?" Aunt Tara asked then continued, "It's not like it's that kid-friendly," and she shot us all a big smile. When none of us responded to her question or even gave as much as a smile, she went on, "Ah, I see, you're all secret antique fans, huh."

Jade nodded to her and said, trying to sound both

defeated and playful, "Oh man, guys, she's on to our obsession of dusty old furniture and second-hand goods." My aunt let out a half laugh, and thankfully, she didn't question us much after that.

Right before we drove past the very last building in town, something caught my eye. For just a moment, I could have sworn I saw the hooded figure standing next to the large "Welcome to Merrow Crescent" sign, but when I looked over my shoulder searching for it, it was no longer there.

Chapter 24

I wasn't sure how much we pleaded and begged for another sleepover during the ride back to the house and subsequently after we got there or during the brief time we had before Chuck's mother arrived to pick them both up. She had pulled up to our house only minutes after we arrived, so we didn't even get a chance to talk, and she practically had to drag him to the car. Sadly all the begging we did was ignored as it appeared there was no way my aunt and uncle were going to let us have another sleepover.

"One sleepover is plenty for one week. Two is overkill," my aunt had told us. Even Uncle James backed her up with some weirdness about one slice of cake was great, but two, and you'd get yourself a stomachache. I wasn't sure if this was the worse comparison I'd ever heard or if he honestly thought we would get a stomachache from having two sleepovers.

The more I was around my aunt and uncle, the more I was starting to understand why they didn't have any kids of their own. I also figured that not having kids and then suddenly having three under their roof at once had proved too much for them. I played back the night before wondering if we had been too loud or made a mess, or perhaps we crossed some kind of line when we headed to the horses first thing that morning. Either way, I wasn't happy at all, and neither were Chuck and Jade. There were so many things that we needed to talk about. I felt like I needed to give myself a swift kick for not using our time wisely in the alley to figure out what we needed to do. Instead, we wasted it all, cowering behind a foul and grimy dumpster, trying to be quiet so no one would hear us.

I did have a fleeting glimmer of hope when Jade said we could just Skype, but that was quickly drowned out when I realized my phone was still MIA. Uncle James noticed this, and with a big grin, he pulled my phone from his back pocket and handed it to me. "I completely forgot I had this. I picked it up this morning for you."

I beamed up at my uncle, my voice coming out in a high-pitched squeal of excitement. "Oh my gosh, oh my gosh! You got my phone!! I love you sooo much!" I felt a bit embarrassed saying that to my uncle, the excitement of finally having my phone back getting the better of me. The past week had been torture.

My uncle's grin changed slightly, looking somewhat nervous, and he began rubbing at the back of his neck when he told me, "Well, I'm glad you're happy to have it back," and he paused just briefly, adding, "but sadly there wasn't much they could do to get it to work out here." I felt my brow furrow, and my smile was replaced with, well, honestly, I wasn't sure what it got replaced with, but the look I was giving my uncle made him gulp. "But you still love me, right?" he asked with a playful grin. Since I honestly regretted that I had said it in the first place, I shrugged, feeling that was the best answer he was going to get.

Aunt Tara did her best to change the tone of the conversation by reminding me they had a landline I could use anytime I wanted. I faked a smile, trying my best to pretend everything was all right, knowing full well that anything I wanted to talk about with Chuck and Jade was way too risky to have within earshot of adults. Besides, it's not like I could talk to them both at the same time on the landline.

After Chuck and Jade had left, I asked if I could see the horses. My aunt was quick to say that it wouldn't be long before dinner, and ultimately, I was too tired to complain anymore. While waiting for dinner, I decided to spend the time lying in my bed, replaying the bizarre and terrifying events of the day in my head. It didn't feel like the day had revealed any answers to any of our questions. If anything, it had created more of them, since the unicorns hadn't been able to tell us anything useful, and the whole library trip had gotten us nowhere except for possibly being kidnapped at Susan's nightmare antiques shop. The only thing I got out of the whole day was a feeling that I needed to be looking over my shoulder anytime I left the house.

The more I thought about it, the more I realized I was bumming myself out. That was until one name popped into my head, Mr. Woodwick. The only thing Jade had told me about him was that he had a lot of money and his family had been in this town forever. Other than that and his name, I didn't know much else. But clearly, it was a name that held some kind of importance. They had contacted him about us, almost like whatever we were looking into wasn't something this Mr. Woodwick or the people working for him wanted anyone looking into.

I grabbed the phone that was resting on the table next to me and attempted to type in Mr. Woodwick into a search box, but of course, nothing happened. I soon dropped it back to where it had been lying on the table with a soft thud and a defeated sigh, and then I heard my aunt calling me downstairs for dinner.

There was nothing special about dinner. It looked to be some form of breaded chicken, a lump of mashed potatoes, corn, and what appeared to be bread but was square and yellow. When Aunt Tara noticed me poking it with my fork, she told me it was corn bread. Yep, that definitely didn't sound like something I'd like, not that I was very hungry with my big lunch anyway.

I mostly moved my food around my plate, only taking a small bite every once in a while, while half paying attention to my aunt and uncle talking about farm stuff and other boring adult things. The food wasn't bad, but it wasn't exactly good either; it was just food. I would have been fine doing that for the rest of the meal, playing with my food in complete silence, but like everything else, today's luck wasn't exactly on my side and my uncle turned his attention to me. "So, kid, how was your day in town?" he asked, only looking half-interested, I thought. I was still a bit annoyed about the whole phone thing, so I shrugged back at him. I thought that would have been the end of it, but he followed it by saying, "Didn't get into any trouble, I hope."

The fork dropped from my fingers with a loud clang, and I quickly sat up straighter before picking it up again. "Nope," I said, feeling suddenly flustered. "Just normal kid stuff." Uncle James smirked slightly, but he didn't seem to be implying anything. So that made me feel a bit better, but only just a bit.

I decided to try my luck with a question of my own "Do you think I could go see the horses after dinner?"

There was a brief thought before Aunt Tara told me, "It's a bit too dark out there now, and I'm sure they're probably fast asleep," which she followed up with a small smile.

I couldn't help but let myself sink a bit into my seat, and I must have looked completely miserable because Uncle James chimed in saying, "I'm really glad to see you're taking a liking to the horses, and please don't feel like your aunt or I have anything against going out to see them."

I stared at my uncle for a long moment, and when he didn't say anything else, I looked at my aunt, but still nothing. I was sure there would be more to what he said, and I almost let myself relax, thinking I had nothing to worry about. Well, I did, at least, until he started talking again.

"It's just," and he paused again in serious thought, "after you got back today from town, all the horses have been acting extremely skittish for some reason."

Aunt Tara nodded at my uncle in agreement. "Something out there definitely got them all worked up. Your uncle and I are worried that snake might be back." I couldn't help but roll my eyes at that last part. I was never going to live the whole snake lie down. Thankfully neither one of them seemed to notice my eye roll, or if they did, they didn't let on.

Uncle James gave me what I would call an apologetic smile when he said, "It's just, I—" He shot a look at my aunt when she cleared her throat. "—er, we, don't think it's safe right now for you to be out there with them alone." He continued, a bit more playfully, by adding, "And besides, I think your dad would have my hide if we let you get bit by a snake, or worse, trampled by a horse."

I tried to smile back at him, but it lasted only for a moment before I said, "I'm not scared of any snakes, and to be honest, the more I think about it, the more I'm sure it was just a stick." I could see my aunt was about to say something, so I cut her off with "And besides, it's not like I'm stupid enough to climb into their stalls. How exactly do you think I'm going to be trampled?" I stared back at them both, trying to look as confident by my statement as it sounded.

Aunt Tara leaned in just a tad and pretended to whisper so my uncle wouldn't hear her. "Well, what your uncle isn't telling you"—she paused to look at him briefly before turning back to me—"is that one of the horses bit him on the arm when he was trying to feed them this evening." With that, she leaned back in her chair, giving my uncle some serious side-eye and trying to keep herself from smiling.

My uncle rubbed at his arm covered up by his shirt sleeve and he muttered something under his breath. There was no way I could argue my safety if it was a biting thing. After all, it wasn't like I could say I'd stand by the stable door and see them from afar or anything like that. Instead, I just asked, "I guess that's not a normal thing for your horses to do, then?"

Uncle James shook his head. "Nope, I've never once been bit by any of them."

My aunt's eyes suddenly widened and she reached out, resting her hand on my shoulder. "None of them bit you, did they?"

I shook my head emphatically at her question, realizing how my question could have implied that. "No. No! Not at all," I protested. "They have all been nothing but gentle when I've been around them." I had to smile to myself thinking about Cliffton fighting me over the book, but that wasn't the same as biting my uncle. Aunt Tara lowered her hand back down, and she appeared to relax more.

I was glad this whole not wanting me to be around the horses thing had to do with some kind of need to protect their niece from any danger, and not just wanting me to stay away because they didn't trust me. But this kink was definitely going to hinder our investigation if I couldn't be around them unsupervised.

I sat there a little longer watching them eat before I asked another question, "Who is Mr. Woodwick?" I was sure my aunt's whole face turned several shades lighter. At the same time, my uncle jumped out of his chair so quickly that it nearly caused it to fall backward, and he looked at me with some alarm.

"Where did you hear that name?" he asked, his voice sounding upset for the first time. I hadn't expected this kind of reaction from either one of them. Honestly, I hadn't expected any kind of reaction.

"I, um" was the only reply I was able to give my uncle. He looked at me inquisitively, picking up on my apprehension. He blinked at me a few times before he sat back in his chair. "I'm sorry, I didn't mean to startle you like that, but where did you hear that name?"

"In town. Jade said he was some rich old guy," I shrugged, trying to look like I didn't care either way. "I just was curious, I guess."

This answer appeared to appease them both. The tension that had filled the room faded as quickly as it had appeared, or at least that's what I had thought because in the next moment, my uncle was on his feet, and with a fast apology, he headed out of the kitchen. I watched him as he left, feeling a bit concerned and possibly guilty that my question had triggered something in him. I looked back to my aunt, giving her a questioning look. Aunt Tara nodded to me, probably knowing I wasn't going to be happy unless she gave some form of an answer about what that was all about.

"Your uncle and Mr. Woodwick are not on the best of terms," she told me.

"Why?" I asked.

She hesitated, deciding if she should tell me, before finally admitting, "He's been trying to make us sell him our land and horses for a few years now." She paused to take a small sip of her iced tea. "And he's become more aggressive in his techniques as of late."

"What do you mean?" I asked as I leaned a bit closer across the table. This was definitely getting more interesting.

Aunt Tara smiled slightly. "Let's just say he was very generous and kind in his first offers, and over time he's become—" Aunt Tara paused for a moment like she was trying to choose her next words carefully. "—a bit more forceful."

I tried to urge her to go on by gesturing both my hands in a circular motion, like the wheels spinning on a bike, but she shook her head at me, adding, "But this really isn't something you need to worry about. Finish your dinner, and we can have some of that pie you so kindly picked up for us."

I felt my stomach sour at the mention of the pie, a sudden worry it had been tampered with. So I was forced to lie when I looked at my aunt with a wrinkled nose, telling her, "Um, maybe we should throw them away." Aunt Tara gave me a confused look before I shrugged, saying "I think I saw Chuck poking at them before. Since I don't know which ones and I'm pretty sure he hadn't washed his hands once today, probably better to be safe than sorry."

Aunt Tara's face looked a bit grim before she nodded in agreement. "Good idea. I think I have some ice cream in the freezer anyway." I smiled at the thought of ice cream. There was just something about it that could somehow make a bad day just a tiny bit less bad. Well, as long as it wasn't all down the front of your shirt, that is.

Aunt Tara had made me a much larger bowl of ice cream than either of my parents would have ever allowed me to eat. For someone who didn't have kids, she sure knew how to make them happy. I couldn't help but wonder if she just felt guilty because of the whole no sleepover thing, or maybe because I had barely touched dinner and I hadn't done a good enough job pretending I liked it.

After finishing our bowls along with the small bit of chitchat, I decided to head upstairs, but before I could open the door, she told me, "Your mom tried calling you while you were out today."

"Oh, really?" I asked without looking back at her. My tone was flat, conveying my mix of emotions to the news. There was a long awkward silence before she spoke again.

"She misses you a lot, you know." I had to swallow back the urge to start tearing up. Instead, I nodded wordlessly before walking out of the kitchen. I had still intended to go upstairs but found myself pausing at the first step, my gaze turning toward the living room doors. Should I call her? I mean, it wasn't really her I was mad at right now, or would it be better to wait until morning? I convinced myself that the morning was a better idea. I made it up one step before I found myself heading into the living room and shutting the door behind me.

It took three rings before someone answered, and I found myself almost startled when I heard my dad's voice instead of my mom's. I had called her cell number just so that I could avoid talking to him. "Hello?" he asked in an overly tired voice.

"Um, hi, Dad. Why are you answering Mom's phone?" The question itself caused me to panic. Had something awful happened?

"Hey, Uni!" His voice was suddenly more awake and happier. "No, no, everything is fine. I just didn't want the noise to wake your mother."

"Oh, um, isn't it sort of early for her to be sleeping?" I asked, unconvinced.

"It's been a very long day of doctor appointments. Someone had a baby before your mom's doctor's visit, and we ended up waiting almost four hours." He stopped long enough to yawn before continuing, "So it left her a bit, well, drained." I felt a smirk on my face at the fact that he wasn't admitting that it sounded like it had a more considerable toll on him.

"Can I talk to her?" I asked.

He didn't reply at first, but he sounded almost worried when he did. "I know your mother is going to kill me in the morning—she's been wanting to talk to you for days." And just like I expected, the next words out of his mouth were "But I really think I need to let her sleep. I'm sorry, Uni."

"I understand." I tried to sound as calm as I could, but the words felt bitter coming out of my mouth.

"We could talk instead?" His voice sounded hopeful.

"It's OK. Aunt Tara said she called and seemed uber-eager for me to call her back. Besides, I'm rather tired myself."

There was another silence, and when he spoke again, I could hear just a hint of regret in his tone. "Sure, sure, I understand. Yeah, me too. I'm super exhausted. We'll just talk tomorrow."

I felt a tinge of pain when he hung up the phone without saying anything else. No "I love you," or "I miss you," not even a simple goodbye. I swallowed that feeling down deep inside me, giving myself a small shake. My life was way too complicated right now for two dramas.

Chapter 25

When I awoke the next morning, my whole body felt sore and stiff. I was also exhausted, and it made me wonder if I had even slept at all that night. If it hadn't been for the endless dreams of being chased by shadowy figures, I would have doubted it. I was starting to miss the life I had just a few days ago before all this madness had started. Back then, all I had to be worried about was the whole baby thing and maybe if I would be bored out of my mind. Now, however, I worried about what new dangers the day would thrust at me and how much at risk my friends and I were.

I had to will every ounce of energy I could to make myself get out of bed. Fortunately, after a doubly long warm shower, I felt just a bit more like myself. By the time I stepped out of the bedroom, the hallway was already wafting with the mouthwatering smell of what I really hoped was bacon.

Before I went into the kitchen, I decided that it was a good a time as any to try calling my mom again. Also, I wouldn't have a chance to be too busy or chicken out. As an added bonus, I figured that my aunt and uncle were already settled in the kitchen, so I didn't have to worry about them eavesdropping. Still, I decided not to shut the doors behind me this time. That way, I could see if anyone came out.

I picked up the phone and placed it to my ear, but rather than being greeted with the weird noise that I had heard previously, there was only silence. When I tried to dial the number, I was met once again with an eerie silence. I even tried hanging the phone up a few times in case some unseen button had been triggered when I lifted it, but there was still nothing. I checked to make sure the wire was hooked into the phone, and it was. I even followed it to where it was attached to the wall, and it was attached there too. "This is really strange," I muttered before heading into the kitchen.

Aunt Tara was spooning food onto the waiting plates while Uncle James was glancing down at a paper in front of him. "What's wrong with the phones?" I asked worriedly.

"A tree fell on the lines, I think," Uncle James flatly said with a shrug like it didn't bother him much.

"I thought someone hit a pole with their car?" Aunt Tara, asked him, sounding a bit confused as she sat down in her chair. He shrugged back at her as a response.

I decided to sit down too before asking, "Is that normal?"

"Normal?" he asked as he eyed me, puzzled.

"I mean, doesn't that seem suspicious?"

This got strange looks from both of them, but it was Aunt Tara who asked, "Why would that be suspicious, sweetie?" Something about the way she asked seemed like she was more suspicious of me.

I don't know why this made me feel so panicked, and sadly for me, the first thing I could come up with to say was "I don't know, maybe it's an alien invasion or something." That probably wasn't the best I could have come up with, but it seemed to work as Uncle James let out a snorted half laugh before going back to his paper, and Aunt Tara shook her head silently like I was being silly as she spread a lump of butter onto her toast.

With those reactions, I decided to keep my mouth as shut as much as I could for the rest of breakfast, instead focusing on eating my food and thinking about how very suspicious it really was. I needed to talk to Chuck and Jade, and soon.

Aunt Tara promised me that as soon as she had washed up the dishes from breakfast that she would take me into town so I could call my mom. I would also be able to give Chuck and Jade a quick call to let them know it would be a lot harder now for them to reach me. Luckily she kept her promise, and it didn't feel like it took much time at all for us to make it into town.

There was an old-looking payphone next to the entrance of a small grocery store that was called the Sea's Harvest, and Aunt Tara had given me a handful of quarters before going in. Honestly, I was starting to think this town needed to ease up on the nautical names already. The store inside wasn't too small, but not anywhere near the size of the ones I am used to. Still, I figured it was big enough to distract Aunt Tara long enough for the calls I needed to make.

Not knowing how long the phone call with my mom might take, I decided it was probably a better idea to call my friends first. I reached Jade first, but she hadn't been able to talk long at all, only long enough to agree that the lines going out was odd and that she wouldn't be able to see Chuck or me for most of the week. Something about her whole family was in town, and she was stuck at home. Apparently, her parents took family reunions very seriously.

Chuck had talked even less. He said he wouldn't leave the house unless he had to. Not until we all could meet at once. He whispered that he was pretending to have a cold so he wouldn't even have to go outside. I know I was feeling pretty paranoid, but it felt like he might be taking it to a whole other level.

With those two calls finished, it was time to call my mom. After double-checking the coins in my hand, partly hoping I didn't have enough, I let myself take in a long deep breath before putting them into the slot and dialing the number.

She didn't pick up right away. In fact, she didn't pick up the first time I called. It took a whole extra call, and on the fifth ring was the answer I had been waiting for. "Hello?" said a sweet yet somewhat curious voice on the other end, and it suddenly became clear why she hadn't picked up sooner.

Some time ago, it had been apparent that a flock of telemarketers must have gotten ahold of her phone number and it wasn't unusual for her to get at least three calls a day. In response, she had gotten into the habit of not picking up at all if she didn't recognize the number.

"Hi, Mom," I said, suddenly feeling shy but not really knowing why. I mean, she was my mom, not some random stranger.

"Oh, my baby girl!" Her voice cracked, and in my mind, I could just see the tears starting to form in her eyes. I suddenly felt like I was about to do the same but remembered I was in public. Not being the sort of person who liked people to see me cry, I took in a long steady breath and forced the feeling deep into my stomach. A sudden worry washed over me as to whether that sort of thing would cause me to get an ulcer. A later problem, I figured.

"Hey, how are you doing?" I asked as calmly as I could. She hesitated before telling me all the sorts of things I had guessed she would. How she was fine, and the baby was fine, and Dad was fine. In fact, she used "fine" so many times that the word lost all meaning by the time she finished speaking. It made everything she said sound like a big old lie.

Soon she switched over to asking how I was. "Are you having lots of fun? Aunt Tara said you made some friends?"

"Yeah, things are OK," I lied. "And yeah, their names are Jade and Chuck."

"Oh, that's wonderful, sweetie!" she said, and she sounded honestly happy about it. "I knew you would love it there once you gave it a shot."

I was overcome with a sudden urge to blurt out to her that I was lying. Open the floodgates and tell her about how there was something honestly creepy and completely horrifying going on and that they needed to pick me up right away. The only words I managed to get out were "Look, Mom, I need to—" when I found myself suddenly cut off by the sound of a deep Southern voice behind me. "Well, hello there, Miss Greenfell."

A chill shot down my spine from the unexpected voice, and without even looking, without knowing the man or his voice, I knew deep down who it was: Mr. Woodwick. I stood there, frozen for a long moment, probably a lot longer than I should have, and it wasn't until I heard my mom's voice ask on the other end of the phone, "Need to what, Jennifer?" that I realized I needed to act.

I had two choices, let myself be scared—and I was truly and utterly terrified—and let this potentially villainous man know he was getting under my skin, or be brave. I decided right then and there that I wasn't going to give him the satisfaction of seeing any fear or worry on my face.

I faked a glance at the window before telling her, "Aunt Tara is almost done shopping. I'll tell you next time. Love you, Mom." I gave her just enough time to reply with an "I love you too" before I hung up the phone and swung around to face the man.

Before me was a man wearing a gray pinstriped suit on top of a matching gray vest and a white dress shirt with a red tie. He had a matching handkerchief tucked inside his front pocket. His collar partially covered a mole that peeked out on the right side of his neck. The dark oak walking sticking in his right hand had a red gem on the handle and he had some kind of hat under his left arm. He definitely looked overdressed and out of place on the sidewalk, and I felt he would have looked more at home in a big city or a fancy business.

Every single gray hair on his head looked to be glued into place, not that it looked stiff, just that every hair on top of his head wasn't brave enough to step out of line. All of that seemed strange after I looked at his face more closely. He was really, *really* old. I wasn't sure how old, but if you told me anything less than one hundred, I would have thought you were lying to me. Something about his face made me wonder if he would have been considered handsome when he was in his prime with his deep, haunting blue eyes that appeared even older somehow than his whole face. Eyes that had seen too much maybe, or lived too long? Either way, it took all I could not to shiver under his piercing stare.

We stood there for a moment, and when he seemed satisfied that I wasn't going to speak, he leaned ever so slightly onto the walking stick before speaking again, his voice almost as rough and scratchy as sandpaper. "I hear you've been busy around my little town lately?" He eyed me suspiciously for a moment, almost like he was studying me.

I was finally able to find my voice, but it didn't come out as calmly as I had intended, as there was just a hint of a squeak at the start. "Just normal kid stuff," I told him, and he gave me another doubtful look with a slight tilt of his head.

"Oh, is that so, Miss Greenfell? Are you sure that's the story you want to stick with?"

"I have a better story," I said before crossing my arms defiantly and giving him an even more doubtful stare. "But it involves adults getting in trouble for attempted kidnapping."

Mr. Woodwick nearly snorted a laugh, and with a smug expression, he attempted to correct my statement with one of his own. "Kidnapping? More like larceny and private property damage."

I so badly wanted to swallow, but instead, I just stared him down, saying, "I guess we could see what the police have to say about that."

Mr. Woodwick eyed me, this time with a bit more curiosity, before his smug look transformed into a coy grin, and he pointed at me slightly. "Well played, Miss Greenfell. I'm quite sure neither one of us want that to happen." I couldn't argue with that, but I wasn't exactly sure where that left us now either.

Much to my relief, I didn't have to do anything because I heard the door open behind me only a few moments later. I then heard the sound of my aunt's voice asking, "Jennifer, did you finish—" There was a moment of hesitation when I assumed she saw who was standing in front of me before she finished what she was asking, her voice now sounding unsure. "—all of your calls?"

I turned away from Mr. Woodwick and greeted my aunt with a small smile and a nod, telling her, "Yeah, I'm ready to go if you are."

She looked down at me and returned the smile before looking back at Mr. Woodwick, and I noticed the smile vanish as soon as her eyes landed on him. She looked like she sucked in a long calming breath before forcing a smile, though a less genuine one, and she spoke politely as she said, "Good day, Mr. Woodwick." Well, that confirmed it. I never had any doubt who he was, but it was nice to know I was correct in my assumption; otherwise, that conversation would have been a lot stranger.

I stepped closer to my aunt and when I turned back around, I saw him put on his hat, a panama hat, I thought.

He tipped it ever so slightly before he responded, "Good day, Mrs. Greenfell," then he paused before he did the same to me, but with a sly grin. "And good day to you as well, Miss Greenfell." I didn't say anything, instead I barely lifted my hand in an almost half wave, which got me a very cold, dark-looking grin in return. His eyes flashed with a hint of mischief before he twisted on his feet and began to walk away.

"What was that all about?" my aunt asked me after he was out of hearing range.

I knew I couldn't tell her anything, especially when it was clear there was no connection between them. Instead, I shrugged, acting oblivious to the situation, and said, "I guess he was just welcoming me to town?" I had a feeling she wasn't entirely buying it, so I added, "I don't know why old people do what they do."

Aunt Tara's smile returned, and she nodded, telling me, "You and me both, kid. You and me both."

Chapter 26

The next week or so felt like an eternity since it was pretty clear that no one was in any rush to fix the phone line. I had no way at all to contact Chuck or Jade to tell them about my strange encounter with the infamous Mr. Woodwick. The fact I couldn't talk to anyone about it made me feel more uneasy the more I thought about it, and not knowing if Chuck or Jade had experienced the same made me increasingly concerned for their safety.

As it turned out, the downed line had been caused by a tree branch snapping it. Part of me wanted to believe things like that happened all the time, but after we took a little trip to see what the damage was, I wasn't convinced. The first thing I noticed was there weren't any trees close to where the line had been broken, and when I pointed this fact out to my uncle, he looked doubtful for a moment before finally shrugging it off, telling me, "It was probably just carried by the wind, then." I didn't bother pointing out that there hadn't been any bad storms that day or winds. I don't even remember feeling a breeze that day.

Aside from having little random panic attacks, I had spent most of my time just being bored. My aunt and uncle stuck strongly to the no-going-near-the-horses thing, even though I had been told they had mostly calmed down. They still seemed too scared that there was a snake on the loose but did promise I'd be able to see them soon. That promise just seemed to get longer and longer, to the point that it felt useless to even ask anymore.

It wasn't all entirely bad, though, I guess. Halfway through the week, my uncle surprised me by bringing home a few cans of paint for my room. At first, I was nervous when I saw the paint since I had no idea what color my uncle may have picked up. But I found myself pleasantly surprised when the color inside was revealed to be a bright ocean blue. True, it might not have been the color I would've picked had I gotten the choice, but I liked it.

My aunt also surprised me with some new bedding she had picked up from someplace in town, I assumed. It had a beach scene with a blue sky, fluffy white clouds, and crashing dark blue waves. Then I noticed the paint almost matched perfectly with the sky on the blanket and the matching blue sheet set. So my money was on the fact that my aunt had picked out the color of the wall and not my uncle after all. There was also a dark blue curtain studded with tiny crystals that glimmered in the light that came in through my window. It seemed a lot thicker than the one I had now, which made me hope I'd stop being blinded first thing in the morning.

My aunt had promised we would try to find some paintings or posters to brighten up the walls when she had time. This made me hopeful that she would let me pick out at least some of the stuff in my room, even if I did rather like what she had already picked out. After everything was painted and put up, my room actually felt like my room, and it made me feel like for the first time, maybe I was actually wanted there after all, and not just a burden they had agreed to take care of.

With being bored and spending a lot of time working on my bedroom, I found it hard to remember what day it was and when Jade had said her family would be leaving. I kept yo-yoing back and forth with maybe it was today, or yesterday, no, no, it has to be tomorrow. I couldn't seem to work up the courage to go back to town just to call to find out. The possibility that I might run into Mr. Woodwick again was too unnerving.

I sat at the kitchen table, finishing my cold bowl of cereal. Aunt Tara hadn't had time to make me one of her standard hot dishes since she'd had to leave early that morning to run some errands. I couldn't remember what they were, but then again, I had zoned out a bit when she'd started going into details about whatever it was. It had mostly just sounded boring. She had apologized a lot, and I mean a lot, about the whole breakfast thing. I'd reassured her that it was fine and that I was used to eating cereal every day when I was at home. She'd looked a bit surprised by that but didn't say anything about it as she grabbed her keys and headed out.

Cereal was always my regular breakfast. My parents didn't have the time in the morning to put too much effort into it. Time was short with trying to get me ready for school and them for work. We did sometimes have something better on the weekends, but that was few and far between, and it was usually doughnuts from a local shop. But hey, they were really good doughnuts, so I wasn't one to complain about it. My dad liked to call it Doughnut Surprise Day.

I had nearly finished the bowl when I heard a sharp knock come from the front door. I planned to ignore it as I didn't feel too safe answering the door when my aunt wasn't there. I knew my uncle was somewhere outside but had no idea if he was close enough to know someone had come to visit. Then there was the fact that there were people out there who had been willing to lock kids in a basement, and I wouldn't put it past them to try it again.

When the knock came again, I decided to go to the window and peak out. There, standing barely in view, was

Chuck and who I assumed was Jade, but I wasn't entirely sure, and standing behind them was Mrs. Dunbar, who was glancing at her watch, looking very impatient. I saw her say something to Chuck, and I'd lie if I said I was good at reading lips, but it felt like it was along the lines of "Don't think anyone's home," because when she finished speaking, Chuck looked very disappointed. He started to turn but stopped when he glanced in my direction and saw me in the window. He brightened right away as he began to frantically point at me, stopping his mother who was already halfway down the steps.

I rushed to the front door, swiftly unlocking and opening it as I exclaimed, "Hey, guys!" and before I knew it, I was wrapping them both in a big hug. I hadn't planned to hug them when I got there, but it was like some deep instinct overcame me and gave me little choice in the matter. It felt a lot less awkward when they both returned the hug.

Mrs. Dunbar smiled at me. "They have been bugging me for the last few days to bring them to see you, but I thought it might be rude to show up unannounced."

Jade pulled me away and asked in a hushed, almost accusatory tone, "We've been trying to call you. Why is your phone always busy?"

I wasn't sure what she was implying, but I figured maybe she was just as desperate to talk to me as I had been to speak to them. I found myself whispering back but wasn't sure why as it didn't feel like a big secret, "The phone lines are down, remember?"

Jade's head jerked back, and she stared at me, confused. "They are?" she asked.

"I told you that on the phone days ago," I responded, suddenly feeling unsure if I had or not, but when Jade slapped herself on the forehead and announced loudly, "Oh, right, I forgot all about that!" she laughed about it, then gave me a strange look. "Wait, you said your phone wasn't working. I don't remember you saying anything about it being down." I couldn't help but bite my lip at my blunder. Jade was right. All I had told her was that the phone wasn't working, but nothing about why. I didn't even know for sure why until after our call.

"What happened to it?" Chuck asked, joining in the conversation.

Before I could tell them why, Mrs. Dunbar cleared her throat to get my attention and asked, "Is your aunt or uncle home?"

"They're both out doing stuff," I replied.

She frowned slightly before she admitted, "Well, I was going to ask if it was all right if the children came over, but if they are not here—"

Before she could finish whatever truly depressing thing that was about to come out of her mouth, I cut her off by saying, "No, it's fine. They told me that Chuck and Jade are welcome anytime." Of course, it was a lie, but I told myself that I was sure that if they were here, they would have said the same thing.

This got me a wary smile from Mrs. Dunbar. A smile that said, "I don't really believe what you said, but I'm in a hurry, so I'll buy it." She nodded before saying "All right, then," and then she kissed Chuck on the top of his head, which instantly caused him to look embarrassed, before she turned sharply on her heels and was to her car driving away. It wasn't until she was almost all the way out of sight that I noticed a rather large box sitting next to Jade's feet.

"What's that?" I asked, motioning to it with my hand.

This got me a large grin from them both before Jade told me, "It's research!"

Not even five minutes later, we were all standing around my bed, every inch covered by various documents and photographs. Chuck had been really impressed by the changes to my room, saying it was very me. I wasn't sure why he thought the ocean was me, but I decided to take it as a compliment, which I'm sure it was meant to be. Jade didn't seem as impressed as Chuck. She said it was all right, but after looking around a bit, she claimed it needed something but never said what that was. I, of course, filled them in on the whole tree branch thing. Both of them agreed it seemed sus, and they looked a bit freaked out when I told them about my encounter with Mr. Woodwick.

"You did all this?!" I exclaimed, eyeing them both, wondering how many days they had been working on it without me.

Jade shook her head before admitting, "No, my aunt did."

"Your aunt?" I asked her curiously before continuing with another question. "You told your aunt about all this?"

"No, no, no," Jade said, waving both hands in front of her almost defensively. "I didn't tell anyone anything. Well, nothing important, that is." I nodded, feeling a tiny bit calmer. Then she continued, "I just brought up how the library had been lacking any real information on the town or the founding families. I told her you needed to do a report for school about the history of someplace you went and junk like that." She finished with a wave of her hand, implying how unimportant she had made it all sound.

Jade then paused just long enough to make sure I didn't have any complaints before carrying on. "Then my tia told me all about how when she was back in school, the whole class had to do a report on the town and one of the founding families. Pretty boring stuff if you ask me." She added the last part with an eye roll, and I couldn't help but smile slightly. "And voilà, lucky for us, my tia and grandparents are hoarders, so they never threw it out," she said as she motioned at all the items on the bed, looking rather pleased with herself.

I nodded, feeling a bit impressed by how Jade had managed to do all this while I had been stuck getting nothing done at all.

"And we just got lucky enough that her aunt had a crush on one of the Woodwicks," Chuck added, which gained another roll of the eyes from Jade.

"Pretty lucky," I admitted.

"Pretty gross more like it," Jade corrected me. This got a small chuckle from all three of us.

"We spent the last day looking through it," Chuck told me, and I found myself feeling a bit more left out. It looked as if Chuck must have sensed that from me because he continued, "We wanted to wait until we were all together, but you know the whole phone thing," and he shrugged.

"I understand," I told them both, "you didn't know when you'd see me. I get it." I did get it, but it didn't make me feel any less isolated or left out. I decided to shrug it off by focusing on what was important and asked, "So, what did you find out, then?"

Jade looked down at all the papers before saying, "Well, most of it is dull, boring stuff, to be honest, but I did think this was a bit strange." Chuck cleared his throat ever so slightly, causing Jade to correct herself by telling me, "Well, Chuck thought this was strange, but I agreed."

She stood up a bit straighter, trying to hold on to her pride as long as she could. When it was clear Jade was focused more on trying to look good, Chuck stepped in by grabbing a lot of the photos from the bed and placing them in a straight line. He rearranged them a few times before he finally looked happy with how he had them laid out. I wasn't sure why that was so important but was anxious to know why. Chuck looked down at the photos and then back at me a few times before I finally took his hint and looked down at them myself.

I wasn't sure what I was meant to be looking at. Yeah, most of the photos clearly had been taken at different points in time, ranging from maybe a decade ago, I guessed, to all the way back to when they only had the black-and-white ones. There were even a few photos of paintings. I assumed they must have been done long before cameras were even invented, that or someone just really liked having themselves painted.

After a good two or three minutes, I looked back at Chuck, who was staring at me with such intensity that I felt a bit guilty I wasn't seeing what he clearly had. I gave him a helpless shrug hoping he would put me out of my misery and just tell me what I was missing. He sighed ever so slightly before pointing to the very last photo on the right. To me, it appeared to be the newest one. "See that photo? That was taken at a family reunion a year or two before Jade's aunt did her project." I gave him a slight nod, still not getting his point. "That man in the middle in the black suit is Mr. Woodwick." I found myself looking back at the photo, scanning it for a moment. There were a lot of people in the photo, so I was glad Chuck had mostly told me where to find him, and before I knew it, I had spotted him.

Mr. Woodwick did look just a bit younger than he had the day I saw him in town, but it was clearly him. I gave Chuck a nod, letting him know I had now spotted Mr. Woodwick so that he could continue. He then pointed to the photo next to it, saying, "Here is Mr. Woodwick again, and based on how everyone is dressed, Jade and I are fairly certain this was taken during the '70s or '80s." I wasn't very knowledgeable about decades, but Mr. Woodwick did look a lot younger, maybe in his late twenties or thirties I assumed. He had, in fact, been a somewhat attractive man back in his prime with thick dark brown hair, and he still had that coy grin that seemed to imply he was up to something. He stood with a group of men dressed up in suits, so even if his face had changed, his style in clothing hadn't that much. I tried not to be weirded out that I let myself think the creepiest old man in the world had once looked good.

I found myself feeling a bit impatient as the only thing I was being shown was that Mr. Woodwick had gotten older over time, which didn't feel too important. I shot Chuck, and this time Jade, an inquisitive look. "Get to the point!" Jade urged Chuck, apparently having gotten bored herself at this painfully slow revival. Chuck sighed, losing his thunder but decided to listen to Jade. He quickly pointed to different spots in all the other photos to what appeared to be Mr. Woodwick at different ages at different times. In some he would be older, the next younger again, and then middle-age and then younger.

I felt a bit lost still, so I asked, "OK, so he looks a lot like his ancestors? That's not so strange." Chuck shook is his head

"Yes, I know. I mean, my mother tells me all the time how I look just like my grandpa when I was his age—"

Jade cut him off by saying, "She said grandma."

This got a glare from Chuck and a giggle from Jade and me. He ignored it to continue, "But if you look closely enough—"Chuck paused just long enough to pull a magnifying glass from his back pocket. "—every single photo, even the painting, shows the man having a mole above his right side of his neck."

That did seem strange, and I had to stop to think about it before a question finally surfaced in my head. "Are all these photos in order? Like in time order?" I asked.

Chuck and Jade both nodded, then Jade said, "As much as we can gather."

"And how far do they all go back, including the

painting?"

Chuck and Jade exchanged a peculiar look before Chuck said, "All the way back to the founding of the town, we think."

I wasn't sure how long I stood there trying as I may to process what I was being told. It all sounded so unreal, even more so than the idea of unicorns, well, maybe at the same level, but it just felt different somehow. Once I was sure I would be able to use my voice without it sounding worried or cracking on me, I looked up from the picture that I had been staring at and asked, "What does that even mean?" Chuck and Jade looked back at me, but the only thing I got from them both was a shrug.

It was Jade who finally responded, sounding more like she was joking than actually being serious, "Maybe it means Mr. Woodwick is a vampire?"

"Or just immortal," offered Chuck, appearing more confident by his idea than Jade's before he added, "Vampires aren't real."

Jade gave him a sharp look before saying, "And unicorns weren't real until last week either." Chuck nodded slightly, but he still didn't look convinced about the whole vampire thing.

Something seemed to click in my head, like finding a puzzle piece you needed that had been under your knee the whole time. "Do you think that figure who was attacking Cliffton was Mr. Woodwick? Maybe he's been living off the unicorns' life force or something to keep himself young?" They both looked at me for a moment before a look of acceptance seemed to cover any doubt they may have had, both agreeing that the idea was quite possible.

"We have to talk to the unicorns," I blurted out without thinking first. I hadn't been given the OK yet from my aunt and uncle, but then again, neither of them was here right now, so I wasn't sure what to do.

Jade looked at me puzzled. "You haven't been talking to them, like, this whole time?" The way she asked the question felt almost bitter.

"I haven't exactly been allowed out to see them," I explained.

Chuck's eyes widened. "What? Why not? This whole time? Did you get grounded or something?" he asked, sounding as dumbfounded as Jade looked.

I shook my head, giving them a smile that showed how stupid I felt about what I was saying. "No. The horses, er, unicorns, were acting all weird. It started after we got locked in the basement, and apparently, I have the most protective aunt and uncle in the world." I paused just long enough to gesture to myself. "It's like they thought I was going to be trampled to death if I got near them or something."

Jade smirked. "Being as you're a city girl, that's a high probability," she said, her tone oozing with ridicule.

I stuck my tongue out at her, which got me a playful grin in return. "So, are you allowed to see them now?" Chuck asked hesitantly.

"Well," I said, letting the word float there as long as I could before finally admitting, "no." This caused Chuck to sink a little, looking defeated. "But I didn't get a chance to ask them this morning," I added. Sadly this didn't change the way Chuck was looking at me.

"Sounds good enough to me!" Jade declared before marching toward the door as if the situation had been handled.

"Wait!" Chuck begged with a squeaky yell. "We don't want to get in trouble, do we?"

Jade looked over her shoulder at the both of us with a devious grin. "So, we just don't get caught, then." This caused Chuck to frown so deeply his whole brow furrowed. I, on the other hand, couldn't help but grin back.

Chapter 27

As soon as we were all sure that the coast was clear and my uncle wasn't anywhere in sight, we made our way as stealthily as possible toward the stables.

Had anyone been watching us, they almost certainly would have found us comical to observe. Jade and I approached the situation a bit more seriously, while Chuck looked to be having a lot more fun with it, moving around more like he thought he was a ninja or a spy. I had to admire him a bit that even in a situation like this, he could have fun with it. I felt that was something I needed to have a bit more of myself.

Once we reached the doors, we all paused long enough to scan the area before pushing them open as quickly as we could and going in, or at least trying to go in. We only managed to get the doors open enough for maybe two people at most to fit through, and as all three of us tried to go in at once in a hurry, that didn't go so well. Jade and I butted shoulders as we both went in, with Chuck coming in right behind us like he was being chased by a pack of wild dogs. This caused Jade and I to fall forward, with Chuck swiftly tripping over our feet and landing on the back of us. It wasn't the most graceful entrance, that's for sure. After a quick look around the stable just to make sure my uncle wasn't there, I hurried to my feet, and with Jade's help, we shut the door behind us as quickly and as quietly as we could.

My heart was racing so fast now, and it felt like it

took a lot longer than I wanted before I managed to catch my breath again. When I glanced at Chuck and Jade, who were also leaning on the door on either side of me, I saw they looked as alert and winded as I felt. I wasn't sure if that made me feel better or worse.

After I was sure that no one was coming to get us, I pushed myself from the door, turning toward the watching unicorns. They didn't look as startled as I had expected them to be, but they were watching us very intently.

I stomped right up to Cliffton and pointed one finger at him accusingly. "I've been waiting days!" I allowed the last word to stretch out longer to emphasize how annoyed I was with that before I continued, "Were you freaking out just to keep me away, or do you actually have a good reason?" I know I probably sounded a lot harsher than I should have, and even more than I had intended, but I was so annoyed that their actions had kept me from talking to them for so long, and it would have been even longer if I had waited until I had been given the OK from my aunt and uncle.

Cliffton said nothing, and he looked like he was watching me with indifference. I felt a brief urge to just yell at him again, but before I could, I was stopped by the Thor behind me saying, "It's not our fault, lass. There have been a lot of strange vibes flowing through the air." When I glanced back at him confused, he asked, "Don't you feel it?" I shook my head, saying nothing, which caused him to hang his head just slightly before he lowered his back out of sight behind the door.

"He means we have been sensing something sinister in the air," Eloise clarified.

Jade stepped closer to her. "What do you mean something sinister?" she asked in a voice that sounded like she was trying very hard not to sound afraid. Chuck appeared to hide his body behind Jade's as if the word was a lot scarier than anything else that had happened to us in the last few weeks.

"Has the word changed its meaning, or are these children utterly and completely hopeless?" Eloise questioned, sounding exasperated as she gazed at Cliffton with some serious side-eye. Cliffton shook his head almost disappointingly, and I wasn't sure if it was from our evident lack of understanding or from Eloise's stark tone.

"She means," Cliffton said then paused long enough to look at each one of us in turn, making sure he had our full attention before speaking again, "after the incident at the horse show, things around here have made us feel more alert. Then, over the past week, we have noticed that someone has been trying very hard to break through our defenses around the farm."

"You have defenses?" I asked, and he nodded.

"What kind? Like booby traps?" Jade asked, sounding a little bit more eager than before. This girl clearly likes action.

Thor snorted after he managed to get his leg over the door again, and I was sure I saw him roll his eyes, or at least he tried to. "No, nothing like that. It's more like an energy we send out that—" He paused, looking like he was trying to find the best way to explain it before he continued. "—is like a force field that keeps out people with bad intentions."

Thor looked pleased with himself on how he had said it. "You mean like shields on the USS *Enterprise*?" Chuck asked excitedly, his whole face lighting up.

Thor sighed and muttered something under his breath before telling Chuck, "Sure, sure. If that's what makes sense in your wee little head." Then he sank down again out of sight.

Eloise wasn't so satisfied by Chuck's statement and clarified, "No, you little creature! Magic is not the same as science fiction. Do you not hear the 'fiction' part of that?" She just about snarled the last of her words as her tone dripped with sarcasm.

This didn't sit so well with Chuck as he looked like he had gotten wholly offended when he turned his attention to Eloise. "Right, because magic is so much more believable than technology?" he said with the same level of sarcasm and snark she had. He emphasized his point by crossing his arms and giving her a nasty look.

"Can we stop with all the eye rolls and name-calling?" I said, just loud enough to get everyone's attention. I felt a tiny bit annoyed when every one of them rolled their eyes at me collectively, followed a few moments later by some giggles. It was annoying, but at least they could find some common ground at being defiant toward me rather than at each other.

"The girl has a point. We should try to work together and not fight," Cliffton said sternly.

"The girl has a name!" I spat while I gave him a look that showed I wasn't impressed.

He stared back at me with indifference, blinking a few times to show he didn't care, before saying, "Anyway, maybe we should start by one of you telling us why you came out here in such a rush."

I crossed my arms over my chest in irritation and mumbled more to myself than to anyone, "It's Jennifer, not girl." Jade pulled out a rolled-up stack of paper that she had somehow mostly pushed into her back pocket. How she managed not to lose a single one on our way here impressed me. She unrolled them, and after finding the one she wanted, she quickly showed it to all three unicorns, asking them if they knew who it was.

There was unquestionably some recognition because Eloise looked away like she was disgusted. Thor pulled his head back down out of sight with a loud thud, and Cliffton bucked at the air wildly, making a loud neighing noise. I tried to shush him in an attempt to quiet him back down. I begged, asking in a hushed whisper, "Please, you have to be quiet! We're not meant to be out here." I had no idea how close my uncle was or if my aunt had come back. I had a feeling if I wasn't at the house when she got back, it wouldn't take long for her to ring the panic alarm to find me.

He landed on his front hooves with a thud and lowered his head, looking slightly apologetic. "Well, that answers that question," Jade stated.

"What do you know about him?" I asked, letting my gaze slowly linger on each of the unicorns one by one. They were all hesitant to respond, but finally, with a nervous hint in her voice, Eloise acknowledged, "That was the man who attacked Cliffton. The one who was trying to steal his life force."

"Life force?" Chuck asked curiously. Eloise just nodded in reply, clearly not wanting to say any more about the event or this life force thing.

Chuck opened his mouth to speak, asking the question again, but only the words, "What's a—" came out before the look Eloise gave him halted him in his tracks.

There was a long awkward silence before Jade said, "All right then." After none of the unicorns seemed eager to offer up any help, she continued, "Do you know who this is at least?"

They all shook their heads at the same time, Jade's eyebrow arching upward in response as she asked, "No?"

They all shook their heads again. Jade's whole body went rigid as she lowered her arms straight against her sides and looked up at the ceiling, then released a low growl. She looked like she was about to either cry or scream at any moment. Neither one would have been good, considering that we weren't allowed to be out here.

I tried to defuse the situation by asking a question of my own. "Do you know anything about him?" None of the unicorns shook their heads to that, so at least that was a good sign, but none of them said anything either, and it made me wonder if all unicorns were as completely useless as these ones.

I walked over to Jade, who was still breathing heavily through her nose. An attempt to calm herself before she had a tantrum, I assumed. I took the papers from her hands, which she barely noticed, or if she did, she didn't care. I walked to each of the unicorns, first to Eloise, then Cliffton, and finally to Thor, showing each of them the photos we had bought with us before finally asking, "Did anything I show you trigger any memory at all?"

Both Thor and Eloise shook their heads, but Cliffton didn't move, and after a long pause he finally nodded. I felt just a hint of hope deep inside me, but it wasn't enough to make me smile. Instead, I nodded and walked over to stand in front of him. "Help me with these," I pleaded, motioning for Chuck and Jade, who now looked like she had calmed down, to join me. The three of us stood in front of Cliffton, each one holding out two different photos so that he could see them all at the same time. "Which one?" I asked, staring at him with anticipation.

Cliffton craned his neck slightly, his eyes scanning over the photographs from left to right, then right to left, and then left to right again before finally touching the one that Chuck was holding with his nose, telling us, "This one."

Looking down at the photograph, I noticed it was different from the others. It had clearly been printed recently as it had a date near the bottom that was only from a few days ago. After looking at it some more, it dawned on me that it hadn't been one of the ones shown in my room that morning.

I peered over at Jade, feeling a bit confused, before

I asked her, "Is that one your aunt gave you?"

Jade glanced over at the photo Cliffton had touched and shook her head. "Nah, Chuck found that one online, right, Chuck?"

Chuck nodded, adding, "It was from an article I found where they were honoring his achievements. I think it's only from a year ago." He paused to think about that before correcting himself, saying, "Maybe two tops."

I looked back at the photo to study it a bit more closely. Mr. Woodwick was sitting at a desk, a large window behind him flanked by tall shelves filled with tons of what I would call rich people knickknacks. I didn't really understand yet what Cliffton had seen, as nothing looked weird or out of place. Besides it being the only photo that hadn't come from Jade's aunt, I was feeling truly stumped.

"What about this photo do you remember?" I asked, looking back at him. Of course, as I had already expected, he didn't say anything at first. This was definitely becoming a thing with them. Either they took forever to say something or didn't say anything at all. So I was more than overjoyed when he responded in a more acceptable amount of time.

"That thing behind him, on that shelf," Cliffton said.

"Which thing?" asked Chuck, looking back and forth between the photo and Cliffton.

"Yeah, there are lots of things on those shelves. Can you, I don't know, be a bit less vague?" Jade added, her voice oozing sarcasm. I so badly wanted to say something to her about this constant attitude she had but figured this wasn't the time or place, so I kept my attention on what mattered, and right now, that was Cliffton.

"Can you tell me which item you're talking about?" I asked hopefully, trying to keep my voice from sounding anything like Jade's had. It wasn't like I thought Cliffton was sensitive, but I had no idea how long he would continue to work with us if he thought we were bullying him.

Cliffton looked back down at the photo again and then back to me like he thought I was ridiculous or I was asking him some impossible feat. You would think I had asked him to juggle a bunch of feral cats or something.

"The thing on the shelf," he said again, letting each word last longer than it needed to, as if he were speaking to someone who didn't understand the words he spoke.

I nodded slowly. "Yes, I think we all got that part, but can you tell me which item in particular you are speaking off?" Even I was having a hard time now not letting my irritation show.

Again he shot me a look that screamed, "You're nuts," but finally, with a long tired sigh, he told us, "The shelf on the left, the circle thing." I glanced back at the photo and had to squint to try to see what he was talking about. Sure enough, on the left shelf, there was what appeared to be a gray circle. I thought it looked hollow, but it was so small, and the image was so distorted that I couldn't tell too much else about it. Looking at it a bit longer, I figured it was about the size of an orange.

To make sure I was looking at the right thing and partly just to make sure Cliffton knew what a circle was, I pointed to it. "This right here?"

He nodded his head like he was frustrated. "Well, yes, girl, that would be a circle," he told me, his voice matching his nod. I had to bite my tongue so as not to say anything to him that would be less than pleasant. After all, I had no idea how much longer we had before we'd get caught, and I didn't really want to have an argument with a unicorn. It wasn't exactly something I had on my bucket list.

"Well, can you tell me what you know about it?" I

274

asked.

Cliffton shook his head.

"Well," I said, letting out a long huff. My mind was blank, and I really didn't know where to go from there.

Thankfully Chuck asked a question instead, "So do you know what it is?"

Cliffton responded, "No."

"How do you know it's relevant then?"

"I just do," Cliffton snapped back.

"But you don't know what it is?" Chuck asked, clarifying again.

"That's what I just said, isn't it?" He looked at Thor and Eloise and asked, "I did say that, right?" Which got a nod from them both.

"But you remember it?" Chuck asked, not letting Cliffton's attitude faze him in the slightest.

There was a pause. "Yes, I think," Cliffton agreed.

"You think?"

Another pause. "It seems familiar," Cliffton clarified.

"How so?" Chuck pressed, wanting to get some useful information.

"It just does," Cliffton snapped back with a low growl.

"But then how do you know it matters?" Chuck asked again.

This just got a short snort from Cliffton before he turned his head away from Chuck, clearly not wanting to talk to him anymore.

I had to admit I was feeling a bit hopeless right now, but I decided I'd better make the best of whatever time we had left. "So all we know is that you recognize Mr. Woodwick but don't know anything about him, and there's something important about this one thing, but you don't know what. Am I getting all that right?" I paused long enough to gaze at all three unicorns to see if any of them would offer anything else up. All Eloise and Cliffton did was nod in agreement.

Thor was the only one who spoke, adding, "Well, I'm pretty sure he's evil. That's all I got, lassie."

I tried to smile at him, though I'm sure it wasn't too convincing. Then again, maybe human expressions were hard for them to read. At least I hoped they were with the way Jade was staring daggers at them now. The knowledge bomb that Mr. Woodwick was most likely evil wasn't exactly news anymore, but I still thanked Thor for that bit of information regardless of how useless it felt. Maybe some positive encouragement would spark something, or at least I wished it would.

I let out one last sigh before telling Chuck and Jade that we had better sneak back to the house before we got caught, and they both agreed, looking almost as defeated as I felt. We made it halfway to the doors when Cliffton called out, "It's a key, at least I think it a key," his words sounding both anxious and rushed.

The three of us spun around in unison, but it was Jade who asked, "A key to what?"

Cliffton looked away for a short moment as if he was trying hard to hold on to something in his head that was trying to escape him. Then he finally said one single word, "Home."

Chapter 28

We almost got caught on our way back to the house. Luckily for Jade and me, Chuck had managed to spot my uncle before he could spot us. He pulled us both down behind a stack of crates just before my uncle walked by pushing a wheelbarrow full of dirt. A tiny sniff at the air sadly revealed that whatever it was wasn't dirt. I was fairly sure Jade wanted to punch him in the arm again, but as soon as she saw he had saved us from being discovered, she looked like she was going to let the whole thing go.

My aunt's truck was still nowhere to be seen, but I made sure to keep my eye out for her the whole way just in case. After we shut the front door behind us, I told Chuck and Jade to go to my room as quietly as they could, and once they made it up the stairs with only a few stubborn squeaks from the old steps, I headed into the kitchen.

My heart felt like it was about to rocket out of my chest when I saw Aunt Tara standing at the sink washing some weird-looking purple things. She turned and smiled at me. "So, what have you been up to this morning?" she asked cheerfully.

"Oh, um," I stumbled, trying to find my words. "Just hanging out with Chuck and Jade."

Her eyebrow arched slightly before she turned back to the sink. "Oh, really, I didn't realize they were here. You kids sure are quiet."

A strained, uneasy laugh escaped my mouth, and I

had to force myself not to sound nervous when I told her, "Oh! Here I thought we had been making too much noise."

She shot me a quizzical look, and I decided to cut off whatever she was about to ask next by asking something myself, "So um, what is that?"

"What is what, sweetheart?" she asked before following my eyes to where I was looking. "Oh, this," she said with a bright smile. "It's an eggplant."

My nose wrinkled up all by itself at the sound of the word before I could ask, "A what plant?" allowing my words to sound both grossed out and deeply disturbed.

Aunt Tara laughed. It was a laugh that matched her previous smile perfectly. "Eggplant, but don't worry, it's just a name. It's not really an egg."

I wasn't sure if that made me feel better, but I confessed, "Well, that's good, I guess."

We stood there for a moment, and when she noticed I wasn't turning to leave, and honestly, I wasn't sure why I hadn't fled yet, she asked, "Did you need something?"

My brain went blank. Perhaps "blank" wasn't a strong enough word—barren, maybe? Void of anything at all? A vast emptiness of all life? Yeah, one of those had to be right, so I grabbed the first thought that came to mind, which was a thought I had a lot. "Oh yeah, I was just going to get us some snacks," and I smiled sheepishly back at her.

Aunt Tara nodded and motioned over to a plate that was sitting at the table. It was full of cookies that I hadn't seen before, "Just take the whole plate," she told me before continuing to wash what I assumed was the dirtiest eggplant of all existence. She didn't have to tell me twice. I grabbed the plate and got out of the kitchen as quickly as I could without looking too fast, just in case she got suspicious.

When I made it into my room, I wasn't looking at where I was going. I was too busy making sure Aunt Tara wasn't following me. I had to tell myself I was probably being ridiculous, but paranoia was starting to take some major roots in all my decisions. When I closed the door after one last peak down the hall, I was absolutely surprised when I turned around to see Jade and Chuck flanking what appeared to be a corkboard with some of the photographs tacked to it.

I walked closer with the plate still in hand to examine it. As soon as Chuck saw the plate, he quickly took it from my hands, exclaiming, "Yay, peanut butter cookies, my favorite!" Jade grabbed one for herself while giving me a proud smile, letting her eyes dart to whatever it was they had done while I was downstairs.

They had put one of the pictures of Mr. Woodwick on one side with a small torn rectangular piece of paper above it that read, "Mr. Samuel J. Woodwick." I hadn't realized that was his full name until now, not that I wondered what his name was at all. Calling him just Mr. Woodwick felt like it was enough for me. Something about giving him a first name made him seem more like a normal person and less like an evil villain, I guessed, and I was pretty sure he was far from normal.

There was also another torn paper under the photograph that read, "Evil," with more question marks than I thought was necessary. Beside it was the sheet of paper that Cliffton had noticed, the weird item had been circled with red ink and the word "Key?" was next to it. I stood there for a while but the only thing I could think to ask was "Where did you get a corkboard and all this other stuff?" Maybe that wasn't the most important question, but I had spent plenty of boring days wandering this house and had never once seen it before.

Jade waved her hands at me like she was wafting away a bad smell, telling me in an unconcerned tone, "That doesn't matter. What matters is, what do you think?" She motioned back at the board, looking just as proud as she had when I walked into the room, if not more so.

"It's nice," I replied, not feeling sure about my answer. I mean, it wasn't bad, but it wasn't spectacular either. Jade lit up, so I was glad that I came off more convincing than I thought. Then again, it's not like I could have done any better in that amount of time. I hadn't even considered putting all our clues in one spot. Not that we had that many anyway. Yeah, we definitely didn't have enough to warrant a board.

I looked at the two pages on the board a lot longer than I should have before finally turning around to see nearly half the cookies were gone. I assumed it had been Chuck since his mouth was smeared with crumbs, and he was currently shoving another one into his mouth. Meanwhile, Jade still looked to be nibbling on her first. "What do we do now?" I asked. They both looked at me, almost shocked by the question, before glancing at each other as if they had hoped the other had the right answer. A look of disappointment passed between them both when they realized that the other didn't know.

I let a long puff of air escape my lips while my arms flopped down at my sides. The air became still and quiet while we all contemplated, saddened that we were once again at a loss for direction.

My eyes widened. No, all our eyes suddenly widened when an unexpected knock came at my door. We looked at each other, fear sweeping over us, before turning to see the corkboard that was in clear view.

"Hide it, quick!" I said in a low rushed whisper to them both. I didn't care who hid it, only that it got done, and done fast, while I quickly headed to the door before whoever it was decided to just come in. I opened it just enough so whoever was on the other side could see only my face. Aunt Tara gave me a strange look when I blurted out, "Were we being too loud?" This got a raise of her eyebrows, and she shook her head. Moments after, there was a loud crashing sound behind me, followed by a few owws and groans, which made me gulp.

"Is everything all right in there?" Aunt Tara asked, concerned, trying her best to crane her head around the door to peek to the other side.

"Sure it is, just normal kid stuff," I confessed. A wrinkle I had never noticed before appeared above her brow.

She clearly wasn't buying that. "That doesn't sound normal," she said, sounding a little alarmed when there was another sudden loud noise behind me.

"No, it's fine. We are, um—" I paused, trying to think what next to say when Jade interceded.

"We are helping her rearrange her room."

Chuck added, "Yeah, it needs to be way more feng shui."

I wasn't sure if she was going to buy it, but when I saw her face soften, I figured we were in the clear. "Oh, well, I brought you some milk to go with those cookies," she told me with a wide smile. Getting my aunt to go away was going to be harder than I thought.

"Well, we're not thirsty," I told her before quickly adding, "but thanks," hoping I hadn't sounded too rude. Then I shut the door. I took a few steps back, just now noticing how hard my heart was beating, and I swear it nearly jumped right out of my body when the door swung open in front of me.

Aunt Tara walked right in, holding a tray stacked with three tall glasses of milk. She glanced behind me, and a smirk crossed her lips. I wasn't sure what I'd see when I turned around, a giant hole in the wall, a broken window? But when I looked behind me, everything appeared, well, everything looked normal. Besides the corkboard being nowhere in sight, nothing looked different at all. Jade was leaning on the wall trying to look bored, I thought, and Chuck was nervously glancing at my aunt and then back down to the plate of cookies in his hands.

"Oh, Chuck!" my aunt told him. "Try not to eat too many, all right? I don't want your mother upset if I send you home with a stomachache."

"Sure thing, Mrs. Greenfell," he told her, quickly placing the plate down on the bed and then backing away, looking somewhat embarrassed. Aunt Tara didn't say anything. She just shook her head and smiled as she placed the tray carefully down on the bed and walked back toward the door. She stopped, turned around, and for a moment, her mouth pursed like she really wanted to say something, but after a moment's pause, she shook her head again, and with a slightly bigger smile, left the room, pulling the door closed behind her.

We all stood there listening to her leave, and it wasn't until her footsteps had faded away completely that we all let out a collective sigh of relief. I only allowed myself to relax for a short moment before I turned around, asking, "Where did the board go?"

Jade nodded toward the bed. "It's under there."

I couldn't help but feel even more confused when I asked, "Wait, under the bed?" which got a quick nod from both Jade and Chuck. "Um, then what was all that noise?" I asked.

They both exchanged a small look, and it seemed like Chuck was about to answer, but Jade cut him off, saying, "Let's just call it a miscommunication of motion." a wide smile spread across her face. Chuck looked almost surprised by her statement, but after thinking about it, he nodded in agreement, which caused Jade's smile to get a tad bigger.

I could have pushed the issue as I was sure it wouldn't have taken much to get Chuck to confess what had really happened, but in the end, I didn't think it mattered that much. "Well, all right then, I guess," I said while sitting down on my bed and grabbing myself a cookie. After taking a small bite, I asked, "So what do we do now?"

"Get help from the adults?" Chuck asked. We both gave him a look that made his shoulders sag as he muttered, "Or not."

"Adults just complicate things," Jade explained as she began to pace back and forth in front of me.

"How would they?" Chuck asked, looking a bit offended.

"She's not wrong," I said, turning slightly so I could face him a bit more before going on. "Even if they somehow believe anything we say, which I have to tell you right now is doubtful, what do you think they would do?"

Chuck moved away from the bed, walking toward the window before replying, "Tell the police, maybe?"

"And that's exactly why we can't tell them," Jade retorted sharply. Chuck turned to give Jade a quizzical look, not entirely understanding her reasoning. Jade started to roll her eyes but stopped halfway when she told him, "We don't know who we can trust or how far Mr. Woodwick's influence goes. He might have full control of the police, maybe even the mayor, for all we know." What Jade said sounded partly paranoid but also partly feasible. When I looked at Chuck, the expression on his face told me that feasible was most likely probable, or at least, the possibility of it was scary enough to make him agree.

"Well, now that we know what we can't do, what can we do?" I said after a long silence had passed and the severity of our situation sank in a bit more. The reply I got back was a pair of shrugs. Then, after a few seconds, I swear I saw just a hint of mischievous glee flash behind Jade's eyes, and when she didn't say anything, I prompted her with "Well, what is it?"

She put both hands up to her mouth as she tried to resist and then failed to hold back a giggle. Her eyes darted back and forth between us before she said in a low gleeful whisper, "We should break into Woodwick Manor."

"Break in?!" Chuck almost yelled the words, which made me jump in surprise, and I found myself along with Jade telling him to keep it down. "What is wrong with you?" Chuck said back in a hushed whisper.

This, of course, caused Jade to roll her eyes. After a long, drawn-out dramatic sigh and an even more dramatic wave of her hand, she replied, "It's our only obvious choice; after all, where else would an insane life-sucking villain keep his secrets, or mystical unicorn key, or whatever?"

I could tell Chuck was about to argue with her, but the only thing he got out before I cut him off was "We don't know that," when I announced, "Jade's right again. We have to break into Woodwick Manor."

Chapter 29

It had taken a lot longer to figure out exactly how to get to Woodwick Manor than I'd had wanted it. Foolishly on my part, I had just assumed they both knew where it was and how to get there since Mr. Woodwick was such a big deal in town. The reality, however, didn't match up with my expectations. Now, to be fair, they did know where it was, or at least a general location for it, but Chuck and Jade couldn't seem to agree on the best way to get there.

Chuck argued that his way was a smoother, more leisurely ride with what he claimed was a bonus because it was more scenic. He had gone on about how he wanted me to be able to see more of the town. He was also very insistent that Jade's way would require way too much peddling uphill and would leave us too tired for the actual breaking in part of our plan. Jade, however, did not disagree with Chuck that her way would be a lot more work, but she was quick to point out that her way would be more fun and be considerably shorter as well.

In the end, after looking at the map, it was decided that since the manor was so far outside the town, we couldn't reasonably ask to be dropped off near it without coming up with a very creative reason. We ultimately agreed that our best option was to tell my aunt that we wanted to go into town and ride bikes. It didn't seem like the best plan at first since the bike my aunt and uncle had for me would have slowed us down to a crawl, but Chuck told me that he was sure his mother wouldn't mind if I used hers.

So with a bit of convincing, mostly from Chuck, that it would be all right, we managed to get my aunt to take us to Chuck's house. Before she drove off, my aunt asked him for the hundredth time, "Chuck, are you sure it's going to be all right if Jennifer uses your mother's bike? Maybe I should go in and talk to her just to make sure."

She started to open her door when Chuck quickly stepped in front of it, keeping it from opening more than an inch. "No, no," he insisted while nudging the door back with his hands. "She's not home right now anyway, and it's fine. If it makes you feel better, I'll give her a call before we leave," he added with a charming smile. I was a bit shocked, as I hadn't known he had it in him to be quite so forceful. I found myself impressed with how convincing he was. I also found myself wondering if I was somehow corrupting him. I had to shake that silly thought away, though. After all, this was Jade's idea, not mine.

Aunt Tara let out a tiny, defeated sigh and nodded. "All right, but make sure you call her right away, and if she says no—"

"We will find something else to do," Chuck cut her off, giving her another sweet smile that looked like it eased the last remaining bit of worry from her face. Without another word, she waved at us through the window and drove off.

I had a bit of time to look at Chuck's house while he ran into the backyard through a white wooden gate, disappearing to get the bikes. I had offered to go with him to help, but he declined my offer, letting me know he could manage by himself. I wasn't sure why, since moving two bikes alone wasn't going to be easy. I had to chalk it up to being a boy thing. Maybe he wanted to act all strong and tough, or maybe he was hiding something?

The outside of his home was simple but cozy. A two-story pale yellow house with a long porch that went from end to end with rows of bright flowers in nearly every color in front of it. The house wasn't as big as my aunt and uncle's, but it wasn't tiny either. Something about the way the place looked made me feel happy. I wasn't sure why but I just got a vibe that Chuck's family was probably the sort that went on camping trips and spent weekends playing board games.

When Chuck finally emerged from behind the house, he struggled to bring the two bikes with him. That wasn't unexpected, I thought with a grin. I found myself instinctively going over to help with them. "I could have helped you with them, you know," I told Chuck with a half smile, and he nodded, telling me, "Yeah, I know," between small pants. His whole face was red, and he appeared to breathe easier once I took one of the bikes from him and wheeled it over to the street.

The bikes were almost identical, both a crimson red with white details and matching horns near the handles. The one Chuck had kept, his, I assumed, was slightly smaller and had a large basket at the front, which was holding two helmets. I had no complaints about wearing one as I didn't want to have to worry about falling down and smacking my head on a rock. I could tell that beneath the two helmets there were other things too.

After Chuck had handed me one of the helmets and finished fastening his own, he began to put on kneepads, elbow pads, and a pair of fingerless gloves, all of which matched his bike perfectly. I must have been looking at him strangely because he told me, "Don't worry, I got a set for you too," and he motioned at the other set in the basket. I was probably a bit too quick to decline his offer. So when he shrugged back at me, looking clueless as to why I refused, and placed them back into the basket, I was relieved he hadn't taken offense. Again I had no problem wearing a helmet, just the rest of the stuff seemed way over in weird-ville.

I was thrilled when Jade finally arrived a few moments later on her own bike. Aunt Tara had offered to drop her off at her house first. She even offered to put Jade's bike in the back, but Jade declined, claiming she needed to do something inside. Aunt Tara had assumed she needed to tell her parents, but that clearly wasn't what Jade had been doing when I noticed the large backpack tied to the back of her bike with some rope. She patted it with a satisfied grin, saying, "Supplies!" I wasn't sure what was in there, but it looked big enough to hold just about anything we might need. I decided not to ask, partly because the mystery of it made it more exciting, and also, if she had something she wasn't supposed to, I could argue my innocence a bit more easily.

On the other hand, Chuck was more curious than I was because after he looked at the bag suspiciously for a second, he asked, "So what do you have in there?" His eyes darted nervously between her and the bag. All Jade did in response was smirk at him before she started peddling off.

It was at that moment that Chuck noticed that Jade was lacking in the helmet department. "Where's your helmet?" he demanded to know.

Her bike suddenly stopped and she looked over her shoulder at him with a wrinkled-up nose and a sour expression. "My what? Oh, helmet, nah, I don't need one." She was pushing off again but abruptly stopped when Chuck cleared his throat loudly, probably too loudly, as it sounded like it hurt.

Jade let out a long, drawn-out sigh, letting both her arms flop down by her sides. "I don't want to go all the way home just for that, Chucky," she moaned.

Chuck winced slightly from the name she used before a slight smirk curled the tip of one side of his mouth up. "No worries, I have a spare." With that said, he rushed back behind the house only to appear a minute later with a bright pink helmet with a cat face on the front and two pink ears sticking out the top.

When he handed it to her, Jade's whole face paled. "You have got to be kidding me," she spat.

Chuck shook his head, still holding that slight smirk. "Safety first, Jade. After all, it's the law, and we don't want to give anyone a reason to stop us, do we?"

She ripped the helmet out of his waiting hand and looked down at it before looking at me. Well, more she was looking at my helmet. "Want to trade?" she asked, sounding hopeful.

I tried not to smile. I failed to, of course, when I replied, "Sorry, this one matches my bike, and I don't want to break up a matching set." Jade let out a low growl before turning away and peddling off. Chuck and I exchanged a glance, and with a giggle, we followed.

There was a strange eerie feeling that all three of us silently shared once we had gotten a short distance from Chuck's house, and when I say short distance, I mean maybe only two houses away. I found myself fighting the urge to peddle faster because Jade and Chuck were both going at a near-snail's pace. They both kept looking at the houses' windows and past them, and I soon followed their example.

No matter how much I tried to push the paranoid thought that was bubbling up in the back of my mind, I couldn't shake the uneasy feeling that some unseen person was watching us now. I never did see anyone peering out from the darkened windows or over the many fences that connected all the houses, but the hairs on the back of my neck told me I didn't need to see them to know they were there. That feeling only intensified after we got to the end of the first street. The distance between us and Chuck's house now seemed too far to get to in a hurry.

It wasn't much longer, even though it felt like an

eternity, before we made our way through the town itself. It was no more or less busy than any of the other times I had been there, but the way some of the adults we passed smiled at us, the kind of smile that was way too big and happy to be natural and didn't quite reach their eyes, made me swallow sharply.

I could tell Chuck was becoming increasingly nervous by the minute. Jade, who I thought had the most I-don't-care-about-anything attitude, also showed signs of similar feelings by the way she kept glancing behind at us. I wasn't sure if she was checking to make sure we hadn't run away or seeing if someone had grabbed us. Maybe it was both.

When we passed a small butcher's shop, something inside caught my eyes, and I found myself stopping in front of it. There was a tall, husky man behind the counter. His long beard hid most of his face, and he wore an apron that looked way too dirty to be considered sanitary for handling food. His eyes were staring right at me, or at least I think they were. He said something that I, of course, couldn't hear, seeing as I was outside and all, but whatever he said made the much shorter woman in front of the counter who I hadn't noticed, turn to look at me too. She wasn't old but wasn't young either. She was wearing a pale blue suit covering a very frilly collared white shirt with a matching brimmed hat that, to me, felt way too dressed up to be picking up ingredients for dinner, but who was I to judge.

Both their faces looked blank but somehow angry at the same time. Then to my surprise and horror, the man jerked out a butcher's knife from the slab of meat that was sitting on the counter in front of him, all while keeping his eyes on us. I looked over to my friends to see what their reactions were to what was going on inside but found that only Chuck was still with me. Jade was a considerable distance ahead of us, and I assumed she hadn't even realized we had stopped.

Chuck and I exchanged a glance that conveyed that we both wanted to get out of there, and this sudden unwelcome realization made us panic as we both hurried to catch up with Jade. The moment we had managed to reach up to her, there was a sudden ruff voice yelling behind us, "Hey, kids, come back!"

Jade took one look behind her, and her eyes widened so big I was sure they would have popped right out of their sockets. Chuck and I followed suit to see what had her so worried, and that's when I saw the man standing in front of the shop, still holding the knife in one hand. What was even worse was seeing the man's apron in the light of day, which made the stains on his apron look more bloody than dirty. I'm not sure how that was worse than a butcher's knife, but that was just the feeling I was getting in the moment.

"Let's get out of here!" Jade cried as she started peddling away at a hurried speed, not even bothering to wait for us. Thankfully it only took a few seconds for both our brains to click on to what was happening, and we went racing after her.

Jade didn't stop for a very, very, very long time. Not until we had gone so far out of town that when I finally got a chance to look behind me, you could no longer see any sign of it. The only reason we stopped wasn't so much that the fear had left Jade, which was still clearly plastered on her face. It had more to do with Chuck practically crying and begging between breathless pants for over five minutes that she please let us take a break. I was glad Chuck had been the one to do it because, honestly, I felt like I was about to pass out myself. The only thing keeping me from asking myself was I didn't want to be the reason the scary butcher caught up with us.

Once we stopped, I found some solace that even

Jade was having a hard time catching her breath. "What . . . was . . . that . . . about?" she said between labored breaths.

"I have no idea," I admitted, sounding at least a little less breathless than Jade did.

"And I don't want to know," Chuck announced in a voice that sounded like a squeaky cry. This caught us both off guard because soon, the fear that we had been fighting to control our every action turned into hysterical giggles. Chuck glared at us both and said in a similar yet demanding tone, "What's so funny?" This caused us to laugh even more.

Once the laughter had died down, along with Chuck's angry glares, Jade said, "All right, well, I'm still not sure what happened back there, but I don't want to give anyone a chance to catch up with us. So we better keep going."

She was mid-peddle when Chuck asked, "Can we go a bit slower, at least?" and Jade looked over at him with a groan.

I interrupted her before she could say no by adding, "I agree with Chuck. We don't want to use up all our energy before we get to the hard part," Jade gave me a doubtful look, so I continued, "I mean, what if we get caught and have to make a run for it?"

She seemed to mull that over in her head for a moment before giving us both a confirming nod. "You're both right. We better conserve some of our energy. After all, we don't know what we might face inside." Chuck gave me a thankful smile before we started riding after Jade again at a more relaxed speed.

We rode our bikes down the road for another ten minutes or so before Jade slowed again, stopping right in front of a gravel road. She stared down it for a minute before pointing and saying, "The manor is down there." When I looked, all I saw was a small gravel road, barely wide enough for one car to go down that disappeared into the trees beyond. There were so many trees I couldn't see anything beyond them.

"Um, where?" I asked, wondering if I was missing something.

Jade sighed as she turned her bike to face the gravel road ahead. "You can't see it yet, duh. It's a good way from the road."

"OK, I was just asking," I murmured under my breath. She didn't appear to have heard, but Chuck did, and he gave me a reassuring smile.

"Let's just get this over with," Jade announced, all the confidence she once had from this plan seemingly evaporating as her eyes scanned the trees nervously. Chuck followed suit, not that I would have said he was confident about this before, but he definitely looked more nervous now than when we started.

"Am I missing something?" I asked, wondering if I should be more worried too.

Jade motioned for us to follow her, and she began to slowly creep her bike forward. "Yeah, we'll fill you in on the way."

We made our way so incredibly slowly down the road that it was barely fast enough for me to keep my bike upright while peddling it. After only a few minutes of struggling with bumping rocks under me, I decided to just walk my bike instead. Jade and Chuck must have been having the same problem because after Chuck almost fell sideways, he copied me, with Jade joining soon after. It was then that they both began to tell me all they knew about Woodwick Manor, or at least the stories they had heard about it.

Chuck started everything off by saying, "They say that Woodwick Manor is haunted." I wasn't exactly surprised by him telling me that. After all, when wasn't a giant old manor in the middle of the woods not haunted?

Honestly, it would be strange if it wasn't. What Jade told me next, however, I wasn't ready for, and it made my blood run cold, and I felt a shiver down the length of my spine.

"They also say the woods around it are haunted." I found my eyes searching the sudden darkening woods around me. Had they been so dark before? Memories of my dream began to surface in my head.

I could have sworn that just moments before, the woods around us felt alive and bright, with light sweeping from the canopy above and birds singing their songs from the branches. Now they felt cold and dark as if the light, and even sound, had been sucked away, leaving only a chilled silence in its wake. No matter how much I tried to look through them, I couldn't see anything. Then again, nothing felt overly haunted either. After thinking about that for a minute, I decided I probably didn't want to know what would make them look haunted.

My gaze was broken when my front tire hit a large rock, causing my bike to unexpectedly halt. I found myself rapidly falling toward the ground face first, and a loud yelp escaped my lips. To my relief, Jade was quick to grab me by the arm before I could make it too far. A group of black birds, apparently startled by my tiny yelp, came swooshing out of the bush right next to Chuck, causing him to let out a bloodcurdling scream.

Jade let go of my arm and her bike, allowing it to crash to the ground as she hurried over to Chuck before I even could make sense of what had just happened. She clasped her hand over his mouth, telling me, "Shh, both of you. Be quiet, or someone is going to hear us." She didn't remove her hand until Chuck nodded that he understood, and she was soon back picking up her bike. I whispered a quick thanks to her, and she nodded at me like it was no big deal.

We all stayed quiet for a few more minutes. When

I was sure no one was coming down the road to investigate all the noise we had just made, I finally felt safe enough to talk again. I asked, "So how are the woods haunted?" I paused, choosing my following words carefully. "Except for being super dark and creepy and filled with easily startled birds, I'm not seeing it."

Jade snorted before looking over her shoulder at me. "Hauntings are worse at night, duh." I wasn't sure that was right. The only thing darkness did was make things scarier. I wasn't exactly sure how it would make things haunted, though.

"That doesn't really answer my question," I said, and all I got was a shrug from Jade in return.

Chuck looked over at me, a hint of fear behind his big brown eyes before he said, "Many hunters and hikers have claimed they have heard the whispers and giggles of children around these woods, but they never saw any." He paused before correcting himself, "Well, sometimes they think they do, but no one has any proof," then he shrugged. Chuck glanced over to the woods nervously before looking back at me, adding, "And it's not just at night either. It's not like a lot of people hike or hunt then." Chuck paused again after a thought, saying, "Well, I mean, I guess some people hunt when it's still dark, but that's normally first thing in the morning." With that said, he glanced at Jade, who then muttered something under her breath. I wasn't sure how she knew he was looking at her, but she clearly did.

I couldn't help myself as the urge to look at the woods became stronger, my eyes searching every section more cautiously now and with a lot more suspicion. Ghosts and haunted houses were frightening enough to me, but something about kid ghosts was in a whole different ballpark all by itself. Right next to creepy clowns and dolls. It was like how I could be OK with zombies on Minecraft, but the tiny, fast ones would cause me to scream and shut the game off. Scary small things always trumped big ones in my book, every single time. Then the whole ghosts outside was also a lot worse than being in a house. I could rationalize going into a haunted house. All you had to do to escape was walk out the door, but how would you escape a ghost if it was already outside? Something deep inside told me you couldn't or it would be a lot harder.

When Chuck started to say something again about kid ghosts, I cut him off, saying, "I think that's enough talking. We don't want to get caught after all."

I wasn't scared about getting caught, well, maybe a bit. In truth, I had no clue at all how much longer it might be before we saw signs of life again. It's just all the ghost talk was starting to set off every alarm in my head. The kind that triggered a fight-or-flight feeling in the bottom of my stomach, except it was just flight, only flight, a run-away-and-don't-look-back kind of flight!

Chuck nodded sadly, clearly disappointed that he wasn't going to be able to tell any more scary tales about the manor or the woods that surrounded it. I didn't think he was disappointed that he couldn't talk about the scary parts, more that he couldn't continue sharing all the facts he knew.

Much to my relief, it took us only another two to three minutes before we came to a sudden sharp turn in the road, and that's when Jade stopped walking. She pointed at something ahead. In truth, I hadn't been paying too much attention to the road ahead of me as my eyes were too focused on the woods. Probably not the smartest thing in hindsight. When I looked down the road to where she was pointing, I was surprised to see a large stormy-gray brick manor surrounded by tall black iron fences and a gate with a semicircular black iron strip above it that simply read, "Woodwick Manor."

Chapter 30

To say Woodwick Manor was enormous frankly felt like an understatement. I had assumed that Mr. Woodwick probably lived alone, and that was still possibly true. But the thought that only one man lived in a manor so huge, all alone, felt like a waste. It looked like a castle in some ways with its stone exterior. Then again, I wasn't actually sure what a manor was supposed to look like, so maybe it was spot on.

The building itself was mainly two floors, with a few random places where it seemed there might have been a third. I had seen houses, though, where they had that one random window that made it look like there was an extra floor, only to find out later that the window led to nothing at all. Something about that always disappointed me for some reason, kind of like getting a big tin of chocolates only to find out there wasn't another row under the first. It's a major scam if you ask me.

Looking at the manor, I found myself wondering if it had a basement. It must! I had no doubt in my mind that a place this old and big had a creepy basement lurking under it and probably an even creepier attic. The most surprising thing about it was that it didn't look haunted at all. I will acknowledge that it was a bit eerie, maybe even a bit gloomy, but other than that, it was rather beautiful. I wasn't sure if the first two feelings I had were more for the reasons we were there and not so much how the building really looked. I might have felt totally different had I been there under other circumstances, but a nagging feeling in my gut told me I wouldn't.

The woods that surrounded the manor felt darker here, and more menacing than they had before. The darkness was threatening to swallow the whole estate and everything else along with it. That wasn't helping my nerves. The longer I looked at the building, the more unsure I was that we should even be there. I could see through the center of the gate a large imposing dark wooden door with a small set of stone steps leading up to it. I couldn't see much else from where I was standing except for the large stone fountain in front of the manor.

"We should get closer," I whispered, which caused Chuck to shake his head in disagreement. Clearly, the sight of the manor had made him lose any nerves he had left.

On the other hand, Jade agreed, saying, "Yeah, we should also get out of sight before anyone sees us," and she motioned for us to follow her off the road so that we were no longer in sight of the front door. Jade's idea to get off the road was probably for the best, but it made the trek toward the front gate a hundred times harder than it should have been. It didn't feel likely that Mr. Woodwick had people just staring out of his windows, keeping an eye on the road for any trespassers. If anything, I would have thought there would be security cameras, the thought of which made me scour above for them.

Once we reached one of the giant gray brick pillars that connected the fence to the gate, I peeked around to better see what was behind it. The gravelly road continued through the gate and circled the fountain, with an ornate stone path leading to the front door. The fountain was hard to make out. Most of it was encrusted with moss and vines, obviously disused and unmaintained for many years. Instead of flowing water, there was a flood of overgrown plants and weeds. It probably would have been stunning had anyone been bothered to clean it up.

The left side of the building felt slightly longer than the right, with a large circular tower attached to the corner. It looked like it might have been one of the highest points of the building, with a tall cone roof topping it. The rest of the building was pretty much just walls, windows, and what I thought might have been intricate stone carvings that surrounded all the windows and lay just under the edge of the roof. It was a bit hard to tell, though, as over 90 percent of the walls was overrun with thick ivy. Even some of the windows were lost behind it. I thought Mr. Woodwick had to be wealthy, so I couldn't understand why he had let nature take over his house the way it did. Maybe I was wrong about him?

My opinions about it were cut short when an arm suddenly pulled me down behind the left stone pillar of the gate, and I found Jade's fingers clasping my mouth shut with a hushed shushing sound. I didn't think I would have screamed, but she was probably so used to dealing with Chuck, it was most likely a habit now. She mouthed the words "Mr. Woodwick." I stole a quick glance, and sure enough, Mr. Woodwick was standing right in front of the door. I felt a bit stupid. I had gotten so taken in by the manor, I hadn't even noticed him coming out.

I didn't think he saw any of us as he appeared more occupied with fixing a button on the cuff of his shirt than anything around him. There was a strange crunching sound coming from behind the fence. I wasn't sure what it was until I caught just a hint of what looked like a black car through the tall bushes and overgrowth on the opposite side of the fence. I felt a surge of panic when I noticed Chuck wasn't with us. After I frantically searched around me, Jade motioned to the pillar on the other side of the gate. Chuck had pushed himself even farther back than we were, which probably was a good idea as I could just barely see him. What I did see looked frozen with fear, and I couldn't help feeling bad that he was stuck over there all by himself.

I looked back just in time to see the car park in front of Mr. Woodwick. He didn't move an inch, but something about the way he stood made me think he was waiting for something, and he didn't appear too pleased to be left waiting for it. The driver, wearing a chauffeur's cap, quickly exited the vehicle and opened the door for him before standing to attention.

Mr. Woodwick's body slumped ever so slightly. He didn't say anything to the man. Instead, he walked down the step and got into the car, not even giving the driver a second look. After the door was shut behind him, the driver paused just long enough to catch his breath, maybe a calming one, before getting back into the driver's seat.

Once he started driving around the fountain to the gate, my brain decided to remind me that Jade and I were probably still too close and would definitely be seen. We both scurried back, trying to hide ourselves along with the bikes in the overgrown weeds and bushes. The gate opened with a loud rusty-sounding squeak that was unpleasant to my ears. The car drove right past us and kept going. Moments later, the gate began to shut, and I found myself wondering if we would have time to get through it before it closed.

Jade must have been thinking the same thing because she started to lurch toward the shutting gate, but it was me this time who stopped her. I caught her arms before she could make it to the road. She quickly spun her head to look at me with confusion. "The car is still too close," I told her, and this made her peek down the road to look for it.

Jade sighed and rolled her eyes, and she muttered something along the lines of "whatever," but I wasn't entirely sure.

We waited until the sound of the car was gone before any of us dared move again, and when it was, it was Chuck who jumped out of his hiding place first. His whole body looked like he had been shaken by the entire event, and he said between uneasy breaths, "That was too close!"

Jade shrugged like the last few minutes hadn't really been that big of a deal, saying, "Well, let's see if we can get over this fence now that paranoid girl over here can see we're all alone," adding an eye roll in my direction to express her annoyance.

I crossed my arms and said, unbothered, "Well, next time maybe I'll just let you get caught." Jade smirked at me in response before she turned her attention toward the fence.

"Um," Chuck said with a hint of worry in his tone, waiting until Jade, who was now standing on her tiptoes trying to reach the fence, stopped to look back over her shoulder at him before he continued, "Doesn't Mr. Woodwick have a ton of staff?"

Jade shrugged like that fact didn't matter and reached once again for the top. "Wouldn't sneaking in the front get us, well, I don't know, spotted?" I asked, trying not to sound sarcastic.

Jade froze there for a moment before her arms swung down, and she nodded. "Fine, if you want to play it completely and unnecessarily safe, then we can just go around the back."

With another dramatic roll of her eyes, she let go of the fence and began to move her bike into the bushes in an attempt to conceal it the best she could. She didn't try too much, really. After trying to jam her bike into a bush two or three times, only to have it push back out, she threw her hands up into the air and began stomping her way along the edge of the fence. This didn't look to be too easy with the incredibly tall foliage in front of it. Chuck and I just stared at each other for a moment before Jade called behind her sounding very frustrated, "Well, come on, we don't have all day." We quickly covered all our bikes before making our way after her.

It took us between fifteen minutes and forever before we made it to a good spot behind the manor. It had become increasingly harder to see the manor this far back since the plants got taller and denser on both sides of the fence. Whoever was keeping up Woodwick Manor might have been doing an awful job in the front, but they had completely given up on the backyard, probably for a long time. That didn't make sense in my head. I always imagined rich people with big houses and perfectly manicured lawns. The house was big, that was for sure, but why he had left the plants to overrun everything was strange.

Jade pointed at a part of the fence that appeared slightly shorter, as the top part had been bent down at a sharp angle. A tree stump near it told the story of how that managed to happen. Jade and I helped Chuck go over first, and when he gave a cross between a meow and what might have been a bird call, I helped Jade over next. She wedged herself at the top and lowered one hand while keeping the other tightened on the fence before helping me climb to the top, and soon we both managed to get to the other side.

The backyard was a jungle of overgrown plants, weeds, and tall hedges that separated the entire backyard into different sections. They were so tall in fact I wasn't even sure how big or far the backyard went. What I could see was that to the left was a large, windowed area away from the house. It may have been a greenhouse, but the muddy-looking muck and moss that had cracked most of the windows made it nearly impossible to see through, so I couldn't be sure. To the right, there was a pool or a pool-shaped area, and if there had been water in it, it too seemed to be overtaken by a film of thick moss. I wasn't going to check, as the idea of something grabbing my arm and pulling me down was enough to kill any curiosity about what it was or was not.

Even with all that, what really got my attention was right in the middle of the oval-shaped hedge area we found ourselves in. There was a small gray fountain, and much like everything else we had seen, it had also been taken over by a mix of vines, weeds, and moss. The weird and honestly disturbing thing about it were the statues standing atop it. They looked like children, or at least to be child-sized. I wasn't sure if that mattered so much when it came to statues. One looked like a girl and the other a boy. Their bodies were facing each other. They appeared to be hugging each other, but their heads were facing the back doors that led into the house.

I found myself slowly circling to the other side of the fountain to better look at it. It was then that I noticed that the statues weren't so much hugging, but more like they were holding on to each other for dear life. Something about the way they looked gave the impression they were frightened too. The really unsettling part was their faces. I wasn't sure why someone would make statues look so terrified or why anyone would want a statue that looked that way. Both faces were frozen in an eternal look of panic and terror. I found myself following their gazes, and sure enough, they were both desperately staring at the back door with wide eyes and gaping mouths. The strangest thing with all this was not just how scary and eerie the statues were. It was that there was something so familiar to me about them. Like I recognized them somehow but couldn't place my finger on why or how.

"Do these statues look familiar to you?" I asked as the words left my lips without even thinking about them first. Chuck and Jade came to stand beside me, looking up at the statues with uneasy expressions.

"Can't say that they do," Jade finally admitted after staring up at them for a minute.

"Are you sure?" I asked, hoping maybe she would change her mind.

"Maybe there was a picture of them in the photo?" Chuck asked, but his tone suggested he wasn't entirely sure that was possible.

"They just seem—" I paused for a moment giving them another good look. "—like I've seen them before."

Jade looked at me for a moment before her eyes darted back up at them, and she snorted, saying with a hint of sarcasm, "Well, I guess the girl looks a bit like you, but"—she gestured her hands at me—"you do have a somewhat generic city girl look, so, meh?"

"Generic city girl?" I asked, spinning to look at her, letting myself forget all about the statues. "What does that even mean?" I let my voice take on an air of annoyance instead of trying to hide it.

The corners of Jade's lips lifted just slightly, but before they could come to a smile, she looked like she was forcing herself not to, and instead, she just shrugged in reply. I allowed a long puff of air to escape my nose before deciding this wasn't the time or place for whatever that was. I turned to face the back door that was just partly visible behind the arched walkway in the hedges. An array of vines and thick moss draped from it like a curtain. The effect gave the manor an almost magical effect, I thought.

"So how do we get in, I asked?" as I pushed away the overgrowth, making my way cautiously through it.

"Break a window," Jade suggested as she knelt to grab a loose rock on the path.

"Any idea that won't get us caught now or even after we leave?" I asked, shooting her a stern look. She thought about it for a moment before rolling her eyes with a long groaning sigh, letting the rock fall from her hands with a thud.

"Maybe we should start looking and stop yapping," Chuck blurted out as he began walking forward without even waiting to see if we would follow. Jade and I both exchanged confused and surprised looks at this sudden change in Chuck's behavior, and without another word, we followed him.

Chapter 31

After a whole lot of looking around for an easy way in and a whole lot more of Jade attempting to pry open every window she could see with a long, bent, rusty nail she had found, we were all out of ideas. Jade didn't actually get to check every window she could reach because she became too annoyed after Chuck started freaking out about how she was going to get tetanus. She didn't look too concerned about it. It was more that Chuck's persistent whining had finally gotten to her, and she gave in to get him to shut up more than anything else.

"This is pointless," Jade stated as she flailed her arms wildly into the air, causing the nail to fly out of her hand and hit the wall with a soft clang.

"You could have taken one of our eyes out!" Chuck snapped at her in a low voice.

"It didn't get anywhere near you," she argued.

"True," I said with a sly smile, "but you came pretty close to taking out that window."

Jade rolled her eyes. "Yeah, whatever, at least then we would have a way in," she muttered back.

Jade had a point. We had wasted I don't even know how many minutes now just trying to get in, and we had no idea how long Mr. Woodwick was going to be away. Even knowing this, it didn't stop either of us from staring up at the manor like it was the biggest puzzle in the world. One neither of us seemed to know how to solve.

It was Jade who was the first to break the silence

when she flung both her arms up into the air and then crossed them over her chest as she turned to walk away, saying, "Well, that's it, then, I guess. Since you guys won't let me break anything." After a few steps, she appeared to realize that neither one of us was following her, and she spun around, asking in a sharp tone, "What, are you two waiting for an invitation?"

Chuck seemed too preoccupied with his own thoughts to respond. So without even looking behind me, I told her, "We made it all the way to the end, and you want to give up now?"

When Jade didn't say anything back, I stole a quick look over my shoulder at her. Her face was contorted, making her seem both upset and annoyed, and she was looking everywhere else but at me. I had a feeling it wasn't typically Jade who was the first to give up on anything, so the fact I outlasted her was probably playing majorly with her ego. Still, just like I figured, she let out a loud sigh, did yet another eye roll, and stalked back to stand on the opposite side of Chuck.

"Fine," she muttered under her breath. "Don't blame me if we get caught just standing out here staring at some creepy old guy's house." Jade paused for a moment, and then the expression on her face conveyed that she wasn't entirely done complaining yet. She pulled her arms a bit tighter to her chest and added, "I mean, if he is anything like my grandparents, or heck anyone's grandparents, he probably just has a key under the mat."

Both our heads turned sharply to look at Jade simultaneously, and the sudden movement caught her off guard by the way she defensively asked, "What? Why are you both staring at me like that?" A hint of understanding quickly filled her eyes before the three of us all looked down at the mat in front of the back door.

"It couldn't be that easy," I said, then asked, "Could it?"

"Only one way to find out," Chuck replied as he took a small step forward, bending down to pull up the edge of the mat.

My heart began to race faster in my chest as a new surge of anxiety and anticipation crept in, only to vanish instantly when we saw nothing but stained lines from where the mat had been. "That's it. I'm breaking a window," Jade said.

Before she could even attempt to grab a stone, she was stopped by Chuck's voice. "Wait," he told her as he ambled over to a huge, heavy-looking ceramic plant pot. He grabbed the rim and, as he attempted to tilt it, said between pants, "Maybe he's more like my nana." The moment the edge of the pot was lifted just enough, Jade gasped, and when I looked, I saw it. One small key had been hidden underneath.

Jade darted over and snatched the key before I could even think to do so, and she lifted it over her head, looking smugly triumphant. I could see Chuck was having a hard time holding the pot up, let alone slowly putting it back without making a loud noise, so I hurried over to help him. He smiled at me when we got the pot back in place and whispered, "Thanks."

As soon as we joined Jade, she slid the key into the lock and, after a couple of failed attempts, was able to get it unlocked. She blamed the key and lock being old, but I wasn't so sure that it wasn't just the nerves deciding to sink in. We opened the door as slowly as we could with only a few scattered creeks and squeaks from the hinges. Once we got it open enough, we stopped and listened for any indications that we may have been heard. When we heard nothing but silence, I peeked inside.

The cold air hit my face like a tidal wave, sending a shiver down my spine. I would have typically enjoyed going into a cold room after being outside for so long in the hot summer sun, but this air was just too cold, almost wrong in a way. Admittedly everything was wrong about this place, but I wasn't sure if that was just my wild imagination finding things that weren't really there. I couldn't tell much about the room beyond the brief look. All I knew was no one was there.

"We need to go in," I whispered under my breath as I moved back from the door. Saying it out loud didn't mean I wanted to be the first in. After a moment of hesitation, Jade pushed the door open enough for us to squeeze our way past one at a time, with Jade being in front and Chuck in the back.

The room we entered wasn't so much a room. It was more of an entryway that stretched about ten to twelve feet forward before branching off to the left and right. Taking a quick peek around the corners, I saw that both directions led into long hallways with numerous doorways lining them. The top half of the walls was finished with a deep burgundy wallpaper covered in an intricate swirled golden design, while the bottom half was covered by dark wood paneling and detailed trim. The wooden floors were slightly darker than the paneling and were covered in long, wide rugs that matched the square one in the nook where we were standing.

It felt really dark and creepier than I had imagined. A scattering of decorative tables lined the walls between some of the doorways, each covered with ornate vases filled with dark-hued flowers. Old, and more than likely expensive, paintings hung from the walls. "Living in a museum much?" Jade asked in a whispered snark.

I couldn't help but chuckle under my breath, replying, "Yeah, you could say that again."

"Maybe we shouldn't, and instead keep our talking to a minimum," Chuck whispered back, giving us both a stern look.

Jade mouthed, "OK," slowly and very sarcastically, before motioning that Chuck should lead the way.

Chuck gulped slightly but appeared as if he was able to push it down before nodding and turning to peak down both hallways. Jade looked a bit surprised, maybe even concerned, but she didn't say anything and instead walked to stand behind him. Whatever power dynamic Jade and Chuck had appeared to be shifting, and Jade didn't seem to know what to do or how to feel about it. I was just glad she realized it wasn't the time or place to figure that out.

Once enough time had passed, or at least enough time for Chuck, he began to slowly move forward, but before he could get more than one step, Jade caught his arm, stopping him. Chuck turned back, staring at her, confused. Jade leaned forward, saying softly under her breath, "Think maybe we should split up, you know, so we can cover more ground?" The expression on Chuck's face seemed to consider this for just the briefest of moments before he shook his head vigorously, showing his disapproval of that idea, and his voice came out in a terrified squeak.

"What is wrong with you?" he asked her, and shook his head again before continuing, "That's horror movie mistake number one and how most people end up dead." He took a long calming breath before adding, "You never split up!"

Jade did all she could not to laugh, but when she saw neither Chuck nor I found the situation funny, she calmed herself. "We're not in a horror movie, Chucky," she told him, emphasizing his name with a bit of a smirk.

Chuck ignored the name this time, not letting it bother him, and he told her with little emotion before turning, "And that's what everyone in horror movies thinks too, Jade."

Chuck resumed his sneaking forward, making way toward the hallway on the right. Neither one of us followed him right away. I think we were both too shocked by the way he was sneaking. It somehow reminded me of an older cartoon, the way they tiptoed, walking with arched backs, and held their hands out like a T. rex. OK, maybe that wasn't the best way to describe it. Either way, it looked hilarious. After a few good steps, he seemed to sense no one was following him, and when he looked back, he frowned. Not so much because we hadn't followed him but because we were both holding back a laugh. He glared at us before motioning that we should follow him. Jade placed her hands in front of herself defensively as she mouthed "Sorry" before copying him, or at least in a less funny way.

As we slowly made our way down, Chuck stopped at each and every door, slowly turning each handle and opening the door just enough to peek inside. So far, there was nothing too important, a lot of closets as well as a few random rooms that looked more like storage than anything. In fact, most of the rooms that had something in them all had white sheets covering everything. A lot like they used to do a long, long, long time ago. I didn't know how long ago or why they did it, maybe to keep things clean? It seemed like a strange thing to do, but perhaps the duster hadn't been invented yet, or people back then really hated cleaning.

We had just gotten to another door when Chuck's hand froze on the handle, and his head turned to look down the hallway. His eyes were frozen, but I didn't see anything when I looked. "What are you waiting for" Jade whispered, sounding a bit annoyed.

"Shh," Chuck replied, and he waited another moment before asking, "Did you hear that?"

"Hear what?" I asked, looking toward the other hall and rotating my head so my ear was aimed down the hall. At first, there was nothing, but then as I slowed my breathing, I heard it too. It sounded like a voice. No, scratch that, two voices and footsteps, and now that I heard them, they were getting louder.

"Oh no!" Jade exclaimed, this time not whispering, and she clasped her hand over her mouth when she realized her mistake. In a rushed whisper, she followed up with, "Hurry. we need to hide."

Chuck opened the door without even looking at what was inside, and we all hurried in to find ourselves in a very tiny and cramped broom closet. There was barely any room to move without bumping someone with an elbow or knocking into the random brooms and mops that had been left leaning on the walls.

"My foot is stuck in something," Jade whispered in a bit of panic. I managed to look down just enough to see one of her feet was inside an old bucket.

"It's just a mop bucket," I told her. After hearing this, the worried look she had before became disgusted. I tried and failed to shrug, instead hitting Chuck under his chin. After I apologized to him, I let Jade know, "Could be worse. It could be wet."

Jade growled slightly. "Says the girl who doesn't have a foot stuck in a bucket." She couldn't help but roll her eyes and sigh about it.

Chuck shushed her as he placed his ear closer to the door. It had the opposite effect to what he had wanted because instead of being quiet, Jade said in a slightly lowered whisper, "Stop telling me what to do Ch—" and before she could finish saying his name, Chuck somehow managed to get one hand free and he covered her mouth with it.

Jade protested at first with many loud, muffled complaints but soon quieted down once Chuck very carefully managed to convey to both of us without a word that someone was getting closer to the door. This was finally enough to make Jade lose whatever fight she had left, and she nodded submissively at Chuck that she would be quieter.

By the time my heart stopped drumming in my ears, whoever we had heard moments before sounded like they were right outside the door, and it took all the determination I had not to let my heart start racing in my chest again. I thought the closest-sounding voice sounded like a woman, a young woman. Her voice was pleasant and sweet, which did a lot to calm my nerves, but the other one, a very deep, almost sandpaper-sounding one, was a bit farther away. For a moment, I thought I recognized the voice. Was that the same person who had come into Susan's basement? The man's voice wasn't as close, but it didn't make me feel better.

"Did you hear something?" the woman asked, sounding more curious than concerned.

The man grumbled something that I couldn't quite make out, but it sounded something like, "It's an old house. They make lots of noise."

The lady didn't reply right away, and when I looked down at the light that was coming from under the door, it suddenly vanished as if someone was now standing right outside it. This time her voice was so loud it felt more like a scream next to my head. "And where does this door lead?" she asked, and then I noticed the handle move slightly as if a hand had grabbed it. It slowly began to turn, and I felt the three of us hold our breath.

Before the handle could click, it was stopped by the man speaking, "It's just another cleaning closet, nothing you need to deal with."

"Right," she agreed, and the light soon returned under the door as feet receded from the other side, causing me to let out a breath I hadn't noticed I was holding. "And this one here?" she asked again, causing the man to let out a long, tired sigh. His voice was low, almost like he was talking more to himself than the woman.

"I have no idea why Mr. Woodwick thinks you need

320

a tour if all you're going to be doing is cooking his meals." I could just imagine the man on the other side shaking his head in frustration, and then his voice spoke a bit louder, this time clearly addressing the woman, his voice sounding very stern and authoritative. "That is Mr. Woodwick's private study. No one is allowed in there unless told otherwise by Mr. Woodwick himself." I couldn't see the expression on my friends' faces too well, but if they were anything like mine, I'd assumed they had wide eyes and a gaping mouth.

"Of course not," the woman replied, sounding very apologetic. After a long pause that felt somehow awkward, she continued, "Maybe it would be best if we cut this short and you show me the kitchen." The man didn't say anything, but I assumed he must have nodded at least because the sounds of footsteps began again, and after less than a minute, they were gone.

"Let's go," Jade said, sounding panicked, almost like the small space had gotten to her.

"Not yet," Chuck breathed out in a whisper before listening at the door a bit longer, then he nodded that he thought it was clear, and the three of us clumsily made our way out of the cramped closet. Mainly because Jade was pushing us both out like the closet had somehow become devoid of any air and she desperately needed it.

"Quiet," Chuck and I said in unison to the frantic gasping sounds that were coming from Jade. Saying nothing, she bent the top half of her body down toward her feet, resting both hands on her knees, and with a few heavy breaths, she managed to calm herself down.

"Which door is it?" Jade asked in a slightly breathless voice. I wasn't sure, since we hadn't seen which door the woman had been standing at, so I gave her a small clueless shrug.

"It's most likely this one," Chuck answered as he motioned toward a door that was opposite the closet.

"Why that one?" Jade asked quizzically, narrowing her eyes to look at him. She didn't look convinced.

A smirk spread across Chuck's face when he told her, "Well, since they were heading that way," and he pointed down the hall in the opposite direction toward where they came, "and since the woman's voice hadn't gotten any lower when she asked about the next door, I'm thinking it has to be this one."

Jade looked at him doubtfully, and Chuck clarified his theory by telling us, "It makes the most logical sense, as this was the direction in which the steps went. Plus, that's an exterior room, which means it has a window, and I doubt someone like Mr. Woodwick, evil or not, would have a windowless office."

I guess it did make sense. After all, it would seem silly if the woman had asked questions about a door they had already walked past. I found myself looking at Chuck in a different light. The more I was around him, the more impressed I became. On the other hand, Jade still didn't look like she believed his theory, and she muttered, "What are you, Watson now or something?"

Chuck smirked again when he replied, "I think you mean Sherlock, but I'll take either one as a compliment." He reached for the handle to give it a turn, or at least he tried to turn it. He sighed after a few more attempts, telling us, "It appears to be stuck."

"Oh, really? You don't say, *Sherlock*," Jade snapped back sarcastically.

Jade pushed Chuck aside so she could try to get the door open herself. She didn't try as long as he had before she started flailing her arms in front of her, saying a bit too loudly, "It's not stuck. It's locked."

Chuck shrugged slightly, asking, "What's the difference?"

Jade's face changed from one emotion to the next, starting with confusion, then annoyance, then something like bewilderment before finally settling on amusement. "What's the difference?" she asked sharply. "What do you mean, what's the difference?" Her voice now even louder than it had been before.

"Did you hear that?" a low voice could suddenly be heard asking from somewhere down the hall. I wasn't so sure it had come from the direction the people from before had went. Ultimately, though, where the sound came from wasn't the most crucial part. What was important, though, was that it was close, and it sounded curious.

A sense of panic washed over us, and immediately Jade and I were both attempting to open the door at the same time. This proved to be pointless as it didn't matter how many times we tried to turn a locked door handle. It wasn't going to just open. "We need to run," Jade hissed between her teeth.

"Or hide again in the closet?" I countered, and Jade's eyes became wide with an almost animalistic kind of fear at my suggestion.

"Move," Chuck demanded as he pulled something small, long, and black from his back pocket. I took a second look at it before realizing it was a bobby pin. That felt like a really weird thing for him to have. Without saying anything, Chuck knelt, took one quick look at the lock, and then shoved the bent bobby pin into the lock and began turning it in such a way I was sure it was moments away from snapping into pieces.

"I'm not sure. I'll take a look," said another voice. This time I was sure it was the same man who had been in the hallway moments before, and it was soon followed by the sounds of faint footsteps in the distance, a not very far off distance. Then, to my surprise, I heard a snap. No, not a snap, it was more like a click. My brain couldn't decide what that meant until Chuck jumped to his feet, whispering just loud enough for us to hear him in a very excited and proud tone, "I did it," and he opened the door.

Jade pushed us both forward and just a split second later she shut the door as quietly as she could.

We all stood there with our backs firmly against the door. Not a single one of us dared to move an inch as the sounds of the footsteps became closer and louder until they were right on the other side of the door. A panicked feeling coursed through me when I suddenly wondered if Jade had locked the door behind her. I let my hand slowly and silently make its way across the wooden door until it had reached the tiny turn-lock under the handle, and my heart began to beat so heavy in my ears that it had drowned out the footsteps. Unless they had stopped. Had they stopped? I felt frozen in debate. Do I turn the lock and risk it making a sound, or do I do nothing and risk someone trying to come in?

Much to my relief, before I could make up my mind, the voice that was so close it almost made me jump said, "Um, I don't see anything," before another voice that sounded like it was full of static replied, "Yeah, everything clear over here too. Probably just echo off the walls, but I'll keep an extra eye out anyway."

"Sounds good," the voice boomed behind us. "I'll go back and finish getting the cook settled in," the voice continued as it walked away. This felt bad. I had hoped the man in the hallway was the only one we had to worry about, but now there were at least two of them, maybe even more, and now they were on their guard.

Jade hesitated for a moment, listening to the door, before she swiftly made her way in front of Chuck, blocking him from moving away from the door. "Since when can you pick locks?" she asked in an accusatory tone.

Chuck shrugged before admitting, "Today, I guess. That was my first time."

Jade took a step back, looking rather taken aback, but she quickly shook it off and asked, "OK . . . but where did you learn how to do it?"

324

"Books," Chuck said as if that made everything clear.

"Right," Jade said, letting the word stretch out. I could tell Jade wanted to ask more about it, but instead, she started checking the room.

I thought Mr. Woodwick's office was a lot darker than it had been in the photo, but I soon realized that was probably because the blinds were shut. It made sense, but something about seeing the room in person was just so much different from looking at it in the photo, and not in a good way either. The photo was just that, a picture of a smiling ordinary-looking man. Granted, a probably dark, twisted, evil man, but still just an ordinary-looking man sitting in an expensive-looking office.

But something about being in the room, knowing what I knew, made it so weird and disturbing. I could almost feel the bad vibes coming from every inch of the room, threatening to engulf me at any moment. Every shadow seemed to be hiding some unseen threat that was waiting there for me to either turn my back on it or look away just long enough to grab me. The longer I looked around the room, the louder the voice in my head screamed at me to run away. That was until my eyes landed on the item we had come for.

Part of me, a very big part, thought it wouldn't be here, if I'm being honest, especially if it was important. But there it was, in the same exact place it had been in the photo. All the fears and worries I had experienced moments ago felt like they had just faded away. They were replaced with relief and maybe a bit of triumph that we had managed to find what we had been looking for.

"It's there," I said, pointing up at the bookshelf as I made my way around the large wooden desk in front of us. Jade and Chuck soon joined me.

Being so close to the once formally known gray circle, I saw it was something different. Yes, it was still gray and circle-shaped, that hadn't changed much, but now with a closer inspection, it looked like the whole thing had been carved out of a rough-looking gray stone. It almost looked like a thick bracelet, just a heavy stone one. No engravings or anything special about it at all. In fact, it was sort of boring, really.

"This seems too easy," Jade commented as she eyed the circle suspiciously, cutting off my thoughts. It made me wonder how long I had been standing there staring at the very dull-looking stone circle.

"True," I said, letting the words linger in my mouth before adding, "or maybe it's just not as important as we think it might be."

"Or he doesn't know it's important," Chuck corrected, clearly still having some hope we hadn't wasted our time.

"Maybe." I shrugged.

Chuck appeared to study the circle wordlessly for a little longer before tapping it lightly with one finger. "Um, what are you doing?" I asked curiously.

"Checking for booby traps," he replied matter-of-factly. Before Chuck could do anything else to test it, Jade reached past him and grabbed the circle from its place on the shelf and shoved it roughly into her front pocket.

"Stop being so paranoid," she told him before adding, "We should check out the rest of the place just in case there is anything else." Jade nodded in agreement with herself, a mischievous grin crossing her face.

Jade had a point. I doubted we would ever get the chance to look around again, and who knows what clues we might find if we took just a few minutes to take a peek. So I nodded in agreement, and we both started looking in drawers and behind books.

"Maybe we should just go," Chuck said in a pleading tone.

"Don't be such a worrywart," Jade told him as she

checked under a green vase. "You heard the guy. No one is allowed in here but Mr. Woodwick."

"Yeah, but what if he comes back," Chuck asked, his eyes darting at the door and then back to us.

"He just left, Chuck. He might be gone for hours. Now stop being a wuss and help us look." He hesitated for a moment before nodding, uncertain, then he started to peek under some papers on the desk.

"I just think this is a bad . . ." Chuck started to say, but stopped before he could finish the last word. He spun around sharply on his heels, eyes wide with fear, before continuing with a panicked whisper, "Did . . . did you hear that?"

Jade shoved a book back on the shelf and turned to face him. "I told you, Ch—" and even she stopped talking before she could finish speaking. This got my attention, and I found myself slowly turning to face the door to listen. There was a lot of talking far off, and the sounds of steps grew louder like they were approaching at a quickened pace. "Is the door locked?" Jade whispered. I found my eyes looking at the lock but couldn't remember if anyone had locked it or not.

Chuck must have known because he took a few small, silent steps forward, turned the lock with a gentle click, and then wedged the bobby pin he had used to pick the lock under it before moving back to us. "It is now," he whispered. Knowing that didn't make me feel any better when a voice called out, "Mr. Woodwick, you're back so soon?"

Followed by the very familiar sound of Mr. Woodwick's voice just feet away from the door replying, "Yes, I forgot something in my office."

We stared at each other in sudden panic, almost frozen in fear, none of us knowing what our next move would be. There was a sound of keys being taken out and then put into the lock, and then nothing.

"Is something wrong?" a voice asked from behind the door. There was a strange grunting sound followed by the sound of keys being forcefully shaken.

"Its . . . errrr . . . the key is stuck," Mr. Woodwick replied, sounding slightly exasperated. The bobby pin Chuck had put under the lock was holding pretty well, but I wasn't sure how long it would buy us.

Whatever fear had kept the three of us frozen there in place was replaced with just a hint of hope. "We need to get out of here," I whispered as I made my way quietly to the window.

"Or hide," Chuck whispered back, pointing to the desk.

"What if he sits down at his desk?" I asked, trying not to sound mean in how I said it. The expression on Chuck's face told me I hadn't been successful. The sound outside the door started getting louder as Mr. Woodwick and whoever was with him started to get agitated.

"She's right," Jade agreed as she came to join me at the window, and together we tried to get the blinds open. They were heavy, almost like they had been made out of thick slices of wood rather than flimsy plastic, and they made an unpleasant sound, like riffling a deck of cards gone wrong, when we raised them up. To my relief, I didn't think it was loud enough that anyone in the hallway heard over all the talking. We tried to open the window but quickly found it stuck. Chuck started to make his way over to help us, and as he did, he knocked into the desk, causing a small item to fall out and land on the floor with a loud thump. None of us dared move. The once loud talking from behind the door was silenced, replaced by an ominous quiet.

That's when it all started to fall apart when a voice asked, "Did you hear something in there?" followed by the sound of what was possibly a person using the full force of their body slamming against the door. I don't know how we did it, but the three of us summoned all the strength and willpower we could muster and somehow managed to push the window up just enough so that we could fit through it.

Jade was through it before I could blink, and she quickly reached back in, grabbing Chuck roughly by the collar of his shirt, and pulled him through the window with a surprised yelp. I wasn't sure if she was really strong or if she had one of those moments you hear about when a mother is somehow suddenly able to lift a car off their child. Either way, I didn't want to have a dislocated shoulder. So, I made sure I got myself through the window as soon as I could. As I was just about to make my hasty exit, I paused when something caught my eye. There, on the table in front of the window, was a file. There was nothing special about it, but at the same time, something deep inside my head told me it was so much more, and without debating it, I snatched it from its place before I could finish going through.

By the time we had hidden behind the hedges near the statues, we heard a loud bang come from behind us and then the voice shouting, "Who's in here? Come out, or I'll shoot." I heard Chuck breathe in a deep startled gasp. There was more silence before Mr. Woodwick's voice was heard again. It was so loud and clear I imagined that he had to be looking out the window, maybe even bending out of it, when he said to himself, "Hmm, I don't recall leaving this open." There was a pause, almost like he was expecting something to happen, and when it didn't, he said in a calm, almost humorous voice, "But then again, I did forget my phone, so maybe I'm just getting old!" And then to our surprise, he laughed.

"But sir, what about the sound?"

There was another pause before Mr. Woodwick told the man, "See that on the floor? It was probably just knocked off my desk by the wind." There was a bit more of a chuckle, and the man joined in this time. "Well then, I'm off again," Mr. Woodwick said, and his voice got quieter, so I assumed he was walking away. The last thing I heard him say was "Make sure this door is fixed before I get back, and, Frank, please shut that window."

Once I heard the sound of the window being shut, I let out a long breath. I hadn't realized that I had been holding my breath the whole time. I wanted to believe that we had gotten away with it, that Mr. Woodwick really did think he had left the window open, but something about his comment about the wind just didn't sit right with me. It took a long moment to figure out what it was until it hit me. There was no wind. There wasn't even so much as a breeze.

My stomach tightened, and I found myself holding my breath again as I clutched the stolen file to my chest. He knew someone had been there, he knew. And yet he didn't want Frank to know. With shaking hands, I lowered the file and laid it on top of my lap, only partly aware of Chuck asking me where I had gotten it and Jade praising me for snagging something. The voice felt miles away in my ears as I made my shaking hand open the file, and there, right in front of us, were pictures. Pictures of all three of us!

Chapter 32

Our ride back to Chuck's house was mostly in silence except for a few random sounds of panic when one of us got spooked thinking someone was following us, and then when the circle almost fell out of Jade's back pocket when she started peddling too hard. After that, she put it in the front pocket of her backpack for safe keeping. That had been Chuck's idea, but Jade tried to pretend she was already going to do it all along. If it hadn't been for the circumstances, I think I might have enjoyed the ride back. It wasn't too hot, and as we got closer to town, I started to feel a light cool sea breeze that might have made me think about all the good summer things if my mind wasn't constantly telling me I needed to look over my shoulder every time I heard a car coming from behind us.

The pace we traveled was chaotic at best, as every time we heard even a hint of noise, we would all start peddling as if our lives depended on it, and for all we knew, they did. I wasn't sure if it was the random pace or the sudden creepy realization someone had been watching us this whole time, taking photos, that made us so quiet. Maybe it was both.

It was a scary feeling knowing someone had been watching me and an even worse feeling that I couldn't tell anyone about it. The logical side of my brain told me I should tell someone. In fact, I should tell someone right away. It's not like anyone would believe me when I had proof of it, but my more cautious, paranoid side told me that would be a mistake. After all, we had just gotten locked in a basement, and there was no telling who was in Mr. Woodwick's pocket. It didn't seem too out there to assume he knew a lot of important people, like the police or maybe even the mayor. When I thought about telling my aunt and uncle, it stirred frightening thoughts in my head that made my stomach sour with anxiety.

If I showed them these files, how would they react? Would they storm down to the police station wanting to have Mr. Woodwick arrested, and if he had his hands in the police department, would they just turn around and arrest them instead, or worse? Then there was a worse thought, in order to prove it was Mr. Woodwick who had these photos taken, I'd have to admit to breaking into his house and stealing from him. Would that get me thrown into jail too? As I thought about it more, the realization struck me that all our actions today would cause nothing but harm if they ever surfaced. It made my stomach ache to the point that I started feeling nauseous. But even knowing all that, I knew I had to go on. I couldn't stop now in the quest to get the truth about everything. Cliffton and the other unicorns were counting on us. They were clearly in danger.

By the time we finally reached Chuck's house it felt like my mind was spinning around in a whirlpool, and it wasn't until a hand caught me by the arm that my brain seemed to snap back into reality and I realized that I was about to fall off my bike. "Are you all right?" Chuck asked, eyeing me with concern. I honestly wasn't sure if I was, but I forced myself to focus, and I nodded to him that I was. He smiled back at me as he released his grip on my arm, but I could tell by the look in his eyes that he didn't believe me.

"She's probably just hungry after all that riding," Jade said, sounding not the least bit concerned. "I know I am. In fact, I'm borderline hangry, so watch yourselves!"

she added with a wink. Jade wasn't entirely wrong, as it was now a lot closer to dinner than it was to lunch, and I hadn't had anything to eat since we left my aunt and uncle's house that morning.

"I could eat," I said, rubbing my stomach with a slight grin. "Shame we didn't bring any snacks with us." Jade's eyes widened slightly, and I was sure she glanced over at the backpack she had brought with her before turning back with a small sheepish expression on her face.

"Yeah, a real shame that," she said with a hint of embarrassment.

Chuck let out a small sigh before ushering us both toward the front door. "Well, let's go find you both something to eat before one of you passes out," and he looked solely at Jade before continuing, "or one of you murders us all." Jade smirked back in response.

It took Chuck almost five minutes before he finally gave up looking in the kitchen for snacks. He checked the refrigerator and freezer more than three times and the pantry and every cupboard he could reach before throwing his hands up in defeat and announcing, "I give up! We're all going to starve to death!"

"I thought your mom always kept you supplied on the snack front, Chuck?" Jade asked while leaning on the island in the middle of the kitchen, looking either bored or tired.

"She generally does," he snapped back, sounding almost defensive. I wasn't sure if he felt the need to defend his mom or if he was just really hungry.

"It's a real shame no one thought to bring any snacks today," I said again before shooting Jade a knowing smile. Chuck didn't seem to hear me because he started pacing nervously back and forth before checking the refrigerator once again. Yeah, he was definitely hungry. Jade seemed to think about it for a moment before she fake-smacked herself on the forehead, "Wait, you know what? I think I might have packed some in my bag." She lifted it from where it had been on the floor and let it drop on the counter with a loud thud.

Jade unzipped the top, and then began digging through it, trying to reach something at the bottom before ultimately giving up and dumping the entire thing on the counter instead. Chuck and I just stared in shock and wonder for a minute, eyeing the bounty—no, FEAST— before us. The bag must have been over halfway full with just snacks. There in front of me was a vast assortment of snack cakes, cookies, crackers, candies, and chocolate bars, as well as a few juice boxes and one large bottle of cola. There were also other things: a flashlight, duct tape, a cheap pair of green binoculars—the kind that came with those kid nature kits—wad after wad of trash, and a pocketknife.

There were a few other items, but I ignored them when I picked up the duct tape and knife, giving Jade a quizzical look. She shrugged at me while munching through a mouthful of cookies. As she spoke, crumbs cascaded out of her mouth. "What? You never know what's going to happen on an adventure." I wordlessly shrugged before placing the items down. I wasn't sure what someone needed on an adventure, but something told me it wasn't those. Then again, maybe duct tape could have been handy. My dad practically lived on the stuff. What he did with it was anyone's guess, but he did use it a lot.

"You had all this food the whole time?!" Chuck asked, sounding just a tiny bit annoyed. But before Jade could reply, I asked him, "So what do we think about the pictures we found in Mr. Woodwick's office?"

"The ones of us?" Chuck asked, seeming to have forgotten all about his question to Jade as he picked up a chocolate-frosted snack cake from the heap. Jade shot me a grateful look before shoving another cookie into her mouth. I nodded at Chuck before finally settling on a small bag of salt and vinegar chips for myself. It was one of my favorite snacks. Don't get me wrong; I loved sweets just as much as the next kid, but salty and savory were my go-to every time.

"Yep, the creepy stalker ones," I said as I opened the bag a bit too roughly, causing half the chips to explode onto the counter. We all giggled at the incident, but it didn't last as long as it should have.

A solemn feeling washed over all of us as we considered the seriousness of the photos. Without a word, we all went into Chuck's living room and sat down on the couch, Jade leaving a trail of crumbs in her wake. The kitchen was pretty much like any other kitchen I'd imagined people had in smaller towns, plain wooden cabinets with tiled counters and pale pastel walls, in Chuck's case, a minty blue green. The living room, however, was not at all what I had expected, well, mostly not what I had expected.

It undeniably had that homie country-style thing going on, with a big buttercup-yellow floral couch and a dark tan leather recliner. A sturdy-looking coffee table sat in front of the couch, a dainty-looking lace doily covering it, and two matching side tables next to it. Each one was topped with matching copper lamps and pale green accordion-style lamp shades. The whole room felt quaint and cozy. I could almost imagine myself sitting in front of the fireplace opposite the couch with a warm mug of hot chocolate and a soft blanket.

What I didn't expect was the massive TV above the fireplace, the enormous surround sound speakers in every corner, and no less than three different gaming systems along with a large antique-looking apple crate full of games.

Chuck shoved nearly the whole cake into his mouth in one bite, and when he realized he wasn't going to get the entire thing to fit, he swallowed hard, making room for the last little bit. It almost looked painful. After he had finished, he set to the task of opening the file and spilling the photos onto the coffee table, making sure we could fully see each one. The pictures ranged from all three of us together in town to a photo taken through my bedroom window, the angle, and the fact that there were no trees nearby that were that tall, told me it had to be taken by a drone. I quickly pointed out that fact to them both. Chuck eagerly agreed. Jade didn't seem so sure as she asked, "Wouldn't we have heard it? Aren't they, like, super loud?"

Chuck replied by telling her, "Not the new, more expensive ones, and I'm pretty sure Mr. Woodwick could afford a fleet of them if he wanted."

Once that was settled, we continued to look at the rest. There were a few with just Jade and Chuck. I assumed it must have been while I was at the house, and I couldn't help but feel a tinge of jealousy again that I had missed out. There were a few of us by ourselves, which included me mostly in my room or outside at the farm or Jade at her house or hanging at the arcade. There were a few of Chuck in his backyard, one of him in his bedroom, but most of them were taken at the library. Jade pointed at those with a sharp snort. I saw the hint of a word forming on her lips, a clear "ner" sound, but before she could add the "duh" to the end, she seemed to rethink it and shrugged instead. Either Chuck had missed the fact that his best friend was about to call him a nerd, or he had decided to ignore it. I was hoping for his sake it had been the former.

"Well, this is a little beyond unsettling," I admitted after the shock of seeing it again passed.

"I one hundred and one percent agree," Jade said as she rubbed at her chin thoughtfully, keeping her eyes fixed on one of the photos.

"But what do we even do with all this?" Chuck asked, motioning in a circular pattern down toward the photos.

Neither Jade nor I said anything. Chuck looked like he was irritated when he added, "What do we do? Go to the police, or what?" His tone at the end was almost a yell.

"Calm down before you hurt yourself," Jade said, placing both her hands out at him. This didn't seem to get the desired effect Jade was hoping for because instead of Chuck calming down, he looked twice as angry, but I figured it was more because of fear than actual true anger.

I didn't let Chuck say whatever he was about to say, which was probably a good idea on my part with how his face seemed to contort. "We can't go to the police," I said, and found both of them staring at me.

"Why not?" Chuck asked, followed closely by Jade asking, "Yeah, why not?"

"Well, clearly," I said, trying my best not to sound like I was talking down to either of them, "we don't know who we . . ." but before the last words could leave my lips, I felt my body freeze when I heard the sound of someone unlocking the front door.

The door began to open, but it didn't make it very far when it suddenly came to a halt, along with a loud metallic banging sound. Then I noticed the door had been locked with a hinged bar lock, just like the ones in some hotels. I hadn't even seen it until now, but I assumed Chuck must have locked it when we came in, and I was extremely grateful right now that he did.

"Chuck, sweetie, are you there?" came the voice of his mother through the small gap in the door.

"Yes, Mom," he replied nervously back.

"Um, sweetie, can you please come and unlatch the door? My arms are full of grocery bags right now." She paused, sounding almost out of breath before continuing in a much more hurried tone, "And they're heavy. Please hurry." Chuck quickly motioned for both of us to do something about the photos before his eyes darted to Jade's backpack with all the food spilled onto the counter, and he motioned at it, looking just as worried about the food as the photos. I wasn't sure what he was more worried his mother would see, the photos or all the sugary treats.

Chuck hurried off to the door, telling his mother he was coming. Jade managed to beat me to the punch when she started picking up the photos. I figured she went for them because it was a much easier job to scoop up a few handfuls of photos than it was going to be to shove all those things back into an already full backpack. I knew this wasn't the time to argue, so instead, I quickly made my way over to the counter and did my best to shove every single treat back into the place where it had come from. I'm not going to lie, I was pretty sure over half of them would now either be broken, squished, or turned into a pile of crumbs. I just hoped Jade wouldn't be too upset about it.

I had just managed to get the busting backpack halfway zipped up when Chuck's mother walked into the kitchen carrying four overfilled paper bags in her arms. She then lifted them with one long huff onto the countertop. She looked exhausted at best, and when she saw me, she looked more startled than anything. It took her only a moment to compose herself, though, and she smiled warmly at me, saying, "Oh, Jennifer, I didn't see you there. How are you?"

"I'm fine, thanks."

I was about to do the polite thing and ask how she was, but I was cut off by Jade walking into the room, the file tucked under her arm, asking a few degrees too loudly, "Hey, Mrs. Dunbar, how are you doing?"

Mrs. Dunbar looked like she was about to jump out

of her skin. Well, she did jump, actually, and she clutched one hand over her heart. Again it took only a few moments for her to regain that calm demeanor when she smiled and giggled slightly. "Jade, sweetheart, you almost gave me a heart attack."

Jade frowned. Well, it looked like a fake frown when she said, "Ah, sorry, Mrs. Dunbar." I really doubted she was.

Mrs. Dunbar smiled again, telling her in a reassuring tone, "Don't worry about it."

She paused as she began to unload one of the bags, then asked with a slightly suspicious tone, "So what brings you girls here?"

"Just riding our bikes around town," Jade said nonchalantly.

"Well, that sounds nice," she replied while taking a large jug of milk from one of the bags and putting it into the refrigerator. Mrs. Dunbar looked like she was about to ask another question but was cut off by Chuck who was struggling to bring in two more bags.

"I hope you got some snacks this time. We almost starved," Chuck said while he put the bag next to the others. Mrs. Dunbar looked just a tiny bit embarrassed but covered it pretty well with a warm smile and laugh.

"I'm so sorry, girls. I'll make sure I'm more prepared next time." Then she paused to wink at Jade and me before continuing, "I wouldn't want you to have to suffer around my son when he thinks he's starving."

Chuck glared in response, and both Jade and I had to stifle a laugh. Whatever tension had been present was evaporating until Chuck's mother suddenly commented, "Now, girls, it's getting pretty late. Do either of you need to call your parents"—she paused, then corrected herself—"or family members to pick you up?"

I couldn't help but notice that it was barely past lunchtime. Was that really late to Mrs. Dunbar? Jade replied first, telling her, "No, I got my bike. I'm good," which caused Mrs. Dunbar to turn all her attention solely to me.

Something about how she was staring at me made me feel unsettled for some reason, even cold inside, and when I said, "I'll go call my aunt right now," the first half came out in a nervous squeak. Mrs. Dunbar didn't say anything. She just smiled and turned back to unload another bag. "I'll just," I murmured before backing away into the den and heading to the phone to call my aunt. Jade came with me with a very confused expression on her face. I whispered to her, "Is that normal?" but all Jade did was shrug, looking unsure.

As soon as I was done talking to my aunt, Jade and I started to walk toward the kitchen, but we both stopped before we came into view when we heard Chuck's mother ask him, in a less than pleased tone, "Can you explain to me why you and your friends were rude to Mr. Kafer this morning.

"Who?" I mouthed to Jade, and she whispered back, "The butcher." I nodded, understanding now, but at the same time, I didn't understand how we had been rude. We never even talked to the man.

Chuck let out a long "Uh" sound before finally asking his mother, "We were?" He sounded just as confused as I was.

His mother tutted and then sounded just as unhappy as she had been before. "Now, Chuck, you know I don't like liars."

"I'm not lying, Mom!" Chuck argued back. His voice was now sounding a bit worried. There was a long pause before he asked, "How were we rude? We didn't even go to the butcher's. Why would we?"

This question must have stumped Mrs. Dunbar because there was hesitation and uncertainty when she replied, "Well, um, I'm not sure, but Mr. Kafer said he tried to give you a message for me about my order being ready, and he said you all ran off."

It all made sense now. I remember seeing the butcher staring at us that morning and coming out holding his knife. We had all ridden off as fast as we could, clearly paranoid he was out to get us. It seemed so silly now that I thought about it more, but then again, after being locked in a basement and now the photos, maybe it wasn't that silly after all. Chuck stammered a bit as if he was unsure how to reply. The butcher had called for us, and we had fled.

With one deep breath, I walked into the room. Until that moment, Mrs. Dunbar had been looking at Chuck, but now looked to me instead, and I tried to look embarrassed and sound just a bit sheepish when I told her, "I'm sorry. I overheard what was being said." Mrs. Dunbar frowned at me, looking cross that I had been eavesdropping. I continued, telling her, "It's my fault."

I paused to look down at my feet just long enough for the right effect before looking back at her, trying my best to have that I'm-trying-so-hard-not-to-cry face I had used a hundred times before, but only in really necessary situations. Like when I forgot to study for my test because I was watching TikTok, or when I forgot to write grandma a thank-you card because I didn't want to, you know, important reasons. "You see, I'm not the best at riding bikes, and I—" I swallowed before continuing. "—I sort of forgot how to stop, and Jade and Chuck were just trying to keep me safe."

I looked away for a moment again before looking back at Mrs. Dunbar. To my relief, the upset, sour face she had before had turned into one that was sympathetic and maybe even just a tiny bit sad. She reached both arms out to me before breaching the gap between us and giving me a tight hug. In a soft mothering tone I thought most mothers had, she said, "Oh, you poor dear! You must have been so scared, and here I just made it all worse by making you feel bad about the whole thing."

She hugged me a bit tighter, but when she released me from the hug, she reached down, cupped my hands between hers, and added with a warm smile, "Don't you worry about it anymore. No real harm was done."

It was weird and awkward, but I tried not to show how uncomfortable it made me feel and instead nodded timidly at her.

I caught sight of Chuck and Jade, who had managed to get over to him without me seeing. Chuck looked relieved, and Jade, well, she looked amused and maybe even a little impressed. When his mother didn't let go of my hand, I smiled at her, saying, "Well, my aunt said she won't be too long, so I better go outside and wait for her."

This, thankfully, made Mrs. Dunbar let me go, and she nodded, telling me, "Well, you tell her hello for me, and no more worrying about this morning."

"I won't," I promised before quickly snatching Jade's backpack from the counter and hurrying past her. Jade was quick to follow after we both mouthed, "Bye," to Chuck, and then we were out the door.

It wasn't until I'd reached the street with Jade that I managed to feel comfortable again. We both just stood there in silence for a long moment before Jade decided to ask, "That was weird to you too, right? I mean, it wasn't just me?" and Jade motioned back at the house, flailing both hands erratically at it like she was swatting away a fly. "That was creepy, right?"

I let out a long sigh of relief. I had been standing there all this time, desperately wanting to talk about it, but at the same time, I was afraid I would hurt someone's feelings if I did.

"I don't know Chuck's mother," I admitted. "But yeah, that was unquestionably intense. Is Mrs. Dunbar normally like that?"

Jade quickly shook her head, then stopped as if she had to think about it first before shaking it again, telling me, "Nah, I mean she's a bit what I would call overly protective of our boy Chucky." A small smirk crossed her face before adding, "But that was on a whole new level of odd."

I was just about to ask another question but stopped when I saw my aunt's truck turn the corner. "This is me, I guess," I said, motioning to the truck just as it parked in front of me. Jade nodded solemnly to me as she jumped onto her bike, letting both feet rest on the sidewalk under her. I was just about to open the truck door when I remembered I was still holding on to Jade's backpack. I turned back and handed it to her. "You probably want this back," I said with a slight grin.

She chuckled as she grabbed for it, but before I could get very far, she called out to me, "Jennifer, wait." When I looked back, she was trying to open the front zipper, and after a few attempts, she got it open. Reaching inside, she removed the stone circle as covertly as possible. She motioned for me to take it from under her turned hand.

I gave Jade a puzzled look as I tried to fit the circle in my back pocket as quickly as possible. It didn't quite fit, so I had to put it under the rim of the front of my shorts and pulled the front of my shirt over it. Jade hesitated for a moment before admitting, "I feel safer with you having it. I mean." She bit her lip then added, "After the photos, I'm just not up to being the guardian to whatever that is." I couldn't blame her, really. I didn't want it either, but maybe it was fitting that I took it. After all, it was probably my fault we were all in this mess anyway. Well, not probably; it most certainly was my fault.

Before I left, Jade made me promise that I wouldn't

go out to see the unicorns until she and Chuck could come over. I promised her, which I instantly regretted. The thought that I'd have to wait until tomorrow or maybe even longer was near painful, but I wasn't one to break a promise, so I knew I'd have to stick to my word. Who knew what Jade would do if I didn't.

I watched Jade in the rearview mirror for as long as I could see her. She had waited just a bit before peddling off toward her home. Besides the usual questions from my aunt, like "How was your day?" and "What did you get up to?" most of the drive was pretty quiet. I was thankful for that. I needed some time to think and reflect on what had happened not just today but since I had gotten here. What it all meant and how in the world I was going to get the three of us out of it without getting in a lot of trouble or worse. The last thought made me swallow hard. Here I thought the worst thing that could happen this summer was boredom. Oh, how I wish I had some boredom right now.

Chapter 33

As we drove up to the house, I noticed a car I'd never seen before parked out front. When I asked Aunt Tara whose it was, she shrugged at me, looking as dumbfounded as I was. The car had been parked right in front of the house, so I had to pass it as we walked by. There was nothing special about it. There was no license plate on the back, just a tag from a car dealership, so I assumed whoever owned it must have gotten it recently. Everything else seemed completely ordinary about it, even down to the black color, but the closer I got to the front door, the more something started nagging at me. I just couldn't put my finger on why.

It all became crystal clear when Aunt Tara and I walked into the entryway of the house to see Uncle James standing there talking to none other than Mr. Woodwick himself. Whatever conversation the two of them were having abruptly stopped when we walked in. Uncle James looked on the edge of annoyance, making me a bit worried I was now in trouble. The feeling only intensified with the smug, almost satisfied grin Mr. Woodwick gave me.

"And what brings you here, Mr. Woodwick?" my aunt asked without missing a beat.

Mr. Woodwick started to reply but was cut off by my uncle sternly telling her, "He was just leaving."

Mr. Woodwick gave my uncle some major side-eye before smirking again and replying in a very calm and cordial tone, "Right you are, Mr. Greenfell. I was just leaving." He paused for a moment, sniffing at the air before adding, "And it's a good time too. Smells like your dinner might be close to burning."

My aunt's eyes widened slightly in shock before she rushed toward the kitchen with a quick "Excuse me."

Mr. Woodwick smiled as he watched my aunt leave, tipping his hat slightly. "Certainly, Mrs. Greenfell," and then he fixed his gaze on me as he slowly made his way toward the door with his cane. His face grimaced ever so slightly as he got closer to the door, and for a fleeting moment, I felt like I was seeing him for who he really was. A very tired and weak old man. When Mr. Woodwick locked eyes with me, it was as if he realized he had let his guard down, and he quickly adjusted his composure and refined his manner, letting a smile return to his face.

As I watched him, I suddenly became aware of the circle hidden under my shirt, and I instinctively brought my arms up to cover my stomach. I thought he was going to reach for the screen door handle, but he stopped just short to look at me, the smile still there, but his eyes cold and distant. "You know, when I was your age, Miss Greenfell, I used to get into a lot of mischief as well." He paused, turning toward the doorway again. He stared ahead for a while, so long, in fact, I couldn't fight the urge to look out the door myself to see what he was staring at. There, of course, wasn't anything, and when I looked back at him, he was still looking out the screen door, but now he was smiling. This time it was a genuine smile. A smile that said so much without saying a word. It said, "I made you look."

Mr. Woodwick spoke again. This time his voice was low, low enough that I'm sure my uncle didn't even realize he spoke, because honestly if it hadn't been for the fact that I saw his lips move, I would probably have missed it. "But I made sure not to get caught." Then he glanced down at me just enough so that our eyes met, and he winked. There was something so unnerving about it, and all I could do was gulp in reply. I hated that I did because he saw my fear, and his smile got a lot bigger. Mr. Woodwick looked away, only saying, "Good afternoon to you both," before walking out and letting the screen door shut with a soft bang behind him.

I didn't bother watching him leave. I shut the door behind him as soon as the screen door closed. I took one steady breath before I turned around to face my uncle. I was sure now that Mr. Woodwick had come to tell my aunt and uncle what we had done. When I turned around, I let my eyes linger on the floor for just a few more moments. Part of me wanted to delay the inevitable as long as I could. The weird thing was when I looked up at my uncle, he wasn't giving me an angry or disappointed look at all. He looked tired and maybe even a bit lost in thought. The feeling of guilt started bubbling up in me.

"Well?" I asked him, waiting to get the punishment or yelling or both over as soon as possible.

Uncle James seemed to snap out of whatever he had been thinking about, and he looked genuinely perplexed when he asked, "Well, what?"

What did he mean "Well, what"? was the only thought that seemed to process in my head. So when I asked out loud, "Am I in trouble, or what?" I realized I hadn't fully thought that sentence out before asking it. I could have denied a whole lot if I hadn't just admitted that I knew I might be in trouble.

Uncle James looked pleasantly amused, like my question was so absurd it had made him forget all about his troubles. He half laughed when he asked, "I don't know, should you be?"

I had to recover from this one fast. The last thing I needed was to be questioned if I had, in fact, done something wrong. So I did what any good kid would do; I

351

lied. "Well when my dad has that look on his face, it's usually because I've done something wrong."

All my uncle did was smirk and shake his head. "Nah, not you, kid," and he hesitated as if debating how much to say before finally saying, "Just adult stuff. Now come on, let's go see if your aunt really did burn our dinner."

After my uncle and I sat down, Aunt Tara placed a large glass baking pan in the center of the table, saying proudly, "I don't know what that man was talking about. My eggplant parmesan is nowhere near being burnt." The only time I had ever heard of the dish was probably from a show or movie, and I was sure I had never seen the thing in my life. I mean, it looked all right, at least from the surface. There was cheese, that was good. Red sauce normally meant it was OK, and there was a large helping of some kind of green herb scattered along the top. That was neither good nor bad. What I couldn't see was any sign of that gross-looking purple thing from this morning, but I knew it was in there somewhere. It wasn't until my uncle scooped up a large circle-looking disk from one corner and plopped it down on my plate that I could see what part was eggplant.

I couldn't help but stare at it for a moment before poking it lightly with my fork. I wasn't sure why I poked it. It just felt like the right thing to do. Luckily neither of them took notice of my hesitation. My uncle was busy pouring himself a glass of what I hoped was lemonade, and Aunt Tara went over to grab, to my utter delight, a basket covered with a gingham cloth filled almost to the brim with garlic bread. At least I knew if the main dish was a bust, I could fill up on that.

Once my aunt had sat down with us, I couldn't help but feel like she was staring at me, waiting for me to take my first bite. I genuinely didn't want to. I had never done well with trying new foods, and I didn't even know if an eggplant was a fruit or a vegetable. It made it that much more terrifying. I didn't, however, want to hurt my aunt's feelings. It was clear from the dish that she had put a lot more effort into it than just ordering a pizza. So with a tiny hidden sigh, I cut off a piece of the mystery food and plopped it into my mouth. My first instinct was to just let the food stay there in my mouth, chewing would only make it worse, but after a few moments of it being there, I realized it didn't taste awful, just a saucy cheese taste. With some hesitation on my part, I managed to make myself chew on the mouthful. I didn't taste anything, but it was a bit mushy in texture, which wasn't my favorite texture, but it wasn't gag-worthy either. I made myself swallow down the bite and smiled at my aunt, trying to convey wordlessly that I liked it. She seemed pleased by the look on my face and went to eat her own food, finally ignoring me.

I'm not going to lie, it wasn't the worst thing I ever had, but it probably wasn't going to be something I'd ever ask for again. There would definitely be some left on my plate, probably a good third. I wanted to leave half, but that seemed too much. A third felt reasonable, I thought.

By the time my uncle and aunt had finished their food, I had almost finished two-thirds of my plate along with two pieces of garlic bread, or maybe it was three. Uncle James looked at me before his eyes went down to my plate, and then he looked back up again with a smirk, telling my aunt, "I told you she wasn't going to like eggplant."

I was quick, maybe a little too quick, to correct him by saying in a hasty voice, "No, no, no, it was delicious, honestly, it's just, I was . . ." I paused when I realized I didn't know what my excuse was. Eventually, my eyes landed on the still half-full basket of bread. "I'm just full," and I patted my stomach for effect.

My aunt smiled sweetly at me, saying with just a

hint of humor, "Well, I'm very glad you liked it so much, but I guess since you're so full, you don't have any room for dessert."

"Well, I, um," I said, stumbling over my own words before I managed to get out, "maybe full was a bit of an exaggeration," and I added a big smile at the end.

This caused both my uncle and aunt to break out in a fit of laughter. By the time my uncle seemed to regain some control, he had to wipe a few tears from his eyes. "Thanks, I really needed a good laugh today," he told me as my aunt gathered the dishes from the table.

I started to stand to help her, but she shooed me to sit back down. "Stay in your seat, sweetie. I'm about to grab my world-famous banoffee pie." I felt my whole face brighten to that. Every time my aunt had come to visit us in the past, she also made some banoffee pie, and it was one of my top favorite desserts. This was also a bad thing because I only ever got it when I saw my aunt. My parents had made a few attempts over the years, and let's just say it was never right. Banoffee goo, maybe, or Banoffee burnt caramel disaster would have been more fitting names for what they had made.

Aunt Tara mainly looked happy, but once she placed all the plates down in front of us, with very large caramel-drizzled slices of pie, her face took on a more serious expression before she turned in her seat and asked my uncle, "So what did Mr. Woodwick want?"

Uncle James shoved a mouthful of his pie into his mouth and chewed it a lot slower than he needed to, almost like he was buying himself some time, before he answered, "Just the normal stuff." Then he shoved another mouthful in.

Aunt Tara sighed deeply. "Oh, that again" was the only thing she said before taking a small bite herself.

I had already managed to eat a good half of my own pie during this, and I had to force down the large mouthful in my mouth a bit too roughly, which nearly caused me to choke in the process. "A little subtext would be nice," I said, trying to sound like it was a joke.

Uncle James looked up from his plate only long enough to give me a half smile before looking away, saying, "It's complicated adult stuff, nothing you'd want to hear about." I let my eyes stay locked on my uncle for a good half minute, and he must have felt it because when he looked back up at me, he grimaced slightly. I guess he knew I wasn't going to let it drop because he said after a very long drawn-out, over-the-top sigh, "He's been trying to get me, well us, to sell this farm for a long time now, and the longer we have said no, the more he makes our lives, well—" He paused. "—complicated."

My aunt snorted at my uncle and muttered the last word under her breath. "Complicated how?" I asked, and I could tell right away that my uncle had regretted his choice of words.

Uncle James sat there for a long moment, and I could practically see the gears working inside his head. I wasn't sure if he was trying to think of the best way to backtrack his last statement or if he was doing that adult thing where they try to tell you the truth but sugarcoat it so much that it's not even close. So, when my aunt cleared her throat to get his attention and not me, I was a bit surprised. He looked over at my aunt before looking at me with a clearly fake smile and said, shrugging, "Well, I mean, you know, it's just complicated."

"Yeah," I said in my favorite sarcastic tone, letting the word stretch out longer than necessary before finishing with, "I think we got that part."

My uncle snorted in response, putting both his hands up in front of him defensively. "Fine, fine," he said with a half laugh in his voice. "You're evidently too smart for that trick to work." I found myself smiling, feeling just a bit triumphant, but the smile faded when Uncle James didn't follow up with what was going on. He let out a long, defeated sigh and nodded solemnly. "Fine. You're clearly not going to let this one go, are you, kid?"

I shook my head in agreement, ignoring the kid comment, which got another sigh from my uncle.

"The first time that Mr. Woodwick came around and offered quite a lot of money for our land, we turned him down. Afterward, a lot of weird stuff started happening."

Before he could utter another word, my aunt cut him off by clarifying, "Not that we can prove any of this as being caused by Mr. Woodwick." A look in her eye implied that my uncle shouldn't cast any blame on the older man unless he had proof.

Uncle James rolled his eyes. "Right, sure, what your aunt said," he muttered, his voice laced with annoyance. "Anyway, right after that, the bank wouldn't give me a loan we had been approved for days before, claiming the paperwork had 'been lost,' and we would have to start the process over again. Then we suddenly didn't get approved at all. Some of the feed stores started charging a lot more, and when I asked others about the price increase, no one else appeared to have been affected by it but us." My uncle paused thoughtfully as if he was trying to remember more things.

My aunt raised her hand, counting on her fingers, and simply added, "Deliveries were delayed, mail took longer or just vanished. Power and water got cut off even when we had paid the bill. Then we started getting weird looks from people we used to think of as friends." She let out a long sigh. "I'm sure there's more, but to be honest, I've tried to ignore it as much as I can."

She gave my uncle a weak smile, and he reached across the table to take her hand, giving it a reassuring squeeze. She laughed. It wasn't a happy laugh by any means. It was an almost hopeless one. "Truly, I thought I was losing my mind at one point." There was just a hint of a tear building in her eye, and I saw my uncle squeeze her hand just a bit tighter.

I couldn't help but feel sorry for them both, and I felt for the first time that I was truly seeing them or at least seeing things I hadn't before. They looked more tired than they had. It was in their eyes. Almost a pleading hopelessness that I hadn't seen there before, and it made me wonder if it had always been there. Somehow just admitting all this to someone had made it appear. "So, how's the pie, sweetie?" my aunt asked, replacing the sadness that had been there with a smile.

I knew it wasn't a real smile, but she seemed to be trying her best to make me think it was, so I did my best to pretend as well. After all, I didn't want to add to her sadness by making her feel like she made her niece worried or upset with whatever list of things she was already dealing with. I took one big bite before telling her, "It's the best one yet." This made her smile look a bit more genuine, I thought. The pie was good, but something about everything I had just heard made it less enjoyable, and it felt more like a chore with each bite I took.

Placing the fork down on the plate next to a half-eaten piece of pie, I asked them both, "Would it be all right if I invite Jade and Chuck over to spend the night again?"

My aunt looked very doubtful about it, and she seemed to look over to my uncle for some indication that he felt the same before she could say no, but instead of a look of agreement, he looked bizarrely happy. If I had to put words to the expression on his face, I'd have to call it a happy, pained look. The force he was using to smile back at her, with most of his teeth showing, and the shrug he gave that went so high I was sure his shoulders were aiming to reach his ears. "Maybe we should let her after all we just unloaded on her?"

That probably was not what he was thinking, but soon my aunt sighed and nodded, saying with a hint of dismay, "Sure, as long as it's all right with their parents." I uttered a quick thanks and darted to the den to make my calls.

I called Jade first, and she was the easiest one. It took no longer than ten seconds for her to ask her dad and get a yes. We spoke on the phone for a few minutes after that, as she wasn't sure if Chuck's mom would agree to a sleepover, with the weird way she'd acted earlier. She convinced me to let her call Chuck first, and then, when she thought enough time had passed since she'd spoken to him, she would give me the go-ahead to call him myself. Something about preparing him to know what to say to his mother in case she was resistant to the idea, and how she had been a bit rude to me and made me cry.

So sure enough, after Jade called me to let me know it was time, I called Chuck myself. As expected, after I heard him repeat my question about a sleepover, I heard his mother's voice firmly say no. Then there was the muffled noise of a hushed conversation that I couldn't make out before Chuck got back on the line and said cheerfully, "Yeah I'll be right over after we pick up Jade." I had to hand it to Jade again, she was clever. Maybe a bit manipulative but definitely clever. I liked that about her.

Less than an hour later, Chuck and Jade were standing on the front porch. Mrs. Dunbar didn't get out of the car like she had the last time. Instead, she gave a brief, half-hearted wave from the window and hastily made her exit. "That's strange," Aunt Tara whispered to me so the others couldn't hear her comment. "I wonder why she didn't come to say hello."

I shrugged, trying to pretend like I was as lost as she was, even though I was sure it had to do with not wanting to make me upset again. "I don't know. Maybe she needed to be somewhere else?" I said. Aunt Tara pondered that for a moment before nodding in agreement. It appeared that my reason sounded logical to my aunt. Whatever it was about Mrs. Dunbar not getting out of the car seemed to be forgotten as quickly as it came, and she ushered us all to go inside with a cheerful smile and a wave of her hands toward the door.

We made a hasty beeline for the stairs, leaving my aunt standing next to the door staring at us with curious amusement, but just as we were about to round the corner at the top of the stairs, she called out, "Do you kids want a snack?" Jade and I didn't bother stopping. We had way too many things to talk about and figure out. Chuck, on the other hand, stopped in his tracks, and by the time we realized he wasn't following us, it was too late.

He stuck his head back down the stairs and told my aunt in a breathless voice, "Yeah, lots of them."

"What kind?" she asked. Even though I couldn't see her face, I knew she was smiling by the tone of her voice.

"Well, do you have any—" Before he finished what he was saying, Jade managed to yank him out of view, and we both started pulling him down the hall. The whole time he attempted in vain to halt our process while whining, "Hey, I didn't get to tell her what I wanted!"

It didn't take long for Aunt Tara to bring up a large tray with three glasses of milk and a wide variety of treats. Several different cookies, some brownies, a plate of fruit, and even a couple of slices of pies. I think it was a bit overboard, but I assumed, since we hadn't let Chuck finish saying what he wanted, she felt it was best to get a bit of everything. Until my aunt had brought the treats, Chuck had done a fair portion of whining about how hungry he was, but once he saw all the food on the tray, his attitude did a full one-eighty.

We hadn't bothered talking too much until my aunt brought the snacks, mainly because we didn't want to risk being overheard at just the wrong time. So as soon as my aunt left the room and we were all sure she had left the area, Jade sat down heavily on my bed, holding a giant chocolate chip cookie, took a large bite, and after swallowing it down, looked at both of us with a lopsided smile. "So, what's our plan now?"

Chuck and I both glanced at each other. His face mirrored mine, or at least how I thought mine looked. A look that hoped the other person had an idea, only to be replaced by disappointment when we both realized that neither of us did.

We didn't have to say a word, and Jade clearly got the hint because she let out a long, annoyed sigh before falling backward onto my bed. "You guys are so useless sometimes," she muttered.

"So, you have a plan, then?" I asked, partly hopefully but mostly sarcastically.

Jade lifted her head up just enough to look at me, and there was not even a hint of irony on her face when she said, "No, why?"

I couldn't help but smile about the fact that she had just thought we were useless when she herself didn't even have a plan. The bewildered expression on her face made me realize that it hadn't dawned on her, so I said, "Pot calling the kettle black much?"

This made her sit up, and she stared at me, even more confused. "Who said anything about cooking?"

All I could do after that was stare at her. No words were forming in my head, let alone making it out of my mouth. So when Chuck told her, "She's saying that it's sort of stupid you called us useless when you are clearly just as useless as we are!" I felt my face fall, and my eyes quickly darted back and forth between the two of them.

Was Jade going to be mad at him for saying it or me for thinking it? Jade just stared at the both of us for a long moment. The longer she looked at us with her expressionless face, the more worried I got, and even without looking at Chuck, I could swear I heard his heart racing in his chest. Then a smile crept onto her face, and she snorted back a laugh. "All right, you got a point." I could feel the both of us relaxing. "When are we going out to see the horses and give them their key thing?" Jade asked, looking rather eager.

As much as I wanted to go out to see them with everything that we had done that day including managing to get the very item they felt they needed, I knew there was no way we could. "There's no way we can get out the door while my aunt and uncle are still downstairs," I told her.

"Why can't we just ask to go out and see them?" Chuck asked as if it was a simple solution, and really it should have been.

"And what if I ask and they say no?" I asked. Chuck shrugged, evidently missing the point I was trying to make. "Then I, well, we would get in trouble if we got caught sneaking out there."

"Ohhh" was the only thing he said in reply, but the expression on his face told me he understood the importance of it.

"We just don't get caught, then," Jade said with a smirk before sinking her teeth into the cookie for another big bite.

"Easier said than done, and besides, I'd rather get caught being out there without asking first than being caught when I was told no." Jade shrugged and gave a roll of her eyes. I wasn't sure why she didn't see the difference, or maybe she did but just didn't want to admit I was right.

I wasn't sure how much time had passed with us just sitting there thinking about a plan and never actually coming up with one. A couple of times Chuck had acted like he was just about to say something, even going so far as to put one finger up in front of his face like he had an aha moment, only to shake his head and slump back to think some more. He was probably the closest to figuring out a plan than any of us. Jade seemed more concerned with eating cookies and staring at the ceiling. While I just kept thinking of how I was going to get myself in so much trouble. I'd be grounded for life.

So when a knock came at my bedroom door, I'm pretty sure it caught all of us by surprise. I hadn't even had a chance to tell the person to come in when my aunt poked her head in and took a look around the room. She looked a bit confused, probably from the way we all seemed to be apart, looking either deep in thought or just spaced out as Jade looked. She probably thought we either had a disagreement or were completely out of our minds, but she shook off the desire to ask which one it was before telling us, "I'm going to be out in the field helping your uncle, and I'm not entirely sure how long we will be."

She smiled at us, but I could tell something was wrong, so of course, I had to ask, "Is everything all right?" I glanced at the window before adding, "You don't normally go out this late." It wouldn't be much longer before it started getting dark outside, and I hadn't recalled any time since I had been here when they went out at sundown.

I could tell she was in a rush to get outside by the expression on her face, and she hesitated before finally telling me, "Part of Maurice's enclosure seems to have been"—she paused before adding—"broken or, or damaged. I'm not sure yet until I see it. But I need to go help your uncle fix it before he gets wise and tries to break out." I just nodded that I understood, and that seemed to be good enough for her because without another word, she shut the door behind her and hurried off pretty fast.

When I turned back around, Jade was already on

her feet, standing right next to Chuck, a smile on her lips soon followed by one from Chuck. "What?" I asked, feeling like I was the last person in the room to get the joke. She glanced at Chuck just for a second before looking back at me, her smile growing bigger.

"If that's not a perfect distraction for us to sneak out to see some unicorns, then I don't know what is." I felt the corner of my lips go up too. She was right. It was now or maybe never.

Chapter 34

It was already starting to get dark before we reached the stable doors. I had a bit of regret that I hadn't thought to bring a flashlight with us. If we took too long, it would be challenging to get back to the house without tripping on something or even, with my luck, being bitten by a snake. So before Jade could open the door, I told them both, "Let's make this as quick as we can before we lose all the light."

Jade looked amused and asked in a teasing voice, "What, are you scared of the dark or something?" She followed it up with a smirk.

I knew this wasn't the time or place to defend whether I was scared of the dark or not. I mean, really, if I thought about it enough, I probably was to a degree, but still, that wasn't the point. "Well, if you want to step on a poisonous snake or something sharp going back to the house, and you want to have to explain to my aunt and uncle why we were outside, then by all means, let's make this take as long as possible."

Jade considered this, but before she could come up with a reply or witty remark, Chuck pushed past her and opened the door, saying, "I am scared of the dark, and if you have a problem with that, then we can talk about it later. We've got a job to do." Jade and I exchanged quick glances before nodding and following in after him.

I couldn't help but smile when I saw Cliffton, and I know it was odd with him not having facial expressions, but I wanted to believe that he was smiling at me too, or maybe even a bit hopeful at seeing us. I was just about to reach into my back pocket to get the stone circle when the sound of someone tutting from the other side of the stable made my hand freeze halfway there. The three of us spun around toward where the sound was coming from, but all I could see was darkness. Where I had been able to see the unicorns fairly clearly after coming in, all I saw on that side now was pitch-blackness. It was almost like the entire side of the stable had been consumed by the darkness.

The sound continued, and it was then that I noticed that the darkness appeared to be shrinking inward on itself until it finally revealed Mr. Woodwick holding a strange wooden walking stick. Its tip glowed faintly as the rest of the darkness swirled inward as though being sucked inside it. He began moving toward us shaking his head and tutting again.

Neither of us appeared to have the courage to utter a word as Mr. Woodwick slowly closed the space between us. That was until all three of the unicorns began neighing and bucking wildly into the air. That was enough for me to reach one hand out protectively, demanding, "Stay back, you old weirdo." Mr. Woodwick eyed me cautiously for a moment, almost like he was expecting something to happen, but when nothing did, he laughed. It was more to himself than at me, I thought.

He shook his head and muttered under his breath, "She's just a child." Then he looked back at us with that caring grandparent look. Leaning on the staff to support his weight, he spoke. His words didn't hold any anger or irritation at all as I expected there to be. Instead, he sounded grateful. "I really must thank the three of you. You managed to do something in weeks that I've been trying to figure out for—" He paused as if the words had escaped him before shaking his head with another charming smile and continuing, "Well, let's just say a very long time, and to think it was right under my nose for so long."

He shook his head again as if it had been so ridiculous that he hadn't figured it all out before this. "I hate to interrupt your evil mastermind monologue and everything, but we have no idea what you're talking about," I told him before firmly crossing my arms over my chest.

Mr. Woodwick frowned, but only for a moment before he pointed his finger at me and cocked his head slightly, waving his finger, his voice almost a laugh. "You almost had me there for a moment, but we both know that you know what I'm talking about. Let's just skip these childish games, and hand over what you took from me."

He turned his hand over and looked at us all expectedly. "Maybe you should think about a care home or something," Jade told him, sounding completely bored. Mr. Woodwick just stared ahead, still holding that same smile, but it faltered just slightly.

"Yeah," Chuck agreed, "there's nothing to be ashamed about, Mr. Woodwick. My gran's in a care home too. Maybe you two could be friends." Mr. Woodwick's eyes darted back and forth between the two of them before settling on me. His smile seemed more forced now, and when I said nothing tightened my arms a bit more to my chest, the finger of his outstretched hand curled in, and his hand fell limply to his side.

Mr. Woodwick looked away for a moment. He appeared almost remorseful with whatever thoughts he was battling inside. I was sure his dark intention was winning out because when he looked back at us, all traces of the charismatic, happy man that had been there before had been replaced with something dark, angry, and determined. "I honestly didn't want it to come to this again, but like so many times before, foolish common people like yourselves seem to think you have the right to get in the way of power." He paused and looked at Cliffton, a smirk tugging at one corner of his lips. "You truly only have yourselves to blame for this."

I placed both hands down by my sides and balled them into fists. Chuck and Jade were quick to follow my lead. "We won't let you hurt them," I shouted, trying to convince myself as much as I was trying to convince him.

Mr. Woodwick tutted again, his voice going cold when he said, "I would be more concerned with yourselves right now if I were you." He paused for a moment as if he was giving his words time to sink in, and they did because a sudden sense of panic washed over me like a wave, and based on the gleefully sinister expression that was radiating now from Mr. Woodwick, he could sense it too. He continued by saying in an almost taunting way, "But don't worry, you won't remember any of this by the time I'm done with you." He quickly rose his staff in one swift motion toward us.

I didn't even have time to think about dodging before a bright light shot from the end and came speeding right toward me. I shut my eyes instinctively as it seemed to be the only thing my body was able to do. I mean, moving out of the way would have been nice, but my body didn't seem to get the signal from my brain like I wished it had. I expected to feel pain of some kind, but when none came, I decided to open just one eye to see what was going on. There, hovering in front of me, was a glowing orb of light only an inch or two from my face. Mr. Woodwick still had his staff pointed toward me, but he looked strained somehow like he was using all his strength to try to will the orb to hit me. "Damn you unicorns," he grunted between gritted teeth.

When I looked at the unicorns, they were flanking us on both sides, still in their stables. I saw that all three of their horns were showing, and not just that. There was a bright blue glow coming from them that surrounded the three of us. It felt almost warm and oddly safe, considering the situation. When I quickly glanced at Jade and Chuck, they appeared to be just as amazed as I was. That was until Eloise said, in a voice that sounded as strained and breathless as Mr. Woodwick looked, "Please move. We can't hold it back much longer." She didn't have to tell us twice as Jade leaped toward Thor's stall while Chuck and I leaped toward Cliffton's. The impact of my body hitting the wooden door with a loud thud sent an ache through my body.

The exact moment we got out of the way, the glow vanished, allowing the glowing orb to hurtle toward the wall. It didn't seem to do anything to it. Then again, I wasn't exactly sure what it was meant to do. I also wasn't sure if we had managed to move out of the way just in time or if they removed the barrier once we were out of the way. Something told me it was the former with the way all three of the unicorns' heads drooped down, looking drained.

There wasn't any time to ask when Jade screamed for us to watch out. I didn't even look. I ducked, and just in time too because another glowing orb smacked right above my head, vanishing into Cliffton's stable door. "Scatter!" Chuck yelled, sounding just as frightened as I was feeling. I found myself looking around, feeling very much scared and panicked as I had no idea where I was meant to go, and that was when our eyes met. Mr. Woodwick was staring right at me in a way that made my whole body freeze up, and the more my eyes darted around looking for a place to hide or run to, the more I felt like a trapped mouse stuck in the corner.

He lifted his staff again, a smile so wicked as if he was taking triumph in a fight that he knew he was about to win. But before he could send another orb my way, I felt a hand clasp me around the arm, and with one hard yank, it pulled me toward the empty stall that was next to Thor's. It was Jade's hand, and even though her eyes looked full of fear, her face told a different story. She looked brave, I thought. The three of us barely managed to get the door shut behind us and duck down before a barrage of orbs flew above our head, hitting nothing but the wall.

Then there was a laugh. It started small and soft at first before it grew into something much louder and darker than anything I thought I had ever heard. "Foolish, foolish children." The voice sounded a bit like Mr. Woodwick's, but something about it now sounded off as it echoed around us. "Thinking you can hide from me in such a ridiculous place." There was another laugh. Something must have happened because I heard Mr. Woodwick wince. Had one of the unicorns attacked him? It was the only thing that made sense because it was soon followed by three loud painful whinnies, and when the three of us stole a quick look over the top of the door, I saw all three of them surrounded by a glowing red force field. The whinnies continued, so I knew whatever he was doing to them was painful and keeping them from helping us anymore.

"Now, now," Mr. Woodwick spoke softly as if he was trying to calm them, "I'll be dealing with you three soon enough, but first—" He turned in our direction, causing all three of us to sink back down behind the door. "—I have other business to handle."

"This was not the best place to hide," Chuck said in a hushed, hurried whisper as he shot Jade a look.

"Well, I didn't see you coming up with a better solution, did you, Chucky?" she whispered back, sounding just as accusatory as Chuck had.

"We need to find something to help us," I whispered back, trying to break up what might have been the last fight that the two of them ever have.

Jade picked up a handful of hay and let it fall out

of her fingers. "What, like throw this at him?" and then she snorted sarcastically at me, adding, "Unless Mr. Wickedwood has hay fever, I don't think we got much to use for weapons."

"Better than hiding someplace without any exit," Chuck snapped back in less of a whisper.

There was the sound of Mr. Woodwick tutting before he finally spoke again. "Now that you children can see you have no escape, I'll go easy on you if you just come out now. Because if you make me come to you, I won't be so generous." There was a sharp edge on the last word. This was enough to stop our bickering, replaced by Chuck breathing so heavily I was sure he was about to have a panic attack, and to my surprise, Jade buried her head in her knees, looking like she was trying to stop herself from crying. Her whole body shivered like she was cold, but I knew she was just scared. I was sure I was about to join them, that was until something leaning on the wall next to Chuck caught my eye.

It was round and about the size of a dinner plate, and after I picked it up and looked at the other side, I saw the murky reflection of myself looking back. It was a very old, dusty, slightly cracked mirror, but still a mirror. I gave it one big wipe, which made it a lot easier to see myself.

The tutting happened again, and Mr. Woodwick's voice called out, "I'm getting bored, come out now or what happens next is all your fault."

I took in a deep breath to calm my nerves. I was about to do something either very clever or very, very, very stupid. "Come and get me, you old crone!" I yelled at the top of my lungs. This surprised both Chuck and Jade enough to bring them out of their fear, and they both looked at me with shared disbelief. Mr. Woodwick started going into some rant about how much pain I was going to be in, but honestly, I wasn't listening too much, and when

I started to get up, both Jade and Chuck grabbed me by the arms and pulled me back down. They both shook their heads at me, pleading with me not to go. "Trust me," I told them in a whisper, trying to sound as brave as I could, and I had to admit I did hide it pretty well despite the fact I was feeling the complete opposite. They both hesitated for a moment, but it was Chuck who let go first with a small nod. Jade held on a bit longer, but after I smiled at her, she did the same.

Mr. Woodwick was still ranting when I stood up to face him. He must not have expected me to do that because he stopped midsentence and just stared at me with a mix of confusion and delight, but before he could say a word, I yelled, "Come get me, you old sack of bones." His face snarled into one of pure hate and rage, and he lifted his staff at me again. An orb of light, which I was sure was bigger than all the others, came hurtling at me, and then everything seemed to slow down. I, too, was going slowly, but my brain was going fast, and it was enough for me to lift the mirror I was holding to just the right spot where the orb would have hit me, and the closer the orb got, the more the expression on Mr. Woodwick's face began to change. From one basking in complete victory and then, just like everything else, slowly changing into one of utter disbelief. The moment the orb hit the mirror, it went right back toward him. I could just tell that Mr. Woodwick was trying to move out of the way, but he was just an inch or two short of being able to miss the orb, and when it hit the side of his shoulder, everything sped back up, and Mr. Woodwick went falling to the ground in a heap of tangled limbs.

As soon as Mr. Woodwick hit the ground, the red force field that had been trapping the unicorns vanished, and they all looked like they relaxed, but only a bit. "Well, that was just several shades of unpleasant," Eloise said before snapping her head back sharply like she was trying to fix her mane.

From behind Thor's door, I heard him groan slightly before panicking, yelling, "I think I shrank, that old monster shrank me!" There was a pause before he clarified, "Wait, no, everything is fine, my bad."

Cliffton laughed. It sounded like it hurt a lot by the way he winced after, but it sounded relieved as well. "I can't believe you did that," he said, looking at me, "and it worked as well. That was really something."

"Thanks," I told him, feeling my cheeks redden slightly, and I nearly jumped when one hand was placed on my shoulder.

"I mean, if I had seen the mirror first, I totally would have thought to do the same," Jade said, giving me a playful wink.

"Sure you would have," Chuck added with a smirk. When Jade didn't get upset or say anything sarcastic or mean back, I was a little more than relieved. After all that had just happened, the last thing I wanted to deal with was more bickering.

"Why were you guys out here so late, anyway?" Cliffton asked, tilting his head to study me.

"Oh right," Chuck said, with Jade quickly adding, "Hurry up and give it to him before something else bad happens." She looked over at Mr. Woodwick like she was making sure he wasn't going to get up and attack us again. With a smile, I grabbed the circle from my back pocket and held it out for him to see.

Cliffton's eyes widened in surprise, and he kept looking back and forth between the stone circle and our faces before saying in a shaking, nervous voice, "You . . . you found it. You really found it!" This was followed by all three of the unicorns bucking excitedly into the air and neighing so loudly I was sure my aunt and uncle were going to hear them.

"Shh! Shh! We don't need my aunt and uncle

coming out here finding us with an unconscious Mr. Woodwick on the ground," I told them. They quickly quieted down, but I could see they were still busting with excitement.

Cliffton lowered his head toward me so that his horn was just in reach. At first, I wasn't sure what he was doing, but after he cleared his throat in a come-on-let's-get-a-move-on type of way, I realized he wanted me to place the circle on his horn. I wasn't sure if it would fit, but as I pushed the circle down, it began to get bigger somehow and, to my complete surprise, became warm to the touch. Cliffton raised his head slightly, so I let the circle go, letting it slide the rest of the way down the horn, and for a moment, I was worried it might break when it hit his head. Thankfully it didn't. In fact, it started to glow. The glow grew brighter and brighter to the point it was very near blinding, forcing the three of us to look away, shielding our eyes with our hands and, in Chuck's case, both his arms. When I looked back, the once gray stone-looking circle had become an intricately designed silver band that briefly shimmered.

All three of the unicorns became alert as if they could sense something outside. Cliffton looked back at me, an almost sorrowful look in his eyes. "I'm sorry, I don't have more time to explain," he said, his voice matching the look he was giving me now perfectly. "But we have to go, and we need to do it fast."

"Wait, what?" I asked, taking one step back, not quite understanding what he meant. "Go where?"

Cliffton sighed as his eyes glanced nervously at the stable doors. "Home."

"But, but," I said, choking on my own words, a steady stream of warm tears starting to flood down my cheeks, forcing me to admit something I hadn't realized until now. "But I'll miss you if you go." I lowered my head, looking at my feet until I felt something warm touching my forehead. Glancing back up, I saw Cliffton was placing his head right against mine. His eyes were closed.

He whispered to me, "I'll miss you too." Then his eyes opened to look into mine when he said, "I can never thank you enough for what you've done for us. I hope that can be enough for you."

"Will . . . will I ever see you again?" I asked between small sobs. I had imagined he was going to say yes, of course, so when he shook his head, I felt my heart sink. Then I heard a noise coming from outside the stables. Whatever the unicorns had heard before was now close enough for me to hear.

"Go!" I told him more firmly than I had wanted, and I knew it made me sound angry, but part of me was hurting too much to care. It made me remember how I had acted when my parents had left and that was the last thing I wanted if we were really never going to see each other again. So before he could go, I wrapped my arms around his neck and gave him a tight hug. "I love you," I said, and then I let him go.

The circle around Cliffton's horn began to glow before it began to spread up to the tip of his horn. Looking briefly after the others, I saw their horns were starting to glow as well. They bowed their heads down at us, looking grateful. There was one big flare of light that was so big and bright it flooded the whole stable. There was an inrush of air, and when the light vanished, I looked back to where Cliffton had been standing and he was gone.

I wanted to cry more, but that feeling was soon pushed aside by the sound of the stable door flying open so hard it banged against the wall with a crash. My aunt then called cautiously into the stable, "Is someone in there?" None of us even had a chance to reply because as soon as the words had left her mouth, my uncle pushed in past her holding what appeared to be a large metal pipe. He held it up in front of him like a baseball player at bat.

His head searched the area, and when he saw us, his eyes widened in shock, though I was sure we probably looked just as surprised as he did. "What are you doing out here?" he asked, but again, before anyone could say a word in reply, he asked in a panicked voice, "And where are my horses?" It wasn't like I could say they went home in a blinding magical light. I mean, he would probably think I let them out myself.

I stood there trying to think of a good reason but was only able to get out, "Well, they were— And we— Well, I um, it's just that—" My uncle tilted his head and looked at me like I was speaking a foreign language.

Jade took a step in front of me, sparing me from making a bigger fool of myself, and she pointed down accusingly at Mr. Woodwick and said coldly, "You should ask him that." My uncle's eyes followed where Jade had pointed, and when he saw Mr. Woodwick lying there, his face twisted in a combination of surprise, confusion, and irritation.

"Why the heck is Mr. Woodwick lying unconscious on my stable floor?" The way he said it and the way he looked back at us implied he wasn't sure who he was meant to blame for all this.

"We heard noises and thought the horses were upset," Chuck said calmly before motioning back at the lying form of Mr. Woodwick. "When we came out, the horses were already gone, and he was ranting on about something and then just passed out."

Aunt Tara had come to stand next to my uncle, and she whispered loud enough that I could hear, "Is he alive?"

This prompted my uncle to kneel next to Mr. Woodwick and check his neck for a pulse. He quickly looked back up and nodded, saying, "Yeah, there's a pulse, and he's still breathing." My aunt let out a long sigh of relief.

I had thought we were in the clear, but my aunt turned to look at us before asking, "What was that light we saw?" I took a quick glance at my friends, and in unison, we all shrugged at her. To her credit, my aunt didn't push the question because the realization of us finding the horses gone and then finding Mr. Woodwick ranting seemed to overshadow anything else. She followed up by asking, "Are you kids all right?" We all nodded, though I was sure Jade was trying to make herself look sadder and more confused than she was. Probably trying to make sure she looked as innocent as possible. It worked because I soon found myself and my friends being embraced in a big hug by my aunt, her voice sweet and caring as she told us, "You poor things, this must have been so frightening to you."

Half an hour later, there were several cop cars, an ambulance, a fire truck, a news van, and Chuck's and Jade's parents' cars spread across the grass in front of the house and leading up to the stables. My aunt had called the ambulance, which made sense because of the unconscious Mr. Woodwick on the stable floor. My uncle had called the cops since he said it was clear Mr. Woodwick was trespassing and must have done something to the horses. I wasn't too sure why the fire truck had come or even how the news van had heard about it, but I guess a rich, old town founder stealing someone's horse and passing out at the crime scene was something that would spread fast in a small town like Merrow Crescent.

Once Mr. Woodwick had come to, and the medics had checked him over, they decided that he needed to be checked at the hospital to determine the cause of his temporary blackout. When Mr. Woodwick came out of the stable with his hands cuffed behind his back and a thick yellow blanket draped over his shoulders, he stopped to look at us. I was sure he was going to start yelling something along the lines of "If it wasn't for you darn kids," but instead, he looked at us confused and so very lost, and his voice was somehow older and raspier when he asked, "Who am I?"

"You're Mr. Woodwick," I said in a flat tone. He seemed to think about that for a moment and then sighed, looking so lost as they ushered him toward the ambulance. I kept watching Mr. Woodwick as they helped him lie down on a stretcher inside. Part of me expected that at any moment he was going to smirk at me, showing it was all an act, but it never happened.

I played back the things he had said before he hit himself with his own magic about not remembering any of this. Had he been trying to make us forget him? Did such power really even exist? I mean, if unicorns were real and there was magic, why not, right?

There was some more talking, mostly boring stuff, but the cops appeared to agree that Mr. Woodwick had something to do with the horses after my uncle filled them in on his insistence on selling the farm to him. They assured my uncle that he would be questioned as soon as the doctors gave him a clean bill of health, assuming he hadn't lost his memory from bumping his head, and they would come out first thing in the morning with more people to search for the lost horses.

It took some convincing on my aunt's part to get Chuck's and Jade's parents to allow them to stay there for the rest of the night. Something had been said along the lines of "The children have clearly gone through a lot tonight. It's probably for the best that they stay together." All the parents agreed, and after some mushy hugs and kisses, mostly just from Chuck's mom, they left.

I was glad to have finally met Jade's parents, though I wish it hadn't been in such a dramatic way. They seemed really nice, and after talking to them for a few minutes, I liked them more than Chuck's mom. I felt a bit bad thinking that, but being around Mrs. Dunbar left me feeling strange now. A feeling I hoped would fade. Mr. Callaghan had the same shade eyes as his daughter's and a neat head of red hair (the name Callaghan made more sense now as I assumed his family must have come over from Ireland or someplace like that). Mrs. Callaghan's skin was a darker shade of brown than Jade's, but other than that, they looked like they could have been twins.

My aunt had asked us if we wanted to talk about it, but we all assured her we were too tired and needed to get some sleep. She reluctantly agreed. We didn't talk much, not like we normally would have. I didn't feel much like talking away. My heart hurt, but at the same time, I was happy. Happy that Cliffton and the others got to go home where they belonged, wherever that was, but sad we hadn't had more time together. Being both sad and happy at the same time was an exhausting feeling, and I felt like I lay there for hours holding back the urge to both laugh and cry at the same time until I finally fell asleep.

Chapter 35

It was probably the most restless, dreamless sleep I had ever had in my entire life. So much so that I had serious doubts I even fell asleep, except for the fact that I found my aunt and uncle gently nudging me awake. I rubbed at my eyes, clearing the fog from them, and when they began to focus enough, I saw that both of them were practically beaming down at me. "We got some good news," my aunt said, way too cheerfully for whatever time in the morning it was. Especially considering the night before. I groaned at her as I shielded my eyes from the light streaming through the windows, which was way too bright for my liking.

"Well, two good pieces of news actually," my uncle corrected. It was clear they weren't going to leave me be until I listened to them, so begrudgingly, I forced myself to sit up in bed. Now that I was upright, I could see Jade and Chuck had much the same reaction that I had. Chuck was sitting up, not looking half as tired as I felt, staring at them, whereas Jade appeared to have taken the other approach, as her head was covered with her pillow.

"Well?" I asked, attempting not to sound annoyed.

My aunt practically bounced in her spot when she said, well, yelled was more like it, "Your baby sister is here!"

"Oh," I said dryly, and I could tell my aunt's mood lowered just a hint when I didn't share her excitement. "And that's good news why?" I asked bitterly and probably with a tad too much sarcasm.

"Well, for starters, you don't have to be tortured by us anymore," my uncle said jokingly, but I could tell the realization that I was leaving had suddenly hit him. He faltered for a moment like he wanted to be sad, but he quickly recovered from it with a humorous grin.

Had I gotten this news weeks ago, I almost certainly would have been happy. No, I would probably have been ecstatic. But now, after making new friends, granted, most of them were now gone forever, something about returning to my normal life knowing what I knew and probably never seeing any of the people I experienced it with felt like a major bummer. I sniffed back a tear, willing myself not to cry, telling myself I'd do that later when no one was watching. "And the other news?" I asked bitterly.

My aunt and uncle looked at each other before they both put one arm over the other's waist and gave me the biggest grin I thought humanly possible. In unison, they both announced, "The horses are back!"

I felt my jaw drop open, and so did Chuck's, and this sudden unexpected news caused Jade to jump up into a seated position on her bed on the floor, causing the pillow to be flung across the room. "Say what!" She practically yelled.

"But how, when, how, that can't be, when?" I asked, knowing I was making no sense at all.

They both laughed, and my uncle told us, "When I went out this morning, I saw all three of them just standing in the field looking like nothing had happened at all."

My aunt added, "It's so strange. We checked the whole grounds last night before we finally decided to wait until morning. I was sure they weren't there."

"Must have been hiding after all the commotion with vehicles and everything," my uncle speculated.

"Can I go see them?" I asked, now not able to hide

the tears that were forming.

My uncle looked like he was about to protest, but my aunt cut off whatever he was about to say, telling me, "Just for a bit. Your parents wanted us to bring you first thing."

I looked around the room, knowing most of that time was partially going to be me having to pack my bags. Something I knew I'd never be fast about even if I tried really, really hard. So when Aunt Tara looked like she was able to read that thought on my face, she placed one hand on my shoulder, telling me, "Just get dressed, and I'll deal with all your things." She paused to give me a playful smile. "So long as you trust me not to forget anything."

I smiled at her before embracing her in a big tight hug. "I trust you," I told her, and I felt her hug me back just as tightly.

I spared no time at all getting dressed and ready. I didn't go as far as just blindly grabbing the first shirt I saw. I didn't want to have another repeat of the shirt incident from one of my first days here, but I wasn't exactly being picky about it either. I opted for a pair of blue jeans and a simple green-and-white striped shirt and pulled my hair back in a less than neat ponytail. It wasn't a mess, for sure, but it probably could have used a tad bit more brushing. When I left the bathroom, I shoved my brush into my backpack and decided I could just sort that out later in the car. That was when I noticed that neither Jade nor Chuck were still there, and their bags were gone. I wasn't sure why I feared the worst, but I rushed out of the room as safe as my feet could carry me and headed down the stairs.

To my relief, they were waiting for me next to the front door, their bags sitting on the bench next to the stairs. "Took you long enough," Jade groaned, crossing her arms and giving a roll of her eyes.

"Sorry," I muttered, trying not to let this kill my

happy mood.

"We just got down here a good thirty seconds before you," Chuck chimed in.

Jade gave me a cocky smile before playfully punching me in the arm. "I've got to mess with you as much as I can, don't I?" she added playfully.

I faked a wince and was about to say something clever when I heard Aunt Tara's voice calling from the kitchen, "You kids want some breakfast?"

"Um, no thanks," I shouted as I urged everyone to head outside before she could stop us. Chuck hesitated with the promise of food, but he quickly reconsidered it. I wasn't sure if he was just as eager as we were to find out what was going on, or maybe he was too scared of Jade's wrath if he didn't come with us.

The moment I got outside, we all went into a sprint toward the fields, and then I saw them. All three of them were waiting patiently near the fence like they had been waiting for us all morning. I found myself approaching them cautiously. I wasn't sure why. Maybe it was that seed of doubt in the back of my head that was telling me I was just dreaming all of this, and any false move I made might wake me up to a less ideal reality.

When I got to the fence, I stretched my hand out by my side before asking, "Why are you back?" I followed it up by adding, "Not that I'm not thrilled you are, but I thought we would never see you again."

Cliffton sighed before looking at Eloise and Thor in turn, and then he simply said, "It's a bit complicated."

I looked at Jade and Chuck, and they looked as confused by that statement as I was feeling about it, "Complicated how?" Chuck asked, giving me a sense of déjà vu from the conversation I had the other night about Mr. Woodwick.

"Like he said," Eloise said with a flourish from her head, causing her hair to gracefully fall back into place.

"It's complicated." Jade snorted back a laugh. "You vanish into thin air acting like this was a forever bye and then come back, and all you got is *it's complicated?*"

Thor jumped up on the fence, letting his front hooves hang over the top of the middle of the slate. This startled Jade, and she took a step back. I was sure I heard Thor chuckle under his breath. "What my friends here are trying to say in a less wordy way is"—he raised his voice just a tad—"we don't have a single blasted idea what the heck is going on."

I felt my face pale. I wasn't sure what that meant but hearing Thor say it made me incredibly worried. "But," Cliffton said in a low, even, calm voice, "we know we will figure it out." Eloise and Thor nodded in agreement, though something about it looked like they were unsure.

"Did you get your memories back?" I asked, feeling pretty sure I already knew the answer, and sure enough, they all shook their heads no.

Eloise spoke softly. "Some things have come back, or at least parts of some things, but honestly not very much. At least not enough to make heads or tails out of any of it."

"What kinds of things?" Chuck asked.

"A few names and places maybe, but not sure whose names they are or where the places are," Thor replied.

"Where did you vanish to?" I asked next. Cliffton hung his head slightly before meeting my eyes.

"It's hard to say. It was all foggy. It felt like we weren't alone, but none of us saw anyone else."

I frowned a bit. "So just some foggy place with invisible people?" I asked, letting the last word linger a bit longer. I mean, "people" probably wasn't the right word, but I'm sure he got my point about what I meant. Cliffton sighed, and I was sure he was attempting something like a shrug. Honestly, it looked weird on a horse, even if that horse was a unicorn.

"Are you going to go back there? To the foggy place that is," Jade asked curiously, now looking worried.

Eloise snorted. "I don't think fog will do anything good for my mane," she mused, "but the matter hasn't been settled yet, at least not without further investigation into it first."

"Do you remember anything else?" I pushed, hoping they might offer up something we could work with in the little time I had left.

Cliffton shook his head at first, but then he stopped midshake and said, "Well, actually, there's one thing, but it's just too strange." I could tell he was losing his confidence to tell us.

"Just spill it," Jade pressed.

With a deep sigh, Cliffton said, "I was sure I kept hearing a whisper. It said . . . " He paused briefly before adding, "Beware the doppelganger?"

"Doppelganger?" I asked, confused as I looked at my friends.

Jade placed both hands on her hips, her words sounding a bit annoyed. "What in the world is a doppelganger? Is that even a real thing?"

Chuck laughed, slapping himself on the forehead like he couldn't believe what he just heard. "Yes, a doppelganger is a real thing. Don't you remember anything from the book report we did last year?"

Jade just shrugged at him nonchalantly. "If it's something I had to read or do a report on, you probably did it for me, Chuck, and besides, I try my best to purge my brain from all things school-related during the summer as much as I can."

Chuck rolled his eyes, ignoring almost everything she had just told him. "A doppelganger is a creature that can take shape and form of someone else or just already looked like it by chance. You know, like maybe your evil doppelganger did it." He snorted as if this was just common knowledge.

Chuck looked like he was about to go into some more facts about it when he was cut off by a soft voice that came from the air between Cliffton and Eloise. "Can I come out now?"

"Of course you can, dear," Eloise replied, looking at the space between the two unicorns. The air swirled around slightly and sparkled under the morning sun before the form of another horse came into view. She was tall, not as tall as Cliffton, but a fair bit more than Eloise. Her fur was a pale caramel, and she had a long deep brown mane. I couldn't help but stare at her for a long moment. She had to be one of the most beautiful horses I had ever seen. Then it dawned on me. I knew her, but how could I know her?

Then it hit me. I had dreamed of a horse that looked just like her the day I had arrived here. "I know you," I said in a low, unsure whisper, fighting the feeling of how stupid I was going to look if I was wrong. But then she nodded at me in agreement.

"I've been reaching out to you from the first moment I sensed your presence."

"Reach out? How?" I asked, not quite understanding.

She stared at me for a moment before saying, "Well, the dream I gave you to start with." The way she said it was cheerful but also hesitant. Well, at least that cleared that up. "Then I led you to find the journal, and if I'm assuming my magic worked correctly, I also managed to save you a few times from getting yourself hurt." The last part she sounded particularly amused by.

I had to think about this for a moment, and then it hit me. "You mean the time slowdowns?" and she nodded.

"What time slowdowns?" Chuck asked curiously.

I tried to assure him it wasn't important when I

said, "It's nothing really. It is, um, complicated." I followed it up with a grin, but all I got was a look from both Chuck and Jade that told me I was going to have to explain it to them later.

"Why?" I asked to get back on topic. "Why me, I mean?"

The horse stared at me with its large brown eyes before finally saying, "I thought I had finally found the one to save them." She paused as she looked me over before saying, "And it appears I was right."

I felt shocked. I had been some kind of special person she had been waiting for to help them. Even I wasn't vain enough to buy that. I shook my head in disbelief, which got a small chuckle in response, and she said, "So humble."

"Who are you?" Jade asked, beating me to my next question.

The horse regarded Jade, and then she told her, "My name is Natara," before she bent her head down in what I figured was a unicorn greeting.

"Oh," Jade said, "I'm Jade."

Natara laughed, "Yes, and he is Chuck, and she is Jennifer. I know who all of you are." Jade muttered something to the effect of that being a bit creepy but shrugged like it didn't matter to her anyway.

I wanted to ask about so many more things, but my uncle walked up behind us before I could. "OK, kid, your bags are in the car, and Chuck's mom is here to pick them up. We need to hit the road."

I did a double take when my uncle didn't notice the presence of the new horse and found myself cut off when I started to ask, "Don't you—" as Natara told me, "He can't see me."

"Don't I what?" my uncle asked, eyeing me, confused.

I shook my head, giving him a small smile.

"Nothing, I'm just a bit tired still."

Uncle James nodded with a smile of his own. "Well, come on. We need to make tracks." And then he began walking toward the house.

I walked quickly up to Cliffton and gave him one final hug before telling him, "I'm glad you're safe." He nodded, and it seemed he wanted to say something more but stopped himself.

"You better go. He's starting to look a bit impatient," he told me, sounding somewhat amused. Sure enough, when I turned around, I saw Uncle James standing there with his hands on his hips. He might have even been tapping his foot too. I found myself quickly running after him. I wanted to look back, but something told me that if I did, they might have had to drag me away kicking and screaming, and I probably had already done enough weird stuff as it was since I had gotten there.

I was only allowed a minute or two to say my goodbyes to Chuck and Jade. My uncle and aunt figured I'd already had plenty of time to do that when we had gone to see the horse. It was a normal goodbye with some hugs and exchanging of phone numbers and email addresses with a promise to call. Quietly Jade and Chuck promised to keep an eye on the unicorns for me and fill me in on anything they found so I could help from my end, and I promised that as soon as I got home, I would write them about the weird dream and slowdowns as Natara had called them.

Chuck and Jade drove off with Chuck's mom before Aunt Tara came out with a picnic basket and placed it on the seat next to me in the back. For the first time, we were taking the car instead of the truck I had been so used to riding in this whole time. To my delight, at the top of the basket was some breakfast my aunt had packed for me since I had run off so quickly as she claimed. It was two chocolate chip muffins. She even put some milk inside a thermos to stay nice and cold. There were also some other drinks and snacks in case anyone got hungry on the long drive.

My uncle figured it would be a six-hour drive, but only if there was no traffic or accidents on the way. The thought of such a long drive made me shudder, and my aunt promised we would stop for a good lunch and as many bathroom breaks as I needed. Uncle James didn't protest to the good lunch, but he said quite firmly, "Anyone worth their grain of salt should be able to hold it for at least six hours, maybe even eight in a pinch."

My aunt and I exchanged looks, and we both said with a roll of our eyes, "Men." Uncle James just snorted and drove off without another word.

I looked out the window at the place I had called home for some weeks now. A longing feeling told me I was going to miss this place. When I saw Cliffton running along the side of the fence, following us until the fence ended near the road, I just stared at him with a smile, placing one hand on the window, letting him know I was thinking the same thing. I think maybe he was going to miss me just as much as I was going to miss him. It felt weird admitting that to myself, especially with him being so stubborn. But then again, so was I.

Once we were out of sight of the farm, my uncle turned on the radio to a station of his, and only his, liking, I decided to hunt for my phone. I found it pretty quickly, but I also found my journal. I normally would have passed the time watching videos or trying to reach my friends back home, but instead, I started my own page in the journal. I drew Cliffton, or at least as best as I could. It didn't come anywhere close to the pictures before it, but I thought it was nice. I also added my own facts about the things I'd learned, even adding places to be filled out, assuming Jade and Chuck kept their word about going to see the unicorns for me. When I was done, I shut the book and placed it in my bag, turning my attention to the world outside my window.

Six hours and fifteen minutes later, we pulled up outside the hospital in my home city. My uncle had done a reasonably good job at keeping time. No traffic, no slowdown from road works, and he had convinced my aunt to get fast-food over a sit-down lunch as she had wanted. He made us rush inside to use the bathroom while he went through the drive-through. He hadn't gone in to use the bathroom, and it showed when he dropped my aunt and me outside the front of the hospital, telling us he'd be up as soon as he parked while he clenched his legs together and said between his teeth, "And find the toilet." My aunt and I exchanged a laugh before we headed in, and after a quick stop to look at floor information, we headed up the elevator.

It wasn't until my aunt walked over to the nurse station asking for a room number that reality hit me. I was a big sister now. I never really thought about that fact too much until now. Well, if you didn't count the times I thought about how awful it would be. But now I was about to meet my baby sister. I didn't even know her name yet, or if she had been given one. Granted, I didn't even know it was a sister until this morning since my parents had decided to do the whole wait-and-see thing. That seemed weird to me; it's not like having a baby was opening a blind bag, but again it wasn't something I had honestly cared too much about.

Now I found myself feeling scared and nervous. Was I going to be a good sister? Was she going to like me? What if she hated me? I had to make myself take a calming breath as I followed my aunt wordlessly down the hall. After all, babies didn't do too much at first, let alone remember anything for at least a few years of their lives. I had at least some time to figure all this sister stuff out, right? I found Aunt Tara looking at me with a big smile, almost like she had been reading my thoughts the whole time before asking me, "Are you ready to meet her?" I took one big breath before nodding at her, and with a wink, she knocked on the door.

There was the soft and familiar sound of my mom's voice calling for us to come in. When I walked into the room past a curtain that was pulled open, blocking the view from the door, I saw my mom sitting in bed wearing a hospital gown that looked way too big for her and looking like she hadn't slept in days. From where I was standing, it looked like she was holding a wadded-up blanket. My dad was leaning over her, holding a frosted chocolate donut in one hand and a camera in the other. He made a cooing noise toward the blanket before telling it, "You have a visitor, sweetie."

"Do you want to hold her?" my mom asked me, sounding both excited and completely exhausted at the same time.

For a moment, I felt really scared. I mean, what if I dropped her? But without even thinking about it, I nodded despite the fear that was starting to churn in my stomach on reflection. The feeling might well have been the greasy burger I had for lunch, though. When I didn't walk over to the bed, my aunt did instead, and after picking up the wrapped cloth and cooing at it for just a moment, she walked over to me, telling me, "Hold out your arms."

"Like this?" I asked, holding them out, in the same way I thought she was. My aunt nodded at me with a smile before placing the blanket gently into my arms.

It wasn't heavy at all, and if I hadn't looked down and seen the small baby that was looking at me or maybe the ceiling, I wouldn't have even known she was there, but she was there, and despite my belief until now that babies were awful, smell, noisy things, I didn't think there could have even been a cuter, sweeter-looking baby than my sister. "What's her name?" I asked as a small tear started creeping into my eye's edge.

"Emma," my mom said as my dad started taking a few pictures of us with his camera. Such a typical dad thing to do, I thought. I didn't care so much this time. On a normal day, I might have groaned at him, but instead, I wanted to remember what I looked like staring down at my sister for the first time. It would remind me when she got older and louder and smellier that at least at one time, I didn't love anything as much as I loved her at this moment in time.

I was only vaguely aware that my uncle had come into the room or that he and my aunt were peering at her from behind my shoulders until my uncle said, sounding a bit amused, "She looks just like you when you were a baby." This made me smile. But then he added, "Hey, she even has the same birthmark on her neck just like you do, kiddo."

My aunt giggled, adding, "Maybe she's your twin," which caused my uncle to add, "Or maybe your doppelganger."

The word hit me like a ton of bricks, "doppelganger." "Beware the doppelganger." Was my baby sister destined to be evil? That couldn't be right. She was just a baby. That wasn't fair at all. I felt my heart begin to beat at the sudden realization of it all. That was until my dad came over to stand next to me. "What do you mean birthmark?" he asked, looking down at Emma before laughing, and then he proceeded to lick his thumb before swiping what now appeared to be a smudged bit of chocolate that had fallen from his doughnut. I let out a tiny sigh of relief and whispered just low enough so no one else would hear, "Well, that was a disaster diverted."

I was sure she smiled at me, and I looked up at my dad. "Did you see that? She smiled at me."

My dad smiled at me, but in that way, like I don't

want to hurt your feelings, and he said, "Babies can't smile yet. It's probably just gas." The adults all giggled at that.

They could believe all they wanted, but I knew deep down that it had been a smile. This girl and I were going to get along, and the stories I was going to be able to tell her when she was old enough were going to be epic. I walked over to a chair and sat down, holding my sister. None of the adults appeared to mind as they did the whole catch-up thing that adults like to do. I just sat there looking at my baby sister and told her, "I got some great stories to tell you." This got me another smile, and I told her, "I know we just met, but I think we will be good friends."

To be continued ...

Lightning Source UK Ltd.
Milton Keynes UK
UKHW011005030323
417983UK00014B/534